THE MATING GAME

Amanda's legs were shaking. Jason's eyes burned her, scorched her, firing a heat inside her such as she'd never known. This was insanity. The man was a savage, a murderer. How could the feel of his hand threading through her hair calm her, quiet her, make her body grow languid, quiescent, as though he were a lost lover returned to her side after a prolonged and unwelcome separation?

"Have you ever seen horses mate, Miss Morgan?"

She swallowed, unable to think, unable to move, unable to do anything but feel. His warm breath fanned the flames that rose higher, hotter with each beat of her heart.

"The filly nips at the stud, Miss Morgan." He kissed her cheek, her chin, her neck. "She fights him, bites him. She runs. He chases. Until finally she knows what it is she wants. She stands still then. So very still. She lets him." His lips brushed hers. "She lets him . . ."

BELOVED OUTLAW

LINDA BENJAMIN

ZEBRA BOOKS

KENSINGTON PUBLISHING CORP.

ZEBRA BOOKS

are published by

Kensington Publishing Corp.
475 Park Avenue South
New York, NY 10016

Copyright © 1986 by Linda Benjamin

First printing: December 1986

Printed in the United States of America

Chapter One

In three hours Jason Montana would be dead. Hanged by the neck at dawn in front of a cheering crowd of San Antonio's finest citizens. From what he could make of the hoots and catcalls outside the adobe jail, the cheering had already begun. San Antonio's myriad cantinas must have considered it their civic duty to remain open through the night, fueling the courage of those on his deathwatch.

Rising from his stone-hard cot, Jace brushed a hand through an unruly mane of dark hair, studying the sliver of night sky visible through the barred windows of his cell. Above the din of the crowd drifted the steady pounding of a carpenter's hammer. He tried unsuccessfully to suppress the shudder that coursed through him.

Cursing, he shook it off, angling a glance toward the dimly lit room opposite him. "Sounds like the town wants to save you the trouble, sheriff," he said, "and stretch my neck for you."

Sheriff Jon Stark sat hunched behind a small oak

desk in the room's far corner. Raising his head, he scraped back his chair and climbed to his feet. "I hope you're not expecting me to stop 'em if they do, Montana. Three hours, three minutes . . . don't make no difference to me. Nobody deserves hangin' more than you."

Jace didn't waste his breath protesting his innocence. He'd done that at the trial, until it had become obvious that his guilt or innocence was of no particular consequence to either the judge or the jury. Philip Welford wanted him to hang. And in 1877 San Antonio, Texas, what Philip Welford wanted, Philip Welford got.

Just thinking the name ate at him, churning in his guts as he paced the confines of the small cell. In three hours Welford would win. Jace's body would dangle in the warm breeze of early morning, stinking of death even before the oppressive heat of midday began its inexorable task. Though it would never be so indicated in the town records, he would die not for the crime for which he'd been convicted, but for daring to defy Welford and his J-Bar-W empire—to start up a ranch on public range Welford considered his own.

Jace swore, again turning his attention to the lawman. "How much of Welford's money did it take to buy out the conscience of an entire town?"

Stark approached the cell, his craggy features set in granite. "It's talk like that that ain't made you no friends in San Antone, Montana."

"The first night I spent in Texas three months ago, somebody took a shot at me." He knotted a fist around the iron bar of the cell door. "That's as friendly as you people got."

"Lyin' right to the end."

Jace's gray eyes narrowed, but he said nothing, returning his attention to the diamond-studded blackness. The last stars he would ever see? Unconsciously, he reached a hand to his throat. Damn, Isaiah would never forgive himself . . .

He jerked toward the sound of glass shattering, grimacing at the fist-sized rock that had landed in the middle of the scuff-worn wood floor of Stark's office. Scattered shards crunched under the lawman's boots as he scurried over to what was left of his window.

"We want Montana!" came the shouted command. "Give 'im over, Stark. Now!"

Jace recognized Gabe Langley's voice. Welford's foreman. No doubt he was doing his damndest to incite the bloodlust of the drunken cowboys milling in front of the jail.

"Just go on about your business, Gabe," Stark said. "You boys can wait another three hours for your fun."

"We don't want to hurt you, Jon," Langley continued. "Just open the door and step out of the way. We'll take care of the rest."

"Three hours," Stark repeated evenly. "Three hours and you'll see the bastard get what's coming to him. Until then I don't want to see your ugly face."

More angry grumbling followed. All the while Stark's voice remained calm, reasonable, though he held his .45 Colt cocked and ready in his right hand. Jace had to give the man his due. In spite of his earlier bluster about not giving a damn about his prisoner, he obviously gave a damn about the badge on his vest.

The noise of the crowd receded. Stark had won. They would wait for the legal circus at dawn. The sharp

9

staccato of the carpenter's hammer never ceased.

Jace swallowed, stuffing his hands into the pockets of his Levi's, his lean body bowstring tight. Damn, but he was trying hard to stay angry, furious at the manufactured evidence that had condemned him to die. Concentrating on the anger kept other emotions at bay.

Like fear? he wondered, padding the length and breadth of his cage. Surely he'd seen death too many times to fear it, after a lifetime of hunting and trapping with Isaiah Benteen in the wilds of the Northwest Territory. Death in all its varied guises. As a friend, ending the suffering of a hopelessly injured Tame Bear three winters past, and as the bitterest of enemies, riding with the drunken hide-hunters who fourteen months ago had murdered Dawn Wind and Bright Path—his wife, his son.

His fists clenched at the torment the last memory brought him. He had vowed on their graves to find the three men who had savaged them. Now the bastards would go free, his vengeance thwarted by a wealthy rancher with vengeful motives of his own.

No, he didn't fear death. He feared the cost of his dying. To Isaiah. To Dawn Wind and Bright Path.

The hope that this was all some grotesque nightmare brought on by Tame Bear's mixing peyote with his tobacco, as he had that long-ago summer when Jace and Isaiah had stayed with the Blackfoot, dissipated with the clank of heavy chains Stark piled next to the cell door—waiting.

Jace sucked in a long breath, expelling it through clenched teeth. Maybe he had no room for complaint. Wasn't his whole life on borrowed time anyway? Only the propitious arrival of Isaiah Benteen thirty-two years ago had spared him the fate that befell his parents. Isaiah had recounted the tale dozens of times. Though the mountain man's natural penchant for tall tales had often altered the sequence of events, the telling never altered the facts.

Jace stretched out on the cot, remembering the first time Isaiah had told him the story. He was five years old, and he'd just helped dress out his first deer, one Isaiah had shot the day before. A late autumn wind was whistling through the canyon out of the north, warning that much had yet to be done to be ready for winter in the high country. Isaiah built a fire and started dinner, while Jace began the tedious chore of scraping down the hide.

"I figure it was a night like this that caught your folks," Isaiah said, rubbing a huge paw of a hand through a bushy black beard mottled with gray. His grizzly bear size and growly voice were merely endearing traits to a boy who had never seen another human being. Jace hung on Isaiah's every word, as if the story the trapper told was not that of his parents' death but just another thrilling wilderness adventure. "This high in the mountains it can snow any time after August. And it was already October when they made camp near Bald Mountain in the Flatheads.

"The blizzard hit around midnight. It snowed a sheet of white for three days straight. I was holed up in a cave, near out of grub at the time. When it let up a bit, I come out trackin' a buck. That's when I found what was left of their wagon. Your father had dug out a shelter, but it didn't do no good."

"Did he do it in the lee of the wind?" Jace asked.

11

Isaiah grinned. "You learn fast, boy. Damned fast. You're gonna know more 'n me in another week."

"I'll never know more than you, Isaiah."

Isaiah reached over to show him a better grip on the knife he was using to clean the deerhide. "The drifts were higher 'n tree branches. Looked like your pa died trying to get the mules free. Found your ma in the shelter. Fire out. Her body still warm. Figure she couldn't have been dead more than half an hour."

He chucked more wood onto the campfire. "No place to bury 'em. Ain't ashamed to admit I was going through their gear when I heard what sounded like a painter scrappin' with a badger. Found you under your ma's body. She kept you warm as long as she could, even when she couldn't keep herself warm no more."

"She loved me, didn't she, Isaiah?"

"There ain't no doubt about that, boy."

"And now you love me." His small chest puffed up with pride.

Isaiah lifted Jace's coonskin cap, ruffling his hair, his voice gruff, "That I do, little painter. That I do."

"I'm glad you're my ma and pa, Isaiah."

The old man looked away, clearing his throat and making an elaborate display of getting supper started. "Let's see now, where was I with all yer jabberin'?"

"You found me under my ma," Jace supplied eagerly.

"Right you are," Isaiah said, stirring the deer meat into the stew. "You couldn't have been no more 'n eight months old. I took you back to my camp, figurin' you'd die soon enough. But you went on squallin' like a mountain cat, 'til I figured out how ta get some food into ya. Didn't have no one to tell me what your folks

12

called ya, so I called you Jason after my father. And I called you after the place I found ya—Montana."

In spite of an appearance that intimidated less stout-hearted souls he and Isaiah had run across in their travels, the old mountain man had never been anything but kind to Jace. Jace suspected, as the years passed and he grew to understand such things, that Isaiah missed never having a family of his own—that Jace had been as much a son to him as Bright Path had been to Jace.

A renewed pounding on Stark's door diverted him from his brooding thoughts. It was not Langley and his bunch this time.

"Get away!" Stark bellowed, not moving toward the door.

Jace couldn't make out the muffled reply.

Stark peered through the window. The disgust on his face was evident. Lifting the bar, he opened the door, allowing a shadowy figure to lurch inside. Stark quickly rebolted the door.

Isaiah.

"I don't know why you're here, Benteen," Stark said, patting down the old man's clothes in a search for weapons. "You said your good-byes last night."

Jace winced at the sight of Isaiah's haggard features. The patches of skin visible between the shaggy, tangled beard and bushy brows were mottled with red. His trail-stained buckskins reeked of whiskey. "Leave him alone, Stark," Jace said. When Stark made a move to cuff Isaiah away from the cell, he added, "Please."

Stark halted.

Isaiah moved unsteadily toward Jace, the hacking cough that had begun three years ago and become more and more a part of him nearly doubling him over.

"You shouldn't have come back," Jace said quietly.

"I had to. It's my fault. All of it. We never should have left the mountains. I shouldn't have made you come here."

Jace gripped the bars of the cell so tight his knuckles whitened. They'd spent their lives in the wilderness, rarely coming in contact with settlements even remotely resembling civilization, trading with Indians, living off the land. But eight months ago Isaiah had insisted it was time to put down roots. "I ain't going to live forever, boy," he'd said. "And the way the wagons are heading west, neither is the peace of these mountains. You should have a home. I ain't never give you one."

Jace had no interest in leaving the forests to come to the bleakness of southern Texas, but Isaiah had been adamant. A cattle ranch, he said. A stake in the future. Though Jace suspected Isaiah's sudden urge to leave Montana had more to do with Jace's brooding over the deaths of Dawn Wind and Bright Path, he had thrown himself into the task because it was what Isaiah wanted, and because a blind man could see the old man was dying.

"Go back to the hotel, Isaiah."

"No, I can't let . . ."

"You had no part in this. It's Welford's doing. We both know that."

Isaiah straightened, looking for a moment at least like the strong-willed mountain of a man who had battled grizzlies bare-handed and won. "I went to that worthless lawyer they stuck you with, painter. But it was a pure waste of time." He shook his head. "Stinkin' town. They broke into my room last night, tore the place apart. I just can't figure it. . . ."

"Go back to the hotel."

"They're not going to get away with this. I swear they're not. They'll pay. By God, they'll pay."

Stark gripped Isaiah's shirt collar and propelled him toward the door. "I want you out of my jail. Montana don't deserve to breathe the same air as decent folks. I seen what he did to that Melendez girl with my own eyes."

"Jace never hurt a woman in his life. You're a fool, Stark, if'n you believe Welford's lies."

"I said get out, old man. It's your lies I don't believe. Montana's knife was buried in that girl's chest. Mr. Welford and two other men swore they seen him in her room that night. And the desk clerk found him standin' over the body."

Isaiah pulled away from Stark and stumbled over to the cell. Shoving his hands through the bars, he gripped Jace's hand in his. "I ain't leavin' ya, boy."

"Don't be there when it happens," Jace said. "I don't want you to see it."

"I was only trying to give you a home. Nobody will listen. Nobody."

"Drunken old sot," Stark growled. "Get out." He again shoved Isaiah toward the door.

"You know what Welford's doing' right now, Stark?" Isaiah mumbled. "He's throwin' a party. At the hotel. A party. Over a man dyin'."

"What Mr. Welford does is his own business. And if I wasn't sheriff, I'd be there myself." Stark checked the street, then opened the door and pushed Isaiah outside. "Don't come back. Next time you see this bastard, it'll

15

be in a box." He slammed the door and threw the bolt, turning toward Jace. "At least you won't have to worry about the old man seein' you die, Montana. He's so drunk, he'll sleep twelve hours the first place he lights."

Jace stood on the cot, fingers circling the bars of the window. He prayed Stark was right. He couldn't bear Isaiah watching him die.

A shadowy movement in the hotel across the street caught his eye—a silhouette in a lamp-lit room. A grim smile touched his lips. Three A.M. and she was still awake. Getting ready for the party no doubt. He'd come to know that particular room well over the last three days, his newly developed voyeurism brought on by the room's newly arrived occupant.

Miss Amanda Morgan.

Philip Welford's fiancée.

He remembered the flesh and blood version of that silhouette. Pale hair, mountain-lake eyes—a vision that at first glance had stolen the breath from his body. He had never seen a woman so fair, in truth, had never seen a blond-haired woman before.

Yet there she had been three days ago, standing in the back of the courtroom, her arm linked intimately with Welford's. Jace would never forget the look in those blue eyes as the judge sentenced him to hang. At first he could have sworn she had seemed almost stricken, but then she had turned to whisper something to Welford, and Jace had seen more clearly that her gaze reflected only an icy contempt.

When the sheriff had started to lead him out of the courtroom, Welford hadn't been able to resist the twist of the knife. The tall, sandy-haired rancher braced himself in the doorway, the lovely blonde at his side appearing regal and aloof in her canary silk dress with its spinster's neckline fastened high on her slender throat. Welford's own perfectly tailored doeskin suit and white silk shirt, complete with beige cravat and diamond stickpin, only further entrenched Jace's opinion of the man as a fatuous prig.

"I'm going to look forward to your death, Montana," Welford said. "Savor it, as I would a fine wine." He curved a hand around the woman's waist, pulling her close. "I've been telling my fiancée of your barbarous crime. She was concerned, newcomer to Texas that she is, that we're a bit more uncivilized here than in Baltimore. But she's pleased to find us as swift and fair at meting out justice as the great state of Maryland."

"Pleased?" Jace cocked an eyebrow at her. "Should I have the sheriff reserve a spot on the gallows for you, miss, so that you can watch justice dealt out firsthand?"

Her voice had been both dove-wing soft and snap-frost cold. "If Philip likes, perhaps the hangman will allow me to drop you through the trapdoor myself."

He'd straightened, studying her eyes, searching their fathomless blue depths for any sign that she was merely being bold for Welford's sake, or self-righteously indignant. But he found nothing but a haughty disdain. And in that instant he hated her.

Hated her, and against all reason—desired her.

He told himself it was the way she looked, so different from any other woman he had ever seen. Porcelain, fragile, not quite real, reminding him of pictures he'd seen once in a missionary's prayer book. The only difference was that Amanda Morgan didn't have a halo and wings.

He snorted derisively, incensed that he should liken the conceited wench to an angel. In his mind he would have her be anything but. He wanted Amanda Morgan beneath him, writhing, naked—her lofty superiority gone, in its place a primitive need that matched his own.

Yet that very need sent a strange, slicing guilt through him as he thought of Dawn Wind, who had had a dark, sensual beauty all her own. There had been no arrogance in Dawn Wind, no false airs, no pretenses. He stuck a hand in his pocket, extracting a round object scarcely bigger than a silver dollar, turning it over and over in his hand. But it was no coin. It was an expertly worked piece of buckskin, plain on one side, the beaded image of a cougar on the other. Dawn Wind had made it for him, made one for herself. He had not worn it since she died. Hers had been torn from her, and either lost or stolen in the struggle. He stroked the snarling cougar with his thumb.

How could he become so preoccupied with someone so exactly Dawn Wind's opposite? Amanda Morgan with her corn-silk hair, mountain-lake eyes, and ivory skin was a pampered goddess with all the warmth of a glacier. Irritably, he chalked up his pent-up lust to his status as a captive audience. He shoved the medallion back into his pocket.

She and Welford were meant for each other. Not a man given to rash judgments or close-minded intolerance, he nevertheless took a peculiar pleasure in making an exception in Amanda Morgan's case. With no real evidence he condemned her—as she had condemned him.

He had watched her stand on tiptoe to plant a swift

kiss on Welford's cheek. He had noticed her hands—
white, slender, soft . . . oh, how soft he imagined they
were. No doubt she'd never done an honest day's work
in her life. An Indian woman earned her way—
cooking, sewing, stretching hides. He was certain
Amanda Morgan bought and paid for hers with the
only skill she likely had—the use of her body in bed.

He kept a stranglehold on the iron bars as his loins
tightened. Damn. Just what he needed. He hadn't had a
woman in a long time. Hadn't wanted one since Dawn
Wind. Even now he was trying to convince himself his
interest in Welford's ice goddess lay rooted in the
bitch's own scornful judgment of him, an interest that
had sparked a strangely compelling desire to teach her
a lesson.

Besides, he was admittedly uncomfortable around
white women, those few he had ever met seemed
cloying, demanding, shrill. The single exception had
been Loretta Jenkins, wife of a missionary who lived
among the Blackfoot for two years. When Jace was
twelve, Isaiah had left him with the tribe for several
months, and Mrs. Jenkins had taught him the only
reading and writing he knew.

He cocked an ear toward the street, trying to decide
what it was that had snagged his attention. Then he
knew. It was the silence. The hammering had ceased.

To take his mind off it, he found himself unwillingly
conjuring up again the firm, ripe curves of Amanda
Morgan's body. He wondered what it would actually
be like to bed her. Jace snorted. He'd likely freeze to
death at her touch.

The silhouette in the hotel moved across the room
toward another shadow. The shadows met. Welford

and his ice maiden making love in preparation for his hanging?

He swore, coldly furious that Amanda Morgan should occupy so much of his thoughts bare hours before he was to die. Welford's motives were clear enough. No interlopers on what he perceived as J-Bar-W land. Kill to keep it. But Amanda Morgan? Why should she gloat over his death? And more the hell to the point, why did it matter so much to him that she did?

He paced to the cell door and back, unable to sit, unable to lie down, unable to eat even the meager meal Stark had brought him last night.

He flexed his hand, studying the simple play of sinew and bone, wondering what it would be like not to be alive. Was there anything after death? Mrs. Jenkins had assured him there was. Isaiah had often enthralled him with Indian legends on their long treks in the mountains. "Land like this, boy, got to be a bigger hand behind it all."

The hand became a fist. What galled him was that Isaiah would likely do something reckless, get himself killed trying to get to Welford. And Welford would be stronger still, proving that he could murder a man legally and get away with it.

A new sound caught his ear now that the carpenter's work was done. His stomach knotted. He didn't have to see to know. A weighted sandbag was being slung from a noose. Seconds later, the trapdoor of the gallows slammed open.

The rope had to be tested.

The rope that in less than two hours would be used to break his neck.

Chapter Two

Amanda Morgan clenched her slender fingers into a tight ball, hoping to still the trembling that threatened to send her to her knees. *God, how was she ever going to get through this day?*

Even taking deep, deliberate breaths did nothing to slow the trip-hammer beat of her heart. It was three A.M. and she was standing in front of the small wardrobe in her luxurious San Antonio hotel suite. In barely three hours she would be expected to accompany Philip to a hanging. A hanging! Her stomach turned over, the hot and cold clamminess she'd been experiencing throughout the night threatening to return full force.

She closed her eyes. *Get hold of yourself, Amanda,* she told herself fiercely. *Now! You have to go through with this. Make Philip angry, and it could cost you everything.* She dragged in a lungful of air and held it, then ever so slowly let it out. Daring a glance to her right, she was grateful to see Delia still busily straightening the quilted coverlet on the bed. She relaxed just a little. If she could fool Delia Duncan, she could fool anyone.

Clad only in an ivory satin peignoir, Amanda forced her attention to the meager contents of the wardrobe. She'd had no opportunity to shop since her arrival in town three days ago, and Philip's last minute decision that she join him in Texas had left her with precious little time for packing. Swallowing hard to conceal the true emotions roiling inside her, she turned to face Delia.

"For mercy sake," she said, affecting an impatient air, "whatever does one wear to a hanging, anyway?"

Delia straightened, planting her hands on thin hips. She regarded Amanda with ill-concealed exasperation. "You can stop right now, young lady."

"Stop what? I don't know what you're . . ." She did stop as she watched the flash of pain in Delia's eyes turn to despair. "Drat it all, don't look at me that way!"

"Look at ye what way? Like I never seen ye before in my life? The way you been actin' since I got here this afternoon, I was almost beginning to wonder. Like maybe I got the wrong room. The wrong Amanda. But it's only that the act has gotten more serious now, hasn't it?"

Amanda paced to the far side of the room. "I do wish you would stop babbling about some 'act,' as you put it. We haven't seen each other in nearly a year. People change."

"Not that much. I know you too well, Mandy Morgan. I've been with ye since you were a babe in your mother's arms."

Amanda stared at the floor. Delia had been her nursemaid, governess—friend, for as long as she could remember. But things *had* changed over the past year. Things had happened that she didn't dare share with Delia. Because if anyone in the world could see through what she was trying to do, it would be this woman, who was her dearest friend.

"You may fool the rest of the world with your put-on spoiled-brat ways, but you'll not fool me, not ever."

Amanda kneaded the delicate fabric of the peignoir. "I am a spoiled brat. I do what I please, when I please. And I don't appreciate your tone of voice at all, Miss Duncan."

"Miss Duncan, is it now? I spend a year carin' for my dear, dyin' sister and it's become Miss Duncan." Delia sighed, the worry lines on her fiftyish face seeming to deepen before Amanda's eyes. "Don't do it, lass. Don't shut me out. I love ye like a daughter. Ye know that. I don't care what kind of a mess you've gotten yourself into. Aggie's dead, and I'm back to stay. And you can be sure I won't be listenin' to such balderdash as 'What on earth do I wear to a hangin'?'" She deliberately mocked Amanda's tone on the last.

"Well, I can see there's no talking to you," Amanda said. "I didn't ask you to come, you know. When I heard about Aggie's death, I left word for you to stay in Baltimore at the house with father."

"Your father isn't my responsibility. You are."

"Not any more. I'm engaged now, and I'm going to be married." Amanda stared at her hands, unable to look at Delia as she forced the cruel words past her lips. "I won't be needing you any more. I don't want you here. You're to go back to Baltimore and that's the end of it."

She glanced up quickly, terrified of the hurt she

23

expected to see in her beloved Delia's brown eyes. Instead the older woman's lips were twisted into a frown of disgust.

"You must really have done it to yourself this time," Delia said. "And there is no way on God's earth I am leaving until I find out what and why you've done it."

Stamping her foot in fury, Amanda turned on her heel and stomped back to the wardrobe. Extracting a lime-green silk with a particularly daring décolletage, she pressed it against her slender body and pirouetted in front of the full-length mirror on the wall opposite the bed.

"You don't suppose it's a tad too festive, do you, Delia dear," she gritted, determined to see the farce through to the bitter end. "After all, a man's hanging is supposed to be a somber occasion, don't you think?"

"I think you're daft," Delia smiled, running a corner of her apron over the headboard of the bed, then moving to do the same to the maple vanity. "But I love ye anyway."

Amanda sighed. Being brutally honest, she had held no real hope of fooling Delia. But the woman's untimely arrival was not going to interfere with her plans regarding Philip Welford. The man was going to be her husband, and that was all there was to it. No matter what price she had to pay to have it be so. "Philip told me what that monster Jason Montana did to Juanita Melendez. Believe me, he deserves what's going to happen to him."

"And you deserve watchin' it?"

That Amanda didn't answer. Too vividly she recalled Philip's assisting her from that abominable stagecoach she'd been forced to endure the last five

24

hours of her journey. She had alighted just in time to see a man in chains being escorted to what Philip told her was the town courthouse. With hardly a breath to reflect on the bleakness of the town, she had been staggered by the sight of a man being treated like an animal. Leaving Baltimore had been bad enough, but to come to this desolate country to be witness to such cruelty . . .

Yet Philip's words were as clear now as they were then. "Montana raped Juanita Melendez repeatedly, while she must have begged for mercy. He beat her, stabbed her, raped her again. I'm sorry, darling. You said there's no excuse for treating him so savagely. I say he deserves worse. Juanita's own mother wouldn't have recognized her."

He brought her fingers to his lips, his breath warm against the tips. "It's so tragic, really. The poor dear was finally putting her life in order. Her father was one of the great dons with roots in San Antonio that go back generations. Unfortunately, after his death Juanita's mother lost much of his money through bad investments. And then about a year ago she died, too. Juanita was just beginning to make it on her own as a seamstress. Menial work for a menial wage. But at least she had her life. Montana even took that from her."

Amanda's heart swelled with pity.

"Such animals need to be exterminated so that they can never harm anyone else."

Amanda steadied herself. Surely Philip had been right. Such a beast needed killing. Then why couldn't she forget the look in the man's gray eyes that day in the courtroom?

"I don't know anything about this Montana fellow,"

25

Delia was saying. "If he killed somebody, hang 'im! But that still doesn't mean you should see it." She fussed with the bristles of the brush she had picked up from the vanity. "Do you want me to fix your hair or not?"

Amanda sank onto the bed, glad for the distraction. *What I want is to bury myself under these covers and not see the sun until tomorrow.* Instead she allowed Delia to begin brushing out her waist-length blond hair. "Philip should be here any time."

"It ain't decent, you know. His coming here at such an hour. And to take you to a party to celebrate a hangin'! What is the man thinkin' of?"

"He wants Jason Montana dead, and he doesn't care who knows it. Besides," she added, hoping to defuse some of Delia's growing resentment, "Philip's been preoccupied lately. His grandfather is very ill, and Philip's very concerned. Some kind of mental deterioration. Philip says J.T. converses constantly with his two sons—except that they're both dead. That's why Philip's had me stay in town. He thinks meeting me would be too stressful for his grandfather."

"Meeting you would likely put the color back in his cheeks," Delia said. "Don't seem proper not to at least introduce you to the man."

"I guess his grandfather was pretty upset about Montana and Benteen trying to start up a rival cattle ranch on Welford property. Philip thinks it led directly to his illness. So, you see, Philip doesn't just blame this Jason Montana for the death of that young woman, but for his grandfather's infirmity as well. Philip just lost his father a year ago. All of this can't be very easy for him."

Delia was not convinced. "I've met your Mr.

26

Welford once before, as I remember it. He seemed a man determined to get his own way no matter what."

Amanda started. "When did you meet Philip?" What did Delia know about her courtship with the wealthy Texas rancher? It had only begun ten months ago, how could she ... She let out a relieved breath as the woman continued.

"Met him at that fancy ball your father gave two years ago. A handsome man, as I recall, though I don't remember your bein' smitten by him."

"A lot can happen in a year, Delia." *More than you can ever know,* she added sadly to herself.

"Aye, that it can."

Amanda didn't miss the wistfulness in the woman's voice. "Do you miss Aggie terribly?"

"No, no, lass, her passing was a blessing at the end. She was sufferin' so. It wasn't the year with Aggie I was thinkin' about. It's what's been happenin' with you."

"Please, don't start that again."

"Amanda, you're goin' to a hangin' this morning. Don't you think I know ..."

"Don't say it!" Amanda snapped. "Don't you dare talk about ..." She couldn't bear to think it, let alone say it.

"I'm sorry, lass. Truly."

Amanda trembled, letting Delia finish arranging her hair in silence. To keep her mind off the other, she found her mind unwillingly reviving the memory of Jason Montana's charcoal eyes the day of his sentencing. He had seemed to hate her. Hate *her.* She didn't even know the man. Why would he ...

She recalled his cynical words about reserving her a spot on the gallows, recalled too her unforgivable

27

response. *If Philip likes, perhaps the hangman will allow me to drop you through the trapdoor myself.* She was certain Montana neither felt nor saw the chilling terror that surged through her at that moment. He couldn't know what the mere suggestion that she be on the gallows would do to her.

Her years of practice at disguising, altering, burying her emotions, had allowed her to maintain her unperturbed facade that day. But she would have to call on every scrap of fortitude she possessed to get her through the man's hanging. And she had to wonder if it would be enough.

"There," Delia pronounced, stepping back to gaze approvingly at her handiwork. "Lovely as always."

Gently Amanda touched the halo of curls now framing her face. It had been a long time since she'd had her hair done up this way. Styling it herself, she'd often had to settle for a tight chignon. How ironic that she should have it so beautifully arranged to attend a . . .

Abruptly, she stood up, crossing to the window. She eyed the darkened streets with a growing unease. Several men, their swaggering movements attesting to their lack of sobriety, circled like vultures in front of the sheriff's office. They, too, wanted Montana dead.

Unwillingly, her gaze skirted past the men to the wooden structure at the mouth of the cul-de-sac, winding past the rear of the jail. A heavyset figure was tying a large weighted bag to the end of a noose. As she watched, the man jerked on a lever, sending the bag plummeting downward out of her line of sight. The force of such a violent drop would most certainly snap a man's . . .

"Stop it, Amanda!" she hissed. "Just stop it!" She hugged her arms tight against her.

"Let me tell Mr. Welford you're feelin' ill," Delia pleaded, coming over to stand behind her. "There's no reason for you to go through with this torture."

"It's all right. It's not Philip's fault. I'm sure he expected the hanging to be over and done with long before I arrived."

"Who're you defendin' 'im for? Me or yourself?"

Amanda twisted her hands together, looking helplessly at the woman who had been her lifetime companion. "Oh, Delia, what am I going to do?" Tears shimmered in her blue eyes. "I can't go to a hanging."

"Then let me tell Mr. Welford. . . ."

Amanda covered her mouth with her hand, the image of Jason Montana being led to the gallows so vivid in her mind that it was all she could do not to be sick. "No, you can't. You mustn't. Maybe this is all Philip's way of making sure I can survive this Texas of his—showing me its worst side first. Please, Delia"—the words were out before she could stop them—"I can't do anything to jeopardize this marriage."

"I hardly see how attendin' a hangin' can make a difference to his wanting to wed ye."

Amanda crossed to the bed and sat down, her shoulders slumping forward. How could she tell Delia, tell anyone, how desperately important it was not to displease Philip in any way. Delia would only try to talk her out of the whole outrageous scheme. But Amanda had gone over every other possibility, and this was the only real choice she had, the only real chance she had to achieve the goal she sought.

Delia came over to the bed and sat beside her, giving

her a swift hug. "Try to relax yourself, Mandy. You're as tight as Mrs. VandeKellen's corset strings when she's primping for your pa!"

Amanda tried to smile but failed. Even picturing the stout Washington widow, who had these past two years set her sights on Zachary Morgan, could not bring her out of her bleak mood. Perhaps because her mind did not settle on the wealthy widow, or even on her father, still grieving over the loss of his wife five years ago. Her thoughts had leaped instead to the one person she had long ago banished from her memory—Matthew. Matthew, her beloved brother, dead thirteen years now.

Her eyes misted and she blinked savagely, holding the tears at bay. She had never cried for him, never would. She had been barely eight years old when he left Baltimore to join the Confederacy in 1861. Though nine years her senior, he had doted on her, spoiling her with almost as much fervor as her father.

"Who's my best girl?" her brother had said on the last morning she was to see him alive.

"I am," Amanda giggled, hugging her squirming birthday present in her small arms. "Oh, Matt, thank you, thank you. You know I've wanted a puppy forever." She squealed with delight as the wriggling pup bathed her face with its velvet tongue. "You're the best brother a girl ever had."

He laughed. "I just hope ma and pa don't disown me for this." He leaned down to scratch the pup's ears. "I didn't exactly check with them before I bought the little moppet."

Amanda freed the tiny ball of brown fur long enough to give her brother the hardest hug she could manage.

"I'm going to call her Moppet. And I'm going to train her to run to the door every night waiting for you to come home." She bit her lip. "You will come home, Matt. Promise me you will."

"I promise," he said, looking away swiftly. For just an instant Amanda thought she had seen the laughter in his green eyes vanish, but she dismissed the notion at once. He would come home. Matthew always kept his promises.

Later, much later, after the letter came, Amanda remembered what had really been in those green eyes—the barest trace of fear and a kind of eerie precognition. Her brother had known he would not be coming home.

"Matthew's dead," her father said, his normally strong voice reduced to a hoarse whisper. The rest of his words were lost forever as she bolted from the room.

"He's not! He's not!" she screamed. "He'll be home soon. The war is over. He promised! He promised!"

She flung herself on her bed, shoving Moppet away as the small dog sought its customary refuge in her lap. "He promised."

No one had questioned the whim of a pampered daughter when six weeks later she had given Moppet away. But Delia had known. Delia always knew. Amanda couldn't bear to look into her beloved pet's wide brown eyes, to be tormented always with thoughts of Matt. Nor watch the dog do exactly as she had taught her to do—to run eagerly to the front door of the house whenever anyone called, waiting, always waiting for Matthew to come home.

Furious, Amanda shook off the melancholy thoughts. Matthew had made his choice. His blasted principles had been more important than his family, than his dumb little sister, who had been bribed by a puppy into believing his lies. And later, when she had learned the true and awful circumstances of his death, her heart had disowned him.

But what did any of that matter now? She couldn't care less. She hated him. Hated him.

The increasing anxiety in Delia's careworn features put an abrupt end to Amanda's musings. Dropping the mask carefully into place once again, she studied her reflection critically in the ornately carved mirror. Slender hips, full, well-rounded breasts, a decent enough face—Philip would have little room for complaint once the bargain was fully struck. "What do you think, Delia? Will I please my husband on our wedding night?"

Delia didn't bother to be shocked. "You and I have had our discussions about the goings-on between a man and a woman. You tell me if you think he'll be pleasin' you."

Amanda shook her head. That was just what she needed. To be reminded of Philip's chaste pecks on the cheek. He was so concerned about her reputation and his own, as he readied himself for the gubernatorial election next year, that they were scarcely ever alone together.

"He's only ever kissed me good night," Amanda admitted. "It's hard to tell."

"Well, I should hope he's only done as much, young woman! You're not married yet!"

"Oh, Delia, what would a little more than a kiss hurt? Sometimes it's such a bore to be a lady. I want so much to feel the butterflies, the magic . . ."

"Butterflies?" Delia gasped. "Magic? Now where would you be gettin' such notions? Hardly from me, missy, my bein' a maid all my life—in the most intimate sense of the word! It sounds like you've been passin' tales with the groomsmen in your father's stables to hear such talk!"

"Well, Peter and James were kind enough to explain a few things to me. You know the sort, where and when to . . ." Amanda tried hard to keep a straight face, but the totally appalled look on Delia's face sent her into shrieks of unrestrained laughter. Oh, how long it had been since she laughed.

"It's not funny!" Delia grumped, but there was a twinkle in her eyes.

Amanda sobered quickly. How dare she find anything amusing when she'd just been thinking about Matthew? When in less than three hours she was going to watch a man die? "It's good to have you back, Delia," she said, her voice shaking. "Very good indeed to have you back."

"So are you going to tell me what you're about with this Philip Welford?"

Amanda worried her lower lip. "There's nothing to tell. I love him."

"And why aren't you lookin' at me when you say that?"

The sound of a cane rapping on the door gave Amanda the reprieve she needed. Skirting around Delia's accusing glare, she rushed to answer it.

"Amanda!" Delia cried. "You're not dressed!"

Staring down at the flimsy nightgown, Amanda scooped her robe from the bed. Throwing it around her, she flung open the door. "Come in, Philip!" She gave the sandy-haired giant standing in the doorway her most radiant smile.

Philip doffed his wide-brimmed white hat, ducking his six-foot-three-inch frame beneath the door jamb and strolling into the room. Leaning down, he planted a quick kiss on Amanda's cheek. She smiled, admiring as she always did Philip's sun-bronzed good looks. Standing on tiptoe, she managed to return the greeting.

"You're not dressed," he chided, keeping his eyes averted from her robe-ensconced body. "The party's already begun. I'll wait in the hall 'til you finish."

"Philip," Amanda said, forestalling his chance to exit, "you remember my companion, don't you? Delia Duncan. You and she met once at one of papa's parties. She arrived in San Antonio this afternoon."

"You didn't tell me she was coming." There was just the slightest hint of displeasure in Philip's warm baritone voice, but Amanda did not miss it. Fortunately, Delia seemed not to notice.

"A renewed pleasure, Miss Duncan." Philip grinned, raising Delia's right hand to his lips. "Most delighted, I assure you."

Delia withdrew her hand, though none too quickly. "Likewise, Mr. Welford, I'm sure."

Amanda giggled. Philip was a master at charming his way into anyone's good graces. But Delia was not about to let matters rest on a pleasant note.

"I must tell you, Mr. Welford. I hardly think it's proper for you to be escorting Amanda to something so barbaric as a hanging."

To Amanda's immense relief, Philip hardly raised an eyebrow to what she was certain he considered a serious impertinence. "Jason Montana is a beast, a

34

monster to be excised like a festering growth. Not only is he a personal enemy for having made an attempt to steal J-Bar-W land, but he is an enemy of society as well, ending the life of a beautiful young woman in a most savage and depraved manner."

"I didn't ask for a speech, Mr. Welford," Delia said. "Nor did I ask the whys of Mr. Montana's dyin'. I asked why you were takin' Amanda to see it."

This time a corner of Philip's mouth twitched ever so slightly. "Amanda dear, perhaps you can explain it to her. I really have to get back to the party. What dress have you decided to wear?"

Amanda hurried over to the wardrobe, wanting only for Philip to be gone. Once she was married to him, she fully expected to have Delia living with them. At the rate Delia was going, however, Philip could hardly be expected to be receptive to the idea.

She pulled out a rust-colored cotton dress she had once worn to the funeral of a family friend. That should make it appropriate enough.

"No, no, no," Philip said, rushing over to yank the drab garment from her hands. "This is all wrong." She followed his gaze to the lime-green silk she had tossed onto the bed. His eyes brightened. "There." He picked it up. "Perfect. Wear this one."

"But, Philip, for heaven's sake, no matter what your feeling about the man, surely . . ."

"Wear it." It was not a request.

Amanda bristled, remembering her own disgraceful behavior with the dress in front of Delia earlier. Festive? Just right for a hanging? Just right to watch a man die. Yet she dare not let Philip think she was not pleased with his selection. There was simply too much

35

at stake. Perhaps, she could try a different tact.

"I . . . I . . . uh . . . tried on the dress earlier, Philip. That's why I have it out. I thought it would be fine, too. But . . . but the hem is . . . is torn."

"Can't it be repaired?"

"Not in time for . . ." she faltered. She could not say the words.

"Very well," he said, though something in his eyes told her he was not altogether convinced she was telling the truth. She was just grateful he had not chosen to examine the hem.

"Get dressed," he continued, "and come downstairs as soon as you can." Then he was gone.

Amid more of Delia's vocal protestations, Amanda managed to get ready. She did not want to keep Philip waiting. When Delia tried to resurrect the subject of why she had agreed to marry him, Amanda cut her off. "It's my life; I'll do what I want with it." With that she left the room.

Downstairs, she was visibly shaken by the size and scope of the celebration going on in the hotel ballroom. More than three hundred people were crammed into the immense, ornately furnished room, most of them happily indulging in the cornucopia of meats and pastries laid out on the massive walnut buffet table.

Philip was certainly sparing no expense. She had seen parties in Washington, D.C. that would be shamed by the activities here tonight. Yet the ghoulish motive behind it all gave her conscience no peace.

She spied Philip in the room's near corner, engaged in what seemed an oddly furtive conversation with Elliott Wickersby, the Welford family lawyer. Normally boisterous and outgoing to the point of embarrassment in a large crowd of potential voters, Philip's back was to her as he hunched toward the diminutive Wickersby and spoke in short, clipped tones.

Amanda stepped toward them, but halted at the buffet, feigning interest in a croissant as fragments of sentences drifted toward her. "Taken care of everything . . ." ". . . couldn't find the damned thing." "The old man likely . . ." She took a tiny bite of the delicate pastry. Surely she was being silly, reading things into their words that were not there. Her imagination had been seriously overworked ever since her arrival in San Antonio.

She had all but decided to retreat, ready to try Delia's suggested ploy of feigning sickness, when Philip called to her. It was too late.

"Ah, darling," he said, "I'm so glad you've arrived at last. You remember Mr. Wickersby?"

She inclined her head toward the stout, balding little man with the ferret eyes. She had never liked Wickersby, and his usual cold assessing look assured her the feeling was still mutual.

"If you'll excuse me, Philip," Wickersby said, "you and I can finish this conversation at a more *convenient* time."

The less than subtle emphasis was not lost on Amanda. A more convenient time, no doubt, would be any time she wasn't around. She gave herself a mental shake. She couldn't possibly care less what private political machinations Wickersby and Philip plotted between them. The less involved she was, the better she liked it.

For now she would smile and be the perfectly

charming fiancée of Texas's future governor. She gave Philip an appropriately adoring look as he clinked a sterling silver fork against a leaded crystal goblet, seeking to gain the attention of his guests. "Ladies and gentlemen," he said, the room beginning to quiet almost at once, "I have a toast."

Scores of filled and half-filled glasses were raised in unison. Nervously, Amanda accepted the goblet Philip gave her.

"To the much-appreciated demise of a most noxious predator," Philip grinned, raising his wine-filled goblet high above his head. "The death of Jason Montana."

"Here, here," came the appreciative murmurs, as drink after drink was consumed to toast a man's execution.

Amanda forced down a sip of her bubbling champagne, swallowing the bile that rose in her throat that she dare do such a despicable thing. It had to be this way. Had to. No one could know . . . She gasped at Philip's low curse. Dear heaven, did he suspect her revulsion? She followed his gaze, relieved to discover his disgust was not directed at her but at the man who had just staggered into the ballroom. Isaiah Benteen.

"You'll get yours, Welford," the burly trapper growled, his words so slurred Amanda had to watch his lips as well as listen in order to make out what he was saying. "You lied about Jace. And I'll prove it if it takes 'til my last breath."

Amanda slid her hand into Philip's. "What's he talking about, darling?"

But before Philip could answer, Isaiah continued, this time looking directly at her, "You look like a smart little lady. Don't let this bastard fool ya. Underneath

38

his smooth hide beats the heart of a lizard, who'd kill his own to get what he wants."

Philip stepped forward to backhand Isaiah across the face. "Drunk! How dare you speak to my fiancée in such a manner! Montana didn't even bother to deny being in Juanita's room the night she died."

The trapper stumbled back but did not go down. "Tell me you didn't have us shot at when we was settin' up our ranch."

"My ranch. *My* land. You'll not steal what my family worked a lifetime to build."

"I'll do whatever it takes," Isaiah said, and Amanda was suddenly, oddly aware that this man who reeked of enough liquor to stock a distillery was really not drunk at all. Bemused, she said nothing as he chose that moment to stumble out of the room.

"I feel sorry for him," she said. "I understand Mr. Montana is all the family he has."

"You're much too kindhearted, my dear," Philip said. "Just remember, the savage brought it on himself. He killed Juanita Melendez."

Amanda nodded. She would not pursue the subject further. In less than two hours it would be dawn. She was surprised to feel the prickly warmth of Philip's cheek against her own.

"You're so lovely," he said huskily. "I can't resist." He leaned forward, the goblet in his hand tipping as he did so.

Amanda gasped, leaping back, but the damage was already done. She stared at the dark-spreading stain on the bodice of her dress. It wasn't until she heard Philip's self-satisfied chuckle that the full ramifications of what he'd just done dawned on her.

"I guess you'll have to wear the green silk after all."

She swallowed the angry words that rose to her lips. Better he get his way than risk his ire. He might call off the wedding. She gave him a demure smile. "Philip, you are a naughty boy."

"Forgive me?"

"Of course. I'll run upstairs to change."

But before she could take a step, he swept her into his arms. This time the kiss he gave her was anything but chaste, stealing the breath from her body as surely as the wondrous tales Peter and James had recounted to her in the musty hayrack of her father's stables. She was certain that any second now the pulsing excitement the boys had teased her about would begin to take hold of her. Yet this was hardly the place to find out. Shaken, she broke off the embrace.

"Philip, I didn't think you . . . I mean, you've never kissed me like that before."

"I've never had Lawrence Adams watching me before."

"What?" She glanced around wildly. "Who's watching?"

"Lawrence Adams." He pointed at a gray-haired, nattily attired gentleman about twenty feet to their left. She was just in time to see the man give Philip a leering wink. "A good friend to people who seek power in Texas. Damned lecher, too." Philip raised a hand in salute to the older man, flashing him a charismatic smile, though his lowered voice to Amanda was openly condescending. "He'll run straight to his extremely wealthy partners and tell them what a great prospect I am for the governorship. After all, how can I be anything but perfect when I can command the passion

40

of such a beautiful woman?"

"You mean the kiss didn't mean anything to you?" She didn't know whether to be insulted or relieved. She had no illusions about their relationship, accepting it as a business arrangement. And yet was it wrong to want more than that from the man with whom she was agreeing to spend the rest of her life? Certainly she had just felt the first rush of physical excitement he'd ever aroused in her. Still she knew better than to expect more.

"Of course the kiss meant something to me, my dear. But as I've told you before, a man in my position must be above reproach. My every action is circumspect. I have to be very careful."

"Careful about where and when to kiss your fiancée? Careful about who does and who doesn't see you kiss me?" Amanda tried hard, but she couldn't keep the edge out of her voice.

"You're angry." He pulled her close. "I'm sorry. It won't happen again. You know I want this marriage as much as you do."

"Yes, Philip," she allowed, "we both want this marriage. And I think now I can finally see that our separate reasons aren't really so different after all. If you'll excuse me, I'll be right back." Before he could respond, she rushed up the stairs.

Back in her room, Amanda allowed herself to hear none of Delia's warnings as the woman helped settle the silk dress over her head.

"But, Mandy, you've got to see there's somethin' not right about how eager Mr. Welford is for this Montana fella to die. Somethin' not right."

It doesn't matter, she thought. Nothing mattered but

41

becoming Philip Welford's wife. She had hidden motives. She could hardly condemn Philip for the same sin. Gathering up her green velvet cape she hurried back to the hotel lobby, going eagerly into Philip's waiting arms. At least she no longer felt so guilty about the game she played. Philip was now openly playing one of his own.

"It's time to pay our last respects to the condemned man," he said, settling his arm around her waist. "And what a pleasure it's going to be."

Saying nothing, Amanda allowed him to lead her from the hotel. Crossing the street, graying now in the first hint of the coming dawn, her eyes were drawn against her will to the shadowed gallows. She shivered, looking quickly away. But the image remained—the empty noose shifting in the breeze.

Chapter Three

Amanda hugged her cape tighter around her shoulders, conceding the thin wrap was more a barrier between herself and the nearness of the gallows than protection against the early morning chill. Her stride grew shorter with each step she took.

"Quit dawdling, darling," Philip chided, his iron grip on her elbow compelling her to quicken her pace. "I wouldn't want anyone to misconstrue your reticence as disapproval of this morning's planned activities."

"God forbid," she murmured acidly, then could have bitten out her tongue until she realized that the noise from the growing contingent of spectators had kept her comment from reaching Philip's ears. Whether or not anyone else approved or disapproved of her wasn't important. But at all costs she must stay in Philip's good graces. Straightening, she affected the haughty exterior that had for so long protected her from the world. "I apologize, Philip. I was just admiring the carpenter's handiwork. I've never seen a gallows before."

He looked at her doubtfully. But she flashed him a beguiling smile and was rewarded by the pleased glimmer that came into his green eyes.

"Hey, Mr. Welford, won't be long now!" The shout came from a tobacco-chewing man in trail-stained Levi's and dingy blue cotton shirt, who prodded his way through the crowd to reach Philip's side. Amanda's practiced pretenses served her well, preventing her revulsion for the J-Bar-W foreman from showing on her face.

"I just wish I could pull the lever myself, Gabe," Philip said, smiling and shaking hands with any and all who came near him. "But I'm afraid I'll have to leave that pleasure to the hangman."

Inwardly, Amanda was appalled at Philip's high spirits. He could as easily have been on his way to a church social as to gloat over a man who was about to die. The people of San Antonio fared no better in her judgment. Men and women both were now jockeying for position in front of the scaffold. Everyone wanted the best possible vantage point to see Jason Montana's neck snap.

The last thought, coupled with Montana's remembered jeer that she get her own space reserved, was like a fist twisting at her insides. As Philip lauded Langley's efforts to transform self-righteous citizens into a malevolent mob, Amanda's gaze trailed to the square of light visible on the ground just outside the rear of the jail. A shadow moved in the light. The man in the cell, the man who in half an hour would be the red meat for these hungry jackals. She shivered.

"You and Jack keep 'em stirred up, Gabe," Philip called as he guided her along the boardwalk in front of

44

the sheriff's office.

Amanda watched as Langley handed a half-empty whiskey bottle to Jack Bates, another of Philip's ranch hands. She remembered too well her introduction to the obnoxious Bates as he'd carried her luggage from the stage depot. Out of Philip's earshot he had grinned, wriggling something he had attached to his belt. It had made an odd staccato sound like dice being shaken in a wooden cup.

"Rattlesnake's tail," he'd leered. "Warn ya whenever I'm around, eh, missy? 'Course, if'n I wanted it to be a surprise, I'd take it off."

She'd decided against informing Philip of the man's contemptible behavior, only because the vile little snake seemed more bluff than substance. Besides, Philip really did have enough on his mind already. And right now, so did she.

She took a deep breath, putting thoughts of Bates, Langley, and the rest of the crowd out of her mind as Philip rapped on the sheriff's door. This would be the hardest part of all. Pretending not to give a damn about a man's life—no matter what he'd done.

"Come in, Mr. Welford," Jon Stark beamed, swinging the door wide. Amanda had to credit his manners when he caught sight of her and managed to *almost* hide his astonishment. "Miss Morgan," he stammered, doffing his hat, "it's sure nice to be seein' you again." To Philip he said nervously, "This . . . ah . . . isn't a real good place for a lady, Mr. Welford."

"Amanda is my responsibiliy, sheriff. You just keep that in mind."

"Yes, sir."

"Is it safe to be opening the door like that?" she

45

asked, turning a wary eye on the raucous crowd clustered ten-deep and growing along the dusty street.

Stark snorted. "Guess you ain't been in San Antone long enough yet, ma'am. Ain't nobody gonna do anything with Mr. Welford in here. So don't you worry your pretty little head."

"Here, let me take your cape, Amanda," Philip said. He'd unfastened the hook at her throat and removed the wrap before she thought to protest.

The deep V between her breasts tingled and grew hot, and she didn't have to look to know that she was now under intense scrutiny from the cell to her left. Shifting uncomfortably, her hand fluttered to her throat. "I'm . . . I'm still a bit chilly, Philip. If I could wear the cape? . . ."

"Nonsense," Philip said without so much as a glance in her direction. "You'll be warm in no time. Just stand by the stove." He strode toward the cell. "A half hour, Montana. A half hour, and you get what I've wanted for you since the day you set foot in Texas."

Amanda did not cross over to the stove, daring instead a look at the prisoner. She had felt him watching her, yet his eyes were now locked on Philip. As though the iron bars were suddenly not sufficient protection Philip took a step back. Amanda felt the gooseflesh rise on her arms at the cold menace in Montana's charcoal eyes. Murderer's eyes.

"Careful, Mr. Welford," Stark warned. "He's like a coiled snake. And he's got nothin' to lose."

"On the contrary, Jon, he's got everything to lose. And in twenty short minutes he's going to lose it—his life." Philip grunted his contempt. "You should have stayed with your savages, Montana. It's where you

46

belong. I hear Indians don't mind their women being raped and murdered." He stepped closer to the cell again, seeming to take an obscene pleasure in his next words. "At least that's the story I heard on how your squaw died. Raped. Murdered. By you."

Amanda gasped.

Montana lunged forward, shoving his arms through the bars, an insane fury radiating from every taut muscle of his lean body. "Fight me like a man for one minute, Welford," Jace snarled. "One minute, and we'll see whose neck breaks first."

Instinctively Philip leaped back, but immediately straightened, brushing imaginary dust from his jacket. "I trust this creature will be properly chained when you drag him up the gallows steps, sheriff. And that you'll cover the bastard's face so as not to offend the sensibilities of the ladies in attendance."

"Ladies," Jace spat the word, "like your whore?" He glared at Amanda. "How often does he put it between your legs in exchange for your never dirtying your lily-white hands with decent work?"

She did not betray the terror that coursed through her, like a river at flood tide, over his unwarranted attack. Wanting nothing more than to turn away, to run from the jail and never look back, she instead never took her eyes from his. But it was a hollow triumph indeed to know that this man had not the slightest inkling of her true feelings.

"Don't worry, Miss Morgan," he continued, his lips curled in a derisive sneer, "there'll be no hood for this prisoner. I wouldn't want to deprive you of the pleasure of watching my neck break, my eyes bulge out, my tongue swell." He gripped the bandana he wore around

47

his neck, jerking it savagely upward, laughing when her hand flew to her mouth. "Just practicing."

The venom in his voice shocked her. But at the same time she could actually feel the frustration coming off of him in waves. From what she had heard of him he had spent his life in the mountains. Such freedom he must have had to come to this—in a cage waiting to die. But then he had brought it on himself.

Her body grew warmer still under the heat of his stare, but now his hate seemed strangely tempered by his intimate perusal of the gentle curves of her body. He laced his fingers around one of the bars, slowly, sensually caressing the iron, and it was as though he caressed her flesh.

She stood, mesmerized, for nearly a minute before being jolted back to reality by Philip's embarrassed cough. Drawing back her shoulders, she was determined to allow Montana no further affect on her.

"You're contemptible," she spat.

"And what are you to wear a party dress to watch a man die?"

She blushed heatedly but dared not let him guess her own discomfort with the dress. "Philip described the depraved things you did to the Melendez girl before you killed her. As a matter of fact, this is precisely what I felt like wearing, Mr. Montana. An event such as your hanging prompts me to wear something festive. It reminds me of the time my father had one of our servants put down a rabid dog."

"Bitch."

A knock on the door was the respite Amanda needed to attend her shattered composure. Never had anyone come so close to breaching the barriers she had nurtured for over half her lifetime. She moved swiftly to Stark's chair and sat down.

"Who is it?" the sheriff called.

"Father Manuel."

Stark's face screwed up in annoyance, but he opened the door and allowed the hooded, brown-robed figure to enter. "Waste of your good prayers, padre."

"Prayers are never wasted, my son," the dark-skinned man said, his softly accented voice at odds with a girth that put Amanda in mind at once of the legendary brigand Robin of Locksley and his Friar Tuck, a thought that given Father Manuel's profession would have amused her if not for the priest's soul-chilling reason for being here. He stepped over to the cell and made the sign of the cross.

Montana surprised her by making no heathen retort, even appearing to be listening to the priest's murmured mixture of Spanish and English. She was grateful when Philip returned to her side. "Come, darling, it's time to go."

"You, too, padre," Stark said. "Sorry. I got to get the prisoner ready."

"Of course," the priest said. He never took his eyes from Jace. Gripping his bible, he said, "Remember, you will be blessed this day, my son."

"By Lucifer," Philip gritted, guiding Amanda out the door. "We'll be waiting, Montana," he called. "Don't be too long now, hear?"

Head bowed, the padre followed them out. Amanda watched him disappear into the crowd.

"I don't suppose you'd let me go to my room?" she questioned, turning back to Philip.

"You can't let Montana upset you, my dear. I won't

have it. You're going to stand right there with me and smile when the hangman pulls the lever."

"Not . . . not *on* the gallows?" Like uncoiling whips, Montana's words lashed through her mind. *Should I have the sheriff reserve a spot on the gallows for you, miss, so that you can watch justice dealt out firsthand?*

"Please, no," she murmured. Even the armored shell in which she'd so long encased herself was no protection against something so monstrous.

"I'm not asking, Amanda, I'm telling you. This is very important to me. I've got to show everyone that the J-Bar-W does not put up with squatters."

"What are you talking about? The man is being hanged for murder. It has nothing to do with . . ."

"Not directly perhaps," he allowed, leading her toward the scaffold. "But don't think I haven't encouraged people to make the connection."

"Philip, for God's sake, he *is* guilty, isn't he?"

"Of course. I saw him in the girl's room that day. So did Langley and Bates. The desk clerk found him there with the body, the knife in her chest. But don't think I'm not going to use that outlaw's stupidity to my fullest advantage."

Her legs shook as she allowed Philip to lead her up the wooden steps. Had he not gripped her elbow she would never have managed the ascent. An eerie feeling stole over her. What would it be like if the hangman were waiting for her? The hangman. Amanda stared at him, standing aloof in the far corner of the platform. How could a man kill other men for a living? Was it such a man who . . . She slammed back the thought, crossing to the front railing.

So many faces—curious, anticipating, eager—called

up to her in the expanding light. Sickened, she turned toward the rear rail, jumping when the empty noose brushed her arm. Her gaze trailed downward. She was standing on the trapdoor. Swallowing convulsively, it was all she could do not to faint.

The crowd cheered as Philip waved. He was wallowing in every minute of this, milking it to his fullest political advantage. Again and again Amanda had to tell herself that all she endured here today would be worthwhile in the end. She turned, her heart pounding at the sound of chains dragging on wood.

Stark had a firm grip on his prisoner's upper left arm. Montana's hands were shackled behind his back. A similar chain fettered his ankles. His long legs were made for lengthy strides, but his movements now were awkward, clumsy. Against her will, she felt her sympathy rise. A man should die in private, not as the main attraction in a public circus with a crowd yelling obscenities.

Head still bowed, the hooded padre reappeared to follow Montana and the sheriff up the stairs.

On the platform the sheriff accepted a black silk cloth from the executioner and offered it to Montana. True to his word, Montana shook his head. If the crowd wanted to see him die, they would damned well see it all.

The padre opened a small prayer book, his huge hands gliding reverently over the gilt-edged pages. Amanda's eyes blurred. She gripped the rail behind her as the hangman settled the noose over Jace Montana's head. Her stomach heaved.

The hangman wrapped a gnarled fist around the lever. Amanda couldn't tear her eyes from Jason

Montana's face. His throat muscles tightened as he swallowed hard. In spite of all the bluster, he was scared. Still, his jaw was set stone tight with an emotion she couldn't read. Futility? Fury?

He turned his head toward her, his eyes alive with contempt. "Hope you enjoy the party, Miss Morgan. I'm saving this next dance for you."

She gripped the rail tighter, driving splinters into her palm to keep from being sick. He turned toward the crowd, staring straight ahead, though Amanda was certain he saw nothing, no one.

"You're going to hell at last, Montana," Philip sneered.

"I'll have your room ready."

It was the sheriff who was to signal the hangman. But Jon Stark watched Philip, waiting for a sign that he wanted the lever pulled. Jace straightened. Amanda closed her eyes but opened them at once. Philip smiled approvingly.

The padre stepped back, halting beside her.

"Let's not keep these good people waiting any longer, sheriff," Philip said. He nodded toward Stark. "Do it."

Amanda screamed.

The padre threw back his hood, looping his arm brutally around her waist. She couldn't breathe as a twelve-inch-long hunting knife was pressed against her neck.

"Unchain him," a beardless Isaiah Benteen growled. "Unchain him before I slit this little lady's throat."

52

Chapter Four

Amanda couldn't breathe as Isaiah's bear-hug grip crushed the air from her body, her instinctive urge to struggle, fight, claw for life, thwarted by the knife he held against her throat.

"Please," she gasped, "let me go."

"Can't," Isaiah said, his voice softening just a little, as though he regretted what he was doing to her. "Not 'til Jace is safe." To the sheriff he grunted, "Let 'im loose, Stark."

In the whirling blackness that hovered over her, threatened to smother her, Amanda's perception of the deadly drama being played out on the gallows platform grew curiously more acute. She listened as the initial shouts and screams of the crowd ceased. An odd, almost expectant silence descended over the several hundred spectators, audience now to a different, though equally macabre entertainment. As with Montana's hanging they seemed content, even eager, to watch.

She heard Stark swear bitterly as he tromped over to

unlock the manacles on Montana's wrists and ankles. "You'll never get away with this."

Montana yanked off the noose, extracting the six-shooter from its holster on the sheriff's hip. "Trying sure as hell beats the alternative."

"You'll be dead before you get to the bottom step."

Amanda sensed the sheriff's threats were hollow, empty, muttered more out of embarrassment than conviction even before the lawman began to back off. He halted beside the hangman who was now standing in the far corner of the platform. The executioner's interest in the proceedings had dissipated along with the need for his services.

Where was Philip? Why wasn't he doing anything to stop this madness? He'd said and done nothing since Benteen had grabbed her. Out of the corner of one eye she caught sight of him pacing near the sheriff.

"Philip," she half sobbed. "Philip, help me. Do something."

"Be brave, my dear," he said, though the fury latent in his voice belied the encouraging words. "These outlaws don't dare harm you. You're the only thing standing between them and the bullets in every gun in this town."

Benteen's grip on the knife tightened perceptibly.

"Please," she whispered as the blade scraped her tender flesh. "You're hurting me."

"Careful," Jace warned, casting a quick glance in their direction. "Don't cut her."

For an instant Amanda could scarcely believe she'd heard him correctly, but the outlaw's next words ended any thoughts she might have formed about his capacity for mercy or compassion. "If you kill her, we won't have a hostage."

Philip was right. She alone was keeping Montana and Benteen alive. Montana especially had grown the most agitated as he scanned the crowd, seeming to search for something—or someone. An accomplice?

At least the mountain man relaxed his grip, though he did not release her. Amanda winced as he touched what she knew must be an angry red welt on her throat.

"I didn't mean that, missy," he said. "I wasn't thinkin' proper. I guess I was just scared about . . ."

She cringed away from him. "Let me go. Please."

"Can't."

Philip's tenuous hold on his temper snapped. "I don't know how you allowed this travesty, Stark," he shouted, "but you'd better get it stopped now."

"And how do you suggest I do that, Mr. Welford?" the sheriff demanded. "Let Benteen kill Miss Amanda?"

Philip whirled toward the crowd, his hands clenching around the wooden railing that edged the platform. "Isn't any of you going to do something? Are you all cowards?"

"You give the word, Mr. Welford," Gabe Langley called. "We'll bring 'em both down."

"Philip," Amanda choked, "for the love of heaven . . ." Would he really allow a fusillade of bullets to . . .

"Perhaps you'd best reconsider," Montana gritted, cocking Stark's pistol and levelling it at Philip. "Call 'em off, or I'll put the first bullet in your head."

Philip seemed to collect himself, spreading his arms wide in a gesture of capitulation, but the challenge remained in his voice. "You'll never get out of town alive. Neither you nor that vermin who's dared touch Amanda."

Montana ignored him, a slow smile spreading across his dark features as he stared into the crowd. Amanda followed his gaze. A young Mexican boy was wading through the throng, leading two saddled horses.

"Maybe it's time to see just what dear Amanda"— Montana sneered her name—"means to you, Welford."

The closer he stepped, the more she tried to shrink away, but Isaiah's huge body blocked her as surely as a bear-sized boulder. Montana's fingers curled like steel bands around her wrist.

"We're leaving," he said. "Anyone sends a bullet in our direction"—he placed the barrel of the .45 against Amanda's temple for emphasis—"and she won't live to be in your bed again, Welford."

To Amanda he grated, "Do exactly as I tell you. Exactly. Try anything at all, and more people than you will die here today." His eyes raked the bold neckline of her dress. "Not that a spoiled white bitch like you would give a damn about anyone else. . . ."

Even in her terror Amanda stiffened. How dare this beast, this murderer, judge her and find her wanting?

"I'll suffer your presence because you have the gun," she said, though her voice shook. "But I'll not suffer your vile insults one more minute."

His eyes narrowed and for just an instant she could have sworn she saw a grudging admiration in their charcoal depths. But then it was gone, and he was angrily shoving her ahead of him. "Move."

Trembling violently, Amanda stumbled down the gallows steps, Montana's hand still locked around her wrist. At the bottom Benteen gathered up the reins of both horses.

"Gracias, little amigo," he said, flipping the boy a gold coin.

"De nada, senor," the boy grinned, turning to disappear into the crowd.

"Of all the despicable . . ." Amanda blurted. "Using a child!"

To her astonishment, Benteen blushed, stammering, "I just told 'im to do me a little favor and I'd pay him for it. He didn't know . . ." He stopped, raising his scatter gun as the crowd pressed forward. "Get back, all o' you."

"You ain't goin' nowhere with Mr. Welford's gal," Gabe Langley snarled.

"So I take it you want to be the first *dead* hero, eh, bucko?" Benteen clicked back the double hammers on the ominous-looking weapon.

Langley straightened, taking a step back. "Now don't do nothin' stupid, old man."

Amanda's despair mounted. She watched the rest of the crowd fade back as a unit, Langley's bluff called.

"Get mounted, Jace," Isaiah said, shrugging out of the padre's robes. "I'll keep these boys honest."

Jace held a hand out to Amanda, his lips twisting into sardonic smile. "After you."

"No!' Her heart turned over. He couldn't mean . . . "Please, no! You can't take me with you. You can't."

"Can and will," Jace said. "Now shut your mouth and get on that horse."

"Do we have to do that?' Isaiah growled.

"Got no choice," Jace said. "They're less likely to shoot as long as we've got Welford's bi—woman."

57

Amanda twisted frantically, searching the gallows for Philip. She would have begged him to help her, yet what she saw trapped the words in her throat. Philip had somehow acquired a rifle and he was aiming it at Montana. What if the bullet went right through him and . . .

Montana must have read the new terror in her eyes. He jerked around, keeping her piniored in front of him. "Don't try it, Welford."

Philip lowered the weapon.

"Mount up," Jace snapped, his fingers digging cruelly into her arm.

"Don't, please don't."

"Get on the horse. Now."

With shaking fingers she grasped the pommel but could not muster the coordination required to make her legs move. "I can't. Please, Mr. Montana, don't do this."

"So it's *Mister* Montana now?" he mocked. Keeping a firm hold on her wrist he vaulted into the saddle, hauling her up in front of him. "Hang on."

Amanda shivered as he locked an arm around her waist. The man scent of him, the sweat, the leather, the feel of hard muscles beneath his dampened shirt, the broad chest so very close—all combined to assault her senses in a most peculiar way, a way that had nothing at all to do with having her life in danger.

"This is unthinkable," she cried, saying the first thing that came to mind, anything to cover the real reason for her suddenly roiling emotions. "I can't ride astride. I'm a lady!"

His jaw dropped, his eyes widening in disbelief. He seemed almost amused, though she perceived the

58

situation would not allow him to show it even if he were. His voice, nonetheless, was deadly soft. "You stay on this horse, *lady,* or a lot of people are going to die here today, including you." He kept the gun at her head, addressing the crowd. "Nobody follows. Nobody. Or she dies first."

Slamming his heels into the bay's sides, he sent the animal leaping forward. For just an instant Amanda struggled, but the cruel tightening of Montana's arm assured her her efforts were in vain. She held on tight as he whipped the bay into a full gallop. Vaguely she heard Stark shout that everyone was to hold his fire. But when she dared a glance back it was to see Philip bracing himself in the middle of the street, sighting down his rifle. "No." She mouthed the word just as the long barrel flashed fire.

She gasped then caught herself, astonished to realize she would not have been surprised at all to feel Philip's bullet tear through her as long as it killed Montana. But his aim must have been off. He would get no chance to fire again, as Stark yanked the rifle from his grasp.

She felt a sense of relief that under the circumstances seemed ludicrous. But then it was gone, as the grim reality of what was happening to her slammed home.

Isaiah's sorrel pounded up beside them, keeping pace with the bay. Side by side they thundered out of San Antonio.

They rode for miles at a hard run, Amanda's fingers twined in a deathgrip on the pommel. The pins securing her hair yielded one by one to the wind whipping her face until her blond tresses unfurled like the horse's mane that lashed her fingers. Within minutes her thighs

59

ached, protesting the unaccustomed position of riding astride. Her calves would pay the price, too. She winced as the stiff leather of the stirrups caught her again and again, her hiked-up skirts leaving much of her legs exposed to the contact. Even the hard ridge of Montana's knees added to her torment. Shifting her body any way at all only brought more pain.

Gradually, gratefully, a creeping numbness settled over her. She paid little heed to the passing terrain except to note that the ravine-slashed expanse seemed as barren as the hope that flickered and died within her.

No one was following.

She was at the mercy of a murderer.

Chapter Five

The first time Montana sent his horse plunging into an arroyo, Amanda clung tight to avoid being pitched off. The second time she let go.

She hit the ground hard on her left hip, rolling, tumbling down the steep embankment to the dry rock-scattered creekbed below. Taking no time to consider broken bones, she scrambled to her feet, gathered up her skirts, and stormed headlong back up the embankment.

"Let her go!" she heard Isaiah call. "We don't need her no more."

But she didn't have to turn to know that Montana had wheeled his horse around and was now bearing down on her like some distorted, malevolent centaur. In seconds the bay was laboring up the incline behind her. Feinting left then bolting right, she held up a hand to ward off the imagined feel of Montana's whipcord body tackling her own slender one. But it didn't happen.

She ran a hundred yards, two hundred, ducking into

a thick stand of cottonwood, stumbling to a halt beside a huge, withered tree. Leaning against it for precious seconds, she dragged air into her lungs in great deep gulps. She closed her eyes at the sound of the horse cantering back down the embankment. She felt no relief. Its rider had dismounted. Montana's boots crunched along the hard ground as he stalked toward her.

She willed herself to move, but her flight had already made her painfully aware of the effects of the unaccustomed hard ride. Her legs felt more like rubber than muscle and bone, threatening to buckle if she even moved away from the tree. Scanning the desolate countryside beyond the trees she let out a mirthless laugh. Where would she go anyway? The only evidence of human occupation in the wild land was the relentless scrape of Montana's boots on rock as he continued to track her.

If she eluded him, she would be on her own. Alone in the middle of nowhere. To die of thirst. Starvation. Or God knew what on the open plain. And if he caught her? She would be at the mercy of a man convicted of a savage murder. Either way she would be dead.

She bit her lower lip to keep from crying out her despair. She would run, she had to. Better the wilds of Texas, than . . .

A hand grabbed at her, fingers twisting into the shoulder of her dress. She knew at once that if she tried to move he would yank it from her body. She didn't move.

"That was stupid," he said, whirling her around to face him. "Get back to the horse."

The dark anger in those gray eyes unsettled her. If he

chose to rip away her clothes, to . . .

She swung at him, her arms flailing wildly. "Let me go! You got what you wanted. You got out of town. Now let me go!"

He pinned her arms at her sides, his lips compressed in a grim line. "Lady, there's nothing I'd like better. But I can't trust that sheriff not to follow. And if he does, I'll feel safer hiding behind you than behind some rock."

"That sounds like something a murdering monster like you would do. Hide behind a woman's skirts!"

"And pretty skirts they are," he said, eyeing the daring cleavage of the dress with infuriating insolence.

She tried to back away, but he held her fast. In that despairing instant she realized just how fragile life was. The strength in those huge, tanned hands was awesome. He could as easily crush her throat as crush a flower. She dragged in a shuddering breath, wishing fervently, ridiculously, that she had listened to Delia and refused Philip's command that she attend Montana's hanging. Would the outlaw kill her now and leave her body for wild animals to feast upon? She couldn't stifle an urge to gag.

He muttered an oath, seeming to read her thoughts, then thrust her away from him. "I don't murder women before breakfast."

Shaken, terrified, she crossed her arms in front of her, remembering all too vividly Philip's description of Juanita Melendez's bruised and battered body.

"Don't flatter yourself," he grated. "I don't rape women before breakfast either."

Amanda tried with everything in her to steel herself from the incapacitating fear that was shrouding her every thought. All of her life she had prided herself on being in control, not allowing anyone to gauge the true depth of her feelings—not about Matthew's death, not about marrying Philip, not about anything. But this mind-numbing, spirit-destroying terror of being captive to a murderer was more than she could bear. Her imagination was becoming her own worst enemy. Over and over grisly dramas were playing in her mind—of how and when Montana would choose to kill her.

If only she could convince him that he could escape more easily without her than with her. . . . And just that suddenly she seized on the tiny flare of hope that sparked inside her.

"Let me go, Mr. Montana," she urged. "Let me go and I'll make certain Philip calls off his search for you. He'll do as I ask. I know he will." She subdued her pride long enough to add, "Please."

Montana chucked a hand under her chin, studying her face with ill-concealed scorn. "Welford isn't going to let it end between him and me, Miss Morgan. Whatever burr is under his saddle, he means to have it out until one of us is dead."

"But that doesn't make any sense."

He shrugged. "Doesn't have to. It just is."

"But I'll ask him. He'll do it for me."

"If anyone could change his mind, sweet lady," he smirked, "I'm sure it would be you—weaving your witch's spell on his poor, besotted body. But the bedroom is about as far as your charm would lead with a man like Welford. Though I can certainly understand how he could be . . . charmed." His eyes blazed along the quivering flesh of her breasts visible above the plunging bodice of the dress. "I've had similar notions about you myself, ever since I first laid eyes on you in that San Antone courtroom. Even though you promised to spring the trapdoor yourself." He reached up a hand, his fingers trailing a lazy path down the side of her face.

She stiffened, refusing to be intimidated by his touch, yet beginning to feel oddly undone by the quaking desire firing in those gray eyes. No, she chided herself fiercely, he would not have such an effect on her. She was angry, enraged that he was forever insinuating that her betrothal to Philip hinged on her prowess in bed. And for this brute to suggest that he too had entertained thoughts of being intimate with her was more than her sensibilities could tolerate.

If he were foolish enough, arrogant enough, to expect her to be flattered, he was about to find out just how mistaken he could be. She would put this outlaw squarely in his place, letting him know that she had him pegged precisely as the savage he was. Arching her neck, she faced him defiantly.

"Philip and I love each other. Not that I would expect vermin like you to understand such feelings. Though I'm not in the least surprised to hear you reduce love between a man and a woman to no more than the rutting of animals."

His charcoal eyes grew dark, his calloused palm skating past the smooth skin of her cheek to tangle in her golden hair, forcing her closer, until her face was bare inches from his own. "A particular pair of rutting animals comes to mind," he said, his voice grown husky. "A stallion mounting his mare."

Her legs were shaking. His eyes burned her, scorched her, firing a heat inside her such as she'd never known.

This was insanity. The man was a savage, a murderer. How could the feel of his hand threading through her hair calm her, quiet her, make her body grow languid, quiescent, as though he were a lost lover returned to her side after a prolonged and unwelcome separation.

"Have you ever seen horses mate, Miss Morgan?"

She swallowed, unable to think, unable to move, unable to do anything but feel. His warm breath fanned the flames that rose higher, hotter with each beat of her heart.

"The filly nips at the stud, Miss Morgan." He kissed her cheek, her chin, her neck. "She fights him, bites him. She runs. He chases. Until finally she knows what it is she wants. She stands still then. So very still. She lets him." His lips brushed hers. "She lets him."

His mouth was bruising, demanding, the bristly stubble of his beard abrading her tender flesh. But somehow she didn't mind. Her mouth sought him, welcomed him. She was alive to the hot, wet feel of his tongue as it parried with her own. Both of his hands were now caught up in her hair as he pressed her down to the dusty earth.

"Damn, damn, damn," he murmured, "I don't want this. Can't want this." But his hands were everywhere, tugging open the tight bodice of her gown to free her breasts to his searing gaze. The paleness of them struck him first, milk-white with perfect pink tips, the nipples already thrusting pebble hard against the deep brown of his hand.

The blood-engorged heat of his sex grew painful, aching for release from the sweet torment that engulfed him as his mouth captured a creamy mound. His heart hammered against his ribs. His need driving him, he grew rougher than he meant to, his hands slipping beneath her skirts in search of the silken softness of her womanhood.

Her legs crossed, an action that seemed instinctively shy, fearful. But he allowed no time to puzzle it out.

Fumbling, hurrying too much he knew yet incapable of stopping, he started to uncinch his belt buckle. He was on fire.

Vaguely he was aware of the sound of cloth rending as he tore her pantalets from her body. But his only reality was the thundering force of his need as his tongue trailed upward from her breasts to seek entry into her mouth. "The stallion is ready, sweet mare," he whispered. "So very, very ready."

Amanda gasped as his intent seeped through the haze of passion that enshrouded her. She had been lost from the moment he had begun his awesomely erotic dissertation about whatever it is horses do when they . . . Though she was drowning in a sea of sensuality, some tiny part of her struggled for the air of reason.

"Get off of me," she whimpered, shoving upward against his descending weight. "Please."

It was the dawning fear in her eyes that stopped him, raw fear that rose up to consume the burning desire he had watched ignite in blue eyes he would have sworn could freeze hell. He tried vainly to convince himself that any woman would have stopped him, here on a brush-covered hillside in the middle of nowhere.

Stopped him, yes, his pride allowed. But only to seek out a more comfortable haven in which to spend their lust. But Amanda Morgan would have stopped him in a chinchilla-covered bed in a queen's own palace. And that his pride would not allow. He rolled off her, but his stinging frustration prodded him to exact a price for his retreat.

"I'm not as . . . civilized, as genteel as Welford, right?" he gritted, levering himself to his feet to glower down at her as he rebuckled his belt. "God forbid that a savage like me should arouse your passion."

"Savage indeed," she snapped, pinching her bodice together in front of her. "You kidnap me, you terrorize me, you . . ." She fought down the quaver in her voice. Never in her life had she felt so out of control as she had under the sweet assault of this man's hands on her body. Yet everything in her begged her to deny it. Never could she let him suspect the power he had just so easily won.

"But then I could hardly expect anything else," she taunted, rising to face him. "Rutting seems to be your favorite activity. Next to murder. You raped Juanita Melendez, then killed her. Philip even said you raped your own wife. . . ."

He took a step toward her, fury contorting his face into a mask of murderous rage. She shrank back, feeling—*living*—the horror that must have been Juanita's in that last hellish moment when the woman had known she was going to die.

But Montana stopped, wheeling to slam a fist into the cottonwood. She winced as the blow shredded his skin and drew blood. Winced, too, because she knew the tree had merely been a stand-in for her face. His arm snaked out, his fingers twisting in her hair, yanking it viciously back.

"You ever . . . *ever* . . . speak of Dawn Wind again, and I'll make you wish you'd never been born." He released her so quickly that she fell. Cursing, his hand curled around her arm, and he hauled her to her feet. "Get the hell back to the horses. Now!"

Her legs balking with every step, she stumbled toward the bay gelding. What in the world had possessed her to say such a thing to him? Was she trying to get him to kill her swiftly and get it over with? Or trying, however pathetically, to convince herself that what had almost happened here had not happened at all?

The fury in his eyes had proved to her as nothing else could that this man was indeed capable of killing. But murder? He had not loosed his rage on her when there had been nothing and no one to stop him. That he possessed a volcanic temper was evident, but for now he had proved himself its master. Could such be said of a murderer? And was it solely for her own peace of mind that she was suddenly so concerned about his guilt or innocence?

Try as she might, she could not accept her own startling reaction to the man. A few words, a few kisses, and she had been about to . . .

Shaken, bewildered by her own behavior, she reasoned desperately that it must have been the shock of being kidnapped. To resist Montana would have been to invite Juanita's fate. *Yet you did resist,* came the condemning thought, *and he stopped.*

Something had happened to them there among the sheltering trees. Happened to them both. For she was suddenly, oddly certain that Montana was not a man to vent his lust on a woman he hardly knew.

That thought did not necessarily establish his innocence regarding Juanita Melendez's death, but that was of no particular consequence. Amanda was still too upset by the obviously primitive, obviously mutual feelings the two of them had stumbled onto. It made her remaining his prisoner all the more untenable for them both. She had little doubt that he was as repelled by what had happened as she was.

But for now she had no strength to run. Each step an effort, she followed him back to his horse. He picked up the trailing reins and walked the bay over to where Isaiah still sat mounted. He stood there, frowning, scratching the back of his head. "You know, Isaiah, in thirty-two years this is the first time I've ever seen your face."

The old man grinned. "Kinda scary, ain't it?"

Montana grinned back, but then he grew serious. "I'm sorry, Isaiah. I know what your beard meant to you."

"Shucks, boy, it had to be done. A grizzly bear padre would never do."

"Uh huh. And just how did you get Father Manuel to loan you his robes? When he passed me that note in the jail, it just said be ready for anything."

"He had his reasons."

"Isaiah . . ."

"You know, you had me worried a minute ago," the old trapper growled, deliberately changing the subject. "I was beginnin' to think I should round up a search party. I didn't think a slip of a gal would give you such a run, painter."

"I caught her, didn't I?" Amanda didn't miss the new edge in the outlaw's voice. Benteen, too, gave him a quizzical look.

"Should have let her go," Isaiah said. "She'll just

slow us down."

"Maybe," Montana allowed, not once looking at Amanda. "But if a posse gets on our butts, she may be the only thing that makes 'em think twice about using their guns."

"If we make it to Mexico, we won't have to worry about no posse."

"That's three, maybe four days of hard riding. And a bastard like Welford may not even give notice to a border. Besides, he and I have a score to settle."

"You can't be thinkin' about that now."

"It's all I'm thinking about. He wants me dead. And I intend to find out why."

Isaiah looked uncomfortable. "We'd best get riding."

Jace gripped the sorrel's bridle. "You all right?"

"'Course I'm all right. I just want as many miles as we can get between you and Welford." He looked ruefully at Amanda. "And I don't think havin' his woman along is a good way of convincin' him to keep his distance."

"Don't worry," Jace said. "I don't like the idea of having her with us either."

Isaiah frowned. "I suspicion your reasons may be a little different than mine."

Jace strode back over to Amanda, shoving her against the horse. "Mount up. *Fall* off again, and you'd best hope you break your neck. If you don't, I'll do it for you."

Trembling, she gripped the pommel and managed to pull herself into the saddle. Her thighs ached and her bare shoulders were beginning to feel the effects of the blazing sun, but she said nothing. The leather creaked its protest as Montana mounted behind her.

"I still say you ought to turn her loose," Isaiah said, patting the big sorrel's neck. "We're close enough to San Antone; they'd find her sure."

"I've been doing my damnedest to make sure they *can't* follow us. We set her loose, she'd be lost in half a minute, dead in a day."

Her eyes widened. Was this some sort of backhanded concern for her safety? As before, his next words ended her humanitarian notions about the man.

"She's worth more alive than dead. If Welford does find us, maybe we can work a trade. Our lives for his whore."

Amanda blushed heatedly. He was even angrier than she had thought about what had happened—or rather not happened—in the arroyo. But to her amazement Isaiah Benteen did not let the slur pass unchallenged. "I'd best not hear you call her that again, painter. She's a lady. And I won't have you talkin' like a guttersnipe in front of her. I raised you to know better."

It was the outlaw's turn to shift uncomfortably. "I guess I just don't know a *lady* when I see one sometimes." He lifted his hat to Amanda. "My most sincere apologies, ma'am." His voice came nowhere near matching his words in sincerity.

But Amanda was still too busy mulling over her astonishment that he had said them at all. Whatever granite core of bitterness drove Jason Montana, he had a definite soft spot when it came to the burly mountain man.

"That's better," Isaiah said. His words grew wheezy as he seemed to fight to catch his breath. A coughing spasm doubled him over.

Montana's eyes narrowed. He started to dismount. "We'll make camp here."

Isaiah's hand stayed him. "No, I'm all right. Just these old bones objectin' to the hard ride."

"We can stay here," Jace insisted. "It's as good a place as any."

"It's got no real cover, no water. Don't you go stoppin' on my account. I mean it." The big man slapped his heels into the sorrel's sides.

Cursing, Montana spurred his mount after Benteen's. As they rode, Amanda sensed a change in him. He was no longer simply on the alert for pursuers but for any sign at all that Isaiah Benteen could travel no farther. The outlaw's obvious concern for the old man touched a deep, personal cord in her, though she was loathe to admit it. It had been so long since she dared risk caring about anyone, that being witness to such obvious and loving affection was like a physical pain.

She forced her mind elsewhere, even to trying hard to shift her position on the saddle so that her thighs would not continue to be chafed raw by her drawn-up skirts.

"It hurts to ride like this," she said, keeping her voice carefully devoid of emotion. "My face and shoulders are getting sunburned and the top of my legs are . . ." She stopped, not quite able to force out the words that would describe her inner thighs.

"I couldn't care less" was Montana's only comment.

Angrily she jerked at her skirts, seeking to tug the first layer of fabric out from under her rear end. She could use it to shield her already reddening shoulders. Slightly off balance, she was nearly catapulted off when the horse broke stride for an instant.

Montana's strong arms circled her with lightning swiftness. "What did I tell you about staying on this horse?" he growled.

She slapped at his hands. "That's it! I would rather be dead than owe my life to the likes of you." His hands only tightened their grip.

"Still afraid of the savage in me, aren't you, Miss Morgan?" He leaned forward, deliberately nuzzling her neck as the horse continued to move in a rhythmic canter. "I really can't go on calling you *Miss Morgan*. Too formal."

"You can do us both a favor by not addressing me at all," she hissed, flinching away from the intimate contact of his lips as they trailed to her shoulder. She was livid that he was again using the one weapon against which all of her defenses had thus far proved to have but a token effect. His blasted body.

"I think I'll call you Andy," he continued, as though she hadn't spoken. "Yes, Andy it is."

"That's outrageous! If you think I'm going to answer to such an impertinence . . ."

She gasped as his hand captured her breast from behind. His thumb and forefinger teased the hardening nipple beneath the silk fabric. He was taunting her, provoking her, deliberately eliciting a reaction. And though she tried with everything in her, she was unable to prevent the reaction she was certain he most wanted. Slowly, inexorably, like a kitten lulled to sleep with gentle, caressing strokes, she molded herself against him, a low throaty moan torn unwillingly from her throat.

She was only half aware that Isaiah Benteen was riding at a steady pace some twenty yards behind them.

If he had been riding next to them, she doubted she could have stopped herself from surrendering to the sensual magic of Montana's hands.

"See," he whispered huskily, cocooning the breast under his large palm, "even a savage can be discreet."

Hot tears of shame burned beneath her eyelids, but she blinked them back with a new, fierce anger. She was not going to allow this madness to continue. She was his prisoner, for God's sake! His actions were no doubt just some sick ploy to gain her cooperation. Well, it was not going to happen. When Philip found her, it was going to be obvious she had fought valiantly for her life, her honor. Her fingernails clawed at the back of Montana's exploring hand until he cursed and snatched it away.

"Don't worry, *Andy,*" he soothed mockingly, "when Isaiah falls asleep tonight it'll take more than fingernails to keep me away from you."

She swiped at an errant tear, outraged that he be the cause of her shattered composure. "I'll kill you. I swear I'll kill you." But her voice was as broken as her spirit now felt. How could she fight his superior strength, his guns, his hate? For that he hated her, she was now certain. It was what drove him to constantly bedevil and belittle her, and while his reasons may have begun with Philip, her own goading behavior had fueled the fire beyond containment.

She did not question why his hands dropped away then. He had promised his vengeance for tonight. And she had no doubt at all that he would have it.

Chapter Six

Amanda had longed for the torturous day to end so that see could find respite in sleep, but now with Montana's threat of rape to mark the night, she wished only that the agonized ride could go on forever. The relentless heat of the sun, the pain in her shoulders and legs, combined with the stomach-wrenching fear she had suffered throughout the twelve hours since these two men had kidnapped her, wore away at even the reserves of her strength. Her senses dulled and there were times she feared she grew incoherent.

Her head lolled back, her emotions so ragged that she no longer cared if she used his body to cushion away a little of her pain. Random thoughts, mere fragments, danced ghostlike just out of reach of her conscious mind. Almost giddily she had come to accept Montana's logic in taking her hostage. The people of San Antonio would not jeopardize the life of Philip Welford's fiancée.

But what toll would this nightmare take on her before it was over? Again and again her mind replayed her scandalous reaction to Montana in the arroyo. How could she have been so wanton with an . . . outlaw? Even now she retained an odd awareness of the latent power in the lean body that guided the horse. Time and again the backs of her knees brushed the taut denim of his Levi's.

As much as she longed to deny it, she could not disavow the compelling effect this man was having on her. She had made a solemn promise to herself when Matthew died that nothing and no one was going to make her vulnerable again. She would not be hurt, because she would not allow herself to feel strongly enough about anything to care.

But Jason Montana with his almighty arrogance, his bullheadedness, and his singularly foul temperament was proving a too real threat to the life she had chosen, clung to for thirteen years. Simply because he was making her feel: anger, fear, and—she fought the word—passion.

"Will we be stopping to eat soon?" she asked abruptly, wanting to shut off her mind from even more dangerous thoughts about the man whose hand rested so casually on her right thigh as he gripped the reins that guided the bay.

"We'll stop when I say we stop."

She closed her eyes tightly. Couldn't he even answer a simple question without being belligerent? "And when might that be?"

"When I feel like it."

She ground her teeth together. He was acting this way on purpose! Of all the . . . His wry chuckle infuriated her further.

To distract her temper, she ran a hand over her

sweating brow. This was exactly why she had to get away from this man. Always she'd held herself under tight rein, but now it was as though every feeling she'd ever denied herself was rising to the surface, waiting to spill through an ever-weakening dam. And once loosed, she feared there would be no stopping them, that she would be swallowed up by them, destroyed— as she had almost been by the crushing devastation of Matthew's death. It was that fear that pushed, demanded, compelled her to control the powerful emotions Jason Montana provoked in her.

She had to, or she would be lost.

The sweat dripped down into her eyes. Swiping at it, she gritted, "Do you mind if I at least have some water? Or do you want your precious hostage to die of thirst?"

"What *precious* hostage is that?"

"If I wasn't a lady . . ."

He laughed, the first time she had ever heard him sound genuinely amused. And of course it was at her expense.

"Lady?" he mocked. "I do wish I had a mirror."

She unlooped the canteen strap from the pommel and yanked out the cork stopper. "Philip was right. Hanging was too good for you."

He laughed again.

She didn't need a mirror to assess the damage the day's ride had done to her appearance. Her dress was a dust-covered disaster. At least toward noon Montana had condescended to give her one of his shirts, but her shoulders still ached from their earlier exposure. The curls Delia had so lovingly arranged in her hair this morning had disintegrated into something she imagined resembled a sweaty blond tumbleweed.

Shoving her damp locks away from her face, she poured a little water into her palm and smoothed it onto her cheeks.

"Take it easy with that," he growled. "I don't know if we'll find more water before nightfall."

With a perverse grin she upended the canteen onto her head.

He cursed, grabbing it away from her, slamming the cork back into its top. "You have a real problem doing what you're told, don't you, Andy?"

She said nothing, refusing to respond to that ridiculous diminutive of her name.

He seemed not to notice as he continued. "Well, before I'm through with you, you're going to learn some manners."

"Manners!" she blurted. "*You* are going to teach *me* manners! That's like saying a gorilla is going to teach Mozart to play the piano."

The epithet she expected was not forthcoming, though he stiffened perceptibly. Probably had a gorilla for a mother came the waspish thought. But she managed to hold her tongue. Manners indeed!

She told herself it was because she was so tired that she lay her head on his shoulder many minutes later, told herself his arm really hadn't tightened reflexively on her waist, told herself she was unaffected by the surging beat of his heart. . . .

But as she drifted toward sleep she remembered all too well how she had been mesmerized by his outrageous tales of stallions and mares. Her body had betrayed her utterly, succumbing to the sound of a husky voice and straying hands. He'd wanted only one thing from her in that arroyo, and she'd come dangerously close to giving it to him.

But sanity had returned in time to forestall disaster. And he had acceded to her wish that he stop. Had he not . . . She shuddered. Had he not her body would have overruled her head. But she was in control now, she was on guard. It would not happen again.

Jason Montana was not going to disrupt her plans to be Philip Welford's wife.

If only she hadn't made him so angry. She truly was ashamed of her horrid remark about his raping his wife. Her own expertise at masking her emotions served her well enough to recognize Montana's attempt to do the same. He had responded with rage, when in fact she had hurt him. Savaged him where he was most vulnerable—with the haunting memory of his murdered wife. It was the look in those gray eyes that put the lie to Philip's words. Jason Montana had most certainly not killed his Indian wife. Amanda would take care not to ever again suggest that he had.

She wondered if logic allowed her to take her newfound knowledge a step further. Perhaps he had not killed Juanita Melendez either. The man had so fully captured her thoughts that she did not at first notice he had reined the bay to a halt.

"We'll make camp here," he announced, dismounting then surprisingly offering up a hand to assist her down.

She hesitated, but only for an instant. His hands lingered on her waist no longer than absolutely necessary as he deposited her on the ground. She told herself she was grateful.

She studied her home for the night—a huge outcropping of rock sheltering a nameless creek that meandered nearby. The lengthening twilight shadows gave the whole place an eerie, forbidding cast that made her shiver though she was certain the temperature still hovered near seventy degrees.

"Run and you're dead," he said, without so much as a glance in her direction.

She sank down onto her rump in the carpet of soft grasses. *No anger, Amanda,* she reminded herself calmly. *No anger. None.*

Now that the reality of the night ahead was upon her, she wished fervently she'd had more time to conjure some plan to hold Montana at bay. Maybe Isaiah Benteen . . . She glanced at the older man who still sat astride the sorrel. He looked more haggard and worn out than she did, if such were possible.

With a soft moan she stretched out on her right side, threading her fingers through the sweetly scented grasses, finding strange comfort in the feel of the earth beneath her exhausted body.

Her lips curved into a half smile that held no humor. She wouldn't have to worry about Montana attacking her tonight. She wouldn't know it if he did. She was going to be dead. A person as tired as she was couldn't possibly survive much longer.

She thought about his latest directive that she not run away. Run? She doubted she'd ever be able to walk again. Now that the blood was again beginning to circulate in her lower body, her muscles were flaming to agonizing life. Her thighs were chafed raw and aching, her bottom hurt, and every other part of her body seemed to scream for its share of relief. Through drooping lids she watched Montana stride toward Benteen, who had yet to dismount.

"You all right, Isaiah?"

She caught an odd note of concern in the outlaw's voice. But she was having a hard time staying awake to find out what might be wrong. Not that it mattered in the least, she assured herself quickly.

"I'm fine, boy," Isaiah was saying. But when he started to dismount he staggered and almost fell.

Montana caught the big man under the armpits and eased him to the ground. His hands came away bloody. "Son of a bitch!" he exploded. "You've been shot!"

Amanda gasped. Philip had not missed after all. She couldn't look away as Montana peeled off the big man's deerhide jacket and vest. How could he have ridden all day, dismounted, mounted time and again, and never so much as uttered a groan of protest or pain.

"Just a scratch," she heard the mountain man growl.

"Why the hell didn't you say something?" Montana demanded, the tone of his voice more telling than his words. He was scared. Scared for Benteen's life.

"Had to put some distance . . ." Isaiah didn't finish.

Montana turned on her. "Get some water from the creek."

She eyed the burbling stream some hundred yards distant. A hundred yards that might as well have been a hundred miles. She couldn't move.

Montana was opening Isaiah's shirt, the tenseness in his powerful body palpable. "Get some wood and start a fire," he said, not bothering to look to see if she did as he commanded.

Start a fire? She'd arranged the logs in her parents' fireplace once, but they hadn't actually let her strike the match. She lay still.

Her heart jumped as she caught the sound of his

boots rustling through the knee-high grass. He was coming toward her.

"Are you going to finish the job?" she asked with no particular emotion in her voice.

"What job?" he hissed. "I thought I told you . . ."

"Killing me. I'm all but dead anyway. You might as well finish it."

He swore, going down on one knee beside her. He caught her arm, forcing her onto her back. She shut her eyes. "Go ahead. I won't stop you. Just please be merciful."

He swore again. "Get the water. Get the wood. Now."

"I'd really rather you killed me." She dared a look at the grim set of his features.

"Only if you don't get the water and the wood." He strode over to his horse and pulled off the canteen. Stomping back over to her, he dropped the nearly empty container onto her stomach. Enunciating each syllable with exaggerated slowness, he gritted, "Go to the creek and fill the canteen. Now."

No. The word was on her lips, but she didn't say it. She remembered her decision to stay as calm as possible around this man. No matter how difficult he made it. Rousing his anger and her own wasn't any way to keep things calm between them.

Struggling to her feet, she gripped the leather strap on the canteen and headed for the creek. When she reached the water's edge she dropped to her knees, and for what seemed a very long time she sat there, trying to remember why she'd come to the creek in the first place. She was so desperately tired, every bone, every sinew in her body hurt.

It took three tries to get the cork out of the canteen. She held the cowhide-covered metal flask under the swiftly moving, though shallow stream, listening to the water gurgle into its small opening. Despite the high temperature, she was suddenly shivering uncontrollably.

A glance over her shoulder assured her Montana was busy ministering to Isaiah, though he had managed to start a small campfire. Scanning the barren countryside, she clutched the filled canteen to her breast. Dare she?

She gave it no more thought, lest she think herself out of it. Staggering to her feet, she caught up her skirts and slogged into the creek. If he were so concerned about his friend, perhaps he wouldn't follow . . .

A bullet gouged out a piece of rock three feet to her right. She stopped dead, the water rushing past her bruised calves.

"Get the hell back here. Now!" came the hard voice.

She didn't move.

"Son of a bitch." He waded out to her, scooping her into his arms. She ignored the all-male body, feeling light and almost secure for just an instant as he carried her back to the horses. She pushed the crazy thoughts away, telling herself she was light-headed and confused after the tormenting day. He said no more to her as he dumped her in front of the fire he had built, prying loose the canteen from her stiff fingers.

Exhausted, wet, and hurting she lay back, staring at the dimming sky. She longed for sleep, but only one thought sifted through her foggy mind—Montana's threat. Who was she fooling by thinking she could talk him out of raping her? She could not stay in this camp tonight. It would be better to face the unknown danger of the open country than the known danger of Jason Montana.

Rolling over, she pushed herself to her knees then levered herself to her feet.

"Now what are you doing?" Montana looked up from his task of dressing the wound in Isaiah's back.

"I'm leaving."

"Again?"

"For good this time."

"Uh huh. The coffee's hot."

Her gaze shifted automatically to the pot, her empty stomach pleading that she could always leave later. But now would be the best time—when Montana was too worried about Isaiah to concern himself with her.

She would take one of the horses. Her eyes widened as she caught sight of Isaiah's rifle propped against a nearby rock. Montana couldn't stop her if she had that. Taking a deep breath to steady herself, she inched toward it. She didn't know much about guns, but surely all she would have to do is point it at him to keep him away from her.

She scooped up the weapon, aiming it in Montana's general direction. "Don't try to stop me."

He gave her about one second's notice, rolled his eyes, then turned back to Isaiah, and she was irrationally annoyed that he wasn't afraid for his life.

Grimacing, she hurried over to the bay. Staring in disgust at the saddle and gear on the ground beside the horse, she waved the rifle at Montana. "Come over here and saddle this animal."

"You want him. You saddle him."

"You'd like me to put down the rifle, wouldn't you?"

"Woman, I don't much give a damn what the hell you do. I've got other things . . ."

"My name is Miss Morgan to you. And you will stop swearing at me! I don't like it."

He gave her the same incredulous stare he had given her in San Antonio when she announced she wouldn't ride astride.

Awkwardly, she tried to lift the saddle with one hand, but let it loose at once. She doubted she could lift the bulky thing onto the horse's back with both hands. But she did manage to get the bay's bridle on, all the while keeping a wary lookout for Montana to make some kind of move toward her. But he was busily tearing strips of cloth to secure as a bandage around Isaiah's middle. The old man was protesting loudly about all the fussing, and Amanda felt a strange sense of relief to know that he seemed all right.

Leading the horse over to a small boulder, she managed to climb onto its back. She sat with both legs dangling over the bay's left side. Even the more-accustomed position brought quick tears to her eyes. Her skirts were hiked up and parts of her chafed thighs rubbed against the animal's coarse hair and sweaty body. She tried unsuccessfully to suppress a gasp of pain as she sought a more comfortable perch. Her gasp brought Montana's head up, and for an instant she thought she saw a flash of concern in his gray eyes. But of course that was ridiculous.

"I can't let you take the horse," he said quietly, rising to his feet. "Isaiah and I are going to be needing it."

"If you try to stop me, I'll shoot you."

"I guess that's a chance I'll have to take." He started toward the horse.

She gripped the rifle tight in one hand while nudging the horse forward.

He sprang at her. The horse shied. Her finger squeezed reflexively on the trigger, her heart stopping as the hammer slammed home. But the gun didn't fire. She had no time to tell him she hadn't meant to shoot.

His eyes narrowed to slits. Reaching her in two strides, he gripped the barrel and jerked it away from her. "You'll have to remember to lever a cartridge into the chamber next time you try to kill me."

Terrified, she whipped her legs around, straddling the horse. Ignoring the slicing pain in her thighs, she pounded her heels into the bay's sides.

Cursing, he leaped onto the sorrel, thundering after her. She had no chance. In seconds he caught up to her, grabbing the bay's reins and bringing both horses to a halt. Dismounting, he dragged her down beside him. His hands trapped her, forced her to look at him.

"When you're on the hunt, always be ready for the kill. Or you might find the prey becoming the hunter."

"Take your hands off me."

"Not yet." In the spreading darkness her hair caught the reflection of the ascending moon, shining like spun gold. He watched as her lips trembled, knowing they did so out of fear. Yet standing here so close to her, he could imagine what she felt was passion. Imagine it, because though he cursed it, it was what he felt himself.

His hands shifted of their own accord, settling on either side of her face, his thumbs feathering across her cheeks, his jaw tightening to find them wet with tears. He grew angrier still to find himself longing to tell her she needn't fear him, that he was no murderer. But in truth he needed her to be afraid. Anything else could prove far too dangerous to a man whose life hinged on a terrified hostage.

He felt more tears as he took his mouth to hers. He meant the kiss to be brutal, savage—a warning. A reminder of his threat for tonight. But her quivering lips fired the heat of his loins.

He groaned, guiding her down to the soft earth, his mouth never losing contact with hers. He had wanted her, here, now, no preliminaries, no niceties, just sex. He had wanted only to teach her a lesson. But he found his lust tempered by the memory of the fear he'd seen in those mountain-lake eyes.

She'd named him an animal, a savage, knowing nothing of pleasing a civilized woman. The words had hurt, stung, partly because he believed them. He'd had Dawn Wind, loved her, felt no shame at the primitive joy they had taken in each other's bodies.

But was his lovemaking such that a woman from Amanda Morgan's world could find no pleasure at his touch? The thought angered him, challenged him. No. A woman was a woman. He had aroused Dawn Wind. He would arouse this ice maiden, Amanda Morgan, and make her know that it wasn't he who was an animal, but she who feared being one.

His hands roamed the soft curves of her body, kneading, massaging, teasing, until he gained the prize he sought—the low moan uttered deep in her throat.

"Ah, Andy, you see, you're not immune to the animal in me." His lips traced the outline of her jaw, moving with growing confidence to her eyebrows, her eyelids, her cheeks, her nose. "You're beautiful," he groaned. "So beautiful. For a civilized woman." He nipped gently at the arched column of her throat. "I want you."

"No. No, please." This could not be, no matter how much her body begged her to surrender to the torturous ecstasy. She dared not succumb to the whimsy of her physical needs. She had other needs, needs so much more important than the touch of this man.

Man. Yes, man, not animal.

Oh, Jason Montana, why did you have to come into my life now? Why now? This couldn't happen. She couldn't let it. Her physical pleasure could not take precedence over . . .

She cried out, her hands reaching to tangle in his hair as he dared suckle her breasts. The sweet, gentle pressure of his teeth, his tongue, his mouth, sent a shattering response to that part of her that had never known the power of man's loving.

"Stop! Please, stop!" she begged. Somehow, someway she had to find the words to end the rapture she wished would never end. "Philip! I love Philip! Please, Mr. Mon . . . Jason . . . don't do this. Please!"

He groaned, not wanting to break the contact but yielding to the plea in her voice. With a low curse he levered himself away from her. Damn, oh, damn. Why was he listening? Why didn't he just . . . Jason—she'd called him Jason. It wasn't much, but the chink in the silky armor was there. He would just have to be patient. Patient. Though God only knew why he was allowing this woman to reach him. Their bodies might touch, but their worlds were as forever separate as the mountains and the sky.

"I have to give Welford credit," he rasped. "He knows how to pick his women."

Amanda jerked back, feeling a hot flush of shame course through her. He'd done it again. Heaven help her, he'd done it again. But, though she sensed he was all too aware of his affect on her, her pride demanded that she try to convince him she'd felt nothing.

"You flatter yourself," she spat. "Philip is a gentleman. He knows how to treat a woman. With respect. With tenderness. With love. Things an animal like you couldn't know the first thing about."

He retaliated with a single word, barely above a whisper. "Liar."

She whirled, heading back toward the camp, unable to face the tall male body holding itself so rigidly still. Though the darkness had hidden his features, she could well imagine the fury in those eyes.

She took only five steps, crying out at the pain that wracked her body from every quarter. She wavered, felt herself collapsing, expecting to feel the ground coming up to meet her, but she was swallowed up instead by Montana's strong arms. She longed to strike at him, fight him, but he had no strength left.

Just before the blackness claimed her, she didn't mistake the words.

"Woman, before you and I are finished, you're going to know just how much of an animal I can be."

Chapter Seven

"You tryin' to scare her to death?" Isaiah grumped as Jace lay Amanda down on the blanket he had retrieved from his horse. "What the hell you bein' so hard on her for anyway? Like it's her fault instead of Welford's we're in this mess."

Jace grimaced, rubbing a hand across his beard-stubbled cheek. "I don't know what it is." At Isaiah's dubious look, he added, "I mean it. I don't. There's just something about her that brings out the bastard in me."

He used a second blanket to cover her, annoyed that her shirt was still unbuttoned. Unwillingly he noted the creamy flesh above her breasts, remembering the salty sweet taste of her. Cursing, he saw too the fiery evidence of the day's ride in the hot sun showing across the exposed part of her shoulders.

"You want to bed her, don't you?" Isaiah said, his voice more statement than question.

Jace tried to pretend he didn't hear, as he dug through their saddlebags rustling up bacon and beans for dinner. But he should have known better. Isaiah wasn't about to let it lay.

"You want her that bad, huh?"

Jace snorted, slamming the fatback in the pot he'd hung over the campfire. In the darkness he kept the flames at a minimum, lest even in their rock haven they be seen from a distance.

"Maybe," he said slowly, carefully, knowing Isaiah was on the prod about more than his lusty fascination with Amanda Morgan. "But I think that's my business." He and Isaiah had never minced words on anything in their lives, though maybe for the first time he wished that the old man he loved as a father would back off and change the subject.

"A woman like that ain't no saloon lady to make her livin' beddin' men. You'd best think it over."

Jace stirred the beans, fighting down his temper. Isaiah was in no condition for one of their rare but explosive shouting matches. Unwillingly, he remembered the last time Isaiah had taken him apart verbally. Seven months ago, almost to the day.

Jace had fought like hell to keep from leaving the mountains that had been his home, his life for thirty-two years. Mountains that had become a self-imposed prison.

"We're going to Texas, painter," Isaiah had said in a tone of voice that brooked no argument.

"I'm not going anywhere," Jace snarled, not even looking up from the filthy pallet on which he lay. He couldn't remember the last time he'd had a bath, the last time he'd shaved, the last time he hadn't woken up screaming in the middle of the night—seeing the torn and broken bodies of his wife and child as they'd been when he'd found them a hundred and ninety-two

94

days ago.

He lifted the small, jagged piece of tree bark he kept beside him, scratching a two-inch-high line in the flame-blackened log to his right. A hundred and ninety-three days.

"We're leavin'," Isaiah said quietly. "It's done. They're dead. There's nothin' you can do for 'em layin' here rotting your life away. Dawn Wind wouldn't want . . ."

"Don't tell me what my wife would want, old man! Don't you tell me what . . ." His voice cracked. God. Oh, God. If there was a God, how could He have let . . .

Isaiah hunkered down next to him. "I've let ya be for pert near seven months, painter, figurin' you'd work through your grief in your own way. But livin' in what's left of your house, barely twenty yards from their graves . . . I can't let you destroy yourself like that."

Jace raked a hand through hair that felt as coarse and grimy as the bear-hide pallet beneath him. "I miss 'em, Isaiah. I liked to die thinking of her here with Bright Path. She must have been so scared. I can hear her screaming my name in my dreams. Screaming for me to help her, help our son."

Isaiah gripped his arm. "There's no sense torturin' yourself like this. You can't undo what's done. I want you to git yourself up. We're goin' to Texas."

"I can't leave. I can't leave Dawn Wind and Bright Path."

"You'll never leave 'em. Don't you see that? And they'll never leave you. You'll have 'em with ya forever. In your heart. But you can't stay here no more."

Jace sat up, reaching for the half-empty bottle of whiskey that shared his bed. He yanked out the stopper and brought the bottle to his lips.

Isaiah said nothing, only watching with eyes that were at once a measure of sympathy and disapproval.

Jace let the bottle fall. "Damn you, don't look at me like that. And why the hell do you want to go to some forsaken place like Texas?"

Buried in the bushy gray-black beard that faced him was the barest trace of a smile "Because we never seen it, that's why. Where's your mountain man sense of adventure?"

Jace swore, climbing unsteadily to his feet. "You've never lied to me, Isaiah. But I get the feeling that this time you're not exactly telling me the truth either."

"That mean you're coming along?"

"Maybe." He stumbled out of the fire-gutted shell that had been the log cabin he and Isaiah had built for Dawn Wind four years ago, when he'd first brought her here to Bald Mountain as his wife. He stopped at the graves, the disturbed earth still evident nearly seven months later. One hundred ninety-three days.

He sank to his knees between them. "I know I should have buried you with him, Dawn Wind," he said, caressing the tiny dirt mound on his right. "But I couldn't face opening his grave. Couldn't face seeing him again, so little, so cold, so . . ." The tears streamed unchecked down his cheeks. "I'm sorry."

His body trembled as he remembered the three days Dawn Wind had lived after he'd found her. Even had the wounds not been mortal, she would have died. He knew that. The light he had loved so dearly was gone from her wide brown eyes. Though he had tried to lie, to shield her, she had known. Known their son was dead.

96

His gaze trailed to the lone wooden cross three dozen yards distant. A stranger. At first Jace had thought the dead man to be one of the men who had attacked his family. But Dawn Wind had told him the man had merely been a trapper, heading north toward the Canadian border. He had tried to help her, help Bright Path, she said. But the three men had struck without warning, stopping at the house on the pretense of watering their stock, then launching into a frenzy of violence that didn't end until the stranger and Bright Path lay dead, Dawn Wind dying.

"The wrong place at the wrong time, mister," Jace whispered, "but I thank you."

Long minutes passed before he could summon the strength to rise. But before he turned his back on the twin wooden crosses for the last time, he stared at Dawn Wind's grave and said in a voice that was as cold as death, "I'll find them. If it takes the rest of my days, I'll find them. And no law, no God, will stop me from butchering them the way they butchered you."

Seven months ago. But the hate that had fired his words then lay smoldering in his gut even now, ready to blaze to murderous light should he ever cross paths with the beasts who had savaged his family.

He cursed as the handle of the stewing pot burned his fingers. Setting the pot back down, he used a spoon to ladle a portion of beans onto a tin plate, then carried the plate to Isaiah.

"You got kinda quiet there, painter."

"Just worried about you."

"Horse manure! You been thinking about Dawn Wind again. Findin' them killers. Thinkin' about how you shouldn't of listened to me about comin' to Texas . ..."

"I'm here, ain't I?"

"With a rope two steps behind ya. Damn, painter, if I'da known . . ."

"Known what? There you go again, talking like there's something you're hiding from me."

"Did I say I was hidin' something?"

Jace slapped a spoonful of beans onto his own plate, conceding defeat yet again. He'd all but given up trying to get the truth out of Isaiah. When the old trapper was ready, he'd tell him and not before.

"She don't deserve your usin' her to get back at Welford," Isaiah said, none too subtly returning the subject to the one Jace most wanted to avoid.

"I wouldn't lose too much sleep over her. She's not exactly a virgin, you know."

"You find that out for a fact, boy?" Isaiah growled, the censure evident in his voice. "You tellin' me you already had this filly, and we ain't even had our first full camp?"

"No, I don't know it for a fact," Jace said, annoyed that he sounded defensive, knowing full well that if Amanda hadn't asked him to stop . . . "It's just that I'd wager a season's hides she's not."

"You ain't going to get me to bet on a lady's virtue, Jason Montana. It ain't decent. I brung you up better'n that. I least I hoped I did." He shoved a spoonful of beans into his mouth, wiping what missed onto the back of his hand. A mischievous twinkle sparked in his brown eyes. "She's gettin' to ya a little bit, ain't she? Makin' ya sit up and take notice. Not that I'm complainin'. She seems like a right nice little girl. A trifle feisty, maybe."

"Feisty?" Jace half shouted. "She's spoiled rotten. Having temper tantrums over not getting her own way."

Isaiah's twinkle spread into a grin. "Damned if you ain't on the prowl. I thought it might be to get back at Welford. But it's her, ain't it?"

"She's a bi—" He swallowed the word, then grew furious that he'd done so. How could she be affecting his behavior even when she was asleep?

Isaiah's voice gentled. "Cut her some slack, Jace. She's scared. She thinks you're a murderer, remember? How do you expect her to act?"

"Like a lady," he gritted. "It's what she keeps telling me she is."

"And that scares *you*, don't it?"

Jace took a swallow of his coffee, cursing feelingly when he found the brew too hot. "Nothing about that woman scares me. I don't know what you're . . ."

Slowly, painfully, Isaiah pushed himself into a sitting positoin. "You never been much of a liar, boy. I remember that time you tried to tell me Tame Bear washed my best pipe tobacco with lye soap." He laughed. "I felt so sorry for ya. I knowed you meant well afterwards. But you'd seen how mad I was."

Jace frowned ruefully, remembering the incident only too well. "You smoked it anyway."

"You went to all that trouble washin' it, I couldn't disappoint ya. But now this little lady makes you feel uneasy about growin' up in the mountains with an old reprobate like me."

"She makes me mad as hell!"

"She makes you remember you're a man."

Jace vaulted to his feet. "Drop it, Isaiah. Just drop

99

it." He finished off his dinner, stalking back to the stew pot for another helping. For half a minute his conscience nudged him to wake Amanda. She hadn't eaten all day either. But then hadn't she accused him of not having any manners? He might as well prove her right. With a nasty grin he helped himself to what was left of the food. He ate the remainder of the meal in silence, then cleaned up the dishes. Padding back to Isaiah he said, "I'm going to stand watch for a while."

"You think they're following?"

"No. That's what worries me. Welford's got to be planning something."

Isaiah nodded. "You wake me around midnight. I can take my turn guardin'."

"You just get some sleep. I'll manage."

"Manage standin' watch? Or manage Welford's woman?"

"Why the hell do you keep bringin' her into this?"

"Because she's in it. And because I get the feelin' you're plannin' something with that woman, maybe even more than you know. It ain't like you to use nobody. I won't let ..." His breath caught as a coughing spasm gripped him.

"Damn, I'm going to find you a doctor."

"I ain't had no sawbones in sixty years. I ain't gonna start now." He coughed, closing his eyes for long seconds. "Hurts some, but I'll be all right. What are you going to do with her?"

"How the hell do I know? Dump her off in the next day or two, I suppose. We're not all that far from Welford's main ranch house. We get close enough in, point her in the right direction, and be rid of her." He eyed the grizzled trailblazer who was his only family.

100

"You feel sorry for her, don't you?" He lifted his hat to brush a hand through his hair. "She would have sprung that trapdoor herself this morning, you know. She said as much in the courtroom the day the judge sentenced me."

"I don't think so. I was watching her eyes when they put the noose around your neck. It was like they put it around her own. She got all gray."

"So she's squeamish. Typical white woman."

"It was more than that."

Jace shrugged off Isaiah's words, though the mountain man's perception of Amanda Morgan jibed too closely with the one his own imagination was busily conjuring. No matter how he fought it, his original impression of a spoiled bitch was being altered by the terrified young woman who'd stirred his lust for the first time since Dawn Wind's death.

"It doesn't matter what she thinks . . . or feels," he said, wondering who he was trying harder to convince—Isaiah or himself. "Get some rest. We'll be rid of her soon enough." Even as he said the words, he knew that even "soon enough" would be too late. He would not be rid of Amanda Morgan until he had had her in his bed. The cost of such a reckless move he didn't dare speculate.

"You take care with her," Isaiah warned. "There's more to her than she lets on."

"I'll keep that in mind."

Isaiah shook his head, "You'd better. 'Cause I'm tellin' ya, the cougar has met his match. That lady has it in her to be one helluva she-cat, whether you believe it or not. And if I was you, I'd be damned careful of her claws."

Chapter Eight

Jace waited until Isaiah fell asleep, then he stepped quietly over to the slender form curled beneath his own blankets. He remembered the promise he'd made to her about tonight. Promise, hell. He'd threatened her. Threatened her with rape, the very crime for which he'd been sentenced to hang.

He hunkered down beside her, listening to the deep, even sound of her breathing. He knew he was being a first-class bastard with her, but he couldn't seem to help himself. Part of him tried to justify his actions, telling himself that if he kept her scared enough she would be less likely to run off, as she had already attempted twice and failed. He did need her as a hostage, didn't he?

But another part of him—the part he was trying hard to ignore—was irrationally furious at his increasing preoccupation with bedding her.

He was being a fool. She'd named him a savage, an animal. And the jabs had hurt. Yet her icy beauty continued to stir his blood like fire. At the same time his common sense warned him that a woman of her background, her breeding, would never settle for a man who hadn't even learned how to read until he was twelve. Though once he'd learned, he'd read voraciously, trading for any book he could get his hands on, his formal education would never be a match for hers. It infuriated him further that he should now think less of himself because of it. He had never considered his life lacking before.

She shifted restlessly. "Don't hurt me. Please, don't hurt me."

The words stabbed at him, until he saw that she was still asleep. *Don't hurt me.* Was it a spectre of himself she fled in her nightmare?

He wanted nothing more at that moment than to pull her into his arms, to tell her not to be afraid, to say that he likely feared her more than she feared him—feared the cost to his pride if he continued his obsessive pursuit of the passion he only half believed lay untapped in her lovely body. More than once today his hand had brushed past a full, rounded breast as he held her against him in the saddle. She had been asleep or unconscious, he wasn't sure which.

Almost instinctively she had burrowed against him, nestling in the crook of his arm as he rode. Even above the scent of horse sweat and leather he had caught the heady fragrance of the jasmine-scented soap she must have used to wash her hair.

Without conscious thought he had hugged her closer, telling himself it was to make certain she wouldn't fall. If she injured herself she would make a less valuable hostage. But he had felt the stirring in his groin when her breath fanned the glistening flesh at the open throat of his shirt.

He'd forced himself to temper his lust with fury. Fury that she could be stupid enough to fall in love with someone as contemptible as Philip Welford. His cynical nature regarding "civilized" women pushed his jaded opinion a step further. Love likely had nothing to do with it. She was trading her body for Welford's wealth and social position. He didn't dare consider whether or not her abilities in bed might be worth the price Welford was paying.

He'd baited Amanda, threatened her, frightened her, angered her. And still been unable to keep his hands off of her. Even now . . .

His hands circled her wrists as his lips brushed her forehead. She came awake with a scream, but his manacle grip kept her from striking out at him.

"I'm not going to hurt you," he said quietly.

"You're going to rape me!" she half sobbed, instantly alert.

"No." He let go of her. "I'm not. I just want you to sit with Isaiah for awhile, while I get some sleep."

She eyed him warily in the flickering firelight as he moved away from her to lie down, her heart still pounding wildly in her chest. "If I don't?"

His silence was all the answer she needed. Climbing nervously to her feet, she gathered up her blankets and trudged over to where Isaiah lay. She placed a tentative hand on his forehead. It was warm, too warm. "Is he going to die?"

His glare kept her from repeating the question.

She huddled into her blankets, pulling them around her like a shawl. She was surprised Montana felt he could rest and leave her unguarded. If she could be certain he had fallen asleep . . . She waited.

Nearly an hour passed before she dared try. She pushed herself stiffly to her feet, grimacing to note Montana's eyes open at once. "I'm just getting some coffee," she said too quickly. "Is there anything to eat? I'm starved. You didn't stop for food all day."

"We ate. You were asleep."

"Surely you left something?"

"No."

She fought down her irritation. "There must be something. Anything."

"Nothing. I suppose if you circled the camp a couple of times you could find a snake or some other crawly thing."

"If I found a snake, I'd pray it was poisonous and I'd wrap it around your neck!"

"Temper, temper."

"I'm hungry! I'm never in a good humor if I'm not properly fed!"

"Then it's my guess you haven't been properly fed since I met you."

"You're despicable."

"You've said that before."

"I still mean it."

"And you're a bitch. I still mean that." He rearranged his saddle blanket, making it into a more comfortable pillow, then lay his head back. "By the way, if you try to leave, I'll tether you to a tree."

"I'll leave the instant you turn your back. If you think I've forgotten your vile threat . . ."

His gaze darkened, and she wished to heaven she hadn't resurrected the terrifying subject. "You can't keep me here," she blustered. "Do you know who my father is?"

"Lady, I don't even know who my own father is . . . or was."

"Why doesn't that surprise me?"

His low growl made her wonder at her sanity. Why was she forever taunting him? She scurried back to Isaiah's side when Montana flung back his blankets as though he were going to advance toward her. But he remained rooted to the spot. It was as though he didn't trust himself to move.

Gaining a small measure of courage, Amanda decided on a new tact. Jason Montana's one known soft spot was Isaiah Benteen. She ran a cool cloth over the big man's forehead. "He needs a doctor."

"He'll be fine."

"How can you claim to care about him and—?"

"Don't say it." The tone was more warning than the words.

"You live like animals."

"How easily you condemn what you don't know anything about. If animals are what we live like, I much prefer it to humans like Welford."

"You stole his land. Murdered a helpless woman. You're worse than any animal."

"You really would've sprung that trapdoor yourself, wouldn't you?"

"And enjoyed it!" she snapped, though she did not look at him when she said it.

He chuckled, resting a hand on one upraised knee. "I wouldn't have given you credit for that kind of guts. I've never found a white woman . . ."

"And I am sick to death of your bigoted remarks . . ."

"Me? A bigot? You're a fine one to talk. I heard the sheriff say you were from Baltimore. Catered to by slaves as a child, no doubt. Don't talk to me about . . ."

She stood up, the slur against her family making her reckless. She didn't stop to measure her words. "My father never owned another human being in his life. Slavery wasn't the only cause in the Confederacy, Mr. Montana. I resent your assumptions, just as I'm sure you would resent mine were I to make judgments about your life among the Indians."

"You have a real viper's tongue for someone who believes me capable of cold-blooded murder."

"I've decided you won't kill me. At least not yet. I'm worth more alive than dead."

His jaw clenched. "Maybe you do have a functioning brain in that head of yours."

"You are a charmer, Mr. Montana. I can see how you might turn a *lady's* head. If the lady were dead!"

The stick he'd been toying with snapped in two. Too late she realized her error. He would take the insult as a reference to his wife, even though such a thought had never entered her head.

"I . . . I didn't mean that the way it sounded. I mean . . ." Merciful heaven, now he had her apologizing to him. He had yet to move, yet to say a word. "Was she pretty?" she heard herself ask.

Silence.

"How long has she been dead?"

More silence. Again she questioned her motives. It wasn't like her to pry into someone's personal life. She was so fiercely protective of her own, she maintained an abiding respect for other's. Was she deliberately trying to provoke Montana? To see how far she could push him? To see for herself if he was a man capable of the kind of violence that ended Juanita Melendez's life?

"Maybe you should just go back to sleep," he said at last. "I'll sit with him."

"No. No, really, I'll watch him."

"So you can try for the horses again?"

"It occurred to me," she admitted. "But let's face it, I wouldn't even know where I was going in broad daylight, let alone in this blackness."

She waited, as he seemed to mull over what she said. She watched him settle back into his blankets. "I'm a very light sleeper, Andy. Keep it in mind."

Your Indian living, she thought, but managed to hold her tongue. Perhaps she wanted him angry to divert his attention from other things. Because try as she might to fight it, her gaze was continually shifting toward him, the covert scrutiny filling her with an oddly exhilarating sense of danger as she studied the dark features illuminated by the flames.

He was lying on his right side, his left hand resting on his rifle. It was on his hand that her gaze lingered. Long, tanned fingers curled around the weapon, almost seeming to caress it. Unwillingly she remembered those fingers trailing down the side of her face, cocooning her breasts, traversing lower still . . . Her flesh grew hot. She moistened her lips.

She had all but been undone by his touch. Why? Why with her? To prove his power over her? His superior strength?

A man like Jason Montana would have no need to prove himself to anyone. The separate yet joined shadings of his character were beginning to paint an all-too-compelling portrait of the man.

She was awed by his deep and obvious affection for Isaiah Benteen. Montana loved the old man and wasn't ashamed to show it.

Standing on the gallows he had parried verbally with Philip to what could have been his last breath. And in her mind Montana had won the duel.

She recalled the range of his temper, how he'd lunged at Philip in the jail when Welford had insulted his dead wife. Montana's anger had not come from Philip's accusing him of her rape and murder but from his outrage that the man had dared suggest Indian women encouraged—deserved—such treatment.

She stepped over to the outlaw, kneeling on the ground beside him, so close that if she reached out she could touch him. "If you take back the threat you made about . . . about forcing yourself on me, I promise you I won't run away."

He lay still, not looking at her as he spoke, "You have my word, Andy," he said softly. "I'll never force you."

The husky sound of his voice made her legs unsteady as she rose to go back to Isaiah. She hadn't mistaken the word so subtly emphasized. *Force.* He would not force her. Because he knew, sensed, felt the same as she. No matter how she fought to deny it. If she didn't get away from him and soon, she would come willingly to his bed.

"Ya think you two could shush up so's a fella can get some sleep around here," Isaiah murmured. "If a posse was anywhere within a hundred miles, they oughta be down our necks with you two lockin' horns every two minutes."

"I'm sorry," Amanda said and meant it. After all, the

man was injured.

"Go back to sleep," Jace said. "I'll try not to strangle her before morning."

Amanda gasped.

Jace cursed under his breath. He hadn't meant it literally. As much as he told himself he wanted her afraid of him, seeing the fear reborn in her eyes when she looked at him was suddenly no pleasure at all.

But he stopped short of an apology. There was little sense attempting any kind of friendly enmity with the woman anyway. She was Philip Welford's fiancée. Once he was done with her, she would go back to Welford's bed.

The last thought enraged him so that it was a long time before he fell back to sleep.

Chapter Nine

Amanda woke to the thump of something landing on her stomach. She opened her eyes warily to the broadening light of a new dawn, ready to fight, ready to run. She did neither, grimacing to find Jason Montana glowering down at her. After barely a day in his company he had her behaving like some sort of hunted animal herself.

"What is this?" she demanded irritably, running her hands over the clean shirt and trousers he'd dropped on top of her.

"They're what you're wearing today, instead of that damned dress."

She felt the heat rise in her face watching his gaze skim the top of her breasts. Angrily, she pinched together the unbuttoned sides of the shirt she already had on. She supposed she should be grateful. Her legs would certainly be better protected from the saddle trappings by the denim. But his pre-emptory manner infuriated her. No doubt he only wanted to camouflage her female curves to make it easier for him to control his male urges. She shivered. Wasn't that exactly what she wanted him to do?

Struggling to sit up, she winced as her aching muscles protested each tiny movement. She could accept the shirt. But the trousers? Even her modesty was not enough to allow for such an outrage. It was simply not done.

"I will not be seen in . . . in . . . pants!" she sputtered. "Whether you choose to ignore the fact or not, I am a lady." She slapped the Levi's away, shoving them off her lap into the dirt.

"Either you put them on, or I'll put them on for you."

She stiffened, studying the flinty look in those charcoal eyes. This was not a man for idle threats, but the odious thought of wearing the trousers prompted her to be bold. "You wouldn't dare."

He took a step toward her. "I was hoping you'd say that."

Swiftly Amanda bent down to retrieve the clothing. "If I weren't a lady, I'd make you sorry for treating me like this!"

His lips curved into a lazy, mocking grin. "You name the time and the place. I'll be there."

Furious, Amanda limped over to a high boulder, the bruises on the backs of her legs from yesterday's bare-legged encounter with the saddle attesting to the sensibility of Montana's decree. But that didn't mean she had to like it. Blowing out a disgusted breath, she ducked behind the huge stone.

Blast the man! It was just like him to threaten to put the pants on her himself. She stilled. Just like him? As though she knew him well enough to predict his behavior?

Her fingers trembled as she undid the fastenings on her dust-covered dress. She'd only laid eyes on Jason Montana four days ago in a San Antonio courtroom. How could she feel she knew him, even a little? She let out a quavering sigh. Except to know that he had a volatile temper, unpredictable passions, and a stubborn streak as wide as Texas.

Just knowing that was enough to give her pause about defying him. Grimacing, she shimmied out of the dress. Tugging on the trousers, she blushed heatedly as she buttoned the fly, checking over her shoulder to make certain the outlaw was at least allowing her her privacy. That was another thing that would be just like him—to come sauntering around the end of the boulder. She leaned against the rock, brushing a stray wisp of blond hair away from her face. No, that wouldn't be like him at all. He might not be a model of civility, but she was beginning to learn he lived by a code of honor all his own.

She scrunched down to turn up the cuffs of the Levi's, since she would be walking on six inches of trouser leg if she didn't. At least the pants fit fairly securely around her hips, as long as she kept the belt tightened. The clean shirt was a tasteless red print that in a strong wind would billow out from her body like a cloud, but it was better than constantly having her bosom come under Jason Montana's scrutiny. And she had to admit it offered her reddened shoulders protection from the sun. Still, if anyone she knew ever saw her in these things . . . She made a face. It was simply too gruesome to contemplate.

Stifling her indignation she stepped out from behind the rock, expecting to be greeted by any number of obnoxious comments from Montana. Instead she was enveloped by the wondrous aroma of brewing coffee and frying bacon. Her knees almost buckled as the scents reminded her of just how famished she was. Montana had allowed her nothing at all to eat yesterday.

Nervously, she approached him. He already seemed to be in surly form over the clothes. She decided it would be better not to ask about the food, to just help herself. Spying an unused plate and fork near the fire, she picked them up and made an unsuccessful stab at a strip of sizzling bacon.

"Huh uh," Montana growled. "You want to eat, you earn it."

She drew back, unconsciously licking her lips, staring forlornly at the food-laden skillet. "I beg your pardon?"

"I said you're going to start earning your keep around here. Since we're stuck with you."

"Stuck with! . . ." she cried, slapping the plate against her thigh. "You kidnapped me!"

"You want to eat or not?"

Her stomach growled in a most unladylike fashion, but perversely she said, "I'd rather starve than do anything to help you."

"Fine." He scooped out a plateful of food for both himself and Isaiah. Striding over to Benteen, he helped the older man eat, all the while sending sidelong smirks in her direction, as though expecting her to change her mind and plead with him to allow her to eat. Fifteen minutes later he plopped himself down in front of her.

"I've got to give you credit," he said. "I didn't think you'd hold out this long." He shoved a forkful of meat

116

into his mouth, chewing slowly, deliberately, while making all sorts of disgusting noises about how delicious it was. "You don't know what you're missing, Andy."

"I know what you're going to be missing," she muttered, her hand balling into a fist, "and that's a couple of teeth."

"Andy, Andy," he cautioned, "is that any way for a *lady* to talk?"

She whirled away from him, her stomach seeming to close in upon itself she was so hungry. But she was not going to beg. With trembling hands she poured herself a cup of coffee. He couldn't begrudge her that. But the harsh liquid only made her insides feel queasier, emptier.

Light-headed, enraged, she snapped, "You have no right to starve me!"

Montana rubbed his chin as though deep in thought. "I suppose you could pay for your meals like you pay for your pretty dresses from Welford."

She charged toward him. "You stinking ba—" She stopped, appalled by what she had been about to say, about to do. She'd never uttered a crude word in her life. And to even think about physically attacking someone . . .

Twenty-four hours under Jason Montana's influence and she was turning into a barbarian. She had to get hold of herself. If Philip should mount a rescue . . . She shuddered to think of him finding her in such a state. She was already certain the wedding was in jeopardy just because she was alone with these two men. She could well imagine the tales being spread by the gossipmongers of Philip's political opponents. But to have her mental state questioned would be the ultimate blow to her goal to be Philip Welford's wife.

"Philip did not buy me my dress," she said, forcing herself to speak calmly. "If it's any of your concern, I brought it with me from Baltimore."

"Where you have several other men at your beck and call, no doubt."

"I am engaged to be married, Mr. Montana. I resent your implication."

"You're a spoiled brat."

She shrank back, her legs folding as she sank to the ground. She was tired and hungry, but more than that, she was inexplicably hurt by his words. All of her life she'd maintained the image of the spoiled pampered young girl, because it served her well. But out here in this barren land as the hostage of two outlaws, how could she still be perceived as spoiled? Had the act become so perfect that she herself could no longer separate truth from fable?

She let the plate and fork clatter to the ground, knowing the battle was lost, resisting the urge to give in to the tears of misery that hovered over her. Not since Matthew's death had she found holding her emotions at bay to be so nearly impossible.

Matthew. His death had changed everything. Everything. She'd closed off the whole world, keeping to herself from the time she was eleven until she was seventeen. And then it had taken the combined urging of her father and Delia to get her to make any effort at all to enter the mainstream of Baltimore society. Her father had thrown one of the most elaborate coming-out parties ever witnessed, and to his mind her debut had been a smashing success. But to Amanda the entire evening had been a debacle.

More than a dozen men had stood on line seeking a place on her dance card. But as she danced with them even the so-called gentlemen among them whispered outrageous suggestions in her ear. Because of her looks, which she had never in her life flaunted at anyone, she found these men assuming she would behave in a certain manner. Her indignant responses had cost her more than one escort—that night and over the next five years.

She sighed, knowing there were times when she had been unfair. Not all of the men who courted her sought to entice her to their beds. And it wasn't even that she feared the advances of those who did. It was that she feared herself. She couldn't chance falling in love with one of them. To love was to be vulnerable to the same kind of agony Matthew's death had brought her.

And so she had earned a reputation of sorts around Baltimore and D.C. She had heard the whispered asides. By her twenty-first birthday she was Queen Amanda—rich, spoiled, and unattainable. Women sniped because they were jealous, accusing her of taking their beaus. Men stayed away, not wanting to add their names to a list of suitors they presumed to be hundreds of names long. In reality she had grown desperately lonely, though she denied it at every turn, telling herself this was exactly the way she wanted to live her life.

Her every action gained her what she said she wanted—no chance of being hurt. No chance of being loved. No chance of loving.

Still, in her elaborate ploys to stay aloof and apart from everything and every one, something had gone

119

wrong. Some part of her had come to believe that no man could ever want her if not for her looks, that there was some real flaw in her character that would make them withdraw at once should her appearance ever suffer some setback. She had played her own game too well.

"Let those fools think what they wish about ye, lass," Delia had soothed on more than one occasion as Amanda angrily paced the confines of her lavish bedroom. "They're not worth one hair on your pretty head."

"I don't know why I even try," Amanda said. "Melanie Stratford is a silly twit. She actually asked me to leave her birthday party because her fiancée was looking at me, not her. I didn't ask him to look at me! I don't want any man looking at me. Being in love isn't worth the heartache." She sank onto the silk coverlet of her bed. "Men accuse women of being treacherous flirts, but men are far worse."

"Not all men, Mandy. Just the self-important ones that prowl Washington. You'll find a man one day who won't be impressed by all that folderol."

Such a man had never appeared. Not that she was looking! But Philip had. Philip with motives far removed from lust. Wealthy, powerful, secretive, he had not pressed her emotional involvement with him. He had understood that a good marriage didn't have to start and end in the bedroom. They had made a bargain, no matter what Philip's methods, that she intended to make beneficial to them both. And now that bargain was in danger of collapse.

All because of one man.

"Men *are* the same the world around, Delia," she

120

grimaced. A thousand miles from Washington and its *folderol,* Jason Montana, outlaw, added his name to those who thought the worst of her simply because of the way she looked. Again and again he had insinuated that her engagement to Philip revolved around her talents in bed.

Her conscience jabbed her just a little. She supposed she hadn't exactly fostered a favorable impression with the dress she had worn to his hanging. But that was hardly an adequate excuse for his continued insults.

Montana saw her as a well-practiced woman. No doubt he would be astonished to find her a virgin. Not that he was ever going to find out. Not willingly anyway.

To really give herself to a man, she would have to love him. And that she would never be foolish enough to do.

She thought of Philip and felt her cheeks grow hot. But that would be different, she told herself fiercely. She would be married to him. She would have to . . . let him. Love would have nothing to do with it. Besides Philip preferred his displays of affection to be in public, where they would garner him votes. In private she would likely not have to submit too often to his wants.

She refused to consider the price to her self-respect— sharing Philip's bed, while never sharing her heart. It was not as if she hadn't told him . . .

She struggled to a sitting position as Montana finished his breakast and ambled toward her. She jerked her cheek away when he made as if to touch her. It was the smirk on his face that infuriated her. Oh, yes, how easily he judged her. And how much harsher his judgment would be if he ever learned the truth of her betrothal to Philip.

"You missed a great meal, Andy."

"When are you going to let me eat?" She had to gain her strength, had to get away.

"Maybe I won't let you." It was as though the devil himself was driving him. He'd watched her sitting there, looking so lost, sure she wasn't even aware of what she was doing. And he'd had to fight like hell to keep from going to her, apologizing. He didn't want to hurt her, scare her. But neither did he want to desire her. Yet he did. More every minute. It had taken everything in him to stay away from her last night. Was taking even more now. Damn, he was being a fool. What could he ever hope to gain but misery from a woman like Andy?

Andy. Hell, he'd meant the name as an insult. But in his mind it had become a caress. Thoughts like that he couldn't allow. He had to make certain they remained adversaries.

That was why he had launched his attack on her where it would hurt the most—denying her the comforts she had grown used to over a lifetime of opulent living. When he was through with her, she would hate his guts. And he would be rid of his need to bed her.

"Like I said, Andy, you'll earn your keep from now on."

"And just what do I have to do to *earn* it?" She was too hungry not to ask.

A strange glint came into his eyes. "You can cook your own breakfast."

She shrugged, surprised. "Fine. I'm a fair cook."

"We'll see about that." He hefted the rifle. "I'll be back in a few minutes."

"Where are you going?"

"To get breakfast."

He stalked off. A few minutes later she heard a shot. She could only stare as he strode toward camp carrying a dead jackrabbit. Surely, he couldn't mean . . . He didn't blink an eye as he deposited the limp carcass at her feet.

"Your breakfast," he pronounced. "Have it ready in half an hour. We'll be riding out soon after."

Her insides lurched as she stared at the small dead creature. "Aren't . . . aren't you going to . . . to do whatever it is one does with it before I can cook it?"

"No," he said very deliberately. "You are."

"What?"

"Clean it to eat it."

"You can't be serious."

"Dead serious."

"But how can you expect—? I can't do this." Her eyes pleaded with him, her hunger subduing her pride. But Montana only handed her Isaiah's hunting knife.

"You can do it, Andy. Gut it, skin it, cook it."

"I will not!"

"Then you won't eat."

"I hate you."

"You don't know how glad I am to hear that."

She was too near despair to note the odd huskiness to his voice when he said the last. Gripping the knife in shaking fingers, she eyed Montana for a single, wild minute. But she quashed the thought. She'd never get away with it.

"I . . . I don't know how. I mean. . . ." She looked

again at the dead rabbit. It seemed so small, so fragile. "Was it a boy or a girl bunny?"

"Oh, Lord, get it cooked, or you don't eat."

Trembling, she held the knife in one hand, reaching out to touch the sleek fur with the other. Her fingers encountered something wet, warm. She pulled the hand back. Blood. She let go of the knife, bolting to her feet, running, stumbling until she reached a small boulder several yards away. She staked her arms on top of it and bent over, her insides heaving.

It was a long time before she stopped gagging, stopped shaking. Her empty stomach ached mercifully now.

Behind her the only other sound she heard was Jason Montana's cynical chuckle. Hot tears stung her eyes. She was so hungry. How could he be so cruel.

She turned, watching him pick up the small body, slitting it down the middle, something gray and steamy sliding out. Then he was peeling back the fur. She couldn't look any more. She sank to the ground, her head resting on the warm stone.

All too soon the aroma of the cooking rabbit drifted over her, promising to drive her mad. Gathering her strength, along with her courage, she stomped over to Montana. "You'll give me some of that."

"No, I won't."

"Damn you! You stinking son of a—" She closed her eyes. She had never said "damn" before in her life, let alone son of anything. With an anger burning inside her such as she'd never known, she watched him take part of the rabbit to Isaiah. The trapper grunted his thanks but seemed determined to remain rigidly neutral in this odd new war of nerves between herself and Montana.

"Mmmm, now that's what I call a meal," the outlaw said, smacking his lips noisily.

Amanda poured herself some more coffee, swearing in that instant that this beast was not going to see her cry.

"Saddle the horses," he told her. "We're leaving."

Something was very close to snapping inside her. But she held on. Not bothering to object, she staggered over to the bay and the sorrel. Weak, exhausted, it took more than half an hour to get the saddles onto their backs. She cinched them down, but knew neither was tight enough.

But Montana had not expected them to be. After he and Isaiah had finished their second breakfast, he strode over to her and adjusted the saddles. "Glad to see you're learning to take orders. Who knows? Maybe you'll get some lunch."

"You're not going to break me, you know. If that's what this cruel little game of your is all about, I just want to tell you that you're wasting your time." Her voice cracked in spite of her resolve, and she took a moment to take a deep breath before continuing. "I've survived the worst that life can ever do to me, Jason Montana. So you just go ahead and have your fun. But hear me well. You won't win. Not against me. Not ever."

She leaned against the horse, hunger and exhaustion taking their toll. But she jerked away when he touched her, making as if to help her mount.

"I'll see to Isaiah," he said quietly, staying his hand from touching her again. When she didn't look up, he walked away.

"She was right, you know," Isaiah said, settling stiffly into the saddle. "You are being a son of a bitch. And it had damn well better stop."

"Don't interfere in this, Isaiah. This is between me and her."

"Not if you're killing her. I won't . . ."

"For God's sake, what do you take me for?" Montana all but shouted. His patience was gone. But his rage wasn't for Isaiah or Amanda, it was for himself. Turning on his heel, he tromped back to her. She was lying in the grass.

"All right, Andy, let's go."

She didn't move.

He gripped her wrist. It was limp. He closed his eyes. She had fainted. Lifting her into his arms, he settled her on the bay's back, then mounted behind her. "It'll be all right, Isaiah. I promise you it will."

The old man said nothing more as they rode out, heading south. They rode steadily for hours through an endless stretch of bunchgrass and little else. An occasional longhorn broke up the monotony. Jace's jaw tightened. Welford's longhorns. They were still on J-Bar-W land.

He reined to a halt around noon. Amanda hadn't stirred all morning. He laid her in the shade of a willow grove near a small stream. With the back of his hand he brushed her hair away from her forehead, relieved to find no evidence of fever. His hand lingered longer than it should have, trailing down the line of her delicate jaw. Cursing, he jerked the hand away. She would hate him. She had to hate him.

He stood up, crossing to Isaiah. "Don't even start," he warned, holding up a hand as if to ward off the

126

verbal barrage he was certain was coming.

"I ain't sayin' another word. It's like I told ya, that she-cat's got claws. And one day she's going to take you apart with 'em, painter."

"I'm glad you're not saying another word." He picked up his rifle and stalked off.

"Is he gone?" Amanda asked, opening her eyes to take a furtive glance around the small copse of trees.

"He's gone," Isaiah snorted. "Huntin'."

Amanda struggled to sit up, her every thought centered on food. She was ready to do just about anything to get it. "He has to be the most cruel human being I have ever met in my life."

Isaiah sat down, obviously weak from the long morning in the saddle. "I don't know what's got into him. I didn't raise him to be so ornery." He told her a little of Jace's beginnings.

"Ornery? You call starving me to death being ornery? My heavens, what is your definition of rotten?"

"He won't let ya starve."

"He's doing a good imitation."

"I'll talk to him."

She gasped. "Oh, would you?"

He nodded, coughing.

Amanda walked over to him. "Would you like some water?"

"Please."

She held the canteen to his lips while he drank deeply. He wiped off his mouth on his shirtsleeve. "I'll talk to him," he repeated.

A shot sounded. "I wonder what he's bringing back this time?" Amanda grumbled. She glanced up to see him striding toward them carrying another rabbit. She turned anxiously to Isaiah. "Here he comes. You promised . . ."

Her heart plummeted. Isaiah had fallen asleep.

Montana set the rabbit down beside her. "Ready to earn your keep yet?"

"Give me that knife and I'll earn it. I'll use it on you!" She swallowed tears of frustration and anger.

He only laughed, then started building the campfire.

Amanda picked up the knife. "You could at least have the decency to tell me how to . . . do this . . . I'm certain even an animal like you wasn't born with the knowledge."

He hunkered down across from her, his gray eyes telling her he didn't believe for an instant that she was going to go through with it. He sighed. "It's all right, Andy. I'll do it."

"No! You can't have this one! It's mine!"

He sat back on his heels, startled. "I mean I'll do it for you. You can eat it."

"I don't believe you."

"Damn it. I'm trying to . . ." He pushed his hat back on his head. "I'll take care of it. Just give me the knife. I promise you, you can eat the whole damn thing if you want."

She gripped the knife tighter. "You're going to tell me how to cut up this rabbit. Now."

He blew out a long breath. "All right. Whatever you say. First, you hold it by its hind legs." He came around beside her, his hand closing over hers, showing her how to grip the feet between her fingers. She felt the heat of his breath on the back of her neck but ignored it, just as she ignored the spongy feel of the dead rabbit.

"Now you peel back the fur up to its head."

She did as he said, finding the process reminding her bizarrely of a banana. She gagged once at the sight of the gray, hairless skin, then steeled herself. That was precisely the reaction this outlaw wanted. Well, she was not going to give it to him. Not any more.

Even when she slit the jackrabbit along its abdomen to remove the entrails, she did not flinch. Her job was not nearly so neat and tidy as Montana's had been on the rabbit's breakfast kin. But it was still recognizable. And when she readied the carcass to skewer onto the spit to cook, knowing she would get to eat some of it, she felt as a wolf must on a kill. Triumphant. Exultant. Oh, the effects hunger could have on a lady! She almost laughed out loud. Later she was certain her rage at Montana for putting her through this monstrous exercise would return. But for now, she was quite simply proud of herself.

He surprised her by taking the jackrabbit from her and setting it over the fire himself.

"You're not going to cheat me out of my share . . ."

He looked at her oddly. "No, ma'am. You earned it. You eat it."

"The whole thing?"

"If you like."

She swallowed nervously. "Why? Was it sick or something? Did you find it dead?"

He shook his head. "No, I didn't find it dead. I'm not trying to poison you, Andy."

"Then why . . ."

"Because you earned it. Like I said." He stood up. "I'll catch another for Isaiah and me."

She watched, fascinated, as he showed her how he would fashion a snare with rope and a pliable sapling.

"I don't think anyone's following," he said, "but I don't want to keep tempting fate by firing my rifle either." Hefting the small noose, he left the camp.

Amanda licked her lips as she watched the meat darken on the spit. She had eaten at the finest dining tables in Baltimore and Washington D.C., recalling especially the time she had accompanied her father to a special state dinner given by President Grant to smooth over some of the remaining open wounds about the Confederacy. But never would anything taste better to her than this scrawny jackrabbit.

She burned her fingers, hardly waiting for it to cool. The meat was tough and stringy and wonderful. She tore it off in strips, shoving it into her mouth, barely chewing.

"Careful," he warned, coming back with some small game bird. "You'll make yourself sick after going without for so long."

She laughed without humor. "Make myself sick? I've been sick ever since I laid eyes on you, mister." She continued to munch down the meat.

"I mean it. Slow down."

She did as he said, only because she feared if she didn't he would take the food away from her.

Montana cooked his own lunch. As angry as she was, she felt a stab of sympathy for him as he hunkered down beside Isaiah, his features drawn with worry. Besides, she was feeling worlds better now that she'd eaten, even her thighs no longer throbbed abominably. Resting against a tree, she savored a hot cup of coffee. She felt almost relaxed and realized absurdly that it was the first time she'd felt that way since she'd left Baltimore.

Emboldened by her resurgent good health, she rose and crossed to Montana. "Is your friend all right?"

"He's tired." Montana's voice seemed as tired and subdued as Isaiah looked.

Amanda knelt in the grass beside him. Together they got Isaiah to eat a bit of lunch, though the older man grew increasingly listless. "Maybe we should just let him rest," Amanda suggested.

Jace studied her, really studied her, seeing that even under the layers of trail dust she was still stunningly beautiful, made even more so by the tinge of pink the sun had brushed across her pale flesh. But his feelings were heading well beyond what she looked like. He had just put her through hell. Yet here she was, helping him with Isaiah. Spoiled? A bitch? Underneath the silk and the affected arrogance lay the she-cat Isaiah had warned him of from the first. Damn, what a fool he'd been.

"You don't think much of me, do you?" he asked, then cursed himself for asking.

"Mr. Montana, I try to think of you as little as possible, though circumstances . . ."

"I didn't mean it that way."

She looked at him squarely. "I'm well aware of how you meant it. But you are a convicted murderer, and I think it would be in my own best interests *not* to tell you what I think of you."

"That bad, eh?"

"Worse."

He smiled, looking from her to Isaiah. "Thank you for caring about him."

"He seems like a good man. He can't help it if he feels responsible for you."

"Responsible?"

"He told me something of how he found you in the mountains as an infant."

"But you wish he hadn't."

"I wish only that you would have stayed in your mountains, Mr. Montana." She ground her teeth together, certain he was laying the foundation for another one of his nasty little tries at making her miserable.

"Can you stop calling me Mr. Montana?"

"What I would like to call you can hardly come from the lips of a lady, *Mister Montana.*"

A muscle in his jaw twitched. "I deserve that."

Isaiah stirred, opening his eyes. "Sorry I'm bein' such a bother, painter."

Amanda frowned, looking at the outlaw. "You're an artist?"

He rolled his eyes. "Painter. Puma. Cougar. Mountain lion."

She couldn't help her smile. "Montana lion?"

He groaned, though his eyes were alive with amusement. "You can be a real . . ."

"Don't say it. Don't call me that name again, or I'm liable to be wanted for murder myself."

He laughed. "You can be almost likable, you know that?" He shifted uncomfortably, as though regretting the friendly teasing. "Get some rest. We won't be riding again until it cools this afternoon."

She rose and crossed to a gnarled tree, miffed by his abrupt dismissal. For a minute they had almost seemed to be establishing some kind of truce, albeit an unstable one.

Well, what did she expect? Friendship with Jason

132

Montana? No, that wasn't what the man was after. She recalled all too vividly her reaction to his kisses, his caresses yesterday. Maybe that was why he'd been so rude today. He hadn't wanted a repeat performance—or worse.

All she wanted, Amanda told herself, was to get out of this hellish situation alive. She lay her head on her upraised knees, giving the trousers credit for something anyway. She could never sit like this in a dress.

Montana studied her. Damn, she'd done it again. Breached his anger. He'd been damned impressed by how she'd handled that rabbit. The woman had some grit to her. Buried deep, maybe, but it was there nonetheless. And the knowledge made it all the more imperative that he keep the wedge between them high and wide.

Isaiah moaned, shifting restlessly.

"You all right?" Jace asked, putting a hand on the big man's shoulder.

"I've felt better."

"I'm going to get you that doctor."

"No. No, I'll be all right. Ain't the bullet hole that's bothering me anyhow."

"Then what?"

"You've got a responsibility with that little gal. You took her out of the life she was used to. You owe her some respect."

Jace sighed. "It's better this way."

"Why? Because you're afraid she'd laugh at you if she thought you cared about her?"

Jace straightened. Damn, Isaiah knew him too well. Maybe better than he knew himself.

"Don't sell her short," the old trapper went on.

"Dawn Wind would have liked her."

Jace bristled.

But Isaiah did not let up. "Dawn Wind is dead. She wouldn't have you grievin' the rest of your life. She loved you too much."

"You saying Amanda Morgan is a replacement for Dawn Wind?" he demanded incredulously.

"No, I ain't sayin' that. But you're a man. Don't shut yourself off from the rest o' yer life." He coughed, the sound harsher than Jace had ever heard it, painful even to listen to now. "I ain't gonna be around much longer."

"Don't say that."

"It's the way of all livin' things, Jace. I won't have you grievin' over me either." He gripped Jace's hand. "You're my son! My son as much as if I'd . . ." The coughing spasm went on for over a minute.

"Don't talk any more," Jace said. "Get some sleep."

"There're things you don't know."

"It doesn't matter. Nothing matters but your getting well."

Amanda brought over the canteen she'd refilled in the stream. "I thought he might be thirsty." Her hair tumbled about her shoulders like a golden halo.

"He's fine," Jace snapped, wishing the harshness back at once but knowing it was too late.

She dropped the canteen and walked away.

Jace cursed.

"See what I mean, painter," Isaiah rasped, holding out his hand for the canteen. "If you didn't give a damn about that woman, you wouldn't cut her to ribbons all the time."

Jace handed him the water flask. "Then heaven help

her if I should ever be stupid enough to fall in love with her."

"Exactly."

"I was joking."

"Were you? You're tight as a stretched hide whenever you get near her. That ain't hate, boy. That's the he-cat after the she-cat."

"For a man who claims to be at death's door, you sure do talk too much, old man."

Isaiah gave him a wheezy chuckle. "I just want what's best for you, boy."

"Amanda Morgan isn't what's best." He started to say more, but changed his mind. Instead he called to Amanda, "Come over and sit with him for a while." When she seemed about to balk, he added, "Don't worry. I'll be over with the horses."

"He is the strangest man," Amanda said, settling herself in the grass beside Isaiah.

"Don't take Jace so serious, miss. He don't bite near so often as he snarls."

"You really don't think he murdered that woman, do you?"

"I know he didn't. I can give ye my solemn word on it."

"The word of a murderer's friend . . ."

Isaiah's face darkened. She had expected anger, indignation, and what she got was hurt. She had hurt his feelings!

"A mountain man's word is his bible, ma'am. I don't lie." He looked uncomfortable. "I mean I ain't lied too much in sixty years."

"No human being lives a whole life of truth, Mr. Benteen."

"So you're sayin' you lie too?"

"I hardly think that's any of your business."

Isaiah grinned. "You sound a lot like Jace. Not the same words maybe, but you get your back up just the same."

"How dare you compare me to that . . . that . . ."

He chuckled again. "You and Jace would get along just fine if you'd both stop spittin' like tomcats."

"I am not about to get along *fine* with a murderer." Yet Isaiah was right. She did not think Montana guilty of the rape and murder of a defenseless woman. He could kill a man, of that she was certain. She had seen that anger. But as angry as he had gotten with her, he'd still held himself in check.

"He's changed this past year," Isaiah said. "Harder edge to him."

"I should let you sleep."

"I'll be sleeping plenty soon enough."

She gasped, as his meaning sunk home. "Please, Mr. Benteen, if you . . ."

"No, let me talk, girl. I want you to know. Jace never hurt a woman. He loved Dawn Wind. He was like a madman when he found her, found Bright Path."

"Bright Path?"

"His son."

"Dear God."

"Just three years old. They killed him."

"Who?"

"Hidehunters. Scum. Come across her and the boy in the cabin. Me and Jace out clearin' traps. They . . . they didn't kill her quick."

She stood up. "I don't want to hear this."

"He's never got over it. Swore on their graves to find

136

the bastards that done it. We followed their trail but lost it when they left the mountains."

His wife. His child. Savagely murdered. His wife raped. A man who knows such anguish would hardly put another woman through the same hell.

The more she found out about Jason Montana, the more dangerous he became. Because he was a man—a man capable of breaking down the facade she had presented to the world for thirteen years. But he was too late. Her bargain with Philip made him too late.

She would escape when he fell asleep tonight. She would tell Philip what she had learned about the man. Philip might be angry about Montana's encroachment on his land, but surely he wouldn't want to see an innocent man hanged.

Impulsively, she stood up, threading her way through the copse of trees Montana had wandered into. She spied him near an aged willow, his lean whipcord body lounging against its thick trunk. Her heart beat faster just watching him. He was not looking in her direction, seeming to be lost in thought about something, but she couldn't take her eyes off of him.

For thirteen years she'd held herself under rigid control. For thirteen years she'd ruled her emotions, not allowing them to rule her.

With each step she took the studied veneer dropped away. Jason Montana—outlaw. He forced her to feel. Forced her. When no one else could. Anger, fear, but more and more—passion. He was danger. He was excitement. He was fire.

She stepped closer.

He started, whirling. In one lightning movement his gun was in his hand.

She jumped, gasping reflexively, "Don't shoot."

"Dammit, Andy," he said, re-holstering the weapon, "don't do that."

"I . . . I suppose you need to be suspicious of every sound." Was she out of her mind to be toying with this kind of fire?

"What do you want?"

"To talk to you."

"We have nothing to say."

"But we do."

"You dare speak to a rapist-murderer with the only witness too weak to intervene?"

"You're not happy unless I'm afraid of you, are you? Or angry with you."

His eyes widened.

"That's it, isn't it? Keep the hostage scared to death so she'll be easier to handle."

"Think what you like."

"I think . . . I think you didn't kill Juanita Melendez."

"And what brought on this revelation?"

"You."

"I beg your pardon."

"Oh, you're quite capable of killing. I just don't think you're a murderer." Her palms were sweating, her heart was hammering against her ribs. She couldn't meet his eyes. All she could seem to do was stare at his hands. His big, powerful brown hands.

"Well, that's certainly a relief," he said, his voice mocking. "Now I can sleep nights." He closed what little distance remained between them, tilting her chin up so that she was compelled to face him. "Why did you really come over here?"

"I . . . I want you to let me go."

"So you can lead your lover here."

"So I can convince Philip you're innocent, and so that I can send back a doctor for Isaiah."

He stared at her. "You mean that, don't you?"

"She gave him a wry smile. "It's amazing that our low opinions of one another should be so similar."

"I can't let you go." He cleared his throat, amending the words. "I mean it wouldn't take much for them to track a doctor back here."

"He needs a doctor."

"I know. But I'll take care of it."

"Then you're not letting me go?"

"Not in the near future, no."

She turned to head back to the camp. He reached out and gripped her arm, pulling her back, his arms surrounding her, crushing her to him. "I may never let you go, Andy."

Chapter Ten

Amanda allowed Jace to mold her body to his long, lean length, one of his large, calloused palms tangled in her golden hair, the other pressed hard against the small of her back. His mouth was a searing flame to the desert dry tinder that had for so long been guardian to her desire. She had waited a lifetime—never knowing what it was she was waiting for. Until now. It was the heat, the spark, the fire that was Jason Montana as he set her passion blazing to life.

It didn't even occur to her to fight him as he urged her down into the carpet of soft grasses.

"I want you, Andy," he breathed. "I want you so much. Don't stop me this time. Don't stop . . ." His kisses rained across her forehead, her eyelids, down her cheeks to her parted lips. "I've wanted you since that first minute, that first minute . . ."

His mouth captured hers in a sweet, moist snare from which she sought no escape. She whimpered, her body moving, writhing, undulating against him in an ancient, primitive rhythm.

"Please," she moaned. "Please . . ."

His hands tore at the buttons of her shirt, shoving the material roughly aside to uncover the treasure within. He traced lazy circles around her firm, pale breasts, awed again by the sensual contrast in the shading of their skin. Porcelain to bronze. "You're so beautiful, Andy. So damned beautiful."

She arched back, her hand feathering down his beard-stubbled cheek, some tiny part of her rebelling against the words. *Don't tell me I'm beautiful,* she wanted to say. *Tell me you like me. Tell me I'm more than a body to spend your lust. That it matters that it's me, and no one else.*

But she said nothing, too caught up in the unfurling rapture of her own feelings as her arms twined round his head, guiding him to her throbbing nipples. "Taste me. Please. I need . . . Oh, Jason . . ."

Calling him by name weakened the barriers, and she knew that very soon they would collapse. He would claim her utterly. She gasped, almost sobbing her joy as his mouth closed over the hardening pink tips of her breasts.

His suckling loosed other deeper emotions over which she was finding she had no defense. No defense because she had never known such feelings existed to defend against. The velvet folds between her legs grew wet, ready.

No, no . . . she wouldn't . . . couldn't . . . A moment's madness with Jason Montana and everything she'd planned for so long would be ruined forever. Philip would never marry her. And if he didn't . . .

Oh, but it felt so good, so good. . . .

"Jason," she murmured. "Jason, please. Please

understand." So good . . . so good. "I can't. I can't. Philip will know . . ."

"Philip won't know," he rasped. "A man can't tell such things unless the woman is a virgin." His hands shifted to unbutton her pants, easing them down past her hips. "And we both know you're no virgin, don't we, Andy?"

She couldn't say the words. Couldn't tell him. Because she knew . . . *knew* . . . that if she did, he would stop. And though her rational mind begged him to stop, her passion-drugged body begged him to continue. To bring her the only end to this madness that the newly emerging woman in her could abide.

She did not object when he tugged off her trousers, then her shirt, leaving her naked on a bed of fleece-soft green canopied by a sky of endless blue.

"Take me," she moaned. "Take me. Now. Hurry."

He stood up, shoving out of his clothes. For an instant she grew uncertain, shy, lowering her eyes at the sight of the rigid proof of his maleness. But just that quickly she raised her eyes to look again, studying the hardness that jutted from the dark circle of curling hair at the apex of his tautly muscled legs. He was magnificent. Tall and dark and so very much a man. With a boldness born of a lifetime of self-denial she raised her arms to welcome him. Welcome what her body now craved—to feel him inside her, feel him fill her.

It was as though she were awakening from a thirteen year sleep—eager to rediscover a world she'd only too briefly known. She sensed the dangers inherent in such a rebirth—much like a plant set to flower in the sun. The right amount of sunlight and the plant flourished.

Too little and the plant was stunted, doomed never to bloom. Too much sun too soon and the plant itself could die.

Yet the chance to live, to flower, seemed suddenly worth risking the danger. The danger that was Jason Montana.

He teased her long, supple legs apart with his toes, then stepped between them. Dropping to his knees, he caressed her thighs, working his hands upward to explore her silken nest. She moaned, sighed, cried out. There was no reality—none save the sweet, sweet torment this outlaw was evoking in her body.

"Andy, Andy, I want, I need . . ." He stretched out beside her, sucking in air through clenched teeth at the feel of her warm, satiny flesh cradled against the hard heat of his own.

His desire had lain dormant since Dawn Wind. Now it was fever-bright, rising out of control. He wanted no cure for the fever, wanted only the woman nestled in his arms. Yet even in the primal grip of his arousal, he forced himself to slow, to take care with this woman so different from any he had ever known.

It was in his mind that Amanda Morgan had known many lovers. Gentlemen all. Were she among her own kind, a man such as himself—hard living, rough mannered—would elicit no more than a haughty dismissal, even ridicule, should he be foolhardy enough to attempt to lure her into his bed. Here on his own ground he was still not sure of her. She seemed pleased, eager. Yet he couldn't forget the ice maiden in the courtrom, in the jail.

She was, after all, a lady, likely to be repulsed by the crudities of sex. Did she keep her clothes on with

144

Welford, merely raising her skirts? He swore.

She stilled. "What is it? I'm not doing something right?"

His breath caught. The ice maiden was gone. The mountain-lake eyes that searched his were anxious, pleading. Against his will his heart joined his body in what he sought with this woman. The vulnerability he perceived in her became his own.

"It's all right, Andy. It's all right." His kisses ignited flame wherever they touched, until he built in her a fever to match his own.

Neither questioned what was happening. The animosities that had gone before were forgotten in the whirling tide of their mutual lust. It was a dream.

He said nothing.

She said nothing.

Yet their bodies spoke a thousand words—suckling, caressing, stroking, knowing.

Instinctively she grasped his hair, holding him to her, threading her fingers through the dark, tousled mane. She arched toward him, gasping as the yielding flesh of her thigh met the unyielding flesh of his sex.

Warm, wondrous feelings splashed over her like seaspray on a sun-warmed beach. And of all people to make her feel so new, so alive, it was this man, this outlaw whom yesterday she would have watched hang. A man who kidnapped her. A man who forced her to dress out a rabbit. A man who was by turns obnoxious, shy, tender, and savage—but always, always blatantly male.

She gasped, then giggled as he nipped at the creamy smooth skin of her belly, the gleam in his gray eyes telling her precisely where that devilish mind of his had wandered.

"Stallions and mares," she murmured, tucking his hair behind his ears. "Be assured this mare knows what she wants. She knows." She scarcely believed how free she felt, how unabashedly wanton.

"She lets him," he rasped. "She lets him." Dominant, fierce, prideful, he rose above her, staking his arms on either side of her.

Yet he was more gentle than he had ever been.

And she was more aggressive than she had ever been.

"Jason, Jason please . . ." She was trembling and couldn't stop it. The fire reflected in his eyes gave off more heat than the sun.

"God, Andy," he said thickly, closing his eyes. "I don't think I've ever wanted anything in my life the way I want . . ." He didn't finish, using his hands, his mouth his body, to tell her what words could not. That he was sorry. Sorry for hurting her, hating her, when all he wanted in the world was to make her want him as much as he wanted her. To make it better than she'd ever had it with Welford. To find again the primitive joy he had known with Dawn Wind.

He did not know that as he thought Dawn Wind's name he spoke it aloud. He only knew that as he eased himself atop Amanda's beautiful naked body the look on her face that had reflected a passion as raw as his own changed, twisted, to reflect only a too-familiar icy contempt.

He started to say something cajoling, thinking perhaps this was her way of being coy at the last. But his own suspicions, his own insecurities stopped him. She had enticed him past enduring, and now she would rob him of his release. A game. The spoiled bitch was playing a game. His pride demanded he halt, his body demanded he not. His body won.

He thrust hard and deep, completing the mating, his breath leaving him in a long sigh. He felt the resistance but its reason didn't register at first. He thrust harder, deeper. She stiffened slightly, but made no sound. His hips moved, rocked, urged her to join him.

His body found its release, but it was no longer the towering pleasure it had promised to be. The body beneath his was rigid, unmoving. Slowly, as if in a daze, he took in what he had just done. He stared at her stricken face.

"No." His voice was strangled. "How? Why? Son of a bitch!"

She felt the trembling in him, the trembling in herself. The regret in them both. She had wanted it, ached for it. But now, now . . . he had spoiled it, spoiled everything. He had called out to his dead wife. It had not been Amanda Morgan who pleasured his body, but a ghost.

"What the hell were you doing?" he demanded, his lust and his anger laced with an overwhelming sense of bewilderment. It had felt so good, so right. "Did your little game go farther than you intended?"

She slammed her hands against his chest. "My game? You used me! You were the one playing games!"

"What the hell are you? . . ." He stopped, running a hand over the back of his neck. "Andy, why didn't you tell me you'd never been with a man?"

"Why? You made up your mind about me from the first, remember? You wouldn't have believed me."

He levered himself off of her, yanking on his pants. She had been a virgin! All the times he had called her

Welford's whore, accused her of sleeping with the man to gain the trappings his money could buy, she had been a virgin. Damn. "Amanda, I . . ." He stared at the ground. "I'm sorry."

"Sorry? That's what you have to say for what you've just done. You're sorry?" She laughed, a high-pitched sound just this side of hysteria. "I'll be sure to tell Philip that you apologized. I'll mention it just after he calls off the wedding."

His jaw tightened. "Don't tell him."

"I won't have to. He'll know. You knew!"

"He may. He may not." He raked a hand through his thick hair, feeling royally like a mule's behind. Was he really trying to suggest ways she might salvage her betrothal to Welford? "If you tell him it was rape . . ."

"That'll make it all right? To have been raped by a savage? He'll forgive that?"

He gripped her arms. "Just tell him it was my doing. Mine. He can't hate you for that."

She jerked away from him, shivering though the day was still warm. The light and the passion that had been in her was gone. She had gotten too close to the sun. No flowers. She had given up everything . . . for nothing. Not even a memory.

"You'll pay for this, Jason Montana. One day you'll pay and pay well. And I am not referring to money."

"Fine." But he wasn't even listening. He was angry. Angry with her, angry with himself.

Why? Why had he allowed it? Why had she? For his own part, he had no reason save one. He allowed it because he wanted it, wanted her. Still did.

But Amanda's reasons? For that he could hazard a thousand guesses, but the only true one was locked behind the glacial stare of those mountain-lake eyes.

Cursing viciously, more to cover his own bruised pride than anything else, he finished dressing. "I'm going to see to Isaiah. When you're . . . ready, you can come back to camp and fix supper." He winced at how that had sounded, but he made no attempt to amend the words.

"Fix supper?" she gritted. He had had what he wanted, and now they were back to captor and captive. Back to? No. That's all they had been from the first. He'd used her, taking advantage of his superior position. He'd exacted the perfect revenge against Philip, violating his fiancée while availing himself of a warm female body he could fantasize was his dead wife.

She climbed stiffly to her feet. "Cook your own supper. I'm leaving." She had heard Montana say that this land was part of Philip's ranch. It couldn't be that difficult to find his house. All she had to do was keep walking. And that's exactly what she intended to do.

"Keep to the shade," he called mockingly. He would let her work off her anger for a while. Give himself time to deal with his own. She couldn't get far.

Jace tried to step quietly, but Isaiah stirred and woke up as he tromped past him. "Where's the little gal?"

"Gone. Go back to sleep."

"What? Welford . . ."

"No. She left. On foot."

"Are you blame out of your mind?" Isaiah tried to sit up. "You go on and get her back here. She don't know nothin' about bein' on her own in country like this."

"She won't get far. I'll find her when she cools down."

Isaiah's shaggy eyebrows arched. "Somethin' she needs to cool down about?"

Jace dug through the saddlebags, extracting a full bottle of whiskey. He sat down, twisted the cork free, pressed the bottle to his lips, and tilted his head back. The amber liquid burned all the way down to his gut. He shook his head, his eyes watering, settling the bottle between his knees. Sucking in a long breath, he wiped his mouth on his shirtsleeve. "You might say that."

"Damn, Jace . . ."

"Don't." He held up a hand. "Just don't. There's nobody who feels worse about it than I do. I thought she wanted . . . Ah, hell." He took another pull on the whiskey, then shoved the bottle back into the saddlebags. For long minutes he just sat there, mulling over what had happened. But it was no use. He didn't know what had happened.

He had been as aroused and as ready to take a woman as he had ever been in his life. A surge of bitterness coursed through him. Savage that he was, he had been fool enough to believe himself pleasuring her as he himself was being pleasured. And then she had turned it all back on him. Why? Why?

Life had been easier with Dawn Wind. Simpler. City living must complicate a woman's mind. What else . . . Dawn Wind? His brow furrowed as he tried to remember. Damn. He hadn't said . . . Oh, God, had he?

City woman. Wilderness woman. No woman wanted to hear her lover call out another woman's name.

He imagined his own reaction if she had called him

Philip. Swearing, he leaped to his feet, crossing over to the bay gelding. Working swiftly, he hefted the saddle onto the animal's back and cinched it down. "You be all right here alone, Isaiah?"

"I'll be just fine. It's the little gal I'm worried about."

"She'll be fine, too. I promise." He made certain he left Isaiah with plenty of food and water. "I'll be back as soon as I can."

"It'll be dark in a couple of hours. I won't be expectin' you before morning."

Jace grimaced. If he were gone that long, it wouldn't be for the reason Isaiah's glint suggested. It would be because it took him that long to figure out how to bring Amanda back without letting her succeed in killing him.

He rode out and at once spied her small shoeprints in the dusty ground. He turned the horse in a full circle but could catch no sight of her on any horizon. She'd been gone more than an hour. His theory that she would settle herself on a rock somewhere and sulk seemed not to be the case.

He kneed the horse into a trot. Fifteen minutes passed and still he hadn't caught sight of her. He dismounted, studying the ground more closely, his eyes widening in disbelief. Damn her scheming hide! She must have watched him cover their tracks out of San Antone. And he'd thought she was unconscious! The little she-cat had altered her trail, retraced her steps. It was an amateurish attempt, but he had not been looking for it, not even considered the possibility. Her ruse had cost him valuable time.

The sun sank lower on the horizon. The night would be cold. She had no blankets, no food, no water, no weapon.

Her words drifted over him, like a sigh brought by the wind. *You'll pay for this, Jason Montana.*

"Is this your revenge, Andy? You going to get yourself lost and die on me?"

He tensed, spurring the horse recklessly in the waning light. It would be just like a spoiled, pampered citified woman like Amanda Morgan to pull a self-centered stunt like that. The perfect vengeance.

Because if she died, he would never forgive himself.

Chapter Eleven

Amanda looked back at the camp only once. The willows obscured her view of the place where she had last seen Montana, the place where they had . . . She turned away. The weeping branches trailing the grasses seemed to be trading secrets, whispering of a foolish young woman. Had she really expected him to be following?

She drew in a deep breath. She had no idea in which direction Philip's ranch house lay, and so she decided to head north. North because Jason Montana was south.

Within minutes her feet ached abominably, her high-button shoes never meant for anything so practical as walking, especially over tufts of bunchgrass and rocks. But she didn't stop.

It occurred to her as she marched across the ravine-cut terrain that Montana might merely be giving her some sort of head start, amusing himself by allowing her to think she was getting away, only to come thundering up to make her his prisoner once again. She couldn't let that happen.

She studied her shoeprints in the dirt behind her. Even she could follow that trail.

Bending down she grabbed a long switch of willow branch ripped loose in some windstorm past. She brushed the tracks away, then made another trail leading to the ravine's edge. She crunched down into the hollow, tracing and retracing her steps, then resuming her original path two hundred yards from where she entered the hollow.

Not a very good job, she was certain. But if it delayed him for even half a minute, she would derive satisfaction from it. Besides it took her mind off the very real possibility of winding up lost, or worse. Took her mind off, too, the reason for her flight.

Odd, how she might have stayed with her captor if he had not . . .

No, she wasn't going to think of that now. Wiping the sweat and grime from her face, she shaded her eyes in the glare of the setting sun and tried to discern from the layout of the land where she might find water. Not having it was making her very thirsty.

An hour later she scaled a small hillock and spotted a thick stand of willows half a mile to the east. A hollow. She broke in a run. It was deeper than she thought. Peering into the darkness she heard what sounded like rushing water along the cut at the bottom. There had to be water where so much vegetation thrived.

She shook her head, marveling at herself and at how much she had picked up just being around Montana and Benteen for such a short time.

"Lewis and Clark could have used me," she announced to the descending dusk. "Sacajawea would have consulted me about which trails to take, how to prepare game, detailing the maps. Chris Columbus might not have gotten himself lost if . . ."

With a wild whoop she plunged into the hollow, skidding, sliding down to the creek. She dropped to her knees, dipping her face into the cool, crisp wetness, drinking deeply. Then she sat back on her heels, tossing in a small pebble. "I christen thee the River Amanda. I don't care if you are a little nothing of a creek. I found you, and that's what you are."

Sobering, she glanced toward the sun to find it fast disappearing beneath ribboned layers of crimson, gold, and violet. With it would go the stifling heat. But she had already learned there was no middle ground. The temperature would drop quickly, and she carried no matches to light a fire.

She wanted only to curl up and sleep but recognized the danger of staying near the creek. The River Amanda, she corrected imperiously. Every animal for miles around likely used it as a watering hole.

Wading through the narrow stream, she grappled her way up the opposite bank, crying out as she peeled back a fingernail. Atop the low rise she stared forlornly at a horizon that seemed to stretch off forever. *Explorers can't think about these things,* she chided. *I have to find the J-Bar-W. Claim it in the name of the queen.*

Oh, Amanda, she thought giddily. *Delia would tell you for certain. You are going purely daft.*

Her journey became less and less a game as she walked. The night grew darker, and she had no idea where she was. Odd sounds seemed more and more to surround her. What kind of creatures prowled Texas during a quarter moon?

Suddenly, she was sprawled flat on the ground. Pushing herself up to her hands and knees, she felt along her calf to her ankle, finding the skull-sized rock that had been lying in ambush. She exacted her revenge by kicking at it, but only succeeded in further aggravating her twisted ankle. The damage wasn't too great, though, she decided, awkwardly climbing to her feet. Except to her pride, which was hopelessly injured anyway. The thought brought with it what she had successfully suppressed for the last two hours—the stinging agony of her humiliation. How had she allowed things to go so far between herself and Montana? Everything she'd worked for, planned for with Philip was lost. For what? So that a man could use her body to make love to another woman?

Dawn Wind. He had called her Dawn Wind. He had aroused her, teased her, pleased her, broken through the wall it had taken thirteen years to build—then proved to her all over again how desperately necessary those walls had been.

Why? Why had she let him? She shook her head, swiping at the sweat and grime on her face, forcing her aching foot to carry her another twelve steps to a massive rock. She sank down beside it, leaning back wearily. A more forsaken vista she couldn't imagine. As forsaken as she felt.

She let her head drop to her upraised knees. She shouldn't have tried to disguise her trail. Shouldn't have . . . She laughed, a harsh, bitter sound. Why did she think it mattered? Montana wouldn't follow. He didn't need a hostage any more. Didn't need . . .

"Damn you, outlaw. What have you done to me?

What have you done?" The dam was breaking, breaking. The tears that had threatened since she left the camp trailed like acid down her sunburned cheeks.

If only she hadn't come to Texas . . . If only . . . The sobs grew harsher. She might as well think, *If only Matthew hadn't died*.

But he had. And she had come to Texas. Because Philip had demanded that she come. And because she couldn't afford his anger.

"Philip, where are you? Why didn't you follow? Why didn't you come for me?"

If he was so intent on having Montana dead, why indeed had there been no pursuit? Perhaps because Philip knew Montana would not leave the territory. He would come back for his confrontation. And for whatever reasons, Philip wanted that reckoning to be private.

The posse, if there were a posse, could well presume her dead by now—or worse. Philip and every other man in the state of Texas would never believe Montana had not availed himself of her body during the time he held her captive.

She trembled. They would be right.

Struggling to her feet, she decided to walk just a little while longer. She no longer concerned herself with hiding her tracks. Montana hadn't found her because he wasn't looking. A mountain man used to tracking quarry would have had no difficulty following a city woman in the wilderness, no matter how well she had disguised her trail. And she was certain she had done a pathetic job.

Two hours past dusk she was still stumbling forward. She fell often, over small stones, animal

157

burrows, tufts of coarse bunchgrass. But always she kept on, the fear of going to sleep to be food for wild animals greater than her exhaustion.

Besides, the more tired she was the less likely her mind would drift back to that horrible moment when Jason Montana had driven himself into her body, calling her by his dead wife's name.

She tripped, falling heavily, the skin scraping from her palms. She tried to push herself up but found the task impossible. Her cheek lay against the hard ground, her deep, gulping breaths blowing tiny wisps of dirt to swirl around her face. Her breathing slowed, reality slipping away.

Why? Why had he said it? Take back that single part of what had happened between them and she suspected she would not be lost and alone in the darkness of this forsaken Texas plain. She would still be in his arms. In the arms of an outlaw who had awakened her to the wonder of her own body.

"Don't think about him. Don't think about anything. Just sleep for a little while. Just a little while." Her eyes closed. She was drifting, floating.

She wasn't sure at first that she heard it. Wasn't sure even what it was. Or how long she might have slept.

A horse? Yes, a horse moving slowly toward her. She felt groggy, dazed. Get away. She had to get away. The outlaw wasn't going to find her. Take her back. Hurt her yet again.

Hide. Hide, Amanda. Hurry.

Jace had been walking for the last three miles. Amanda was listing in circles now. And he had to be careful not to pass her in the darkness.

Damn, but he wanted to call out to her, but he feared she wouldn't answer. He told himself over and over that she would be all right. That one night out in the cold wouldn't hurt her. But that didn't stop him from imagining the worst.

He had crossed other signs in the night, too. He held a match above the hoofprints. Four horses at least, maybe six. He'd found the posse.

He heard a soft moan then. Quickly he put his hand over the horse's nose to keep the gelding from blowing. Then he listened, walking slowly, listening again. He caught the sound of her breathing.

"Amanda, I know you're out there. Let me take you back to the camp."

Silence.

"Amanda, you can't stay out here alone."

More silence.

He cursed, circling toward the place where he thought she was hiding. Like a cornered rabbit. Terrified. "I'm not going to hurt you."

"It's a little late for a promise like that."

He swore again. How well he knew that. She sounded half hysterical. "Just stay right there. I'm coming to get you."

"No!"

"Dammit, Andy . . ."

"I'm not going anywhere with you."

"I have food. I have water."

"What do I have to do to *earn* them!"

"Nothing. Just come out here."

"No. You get away. You've ruined everything. I planned it. I worked for it. And now . . . And now . . ."

He circled toward her, but she saw him and bolted. She ran, crying out, her feet agonized until at last her sore ankle gave way, sending her pitching headfirst down the side of a ravine.

Jace scrambled down after her. She didn't move. Gently, he eased her onto her back, cradling her against him. Her eyes fluttered open.

"Thank God," he muttered.

"Haven't you done enough to me?" she whimpered, struggling against him, loathing herself for wanting only to burrow against his hard chest. "I hate you." She could have sworn she felt him wince. But that was absurd. "I just want to go to Philip. Please."

His voice was cold. "You'll see Welford soon enough. And I'm sure you'll be able to talk him into anything. Just bat those big blue eyes at him."

"I don't have to take that from you! Not after what you've done. I love Philip. Do you hear me? I love him."

"Then what was that you were playing with me in the grass back at the camp. I'm sure your beloved Philip would be fascinated with the way his fiancée behaves when he's not around."

Hot tears burned at the corners of her eyes. "Take your hands off me." To her surprise he did so. With every muscle in her body protesting, she forced herself to rise.

"You're going to get lost again."

"Who said I was lost? I'll find Philip's ranch."

"Not that way you won't."

"I prefer it to living out another day in your company." She limped into the darkness.

"Get back here."

"Go to hell."

He reached her in three long strides, twisting her around. "I'll lash you to the horse."

"That seems your style."

Muttering a low curse, he spread his hands wide, releasing her arms as though touching her were suddenly distasteful to him.

She continued her walk.

"There's nothing for fifty miles in that direction."

"You're lying. Philip's ranch is here somewhere."

"You're standing on what he claims as part of his ranch. But then he claims a half million acres."

"I don't believe you."

"Amanda, I can't let you go off by yourself."

She grimaced at the exasperation in his voice. He was treating her as though she were some petulant child. "You don't need a hostage."

"I'm not going to have you killing yourself, either."

"Don't tell me you have a conscience."

"What I have is one helluva temper, woman. Don't make me lose it."

"Your threats don't frighten me any more, Mr. Montana. There's nothing worse you can do to me."

His jaw clenched. "You're going back to camp."

"So I can make your supper."

"So you can get some sleep."

She stalked off.

He followed.

"Amanda, please."

Her eyes widened. A request? Not a command. She sank to her knees. She really was so very tired.

She woke to a cool cloth on her forehead.

"You'll be fine."

With an involuntary moan she arched her neck, allowing him easier access as he ran the cloth down the side of her face, along her neck, and down to the V of her shirt.

She was too tired to push his hand away, wondering if she would, even if she had the strength. Her brows furrowed at the look in his eyes. That couldn't be guilt?

"Tomorrow I'll take you back to Welford."

For long seconds Amanda simply stared at him, uncertain that she had heard him correctly. "You mean that?"

"I'll take you to his ranch. Leave you close enough so that you can walk with no difficulty." He seemed to want to say more, but decided against it as he rose to stride over to his horse.

Amanda watched as he brushed down the gelding and tethered it for the night. "Don't you think you should get back to Isaiah? What if he needs something?"

"He'll be all right."

"But that cough . . ."

"Will eventually kill him."

"You say it so easily."

His eyes drilled her and she knew how very mistaken she had been. It wasn't that he said it easily, but that something in him accepted things he couldn't change. But accepting the inevitability of Isaiah's death was a far cry from accepting it as actual fact.

Snapping his blanket open, he lay down. Amanda tried, but she couldn't take her eyes off of him. Though he had hurt her time and again, sometimes deliberately, it gave her no pleasure to hurt him back. "I'm sorry. I meant no harm about Isaiah."

He sighed. "I know. Go to sleep."

Sleep? Near Jason? She sank to her knees. Excitement, danger, and the very real vulnerability she had discovered in this man aroused her senses past enduring. She longed for him, yet wished paradoxically to be gone from him. Only then could she find peace.

A strange sound caught her ear. Like dice rattling in a tin cup.

"Don't move."

"What is it?"

"Just don't move."

He stood up, padding around behind her. She had not missed the warning in his voice, and something else—fear. She swallowed. "What? Please, tell me."

"Don't move, Andy."

He pulled out his gun and fired.

She jumped, then her eyes flew wide with horror as she watched him pick up a six-foot snake.

"Are you all right?" he asked.

She nodded weakly.

"Well, at least we've got ourselves some breakfast." Grinning, he sat down on a small boulder and began skinning the snake. "Tastes like chicken."

"I do hate you, Jason Montana."

"Why? I didn't ask you to clean it."

"I'm not going to eat that thing."

"You don't eat meat back in Baltimore?"

"I don't get involved with it until it's on my dinner plate. I try not to think about it clucking, or mooing, or . . . or hissing." She smiled in spite of herself, grateful for the distraction of the snake. It took her mind off other more dangerous animals. Like cougars.

"Kind of hypocritical, I suppose."

"I don't kill something unless I intend to eat it. Despite your low opinion of me, I have a great respect for life, even snakes, when they're not trying to take a bite out of pretty ladies."

His voice had grown husky and she felt the characteristic response in her veins. But there was more danger now. She was alone with him. He had saved her life. And he was speaking to her not with deference or condescension, but as an equal. It was time for a change in subject.

"How are you going to prove your innocence about Juanita's murder?"

"I doubt if I ever can. Not with Welford's stacked deck." He finished with the snake, then cleaned his hands with water from his canteen.

"But why would Philip want you dead?"

"You tell me."

"How would I know? Are you suggesting that I'm some sort of accomplice in his framing you?"

"No, I don't think that. He wouldn't take you into his confidence. Not with something like that."

Though she had her own secrets from Philip, she took offense at Montana's casual assertion that Welford didn't trust her. "Philip and I share everything."

"Everything?" His gaze caressed her face as surely as if it were his hands.

She looked away. "He doesn't keep secrets from me."

"Then what you're telling me is that you *are* in on his setting me up."

"I'm saying that if you are innocent, the conviction

was an honest mistake. The evidence was there . . ."

"Evidence. My knife, which someone stole."

"You weren't in Juanita's room the day she was killed?"

"I was there."

Her jaw dropped, her voice shaking. "You were?"

"It doesn't mean I killed her."

"Then what were you doing in her room?"

"She was selling me something."

"What?"

"Aren't you going to assume it was her body?"

"No! Why should I?"

"You continue to surprise me, Andy."

"In other words you would have expected such an assumption from a bitch."

He stared at the ground, and she knew, finally, she had embarrassed him.

"I'm sorry," he allowed. "You can be bitchy, but you're not a bitch."

"Thank you. I think."

"Get some sleep."

"No more snakes?"

"I'll keep an eye out."

He watched her settle into her blankets and thought about sending her back to another man. Damn, but he wanted that woman. It made no sense, but he did. Wanted a different ending to their lovemaking. Had he really called out Dawn Wind's name?

His loins tightened, but he ignored it.

Amanda couldn't sleep, her body aching, her shoulders seeming especially tender. Giving up, she climbed to her feet and retrieved the canteen. Opening the first couple of buttons on her shirt, she shrugged it

165

past her shoulders, then drew in a long breath through clenched teeth as she daubed the cool water along her sunburn.

"Maybe I could help," he offered.

"Help?" she grumbled. "I wouldn't need your help if you hadn't kidnapped me in the first place. I would be snuggled comfortably in my hotel room, silk sheets and all." She stopped, appalled. Her choice of sheets was none of this man's business.

But he apparently took no notice.

"I'll get something." He took no time to argue, riding bareback into the night. In fifteen minutes he came back, carrying an odd-looking plant. "Aloeverde," he pronounced. "Now let me take a look at your back."

"No. Please." She wanted no repeat of this afternoon.

"It'll get worse if you don't let me see to it."

She lay still while he hunkered down behind her.

"Take your shirt off."

Her fingers fumbled with the remaining buttons, her hands shaking so badly she accidentally popped off one of the buttons. "Could you turn your back?" she asked softly.

With obvious reluctance he did so.

Trembling, she tugged off the shirt, then stretched out on her stomach, her bare breasts itching on the coarsely spun blanket.

He turned, his low curse confirming her fears. "Why didn't you say something sooner?"

"I did. I said 'let me go'." But his letting her go was the last thing on her mind right now. She lay there, naked from the waist up, waiting, aching to feel his hands on her bare back, even if they hurt.

"Hold still," he said.

He squeezed the odd-looking plant, forcing out the juicelike substance from its leaves.

"Move your hair; I don't want to get this stuff in it."

Swallowing hard, she lifted her blond hair away from her back, even its silky texture an irritation to the injured skin. She flinched when his fingertips made first contact.

"Sorry," he murmured, and now she was certain his voice seemed hoarse and unnatural.

"Do you"—he paused to clear his throat—"do you need this anywhere else?"

She didn't answer.

The juice from the plant was cool from the night temperature, but it was warmed instantly by the elevated temperature of her skin. She was hot and cold at the same time.

He stared at the creamy flesh of her back, naked and hot beneath his fingers. Too hot. His hands trembled slightly as he smoothed the aloe juice over the burn. It would help, but she would still be stiff and sore tomorrow. The shirt he'd given her wouldn't feel very good on the tender skin. What she needed was a cool bath and the silk sheets she'd mentioned earlier. He thought of her body writhing naked beneath his own on those silk sheets. The thought jabbed him about Dawn Wind . . . on buffalo robes.

His hands grew harsher in spite of himself. Her gasp of pain slowed him. Damn. "It hurts that bad?"

She said nothing. She had her share of pride.

Slowly, gently, he massaged away the stiffness, the pain. Unwillingly he remembered the firm ripeness of the breasts that pressed against the blanket beneath her. He tried to ignore the spreading tightness in his loins.

Leaning closer, he skated his fingers over her shoulders and down her arms, feeling her tense. "I'm sorry. I don't want to hurt you." His hands were shaking now. He was losing control. "I think it would be best not to put anything on until morning."

She gripped the blanket to her chest, sitting up a little. "Thank you."

He bolted to his feet, striding over to the fire and making an elaborate display of adding a couple of sticks to the crackling flames. He swore his body was giving off more heat than the snapping blaze. Damn, what was it about this woman? He was no cuckolded boy. She had been the virgin, not him. Not since he was fifteen and Isaiah had arranged for his introduction to the opposite sex with a bawdy, free-spirited trapper's widow named Mazie.

With Dawn Wind he had found harmony, a kinship with a woman who loved the wild land as he did. Their lovemaking had been warm and good, with her earthy beauty and her complete acceptance of her womanliness.

Amanda Morgan was no bawdy free spirit. Nor did she seem to have any particular affection for even being outdoors. But there was something about her. Isaiah had alluded to it. Something hidden, buried, secreted away. And if he could just find the patience to seek it out, he could well believe he would hold a treasure beyond imagining.

She was a fire in his blood, the fever rising with each beat of his heart.

He looked at her.

She looked at him.

She let the blanket drop away.

"Damn . . ." He clenched his fist. "Andy, what are we doing to each other?"

"I don't know." Her voice was a throaty whisper.

He knelt beside her, his hand looping her hair behind her ear. Her lips parted, the tip of her tongue unconsciously tracing a moist outline. With a fierce groan he pressed her down, mindful of her sunburn.

"I want you, Andy."

In spite of her best intentions her body grew languid. She couldn't deny the message of her newborn passion. Her flesh wanted his flesh. Nor could she deny how entwined her heart had become in her need to make this man part of herself.

He molded his hands to her face, his mouth savoring the petal-sweet softness of her lips. The kiss was long and deep and might have gone on forever had he not thought of Dawn Wind, that he was being disloyal. That the night air was affecting his mind. But her fingers threaded through his hair, holding him to his erotic task as his hands charted a path to her breasts. "Thank God there's no burn here," he rasped.

His name was a breathless sigh as she arched against him. "Oh, Jason, please. I . . . I want you to do it . . . I mean . . . because you want me. Me. Not . . ." She couldn't say the name. Couldn't risk his anger.

"I do want you. Very much."

But suddenly she had to be certain. No matter what the cost. She kissed his cheeks, his eyelids, his forehead. "Then why . . . why this afternoon . . . did you call me . . . Dawn Wind?"

"Damn. I wasn't certain . . . Damn."

"I thought you wanted me, but . . ."

"If I said her name, I didn't mean it to hurt you. I . . . oh, damn, Andy, I'm not going to tell you I didn't love her. I did. And I don't think you expect me to love you . . ."

"No, of course not," she said, her voice more vehement than she meant it to be.

"But I do want you. I want you very much. You're so beautiful."

She closed her eyes. "You wouldn't want me if I was plain, or had a wart on my nose, or had crooked teeth, or . . ."

"Now what are you . . ."

"Nothing. Nothing." It felt so good in his arms. She didn't want to spoil it. Right now she needed whatever it was about him that freed her from her self-imposed prison. She needed Jason Montana, outlaw.

He held her, caressed her, kissed her. "This time will be different, Andy. I promise."

She was ready, so very ready. "Then show me," she murmured. "Show me how different." She opened herself to him, welcoming his hardness into her own velvet softness, revelling in his cry of raw pleasure. Dawn Wind was gone. It was she, Amanda Morgan, making him feel this way, making his strong, powerful body tremble with need.

Instinctively, she wrapped her legs around his hips, locking him to her as her own body suddenly threatened to shatter apart in a mindless rapture that seemed to spiral into forever.

Long minutes later she relished the look of astonishment in his eyes.

"I was all right?" she asked shyly.

170

He swallowed, unable to speak. Only nod.

"What is it?" she asked gently as his eyes grew troubled. She stiffened. He was thinking of her again.

"No," he said, petting her, stroking her, as she bucked upward. He held her tight until she quieted. "I don't mean it like you think. I wasn't thinking of her when I . . ." He stopped, rolling to one side. He was only making it worse. "It was good, Andy. It was damned good, what we just had. I guess that's why I thought of her. I feel guilty about just how good it was." He sat up, angry that he had said so much. "It still hurts. I wasn't there. If I had been . . ."

"Then maybe you would be dead, too."

"Maybe I'd rather be than live with what happened to them."

"So you let guilt cripple you, cripple your life."

"Is that experience speaking?"

"Maybe."

"As long as we're flaying at open wounds, when are you and Welford getting married?"

The rapport was over. Why not finish it completely? "We haven't actually set a date. Soon."

"Send me an invitation?"

"I think not."

She thought of Philip—his arrogance, his shrewdness, his ability to know exactly when and where an opponent is most vulnerable. She thought of herself married to him for the rest of her life. And for just an instant she thought of herself free of everything, free to discover what a real mountain lion looked like, free to follow where her heart begged to lead.

"Philip can give me everything I want," she said, hating herself but seeing no other choice. "Money, comfort, power. The important things, the things I value in my life."

"I don't believe you," he growled. "Not any more."

"You'd better," she supplied as icily as she could manage. "Oh, I suppose I have found you an amusing diversion." He had to think the worst of her. Had to. She didn't want love, pity, or even friendship from this man. He was much, much too dangerous.

"Diversion!" he roared, twisting to capture her wrist in a viselike grip. "You're a liar!"

"No. I'm a bitch." Her tone was flat, emotionless. She held her breath.

"Yeah," he said at last, seeing no change in those fathomless blue eyes. "I guess maybe you are."

She watched him lever himself to his feet, adjust his clothes, then stalk over to the horse. Again he had confounded her. She had expected fury, wounded male pride. Instead he seemed to make no effort at all to hide the fact that she had hurt him.

He couldn't know she had hurt herself more. As bleak as it might be, Philip was her future. Her only future.

Chapter Twelve

Amanda was used to the dream, but she never got used to the pain. Moppet wriggled in her small arms, whining anxiously as though she sensed her mistress's intent. Hugging the dog close, Amanda drew in a long, steadying breath, then stepped up to the doorway of the imposing two-story red brick house. She stood on her toes, lifted the brass door knocker, rapped twice, and waited.

A minute later the heavy oak door swung open. Amanda stared up into the stern countenance of the wasp-thin woman who stood in the entryway, a huge yellow tomcat ensconced comfortably in her arms.

Moppet yapped wildly, but the cat only yawned and closed his eyes. "Hello, Aunt Claudia," Amanda said, trying to keep Moppet from eating the cat and spoiling everything.

The woman frowned. "What in the world are you doing here, child? Does your father realize—?" She paused. "Just what are you up to?"

Amanda swallowed, knowing she was on shaky

ground. But she had to try. Zachary Morgan rarely saw his spinster sister, since Aunt Claudia had announced her support for the Union. Her father's outspoken belief in the Confederacy had strained relations between siblings beyond the breaking point. But she couldn't just give Moppet to anyone. . . .

"I can't keep her any more, Aunt Claudia," she said, giving a practiced sigh. "I have more important things to do with my time than take care of a silly little dog."

With a reproachful sniff Aunt Claudia released the cat into the house's interior. "Your papa lets you get away with entirely too much, young lady. The dog is your responsibility and you should take care of her."

Amanda tossed her head, brushing at her silken curls as though her aunt were being purposefully dull, though inside the young girl's rehearsed indifference was threatening to crumble. She must see this through. She must.

"I have parties to attend, dresses to shop for," she said as pre-emptorily as she dared, since she was after all only eleven years old. "I don't want the scruffy thing. She sheds hair all over the silk coverlet of my bed."

Flashing a bright smile she neither felt nor meant, Amanda bolted through the house, darting out the back door. She whirled, skipping backward, waiting for her aunt to join her in the perfectly manicured yard. Then she knelt in the lush green grass surrounded by its three-foot-high white picket fence and let the dog run free. "See, she loves it here already."

The cat hissed, slashing at Moppet's nose, sending the dog yowling back to Amanda. "Behave," Amanda said desperately. "You're a guest. The cat lives here."

174

To her aunt she said, "I don't want to give her to just anyone. I know you'd love her like I . . . I used to."

She watched the play of emotions on her aunt's face. In spite of her stern demeanor Aunt Claudia had a genuine soft spot when it came to animals. But she wasn't going to let Amanda off easily.

The woman waggled her index finger in front of Amanda's nose. "I suppose I can take her. She'll give Tristan a fine companion to play with. But I hope someday you learn your lesson. Tossing off something that loves you so dear, like it was a used-up toy. It's just a disgrace. But then I couldn't expect much different from Zachary's daughter. Entirely too self-indulgent, the whole family."

"Not Matthew!" Amanda blurted, then gasped. "I mean . . ."

Aunt Claudia gave her a reproving glare. "High-strung, like your mother. Insensitive, like your father." She tapped her foot on the flagstone footpath. "You do have a point. I don't know how a dear boy like Matthew ever found his way into such a family. So selfless, so . . ."

Amanda called Moppet over, giving her a swift kiss, then whirled to hand the small dog to the woman. "Well and done with," she pronounced, glad to see that her tsk-tsking aunt had taken no notice of the quaver in her voice.

Streaking out of the house, she hailed the groomsman, who drove her back to her father's estate. But she didn't go to the house, running instead to the apple orchard adjacent to the colonial mansion. Under the heavy scent of ripening fruit, she sobbed for hours, clutching the tiny braided leash to her chest. "Moppet,

Moppet, I'm sorry. Forgive me. Aunt Claudia will be good to you. She will. She will!"

The sobs seemed destined to tear her small body apart. "It's all your fault, Matthew," she said fiercely. "All your fault." She used the hem of her lime taffeta dress to blot the tears. "Don't think I'm crying for you, Matthew. 'Cause I'll never cry for you."

It was going to be hard pretending not to care about things any more. But she would rather have people like Aunt Claudia accusing her of being a spoiled brat than allowing them the power to hurt her. Matthew had taught her well. Promises meant nothing. He had only cared about himself. And now so would she.

She shivered, remembering the ugly scene in the family parlor yesterday afternoon. No, she would never care about anyone again.

She had come in from riding her pony to find her mother sitting alone on the veranda, a wool blanket on her lap, though the August temperatures were exceptionally warm. Her mother stared off vacantly, seemingly aware of nothing. She had been much the same ever since word of Matthew's death three months ago. Still, Amanda sensed there was more than the usual withdrawal in her mother's behavior.

"Mother, you really must start to do your needlework again." She took a deep breath. "Maybe tonight, after dinner, you could read to me?"

Her mother made no response. She didn't even look up. She just twisted her hands in the blanket.

Frightened, Amanda rushed into the house. She was about to call for Delia, when the sound of voices coming from the parlor stopped her. Her father's voice. And another man, a stranger. The voices were heated, angry. And she heard Matthew's name mentioned.

Walking on tiptoe, she crossed to the door and peered inside. Her father had his back to her. The other man, who was of medium height with silver hair and black broadcloth coat, was bent over the gateleg table helping himself to a smoke.

Amanda used the second's distraction to sneak into the room and scoot behind the settee. It wouldn't be her first experience at eavesdropping, though always before she herself had been the subject under discussion, most often between her father and Delia. She'd had to work hard to keep from giggling as they planned how best to curb her exuberance at such things as pretending to be Magellan or Cortez or Columbus in the acres of timberland that were part of her father's plantation.

There was nothing amusing about what was taking place in the parlor now.

The voices rose, her father's increasing agitation evident. She had heard him get that high pitch to his voice before, usually when he was losing an argument with Delia or mother.

"You're mistaken about Matthew, Major Bailey," Zachary Morgan said. "I don't give a damn what kind of proof you say you have. It's all a lie. All of it."

"It's *Mister* Bailey, Mr. Morgan. The war is over. And I'm sorry about your son, believe me. But there's been no mistake."

Her father's voice was stricken, agonized. "You can't come into my home with these abominations, sir. My son died a hero in Virginia in March of this year."

"Your son died two days before Lee surrendered. And it was in no battle, sir. The evidence that led to his death was irrefutable."

What were they saying? She ducked farther behind the settee as Delia entered the room with a silver tray laden with pastries and a tea pot.

Zachary Morgan fell silent, only nodding as Delia quickly poured tea for himself and the former CSA officer.

"Begging your pardon, Mr. Morgan," Delia said, "but Mrs. Morgan is deeply distressed. I found her in her bedroom this morning reading . . ." She faltered, shoving a paper toward Amanda's father.

Amanda watched her father's face go chalk-white. "Dear God, I never meant for her to see this." He stiffened, boring a hard look at Delia. "Did you read this, madam?"

Delia faced him squarely. She had never been a person to back down, not even from Zachary Morgan. "I did not read it, sir. But Mrs. Morgan did read parts of it aloud as she was . . . was crying, sir."

Amanda's heart ached at the sight of her once-proud father slumping to the chair. "You recognize your letter, Major Bailey? Now my wife has discovered the lies being spread about my son." He rubbed a hand across his face. "I would have given my life that she never find out."

"Then you believe it," Mr. Bailey said. "Because I assure you, there is no mistake. He was a traitor. Matthew Morgan was a Union spy!"

"No!" Amanda leaped from her hiding place. "Papa, what is he saying? How can you let him talk about Matthew like that?"

His eyes beseeched her to understand. "I wanted no one else to know the shame of it."

"It's not true!"

"I'm afraid it is, Mandy. The major has sent me proof."

"No!" She hadn't been old enough to be involved in the war and its causes. But she understood betrayal, because she could see it in her father's eyes, feel it in her heart.

She had been angry with Matthew for dying; now her rage was magnified a thousandfold because he had all but chosen to die. To die a traitor to his own family.

She marched over to Bailey. "You didn't know my brother. If he did what you say, it was because he believed it was right." She said the words, screamed them, but she never accepted them as truth. That Matthew had died in the war, a soldier doing his duty, had been hard enough to bear. But to discover his duplicity was unforgivable.

She remembered his promise to come home, a promise renewed again and again in his letters as he told of fighting for the glory of the South. The promises, the letters, the words. Lies. All lies.

Her father tried to put his arm around her. Delia called out to her. But she'd stormed out of the room on the dead run. She'd spent the night in the hayloft of the livery. And that's when she made herself the promise.

"I believed you, Matthew. I believed all of your promises, all of your lies. Well, I'll never be so stupid again. I'll never love anybody again. Never." The tears fell. "Never."

More images swirled through her mind. Her father, his spirit broken. Nothing ever the same after Mr. Bailey's visit. The odd fight she had heard her parents have three nights later. Her mother seeming to gather

her strength one last time to confront Zachary about something. The next morning her mother had moved all of her personal things into a separate bedroom.

Amanda had never understood it then. Not until Philip had . . .

Papa, how could you? How—? And to be so self-righteous . . . to pretend . . .

The dream spiraled outward . . . changing focus. She saw Matthew as he had been the day he had left home in his Confederate grays. Smiling, happy, promising to come home. Then she saw the other Matthew. The Matthew she had imagined so many times after that day in the parlor.

The drums . . . the soldiers . . . laughing, jeering, shouting obscenities.

Matthew, a spy.

Matthew condemned.

Matthew on the scaffold. The trapdoor sprung.

His body twisting in the wind.

The face . . . blotched, disfigured . . . eyes open . . . staring at her. Matthew.

Hanged by the neck until dead.

She woke, screaming.

Strong arms held her, quiet words sought to soothe her.

"Don't touch me! Don't you touch me! I hate you, Matthew. I hate you!"

"It's all right. All right. It's just a dream. A dream." The arms didn't let go. They circled her, pulling her close. "It's all right." The voice, calm, comforting, repeating over and over, "It's all right."

Fighting her sleep-drugged despair, she allowed the intimacy, the warmth to seep over her, through her. Felt so good, so good. Her breathing slowed, awareness taking over. Her eyes widened. Montana. With his hands on her yet again. Angrily, she pushed him away.

"How dare you!"

Startled, he backed off. "I was just . . ." His eyes trailed down, assessing the direction of her thoughts. His lips twisted derisively. "Think what you like." He stood up. "It's almost dawn. Get dressed. We'll be leaving soon."

She sat there trembling, remembering the dream, trying to remember what had come afterwards. Was that really Montana who had held her cradled to him whispering soothing, gentle words as though she were a frightened child? Even after the horrid things she had said to him about marrying Philip.

She wiped at an errant tear. No, Matthew, I won't cry for you. You chose your path. Being a war hero for the Union was more important than coming home to your family. A traitor. A Yankee traitor.

And her father. Oh, God, what her father had done. No one could ever know the shame of it.

She shivered, wondering if she had called out anything in her sleep. If Montana knew . . . No, it wouldn't matter. Her father had buried the proof, paid off a detective to excise the truth from the government files. No one was ever to know.

It was just that her father hadn't reckoned on Philip.

She sat there, watching Montana covertly now as he saddlèd his horse, realizing that it was he who had jarred loose memories of Matthew right from the first. Just by virtue of the fact that he was sentenced to hang. She closed her eyes. Even if Montana were guilty, she would never have been able to watch his hanging.

Because she knew, knew that forever after it would have been Matthew's face, Matthew's neck that had broken for her that morning.

Montana continued to step lightly around her, oddly subdued, almost deferential. Now she was certain he had heard something of the dream, though she had no idea what, or how he might have pieced her murmurings together.

Her heart seemed to catch as she remembered the wonder of last night, before the nightmare. When the outlaw had held her in his arms, it made her feel whole and alive. Made her feel the yearning, the rapture, the wonder of her own body.

Then the guilt came. No matter that she didn't love Philip, that their marriage was arranged for the benefit of them both. She still owed him some bit of loyalty, didn't she?

She stiffened, thinking of the bargain Philip had wrought. No, she didn't owe him anything. But she owed herself. Owed herself the courage to keep the vow she had made thirteen years ago. To shield herself from exactly the kind of pain she sensed Montana could bring her should she ever be foolish enough to care.

Care? For Montana? Never.

He was on the run. He would likely never be able to get out from under the charges against him. Never be free. More than that, he would never be free of his memories of his dead wife.

No doubt his newfound compassion stemmed from not wanting a hysterical woman on his hands. Doing what he could to keep her calm.

"Whatever I said in my dream," she said, her voice defensive though she fought it, "is none of your concern."

He paused in his task of tightening the cinch on the bay. He took a step toward her, but stopped. "Andy . . . Amanda . . . I think I know . . ."

"None of your concern. Do you understand?"

He straightened. "Whatever you say." He returned to the horse, but as much as he wanted to do as she asked, to dismiss her from his concern, he found he could not. Her brother had been hanged. He hadn't gotten much else out of her frightened cries, but of that much he was certain. No wonder Isaiah had said she turned gray on the gallows.

Then why the bold pronouncement that she would spring the trapdoor herself? It didn't make sense. He shook his head. Not much in his life made sense lately. Most especially since Amanda Morgan had stepped into it.

The horse snorted as he jerked the cinch too tight. Grimacing, he let the thick strap out a couple of inches. "Sorry, horse," he said, scratching the bay's ears. "Got my mind on other things besides your breathing."

Other things like Amanda Morgan. The sooner he got rid of that woman, the better off he would be. He preferred his women simple, uncomplicated. She had to be the most contradictory female he'd ever met.

His image of her as a spoiled bitch, deriding him as a savage and always getting her own way wavered perceptibly when butted up against hard facts. Her concern for Isaiah was genuine. The agony in the voice that cried out in the dream could not be feigned. And she felt guilty about eating "bunnies" when she was starving!

Oh, but more than that, more than that was the woman she became in his arms when for that brief span of time she allowed the real world no intrusion. Not who he was. Not who she was. And it was that woman who frightened him the most. If she ever set herself free for good . . . He was grateful when she interrupted his increasingly disturbing musings.

"So are you taking me back to Philip or not?" She planted her hands on her hips, hating the look in those gray eyes. Instead of the hate she had so carefully sown there last night there was sympathy, and a kind of sad understanding that made her very nervous. "Did you hear me?" she demanded irritably.

"I'll take you back," he said at last. "But the ranch house is half a day's ride. I want to check on Isaiah first." He didn't say it, but he couldn't shake having seen signs of Stark's phantom posse last night. The tracks could intercept the camp.

"Whatever it takes," she said. "Just so I'm free of you by tomorrow."

"You'll be free, Andy. By tomorrow."

She did not mistake the words he added, "And so will I."

Chapter Thirteen

A sharp popping noise shattered the dawn stillness. Jace reined to a halt, listening. They were still a mile from the camp in the willows.

"What is it?" Amanda asked, alarmed by the tightening of the arm settled about her waist.

The distant crack sounded again. And again.

"Gunfire," Jace gritted, spurring the horse into a hard gallop.

Amanda hung on, her heart pounding to match the beat of the bay's hooves on the grassy turf. She said nothing more as Jace manuevered the horse in a wide circle, coming up on the opposite side of the encampment. Atop a small knoll he sawed back at the reins, all but setting the horse on its haunches. Leaping from its back, he flattened out on his belly, snaking to the edge of the rise.

Her gaze darted from Jace to the willows as she assessed the grim reality below. The brunt of the gunfire was coming from the trees—from Isaiah. She steadied the nervously prancing gelding as she checked the reasons for Isaiah's defense. She counted five men in the rocks above and to the right of the circle of willows. One by one they were moving closer to the nearest of the trees. Shading her eyes, she could just make out the only man seeming to hold back. She gasped.

Philip. He had come for her after all.

Her fingers curled around the reins. Montana had yet to rise. All she had to do was dig her heels into the bay's sides and she would be free. She could ride toward the posse. The outlaw would not shoot her. Not stop her.

But to ride away was to condemn him and Benteen to death. She had no doubt the posse would fill the air with bullets as soon as they saw her safe.

Jace levered himself up, coming toward her. He grabbed hold of the bridle, quieting the horse as he spoke to Amanda in short, clipped tones. "I'm going in. Isaiah's dead if I don't. You ride out of here. I don't want you with Welford if Isaiah or I have to shoot in that direction."

Her hands twisted on the pommel, considering the irony of what Montana was saying. She was his hostage. Yet he was setting her free.

His gaze held hers, but he kept his thoughts to himself. With a mocking half grin he tipped his hat, then started down the incline.

"No! Jace, don't . . . You can't . . ." But he didn't stop. Terrified, she dismounted, edging her way to the rim of the knoll, keeping low and out of sight. She told herself she wanted no one hurt here today, yet it was on Montana her eyes rested, her eyes and her prayers.

He ducked low, skirting behind any available cover.

The posse's concentration was still on the trees. They had yet to spot him. Likely, they assumed Montana was pinned down with Isaiah. That would explain their sporadic fire. They feared she was hidden amongst those trees too.

"Come on out, Montana!" Sheriff Jon Stark called, rising up from behind a huge boulder. "We know you're in there. There's no sense making this harder on any of us. Just let Miss Morgan come out first. Then you and Benteen throw out your guns and come out with your hands up."

Amanda sank back, taking care not to be seen. As long as the posse thought she was still with Isaiah and Jace, they stood a chance of surviving.

Jace was almost to the trees, keeping to the rocks and the rises. The posse had not covered the rear of the grove, evidently crediting the high west bank of the creek with being too steep to scale on horseback.

"You're dead, Montana," Philip called. "If you've so much as put a bruise on Amanda, I'll kill you myself." He gestured to Langley and Bates, who instantly raced forward, dropping to prone positions behind the first sentry line of trees.

"Watch out for Amanda," Philip shouted. "I don't want her hurt, Gabe."

Amanda held her breath as they disappeared from her sight, swatting at the trailing branches. She was surprised and touched by Philip's obvious concern for her safety. She did not question his courage that he sent others to do his fighting for him. She had seen it was a politician's nature to delegate.

A barrage of bullets sounded inside the shrouding trees. She knew Jace had joined Isaiah. Her heart was pounding so hard she thought it might jump from her chest.

The gunfire ceased, the ensuing silence more ominous still.

She bit her lip to keep from screaming to Jace, desperate to know if he was all right. In that instant Gabe Langley bolted from the trees, helping an injured Jack Bates back toward the rocks.

Scrambling up the embankment on the opposite side of the grove was Jace. He was pushing, prodding, pulling Isaiah along with him. She couldn't tell if Isaiah had been hurt or if it was simply his weakened condition that slowed him.

Wheezing, coughing, Isaiah hugged the ground on his way up to the knoll. She found herself holding her breath, waiting for Jace to follow. But instead he slid back down the embankment and into the trees, laying down a cover fire, distracting Stark and his men.

"No, no, no." Tears stung her eyes as a minute later he came pounding out of the trees on Isaiah's horse, directly into the teeth of the posse.

Pistols in both hands, he let out a spine-curdling yell, firing as he rode. His shots missed, and she knew it was by design. But the bullets came close enough to send the posse diving for cover. Digging his spurs into the sorrel's sides, Jace put the horse into a dead run away from the willows and the rocks, away from Isaiah, away from her.

In seconds the posse was scurrying for their mounts, ready to ride after Jace. All but Philip.

"Amanda's not with him," Philip shouted. "I'm going down there. See if that bastard hurt her . . ."

"We'll get him, Mr. Welford," Stark yelled, as he

swung onto his chestnut.

"See that you do," Philip yelled back, signalling to Langley and Bates that they were to stay behind while Stark and the other two men thundered off in pursuit of Jace.

Amanda gave no more time to Philip or the posse. The thought of calling out to them was ruled out even before it had a chance to fully form in her mind. She had to make certain Isaiah was safe. If Sheriff Stark were down in the willows, perhaps she would have given the mountain man over to him, ending her own participation in this bizarre turn her life had taken. But she dared not give him up to Philip. She would never have been able to forgive herself if Philip had attacked Isaiah to get to Jace. And Philip's core-deep hate for Montana left her with little doubt that he would do just that.

When Isaiah made it to the top of the knoll, she helped him onto the bay, her eyes widening at the patch of red that stained his trouser leg.

"I'm all right, miss," he rasped. "Just leave me be."

"I'll do no such thing." Quickly, she rummaged through the saddlebags. Yanking out Jace's last remaining shirt, she ripped it into long strips, tying them securely around the wound. Only when she was certain the bleeding had stopped did she pick up the trailing reins and start walking.

"Don't, little lady," Isaiah said, his voice barely audible. "I can take it from here."

"You're hurt."

"This ain't your fight. I'm sorry I got you into all this. You go back to Welford. He'll take you where it's safe."

She looked at Isaiah, looked back toward the

direction she knew Philip to be. Maybe she was out of her mind. But she couldn't leave Isaiah like this. It was partly her fault he had been ambushed. If she hadn't run off last night . . .

She checked herself. She was being ridiculous! Was she really trying to tell herself she was wrong to try and escape from her own kidnappers? No, it wasn't her fault Isaiah was hurt. It was simply that she didn't want to leave him wounded and alone. He could die, and then she would be responsible. She paused to examine the bandage. The leg was bleeding again.

"Find a stick," Isaiah said.

Swiftly she did so.

He jammed it under the bandage, twisting it until the bleeding stopped. "Let it loose every so often," he said, leaning forward, his head brushing the bay's mane. His eyes rolled back. He was losing consciousness.

"Is there any place Jace said he would try and meet you?" Amanda asked urgently.

"The ranch," Isaiah gasped.

"What ranch?"

"Our ranch."

She didn't raise any objections to the question of ownership. "Where is it?"

"'Bout ten miles north. A place we built in a hollow. A hideout near where the ranch house was supposed to be."

"How appropriate," she muttered. She kept to the arroyos to avoid being skylined and to make sure she wasn't spotted by Philip. And as she walked she told herself again and again that she was being a fool. Jason Montana would not be pleased to find that he had not rid himself of her after all. She shook her head ruefully, realizing that to imagine his displeasure was to imagine him free of the posse. She only hoped she was right.

When her feet hurt so much she couldn't go on, she climbed onto the horse and rode behind Isaiah. He was out cold, and she was terrified she was going to pass by the hollow he had told her about. When she thought she had covered at least ten miles, she shook Isaiah gently to rouse him.

His eyes were glazed and dull, but somehow he took in the surrounding countryside and pointed her in the right direction. Nowhere was there a sign of Jace. What if Stark had caught up with him? What if they'd shot him? Taken him back to San Antonio to hang?

Isaiah groaned, and she put everything out of her mind but getting him to a place where he could rest. Near dusk she found the hollow. She guessed it must run on for miles. Steeply troughed on both sides and thickly wooded, a stream no more than two feet wide meandered through its bottom.

Deadwood splintered and cracked under the bay's hooves as Amanda maneuvered the horse into the basin. The descending darkness would have put an end to her chances of finding the hideout Isaiah described, but the trapper came to long enough to point her to it.

She stared at the heavily shadowed structure that was an insult to the word *shack*. Barely six feet by ten feet on the inside, the crude wooden hut was camouflaged by the heavy circle of trees that all but smothered it. Amanda doubted it would even be visible from more than a foot away in broad daylight. The only decent thing she could say about it was that at least it would be a roof over her head for tonight.

Tying off the horse, she helped Isaiah inside,

easing him onto a pallet lying on the floor near the left wall. She couldn't see his face in the darkness, but she could feel how stiffly he was holding himself and knew he must be in considerable pain.

"No fire," he groaned.

"But your leg."

"It'll keep. It ain't bleedin'. Wait . . . wait 'til morning."

She placed a tentative hand on the man's forehead, letting out a small sigh of relief. No fever.

"I told ya," he said, and she thought she detected a smile, albeit a feeble one, in his voice. "I'm fine."

"Jace would likely starve me again if I let anything happen to you."

"You're worried about him, too, ain't ya?"

"Of course not!"

The old man chuckled weakly and lay back. "Never heard ya call him Jace before."

She grimaced, but Isaiah wasn't finished.

"Don't worry. He's got more lives than a cat. He'll be here. Might take him a while, but he'll be here. I'm glad he found you all right last night."

"I'll—uh—I'll get us some fresh water from the creek." She stood up abruptly and went outside, getting the canteen from their gear. She was in no mood to discuss Jace with Isaiah. She hadn't even settled in her own mind why she had brought the trapper here. Why she hadn't saved herself when she had the chance.

Kneeling by the shallow stream, she held the canteen under the current. Somewhere close by a twig snapped.

It was pitch-black. No moon. She was glad she had thought to bring Isaiah's rifle, even if she wasn't adept

192

at using it.

A dark outline padded toward her. The way he was moving, gracefully, like a mountain cat, she knew at once who it was. She felt herself grinning, then quickly suppressed it, wondering what his reaction would be to finding her here.

"Isaiah?" he called, creeping closer.

"He's in the shack," she said quietly, rising to her feet.

She almost laughed at the way he jumped. She had actually startled him. He eyed the gun in her hand balefully.

"Don't worry. I remembered to cock it," she said.

"Glad to hear that. How's Isaiah?"

"He has a leg wound. He's resting."

He spread his hands wide in an odd gesture of surrender. "Can I see him?"

"Of course." She lowered the rifle, following him to the shack.

Isaiah was asleep, but Jace struck a match to check the wound. He looked at Amanda. "You did a good job."

She stayed in the doorway. "Thank you."

"Now you want to tell me what the hell you're doing here?"

"What was I supposed to do? Let him bleed to death?"

"Welford would have seen he got to a doctor."

"You believe that?"

"No."

"Neither do I."

"I can't figure you out, Andy."

"That makes us even then, doesn't it? I take it you

managed to elude Sheriff Stark."

"That wasn't exactly difficult. The man isn't much of a tracker. Neither are any of his men."

"Maybe they just haven't spent thirty years learning the craft."

He smiled. "Maybe." He stepped closer to her. "I—uh—want to thank you again. For taking care of Isaiah."

"Aren't you going to suggest that if I hadn't run off . . ."

"I can't fault you for that." He turned, scratching absently at the back of his neck. "I saw the posse's sign last night. I should have come back then. But I couldn't leave you out there alone."

"I can certainly understand that. Philip might have found me and saved me that whole experience this morning." She hadn't meant the sarcasm, but she was suddenly achingly tired. And all too aware of Jace's presence in the cramped quarters of the one-room shack.

He lay out his blanket with a sharp snap but otherwise ignored her mood. "How do you like my ranch?"

"It's lovely. All the comforts I'm used to having when I'm around you. None."

He chuckled. "It's got running water. What more do you highly civilized ladies want?" He waved a hand in the direction of the creek.

"I am not amused, Mr. Montana. However, I will indulge myself in the running water in the morning. I intend to take a bath. It seems like forever . . ." She stopped, sensing the sudden heightened tension in the room. He was not accepting her notion about a bath with indifference.

A long minute passed when Amanda could have sworn he touched her, though he was sitting on the floor four feet away from her. Then he gave her an exaggerated yawn and lay down. "Just be careful."

"I intend to be." She curled into a corner of the room farthest away from him, though in reality there was barely a foot between his boots and her knees. She was grateful then for the exhaustion, because in less than a minute she was asleep.

She woke to the smell of beans and bacon. In an instant she was alert, hurrying outside to see Montana busily preparing breakfast. He looked up, grinning. "Good morning."

She smiled back, awed by the warm feeling that swept through her just seeing that boyishly pleased look on his face. "Isaiah's better?"

"He seems to be. He's asleep instead of unconscious."

"I'm glad."

The look in his gray eyes crackled with the same heat as the cookfire. "Go on and take your bath. I'll see to Isaiah and make sure there's plenty of food left for you when you get back."

She didn't argue, skirting quickly to the saddlebags and extracting a bar of lye soap. She ambled several hundred yards upstream to find a secluded spot. The water was only six inches deep, but it was cool and clean and wet. Not even bothering to undress she sloshed out to midstream and plopped herself down on rock that just barely broke the surface. Using the smooth stone as a stool, she shed her clothes and gave them a good, hard scrubbing. Prancing out of the

195

water, she tossed the shirt, trousers, and undergarments over a shrub to dry, then hurried back into the water.

"Is this really you, Amanda Morgan?" she asked aloud, pirouetting in the cool waters. "You are standing in a creek stark naked in the middle of God knows where, and you feel like . . . like"—she kicked at the water, dancing and splashing—"like you could stand here forever!"

Even after she'd given herself a thorough bath, she was reluctant to leave. She just stood on the smooth, pebbled creek bottom, wriggling her toes and staring up at the cloudless sky through a tangled web of towering tree branches. Never had she felt so free, so abandoned.

Amanda brushed her still damp hair away from her face, sighing. She supposed she really ought to get back. She started toward her clothes, then stopped dead.

Swallowing hard, she turned her head toward the exact spot where she knew he was standing.

A muscle in his jaw twitched, and he immediately looked at the ground. "I'm sorry," he gritted. "You were gone so long, I . . . got worried."

Her arms automatically covered her breasts. She knew he was telling the truth but knew also that once he had ascertained she was in no danger, he had not gone back to the camp. She could only guess at how long he'd been watching her.

"I am sorry, Andy." He turned away.

"Jason . . ."

He stopped, but did not turn around.

"Why?"

"I can't seem to stay away from you."

She expelled a shuddering breath. "Then don't. Stay away, that is."

He straightened, his hands clenching and unclenching at his sides. "Damn." He twisted around and in three strides she was in his arms.

His mouth devoured hers, his tongue exploring her mouth with a fiery need that consumed her. Her hands gripped the back of his neck, holding him to her as her tongue parried with his, taking, taking, taking as much as she gave.

The palms of his hands were firebrands on the cool flesh of her breasts. She gasped as he ever so gently teased the nipples, his fingers circling, caressing. Her knees no longer supported her.

Her hands worked the buckle of his belt, the buttons of his shirt. She pressed her breasts against his chest, feeling him suck in his breath, cry out his need.

Almost worshipfully, he eased her down in the shallow water. As if in a dream, she felt it rippling by, caressing her head, her shoulders, the backs of her legs.

Jace shoved out of his clothes, his body demanding release. The water trailed over the tops of his toes, then his knees as he knelt between her legs. The coolness of the water only added to the fever in his blood as she opened herself to him.

"Now, Jason. Now, please."

He stole inside her an inch at a time, revelling in the way she drew him in. "No anger afterwards, Andy. Not this time. Please."

She lay trembling fingers against his lips. "No anger. None."

She moaned, her body writhing, her legs twining

round his hips.

He held himself still, his breath hot and wet against her ear, savoring the passion he'd loosed in his ice maiden. "Tell me you don't mind my being a savage. Tell me."

She snared her fingers in the hair of his chest, her head arching back. "Yes, savage. You are a savage. My sweet, sweet savage. Mine." She screamed his name as he took her where she'd never been, never wanting to be anywhere else.

Afterwards, she nuzzled against his chest, kissing his nipples, nipping at the hard-muscled flesh. "It's going to be all right. I promise. I'll talk to Philip. I'll make him understand you're innocent."

He tensed. "No. It's not that simple. I don't know what he wants, but it can't be finished between Welford and me until I get some answers."

"Jason, please . . ."

He pressed his lips to her forehead, then sat up, shaking off the cool water. "I'd better get back to Isaiah."

She bit her lip. She was not going to regret their time together. Not again. No matter how stubborn and unreasonable he was, no matter how foolish she felt.

He cupped her chin in his hand. "You're not going back to Welford just yet. I won't let you." He kissed her, then drew back. "Andy, I don't pretend to know what's happening between us, but if I have my way we're going to have more time to find out."

She trembled, struck by how straightforward he was about his mixed-up feelings for her. She wished she could be as candid with him. But he would never understand, and she could never explain.

"You go on back to the shack and have yourself some breakfast and sit with Isaiah. I'm going to hunt us up some lunch."

She tried to smile. "Will I have to clean it?"

"You could use the practice."

"Right. I'll need to know how to skin game to be a governor's wife."

She could have bitten her tongue. His gray eyes darkened. Without another word he dressed and stomped away.

Miserable, she trudged back to the camp. It was past noon before Jace returned astride the bay, a dead longhorn in tow. She stepped out of the shack, not meeting his eyes as he dismounted and went to work dressing out the carcass. The thought of beefsteak appealed to her suddenly ravenous, carnivorous self. And she was again struck by how easily mere days in this man's company had stripped away the veneer of her civilized upbringing.

"You two just won't admit you're more alike than different."

She gasped, startled, twisting to see Isaiah limping toward her. "You shouldn't be up."

"A man can't sleep what's left of his life away."

"Don't talk like that." She came under his arm and helped him outside. He sank down beside the outer wall of the small cabin. His eyes were on Jace some twenty yards away, but again he spoke to her. "Don't sell 'im short 'cause he was brought up different than you."

"Different?" she choked. "That's a rather mild way to put it."

"And do you think he'd be a different man if he'd

199

been raised in Baltimore society. That he'd be all duded up, a real dandy, a banker or accountant or maybe a politician like Welford."

She laughed as the image flitted through her mind of Montana in a suit complete with cravat and top hat. Like putting clothes on a bear. But she was feeling defensive of her own upbringing, "If he'd been raised in gentility, of course he . . ."

"People don't kill people in Baltimore? No murders? No robberies? No . . ."

"Well, of course there are bad seeds, Isaiah. No matter what ground they fall upon . . ."

"The same can be said for good seeds. No matter where Jace woulda growed up"—his voice grew fierce, proud—"he'd be the same man. Decent, hardworking, make any woman a good catch."

Her eyes widened. Isaiah Benteen wasn't even attempting to be subtle. The man was matchmaking! Herself and that . . . that . . . She looked up to see Jace bending, sweating half naked over the longhorn carcass, butchering the beast, blood smeared up to his elbows. He looked to be as much a beast as the one at his feet. Yet she couldn't help but notice too the rippling muscles of his back, taut with exertion. The strength in his arms, the gentleness in those hands. Such big hands he had.

Ludicrously she could hear in her mind Delia telling her the story of Little Red Riding Hood and the big bad wolf. "Oh, grandmother, what big hands you have!"

"All the better to caress your breasts, my dear!" Only this time the voice in her mind was not Delia's, but Jason's. A deep, growly Jason's voice. She started laughing and couldn't stop.

200

Montana strode over to her, bare-chested, his eyes narrowed with concern. He looked at Amanda, then at Isaiah. "What the hell's the matter with her?"

Isaiah shrugged. "We was just talking and it started all of a sudden."

Amanda tried very hard to quiet herself, but every time she glanced at Montana her eyes settled on some part of his anatomy, and he was suddenly no cougar but every bit the big bad wolf. What big eyes you have . . . The better to see you with . . . What big hands you have . . . The better to feel you with . . . What big . . . Her eyes slid scandalously below his belt buckle.

Mortified, she looked away, though the heat that suffused her skin had nothing to do with embarrassment. She had to put a stop to the outrageous direction of her thoughts. He was an outlaw. She was deluding herself with some sort of romantic notion, not unlike those found in the penny dreadfuls Delia secreted into the house for years.

More than once Amanda had pressed a rug against the bottom of her bedroom door so that her father would not notice she still had her lantern turned up well after her bedtime. She read the trashy books voraciously.

It was as though her life had become a penny dreadful. She was a hostage to a convicted murderer, who only a few short days ago had terrified her. But then she had been seeing him through Philip's eyes. Now she saw him through her own. Jason Montana had come into her life with all the unpredictability of a summer storm. He could be violent. He could be gentle. He could frighten her. And he could make her

201

feel so very, very safe. Even now, as she sat on the ground nearly hysterical with laughter, his eyes were not angry but concerned, as though he feared she had misplaced her mind.

"Miss Morgan," he began, "uh, Amanda, are you well? I mean did you eat something you shouldn't have? Are you sick?"

"Because I'm laughing I'm supposed to be sick!" She laughed harder.

He wiped off his hands, stooping down to grip her arms. She stared at his hands and laughed all over again. "What big hands you have, grandma!"

"She's gone round the bend, Isaiah," Jace said. "I thought she was doing all right."

Isaiah started to rise but fell back with a groan.

"Oh, Isaiah," Amanda cried, "please don't get up."

Jace glared at her. "What the hell is the matter with you?"

"Well, pardon me for being amused!" She stood up, brushing off her trousers.

"I want you to tell me what that was all about."

Her gaze trailed the length of him, head to foot. Eyes, hands, and lower. "Not on your life, Mr. Montana. Not on your very life." She giggled again.

"I'm pleased you find me so amusing." He stomped away.

Her shoulders sagged. Drat him; she hadn't been laughing *at* him. Why in the world would he think . . . Oh, what did it matter anyway. For a brute and a bully he could be excessively sensitive on occasion.

Isaiah chuckled. "Ah, missy, I'm real glad I kidnapped you. I figured you'd be the perfect one."

She frowned. "The perfect what?"

"I seen the way he looked at you in the courtroom."

"Men have looked at me before."

"Not like that, missy. More than just a man lookin' at a purty woman. He ain't showed no interest in any female since Dawn Wind. But when I seen that look, well, that's when I picked you to be my hostage."

"You! Picked me?" All this time she had imagined she had merely been in the wrong place at the wrong time.

"Of course I picked you. You don't think Jace woulda picked ya. A lady like you. Never. But for all your sputterin' I seen the way you looked when you didn't think nobody was watchin'. When he talked to ya in the courtroom. When they put the rope around his neck. Even if you wouldn't have been on the gallows, I'd have found a way to make you the one."

"But in town that day you made it sound like you didn't want to take me with you at all."

He smiled. "I didn't want Jace gettin' no notions that I was plannin' anything but gettin' him out of town."

"But you were . . . deliberately forcing the two of us to be together? That's . . . that's unconscionable!"

"I ain't sure I know what a big word like that means, miss. But I know Jace is fightin' like hell not to like you. And I know you're doin' the same with him."

"This is the most absurd conversation . . ."

"He'd never in his life figure a lady like you would be interested in the likes o' him."

She shifted uncomfortably, accepting the gentle insult as a valid one, knowing that until the day she became Jason Montana's hostage she likely never would have noticed such a man.

"And you, Miss Morgan, you've got 'xactly the

opposite problem. How could a lady like you ever land a wilderness man?"

She grimaced. She'd never considered the reverse. "I don't have to listen to . . ."

"No, ma'am, you don't. Just listen to your heart. If he gives ya his, you won't need nothin' else in this life to make ya happy."

She tromped off into the woods. Jason Montana give her his heart? Love her? Her throat constricted. Even if he did, even if he did, she could never stay with him. She walked aimlessly for hours, though she never left the timbered basin.

When she returned to the camp it was to find that Jace's edginess had grown along with the afternoon shadows.

"Where the hell have you been?" he snapped.

Her angry retort never left her throat. She stared at the haggard lines of his face as he hunkered down beside Isaiah. She pushed away her own tortured doubts at once, hurrying over to him. "What is it, Jace?"

"He hasn't been able to keep any food down all day. I can't take this. I'm going for a doctor."

"No," Isaiah rasped. "It's too dangerous. I didn't save your neck from that rope so you could stick it right back in the noose yourself."

"I'm going," Jace said. "That's all there is to it."

Amanda followed him over to the horses. "Don't worry. I'll watch out for him."

"I know."

His bronzed hand captured the side of her face. "You're starting to look less like a bedsheet." His voice was husky. "A little more sun, and you'll look like an

204

Apache yet."

She tried to smile. She supposed he meant that as a compliment, but she couldn't help thinking he was recalling his wife again.

"Don't worry," he said softly. "You could spend the rest of your life in the sun, and you would never ever look like Dawn Wind."

His eyes caressed her and she knew he was going to kiss her. And she knew she wasn't going to stop him.

His lips were warm but tentative, as though gauging her reaction before he continued. When he encountered no resistance, he grew bolder, pulling her against him. But he did not press her further, seeming to content himself with the kiss.

A long, languorous minute later he released her. "Take care of him. I'll be back as soon as I can."

"You're going to San Antonio?"

He nodded. "It'll probably take three days to get there and back."

"Be careful."

He stroked her hair. "What were you laughing at before?"

"I can't tell you." At his frown she added, "I wasn't laughing *at* you, Jason. I promise."

He swept her into his arms, crushing her against him. "Give us a chance, Andy. Maybe it won't work. Maybe we're too different. But at least give us a chance."

She said nothing.

He pulled away. "I'll be back." He mounted, gigged the horse into a trot, and was gone.

She stood there, watching him ride away, her eyes burning with unshed tears, recalling his words. *I'm not sorry we're going to have more time.* Recalling Isaiah's.

Listen to your heart. If he gives you his, you won't need nothin' else in this life to make you happy.

Jace was asking for that chance, the chance to see if she was the woman to whom he could give his heart. He didn't know it. Could never know it. Because she would be Philip Welford's wife. But she had already given him hers.

Chapter Fourteen

Jace tied off the bay behind the doctor's office, pulling his hat brim down to further shade his eyes. Though it was nearly midnight, he wanted to take no chances on being recognized by some nocturnal San Antonian with heroic delusions. He lifted the .45 from its holster and spun the cylinder, checking the load. Nor was he in any mood for arguments from the medical man. Testing the latch on the rear door, he smiled grimly to find it unlocked.

Anxiously, he prowled the darkened house, a fear goading him such as he'd never known. Fear for Isaiah's life.

He cursed to find the doctor gone, the home's only apparent occupant a young boy asleep in an upstairs bedroom. He was about to exit through the kitchen, when he sensed more than saw a shadowy figure hiding near the pantry. He cocked the revolver.

"Please, don't shoot, senor," came the quaking female voice.

Jace grimaced, letting the hammer down easy. "I

won't hurt you. Who are you? And where's the doctor?"

"I am Teresa Perez, Dr. Adams's housekeeper. The doctor is out at Senor Welford's ranch. He has been gone two days now."

Welford, Jace thought viciously. Perfect. He jammed the gun into its holster. "I didn't mean to frighten you, senora."

"I do not fear you, Senor Montana."

"You know who I am?"

"Si. Padre Manuel is my priest and my friend. It was my son who brought Senor Benteen your horses. Estaban is upstairs asleep." The woman stepped away from the wall, moving with the confidence of familiarity across the darkened kitchen. Jace heard the scrape of a chair as she positioned it so that she could sit down. "I was hungry. I came down to have a little bread. Would you like me to fix you something to eat, senor?"

"No, thank you." It was disconcerting to speak to a shadow, but he couldn't chance turning up a light. "May I ask why you allowed your son to help me, senora?"

"Juanita was a good girl. I do not believe you hurt her."

"But I was convicted of killing her."

"Poor child. She was so mixed up. Ever since her madre died. She really tried to make a living sewing for rich gringos."

"Is there something you know about Juanita that would help my case with the law? If there is . . ." Perhaps this woman was privy to some bit of unknown evidence that would help clear him. Why else would a stranger be so convinced of his innocence?

"I believe you did not kill her because Padre Manuel says it."

Jace suppressed his disappointment. "I see."

"The padre also asked me to tell you, if I should see you, to go to the mission and speak with him."

"Why would he have expected me to come here?"

"He knows Senor Benteen is not well. He thought you would eventually come for the doctor."

"Well, I can't stop to see him tonight. I have to get back to Isaiah."

"Please, senor, Padre Manuel was very insistent you speak with him."

Telling himself he was wasting precious time, he left the doctor's office and skirted through back alleys to reach the adobe mission. On the way he spied a wanted dodger nailed to a post. His eyes were accustomed to the darkness, and he found the dim starlight more than adequate to make out the bold letters that proclaimed: Jason Montana—WANTED—DEAD OR ALIVE. The list of crimes credited to him would have kept a gang of ten men busy around the clock for months. Swearing under his breath, he folded the poster and shoved it into his pocket.

Skulking around the back of the mission, he eased the heavy oak door open as silently as he could. He grimaced ruefully. He was becoming entirely too adept at playing the part of the thief in the night.

"Who's there?" came the soft voice.

"Padre?"

"Si."

Jace closed the door. "Jason Montana."

A match was struck, a lantern lit. Jace found himself

face-to-face with a large figure in a white linen cossack.

"You are well?" the priest asked, as though this were the most ordinary of social calls.

"Thanks to you. I don't know why you helped Isaiah, but I'm grateful."

"Because I know you are innocent, my son, and I could not let them hang an innocent man. Since your escape they have accused you of many more crimes in and around San Antonio."

"So I've noticed." Jace paced the confines of the small room. "I'm in a bit of a hurry, padre. But Senora Perez insisted you would want to see me."

"Yes. I want you to take me to your friend."

Jace rubbed a hand across the back of his neck. "You want me to what? Padre, I am on the run. Forgive me, but I have to hide my trail out of town and . . ." He stopped, embarrassed, assessing the priest's size.

"Do not let my appearance deceive you, my son. I can ride a horse as well as Isaiah. Please, we are wasting time. Time he does not have."

Jace stiffened. "Why don't you just tell me what this is all about? It's my life that's on the line here. If there's some problem you have with Isaiah . . ."

"I can only speak of it with him."

"There are men out to kill me. You'll be in danger."

"Shall we go?" The burly priest pulled on his robes and stepped toward the door. "We're wasting time, no?"

Jace followed, drawing rein on his mounting temper. Something was going on, something well beyond what Isaiah had told him. But he sensed there was little use asking the priest. The man would tell him nothing. He waited in the small livery behind the mission while the priest saddled a big roan gelding.

They kept to the side streets on the way out of town. Jace was relieved to find that Padre Manuel rode well enough, though not as well as Isaiah. He guessed it would take nearly twenty hours to make the trip back.

He chafed at the delay but still paused frequently to blot out their trail. The horses, too, needed the rest. He used one such occasion well past dusk to prepare a meager meal for himself and the priest. Biting off a hunk of hardtack, he eyed the holy man. "Why are you doing all this? Risking so much for a stranger?"

"No one is a stranger to God, senor."

"That may be true, padre. But that doesn't answer my question. Welford is a powerful man . . ."

"No man is truly powerful."

Jace could see he wasn't going to get the kind of information he wanted from the priest. He thought of Amanda, hoping she was doing all right. If Isaiah should worsen . . . He knew she would blame herself if anything happened before he returned. Damn, but he missed her. And then he cursed himself for the feeling.

"Do you still have Senor Welford's fiancée with you?" the priest asked.

Jace nodded slowly.

The priest's normally placid gaze turned darkly reproachful. "Senor Welford has promised death if she is harmed."

"I've no intention of harming her. Or anyone."

"There is something you should know. About Miss Morgan herself."

Jace waited, growing increasingly uneasy.

"Does it not seem odd, given Mr. Welford's and Mr. Morgan's money and social position, that you should still hold her hostage? That these men have not turned the state of Texas inside out to rescue her?"

"Welford tried."

"But how hard, senor? Sheriff Stark is a good man, but he is not that good at—how you say—tracking game?"

"So Welford's being cautious. He doesn't want to chance having her caught in a crossfire."

"And yet he let a convicted rapist—a convicted murderer—keep her prisoner?"

"Just what are you getting at, padre?"

"That Senor Welford has planned something. Something evil. I do not trust him, senor."

"That's hardly a revelation to me, padre."

"I do not repeat false rumor. But the chance that you might lose your life makes a warning necessary. You should not be surprised to find that his fiancée is as well informed of his dealings as Philip Welford himself."

"I don't believe that."

"I just thought you should know."

Jace stood up. The horses hadn't had as much rest as he would have liked, but he suddenly didn't want to lose any more time. Quickly, he mounted and rode out. He had to get back to Isaiah. If the priest couldn't keep up, then he would be left behind.

Taking a circuitous route at the end—only because it would lessen the chance of the posse finding Isaiah—he made his way into the hollow, the priest bringing up the rear. Jace vaulted from the saddle, his stomach tightening at the worried look on Amanda's face as she rushed out of the shack to greet him.

"He's not good, Jason."

Jace hurried past her.

She stared at the huge man dismounting the roan. "What on earth? Jace was going for a doctor."

"Senorita Morgan, I am Padre Louis Manuel."

She crossed her arms in front of her. "You helped these men take me hostage."

"That was not my intention. I wished only to spare Senor Montana's life."

"Then you know he's innocent?"

"Si."

Her heart jumped. "You have proof? Something a lawyer could use in court?"

He shook his head sadly. "Unfortunately, that is not the case, senorita."

"Then you only think he is innocent."

"And what do you think, senorita?"

She straightened. "Why are you here? It's very dangerous for Jason to have let you come. You could have been followed."

"I must speak with Isaiah. Excuse me." He stepped past her into the cabin.

Isaiah groaned. "Thought you were going for the doctor, painter. Figure I need a padre more?"

"Don't try to talk," Jace said.

"I'd better. Ain't got much time left to say things in. I'm wonderin' if you'd let me talk to the preacher alone."

Jace stepped outside, his gaze locking for just a heartbeat with Amanda's. Then he stalked into the timber alone.

Amanda ached for him. But there was nothing she could do. Nothing she could say to ease his pain. She sank beside the open doorway, thinking she should start supper but needing the few minutes of solitude.

She had spent the day at Isaiah's side, helping him eat, helping him any way she could. But the old man had weakened before her eyes. And all she could think of was Jace, and how much Isaiah's dying was going to hurt him.

As she sat there, the sound of voices carried from the interior of the shack. At first she didn't mean to, but something about their tone caught and held her attention. She shifted, hating herself but listening just the same.

"You . . . you didn't bring it with you, did you?" Isaiah asked.

"No. No, my friend. Do not worry. It is safe in the mission."

"Thank you, padre. For everything."

"Do you not think it would be best to tell Senor Montana what you have told me?"

"Tell him I lied, tell him . . . Padre, I can't do that. I can't see it in his eyes right before I . . ."

"Calm yourself, Isaiah. I did not come here to upset you. And you must do what you think is best."

Amanda scrambled away from the door just as the padre stepped through it.

"I . . . I was about to start supper," she stammered. "Will you be staying, father?"

His gaze shifted from the interior of the shack, then back to her. Amanda toed the dirt, feeling as though she had been caught pilfering the Sunday collection plate. But she had understood nothing of the priest's bizarre exchange with Isaiah and so she was determined to bluff her way through this.

"I must be getting back to the mission," the priest said at last. "I will suggest to Senor Montana that you

214

accompany me."

She gasped. "No! I mean, he'll never agree. He . . . he needs a hostage."

Now he really did give her a peculiar look. "You are being held here against your will, senorita?"

"Of course! Whatever would make you think otherwise?" She crossed to the cache of supplies near the campfire, extracting a bag of coffee grounds. "You're certain you won't stay for supper?"

"For a hostage you seem remarkably at home here."

She squared her shoulders. "Perhaps you could be a bit more candid, padre."

"Jason Montana is innocent, senorita. What weighs on my mind is your betrothal to his sworn enemy, Philip Welford. I must wonder where your loyalties will lie should your marriage be jeopardized by your continued association with Montana. Look at me and tell me you would choose Montana's freedom over your marriage to Welford."

Amanda couldn't breathe. She felt as if a huge stone were weighting her chest. It was as if the priest knew how desperately important it was that she marry Philip. What he couldn't know was how strong her feelings for Jace had grown, how much she wanted him free. But to make a choice? Oh, please God, don't ever let me have to make such a choice.

"Why don't you answer the man, Andy?"

She whirled, startled to see Jace standing just three feet behind her. "I . . . it was a ridiculous question. I have no power over whether or not you have your freedom. That's for the law to decide." Abruptly she returned to the task of preparing supper, though her hands trembled so badly she spilled more coffee onto the ground than into the pot.

"You're leaving, padre?" Jace asked.

"I can find my way back to town."

"I would appreciate it if you'd take a rather roundabout way of getting there."

"I will do my best to keep your secret, my son." The priest walked over to the roan. Before he mounted he looked back at Jace. "Sometime you must come again to the mission. There is something I must give you."

"It'll have to wait awhile."

"I understand. But do not wait too long."

The burly priest mounted and rode out.

Amanda paused in her stirring of the beef stew she was preparing. "You trust him not to tell Philip where you are?"

"Yes."

"But you can't say the same for me?"

"Andy, don't. Not now." He disappeared into the shack where he stayed until long after the sun had set.

Amanda fixed Montana a plate of food and took it to him, halting just inside the doorway. He was tucking Isaiah's red and blue Indian blanket under the big man's chin. Taking a deep breath to steady herself, she crossed over to him. "You have to eat something."

"I'm not hungry."

"Starving yourself isn't going to help him."

He took the plate from her, picked up the fork, but let it drop. He set the plate down. "I'll be back." His voice was hoarse, unnatural. She watched him jam his hands into his pockets and stride outside. She rose to follow him, but Isaiah's voice stopped her.

"You heard the padre and me, didn't you, gal?"

Embarrassed, she nodded.

216

"You don't understand?"

"Please, it's not my business."

"But you care about painter."

"Isaiah . . ."

"There's somethin' between the two of ya," he rasped. His voice had grown so weak she had to kneel beside him to hear. "I seen it that day in the court. He looked at you. You looked at him. Put me in mind of an old Indian legend about two rivers comin' out of the mountains. Both of 'em roilin' and tumblin', goin' their separate ways, not whole, not happy. Lonely."

"I hardly think of rivers being lonely, Isaiah." She knew where he was leading, but she didn't want to hear it. Couldn't bear to hear it. But he continued relentlessly, as if knowing he would never have another time to tell her.

"Two lonely rivers to make one mighty river."

"Really, Isaiah . . ."

"No, it was there. I seen it in his eyes. Just for a second. Then he remembered Dawn Wind. He stopped himself from feelin' what's gotta be between ya. He don't remember it, don't let himself remember it since she died. But before Dawn Wind and Bright Path was killed, Jace was gettin' restless. He wanted to bring 'em out of the mountains, see what some of the rest of the world looked like. When they died it was like he buried that need with 'em. Like he felt guilty for thinkin' it. For thinkin' of takin' Dawn Wind from the mountains.

"You see, she didn't want to go. She was afraid of the white man's world." He coughed, gasping as a pain sliced through him.

"Isaiah, please, let me call Jace."

"No, not yet." He closed his eyes. "You done the

same, don't you see? Stopped yourself from lovin' him. I don't know what secrets you're carryin', little lady. But in the end it's gonna be you that's gotta go to him."

"He's an outlaw. I'm engaged to be married to the man who . . . wants him dead."

"You're separate halves of the same whole. Welford ain't your destiny, gal. Like it was painter's destiny to live, his parents to die. Mine to find him, love him, teach him all I know . . . I just hope I done right. I hope he knows how much . . ." His efforts to breathe grew more agonizing still.

She bolted to her feet, rushing for the door. "Jace!"

He was there instantly. She couldn't speak, turning away from the anguish in his gray eyes. But he knew. He crossed the room to sit on the floor beside the big mountain man, lifting a gnarled hand into his own.

"Ya remember the time Tame Bear took ya on your first buffalo hunt and ya came back with the biggest bull I ever seen in all my days?"

"I remember."

"I was so proud of you."

Jace gripped the calloused hand tighter, hanging on, trying with everything in him to hold back what had to be. To keep Isaiah from leaving him. "It was just a lucky shot."

"No. You're the best son a man could ever have, painter. The best." He coughed, his own grip weakening, his brown eyes dulling.

"It's time for me to go, painter. I walked one too many trails."

"No."

"You made an old man's life mighty happy. I just hope you can find it in your heart to understand why I

218

done what I . . ." The coughing took on an ominous rattle.

"Isaiah . . ." The bear paw hand in his own grew slack. "No." Jace's broad shoulders heaved. "No."

For a long time Jace just sat there.

Amanda watched him from inside the door, feeling like an intruder. Finally she couldn't just watch. She crossed over to him, sliding her hand over his shoulder. "I'm sorry."

He didn't look up. "Take Isaiah's horse. Go. I won't stop you. Welford's ranch is ten miles northeast of here."

Of all the things he could have said, that was the last . . . "Jace . . ."

"Just go. Now." His voice shook. "Please."

Woodenly, she walked to the door. He was giving her her freedom. But she didn't want it. Not now. Not this way. She turned, her eyes burning, watching Jace sit there, hunched and hurting. "I can't leave you like this."

"I'm all right."

Slowly she crossed back over to him. Kneeling beside him, she put her hand in his. He was trembling, blinking his eyes rapidly. He didn't want her to see him cry.

"Get out of here, Andy. Go back to Welford."

"No."

He turned into her arms.

She held him until he fell asleep.

Chapter Fifteen

Amanda woke before sunrise, stiff and sore from sleeping in a half-sitting position. Even so, she didn't move, not wanting to awaken Jace. He still lay with his head pillowed against her breasts.

She listened to the deep, almost peaceful sound of his breathing, knowing that his peace would be gone the instant he opened his eyes. Isaiah's death had hurt him badly. She had seen the deep affection the two men had for each other, but until now she had not realized just how strong the bond had been between them.

Against her will in the predawn darkness, she found Jason Montana's grief forcing her to confront her own. Grief never acknowledged, never shared with anyone. Grief for her brother, for Matthew. For the first time in thirteen years she allowed herself to feel the pain of his loss and in feeling it to see just how unfairly she had judged him. Judged him through a child's eyes, because the child she had been had expected the impossible. Expected him to be perfect. To keep his promise to come home.

But Matthew had not just been her brother. He'd been a man with principles and the courage to stand by them even if it meant going against his own family, even if it meant dying.

He had not betrayed the Confederacy. He had believed in the Union.

"Forgive me, Matthew," she whispered, not minding the tears. "Forgive your dumb little sister who loved you so much."

Jace stirred, shifting to look up at her. His brows furrowed. "Are you hurt? Why didn't you say something? Just push me off of you . . ."

"No, no," she assured him quickly. "I'm fine. Better than I've been in a long time, as a matter of fact."

He sat up, stretching his long arms high over his head, the unfamiliar position evidently as cramping for him as it had been for her. But his voice was as warm as his eyes when he said, "Thank you."

"You're welcome." Amanda wanted to add, *My pleasure,* but she didn't.

He stilled as his gaze shifted to the blanket-covered body barely three feet away. "I'd better start on the grave."

"If you need me to do anything . . ."

"No, I'll do it."

She caught his arm before he could move away. She wanted to say so much, but there were suddenly so many emotions and not enough words.

But it was as though he understood. He touched the back of his fingers to her cheek, a caress as light as a butterfly's wings, yet it had a more profound affect on her than if he had crushed her in his arms. It was all she could do to keep from pulling him to her, telling him

222

how very much she had come to care for him.

But she didn't. Instead she climbed stiffly to her feet and made some inane comment about fixing breakfast.

"I'm not hungry," he said.

"You'll need to eat."

He didn't press the subject, instead crossing to a small chest in the tiny room's far corner. From it he extracted a shovel with which to begin his somber chore. Shedding his shirt he stepped outside.

Amanda stood in the doorway, watching. Even in the dawn chill in minutes his upper body glistened with sweat, the muscles rippling as he tore at the soft earth beneath a sprawling willow tree.

Forcing herself, Amanda crossed to the ashes of the previous night's cookfire. She didn't feel like eating either, but she was determined to stay strong for Jace. She wasn't fooling herself, though. Very shortly he would send her back to Philip. And she would not make any attempt to talk him out of it this time.

Jace was alone now. As tragic as Isaiah's death was, Jace was free now to deal with Philip any way he chose. And she had little doubt that such a confrontation, when it finally occurred, would end in violence. She knew she couldn't stop Jace. But maybe, just maybe, she could stop Philip, convince him of Jace's innocence, convince him to leave Jace alone. Leave him alive.

Jace finished the grave at the same time she finished preparing breakfast. They ate in silence, Amanda allowing him his private thoughts, his private grief. Afterwards, the silence grew awkward. Finally, Jace cleared his throat, setting the tin plate beside the dying campfire. "I want to thank you for understanding.

223

I . . ." He stood up, pinching his eyes shut, then he straightened. "I'll get him ready."

Amanda nodded. She waited outside the doorway while Jace hunkered down beside Isaiah. The big mountain man was cold and still now, so unlike the blustery bear she had been allowed to know for far too brief a time. She watched Jace's big tanned hands tenderly straighten Isaiah's buckskin jacket, button his shirt, smoothe the beginnings of a bushy beard that hadn't had time to return to its full glory.

A grizzly bear padre would never do! She smiled, remembering the booming voice, swiping at a tear that blurred her vision.

Her heart ached for Jace, but all she could do was watch as he gathered the brightly colored Indian blanket around Isaiah, tucking it around him just so, making certain no dirt could accidentally fall on that beloved face. With infinite care he used a second blanket as a travois to transport the body to the grave. Ever so gently Jace eased the old trapper the final three feet of his journey. For a long minute Jace sat there, staring into the open grave. Then he reached down to touch the blanket one last time and slowly began to fill the hole.

Amanda couldn't bear to see the strain in Jace's face any longer. She turned away, swallowing a sob. Wanting to do something, anything to help him, she searched the shaded ground until she found two sticks she could tie together with rawhide to form a cross.

Jace gave her a grateful smile, staking the wooden marker at the head of the grave, going down on one knee beside it. "Damn, Isaiah," he said, his voice reflecting the anguish in his heart. "I hate this. You shouldn't be in this forsaken valley. You deserve your mountains. You only came to Texas because of me."

Amanda reached a hand toward him but decided it was best not to intrude. Bowing her head she began in the barest whisper, "The Lord is my shepherd, I shall not want . . ."

Halfway through, Jace's voice—stronger, steadier—joined hers, staying with her to the end, "And I shall dwell in the house of the Lord forever."

He stood then, turning toward her, saying nothing else, and she went quietly into his arms. For the longest time he held her, neither speaking, each drawing on the strength of the other.

At last he cleared his throat, giving her a swift kiss on the top of the head. Then he put her away from him. "I guess it's time I took you back to Welford."

"There's no hurry," Amanda said too quickly, though she had promised herself she would say nothing.

"Yes, there is. Somehow he's at the bottom of all of this, and I intend to find out how and why. You'll only slow me down, Andy. I don't want to chance your getting hurt."

She stooped to pick up a small stone, ambling toward the creek. Her voice was not at all steady when she spoke. "Is this the same man who said he would rather hide behind my skirts to dodge bullets than behind a rock?"

"That man was just trying to scare you."

"That man?"

"That other nastier me."

"God help the world if there are two Jason Montanas. I find one more than impossible . . ." She stopped as her voice caught, praying he didn't notice.

He followed her. "You don't need to get my mind off of . . . anything."

"I know." She tossed the stone into the shallow stream. "Maybe I'm doing it for me."

"I'm taking you back, Andy. Today. Now."

She could only nod, not trusting herself to speak. Too many emotions, too few words. Isaiah had been right, so very right. Two rivers. But each with dams a mile high and a mile wide.

She waited while Jace saddled the horses, plucking a tiny wildflower and tucking it behind her ear. She would press the flower between the pages of a book, and whenever life grew too tedious with Philip she would open the book and remember . . .

"Ready?" Jace called.

"Ready," she said softly, tugging the flower from behind her ear. She gave the silky petals a last caress, then let the flower slip through her fingers.

Crossing to the horse, she swung easily in the saddle. He gave her a half smile. "You've gotten used to riding astride."

"I've gotten used to a lot of things lately." She led out at a trot, Jace following close behind.

They rode in silence for a while, settling into an easy canter. As usual Jace kept them to washouts and gulleys, avoiding any chance of being skylined. "Isaiah gave me a pretty rough time about the way I was treating you," he called as they splashed their way through another of the area's ubiquitous, nameless creeks.

"And well you deserved it," she shot back. "How a gentleman like Isaiah could raise an ill-mannered

226

ruffian like you . . ."

He grinned, and it warmed her heart to see it. She just wished he hadn't spoiled the sassy rapport with his next words. "We'd best hurry. I want to get you to the ranch by nightfall."

Neither of them said much of anything the rest of the morning, stopping only for a perfunctory lunch of hardtack and water. She guessed he was trying to make their parting easier on the both of them, but his deliberate silences only succeeded in making her miserable.

It was well past noon when he reined to a halt atop a shallow knoll. "We'll be able to see the ranch soon," he said, lifting his hat and mopping the sweat from his brow. "I think we'd best wait 'til it gets dark. I don't want any gun-happy ranch hand trying to please the boss with my carcass."

"You're that certain Philip wants you dead? That he would have you murdered?"

"You might say I'm dead certain."

"That's not amusing," she snapped.

"Sorry." He dismounted, loosening the cinch on his saddle.

She followed him into a fissure of rocks where he tied off both horses.

"Might as well make yourself comfortable," he said, sitting down in front of a high boulder. "We'll be here 'til midnight."

She slid down in the shade of the rock, making very certain her shoulder pressed hard against his. He shifted, and she thought she had lost the subtle battle, but he only moved so that he could settle his arm around her shoulders, pulling her against his chest.

"Just how much do you know about my trial? My supposed murder of Juanita Melendez?"

"Only what Philip told me."

"Which was?"

She swallowed, a strange division of loyalties assailing her. But her belief in Jace's innocence made the decision an easy one. "He told me you were having a . . . relationship with her. That she tried to break it off and in a jealous rage you raped her, stabbed her."

"Well, that's close," he gritted sarcastically. "She was a seamstress. Isaiah asked her to make some curtains for the ranch house, some serapes for us. I think Isaiah may have had it in his head that I would see her as more than a seamstress, but that didn't happen."

"I heard she was very pretty."

"Very."

Amanda could have hoped he hadn't been so quick with his affirmation. Juanita would have been dark-haired, bronze-skinned, the way Jace preferred his women. She eyed her arms with their upturned sleeves, wrinkling her nose. Hopeless. Even after four days in the sun she was still a bedsheet compared to Jace. And always would be.

"You didn't court her?" she asked in a small voice.

He hesitated, and when she looked at him she knew he had done it deliberately to goad her. She slapped at his chest. "This is serious."

He sighed. "I know. No, I did not court her. I was in her room that day for one reason only. To get the curtains she had made for our windows."

The incongruity of Jason Montana carrying window curtains was simply too much. "Did the poor girl have to make them out of your old socks? It's the only

228

pattern I can imagine being acceptable to you and Isaiah."

"They were some sort of sturdy stuff," he growled. "But definitely not socks."

"Uh huh." Just to sit here and talk to him, have him all to herself, was heaven. If only the subject didn't have to eventually lead to Juanita's tragic death.

Suddenly Jace jerked away from her, slapping at his arm.

"What is it?"

"Bug." He cursed, seeing that he hadn't dislodged the little beast. "Damned tick. Having himself an easy lunch."

Amanda made a face at the disgusting-looking creature engorging itself on Jace's arm. "Do something!"

He struck a match and held it to the insect's back until it retracted its head, then he flicked it off his arm and gave it a summary execution with his boot. "Pest."

"He was hungry," she said. "I can sympathize with that."

He grinned. "I can take a hint." He pulled some hardtack from his saddlebags. "Enjoy."

She sighed. "I'd even clean a rabbit if you'd catch one."

"Can't take the chance. We're too close to the ranch."

She nestled against him. "What do you know about how Juanita died?"

"Not a whole lot actually. Only what I could piece together from what I overheard the sheriff saying, what my worthless lawyer told me." He snorted. "Lawyer! I swear the man was on Welford's payroll."

"Couldn't you get someone else?"

"I couldn't get the time of day. Three months I was in Texas. Three months. The first night someone shot at Isaiah and me while we stepped off what we thought was our land, since this is public range.

"That only made us mad. We started building the ranch house the next day. They let us go at it for about a week, then they burned us out. I was starting to get a little testy."

Amanda smiled. That she had no trouble imagining at all.

"Welford rode in with Langley and Bates, after we'd been here about six weeks. He wasn't exactly subtle. I believe his precise words were 'Leave or you're dead.'"

"You didn't leave?"

"Does that surprise you?"

"Not in the least. What surprises me is Philip. If he believed he had legal grounds to evict you, why didn't he go to the law?"

"Welford seems to use the law when it suits him. If it doesn't, he uses other means."

"You're not suggesting he had Juanita killed! That just isn't possible. The man is running for governor. If not for moral reasons, then merely to keep his reputation above reproach he would never involve himself . . ."

Jace gripped her arms, his eyes boring into hers. "I think Philip Welford is capable of just about anything to get what he wants. And I'd give just about anything to convince you of that."

"Not murder, Jace. I won't believe that. Someone killed her, and maybe, just maybe, he decided it would be convenient to blame you. But he couldn't . . ."

Jace swore. "Don't defend him to me, Andy. Just don't. I was in that jail for a month. I watched his comings and goings all over town. The man has San Antone in his hip pocket."

"Jason, you yourself admit you were in Juanita's room the day she was killed. Don't you see how an honest mistake could have been made?"

"Juanita was attacked sometime between seven and eight that day. The door hadn't been forced, but then it hadn't even been locked when I came to see her. I remember she'd just called 'Come in.' She was working on the damned curtains."

"She hadn't finished them? Maybe she wanted you to come back to her room at a more seductive time."

He groaned. "They just weren't done, that's all. why would you? . . ."

"Because I would have done the same thing."

He squeezed her waist. "I'll remember that. Unfortunately, I did go back to Juanita's room that night."

"Then you saw her dead?"

"With my knife sticking in her chest."

Amanda winced.

"I'm sorry. Damn!"

"It's all right, I want to hear it all. How . . . how did the killer get your knife?"

"It was stolen the same night the ranch house was burned. I hadn't seen it for nearly three months."

"How would anyone know it was yours?"

"Isaiah had it made for me. It had my name carved into the ivory handle."

"Jace, my father knows a lot of excellent lawyers in Baltimore and D.C. I'll find one and hire him to help you."

231

"What will Welford say to that?"

"I don't care what he says. I mean . . ." she sighed. "I won't tell him. But I want you to tell me everything."

"Not much more to tell. The desk clerk came up to the room, saw me standing over the body, and went for the sheriff."

"You didn't run?"

"I didn't kill her. Like a fool I didn't see that the setup was perfect. Perfect."

"You make it sound as if Juanita were in on her own murder."

"No. But I think she was a pawn. A part of someone else's elaborate frame."

"If Philip wants you dead—and I'm not saying he does—I assure you, he has the power to simply hire someone to kill you. Very discreetly, very permanently. Why go through all this?"

"It's nice to know you have such confidence in your fiancé's ability to get things done."

"I've been around political animals all of my life, Jace. They're not so different really from the animals who prowl your mountains. They do what needs to be done. I'm not saying they resort to murder, for heaven's sake. But I've heard more than one scandal created to end an adversary's career."

"I'm not Welford's adversary."

"He said you settled on his range."

"Public range."

"Not if he thinks otherwise."

"And that's reason for murder?"

"No," she said, "it isn't. And I promise you, if there's more to this than an honest mistake, I'll find it."

"No. It could be dangerous."

232

"Philip won't hurt me. We're going to be married, remember?" She wished the words back at once, as she sensed Jace's instant withdrawal. But the damage was done.

"We might as well rest until we're ready to go in."

"Jace . . ."

"Don't say anything. You don't owe me any explanations."

"No, I don't."

He flinched.

"But it's not explanations that are important right now." She wanted him. All of him. Here. Now. Because she might never have the chance again. "Hold me, Jace. One last time. Please."

"No." He shifted away, but there was nowhere to go in the small enclosure.

She reached out to him, snaring his left hand and bringing it to her mouth. She kissed his palm, then settled it on her upraised knee, studying the lines in a hand that seemed twice the size of her own. Her voice was low and throaty. "A gypsy read my palm once. A band of them were passing near Baltimore when I was about fifteen. My father had them chased away, but not before I'd met Madame Rosa."

"A young beautiful girl should stay away from gypsies."

"I wasn't afraid." She traced a finger along the deeper lines of his palm, keeping the touch featherlight. She smiled as his arm tensed. "Madame Rosa said that one day I would find the love of my heart. I assured her I was not looking, but she insisted. He would be tall and dark and "—her gaze skated up his arm to his face—"he would look like a gypsy himself."

She watched a muscle in his jaw twitch, his eyes darken. Her own breathing grew shallow. "I don't remember much of anything else she said." She brushed the backs of his fingers with her lips. "But your heart line cuts deep and strong. Madame Rosa would say you were a passionate man, a man who knows well the power of love." Her voice was barely audible now. Her whole body quivered with the need to touch and be touched by this man.

"Jason, please." She tugged open the buttons of his shirt, but he laid his hand over hers, stopping her. "No."

Her mouth found his, her kisses hungry, desperate, wanting him, needing him, as she'd never wanted or needed anyone before.

With an explosive curse his hands went to the buttons of her shirt, her pants, all but tearing them from her body. His sex was hard, ready, and it was obvious his thoughts had travelled the same path.

She was just as ready, crying out her pleasure as he linked himself to her, though his mouth silenced her cries.

"We don't need any company," he groaned, driving himself inside her.

No, she thought wildly, savagely, *all I ever need is you.* She reached the peak before he did, then brought him with her, revelling in the trembling power of their release.

"Oh, God, Andy," he said afterwards, holding her to him and giving her a lopsided grin. "I apologize for every thought I ever had about your being made of ice."

She smiled and lay back, closing her eyes, telling herself it would only be a few minutes. It was dusk when she opened them again. She gazed wryly at the blanket Jace had tossed over her naked body. She started to thank him, then noticed the look he was giving her, as though he had sat there watching her for a long time, a look that seemed part awe, part fury. And she knew at once what he was going to say.

"How can you marry him?"

Somehow she maintained a facade of control. She didn't want to think about it, but in minutes Jason Montana would no longer be a part of her life. It was time to play the game again, though she found the task infinitely more difficult than she ever had before. "Philip is going to be governor of the state of Texas. I want to be the governor's wife. It's that simple."

His gray eyes narrowed with disgust. "Just when I think I know you . . . Ah, hell." He turned on his side.

She made certain her tears were silent as she watched him lie there, so rigidly angry. Why? Why did she have to meet this man? Marrying Philip would have been so easy four days ago. She had held no delusions about romantic love, believing herself incapable of it. Feelings were something she had excised from her life since Matthew's death. Now she had even dealt with the trauma of that. All because of this man, this outlaw.

Two rivers. No, Isaiah, she thought, not two rivers. Two solid walls of rock. Destined never to move, never to meet. For she would still marry Philip. But now she would hurt every day of that marriage, every day of her life.

And she would never even be able to give Jace the explanation he deserved. She couldn't tell him why. She could never tell anyone why.

Chapter Sixteen

Jace's mood matched the sky. Black. Amanda shook her head wearily as they walked the horses the last mile toward Philip's ranch house. Her every attempt at humoring him had failed miserably. This was not the way she had wanted to end it. But he seemed determined to be unpleasant.

He tied off the horses behind one of the farthest outbuildings.

"So this is where Philip lives," she murmured, almost to herself. The Spanish-style main house with its perfectly manicured center court bespoke the quiet elegance she would have expected from Philip.

"I can't believe you've never been here."

"You can still talk?" she remarked acidly.

He ignored that.

She sighed. "I'd only been in Texas three days, remember? Your trial was too important for Philip to be making trips back and forth to the ranch. So I stayed at the hotel."

"I used to watch you in your room. You made a

237

lovely silhouette."

"I beg your pardon?" When it was obvious he wasn't going to explain himself, she said quietly, "I can make it alone from here. You'd better go." Telling him to leave was the last thing she wanted to do, but her fear for his life was greater than her fear of never seeing him again.

"I'm going in with you," he said. "I want to see how a wealthy rancher lives."

"Are you out of your mind?" She couldn't make out his features in the new moon darkness. But she sensed what she couldn't see. "You're up to something. What?"

"Just get moving."

They wound their way past a large bunkhouse, then on to the home Philip would have her share after their wedding. If the interior was as imposing as the exterior, she could be certain that her future husband would not be a man to give up the comforts of city living just because his home was on a Texas plain.

Jace tested a window in a darkened corner of the house. It slid up easily. "I'll give you a boost up," he whispered.

She tensed as his hands banded her waist, lifting her onto the window ledge. "Get out of here," she hissed. "You're going to get yourself killed."

"I'll take my chances."

"But why?"

"Get the hell into the house! I'm not going to discuss it standing here in Welford's courtyard."

Amanda slipped into the room, seething when Jace vaulted in after her. Now she knew he was out of his mind. What other explanation could there be for him to challenge Philip on his home ground.

"Calm down," he said, keeping his voice a bare whisper. "Welford may not even be here."

"But somebody will be! Don't you understand? You're not going to find any friends on Philip's ranch!"

He didn't answer, hunkering down in front of a large shadowed square object abutting the near wall. He patted the object, giving it a long, low appreciative whistle. "I think this little visit is going to work out just fine."

"What on earth are you doing?"

Instead of telling her, he rose and crossed to the door on the opposite side of the room. Cautiously, he cracked it open and peered out. The whole house seemed dark. "Stay behind me."

"Stay behind *you?* Jason, you are the one who should stay behind me. I'm not going to be shot on sight." She stepped in front of him and swung the door open, moving out into a narrow corridor.

He muttered an oath but allowed her to take the lead. Grimacing, he wondered how he was every going to let this woman marry Philip Welford. Could she really be that grasping, that money hungry? He shook off the thought. He had to have his full concentration focused on his reason for being here. Welford was very likely in the house. At least he hoped he was.

"Watch it," he hissed when she bumped into a piece of furniture.

"I'm not a bat!" she gritted.

"Just be careful."

She gripped his arm. "You're the one who has to be

careful. Please, Jason. Get out of here before someone finds us. They'll kill you."

"Does that mean you care?"

"Damn you," she snapped, edging her way into the massive living room. "I don't want you dead."

His hand curved over her shoulder. "I'll be all right. Don't worry."

Don't worry, she thought despairingly. *If anything happens to you . . .* She forced her attention to the shadowed room. A fieldstone fireplace dominated the inner wall, the glowing embers of a fire giving off the only light in the room. A bearskin rug lay sprawled on the hearth. Her eyes widened, a totally lascivious thought flashing through her mind. Bearskin. Bare skin. She and Jace on the rug. In front of a crackling fire.

Stop it, she warned herself fiercely. Those were exactly the kind of thoughts she didn't need.

She jumped when Jace grabbed her hand. He pulled her across the room, leading her up a short flight of stairs.

"Where are you going?" she whispered. Had he completely lost his senses?

She gripped his arm, but that didn't stop him from easing open the door to the room at the head of the stairs. Amanda's hand instantly flew to her nose at the smell of sickness that rolled out of the room in waves. Breathing through her mouth, she allowed Jace to lead her inside and close the door behind him.

"Is that you, Philip?" came a frail voice from the bed that abutted the outer wall. A kerosene lamp, its wick set to give off only the barest light, sat on the small

240

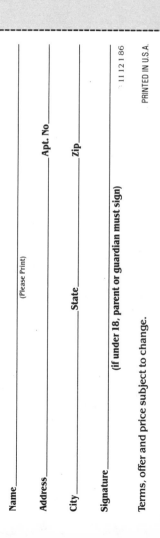

MAIL THE POSTAGE PAID COUPON TODAY!

START YOUR SUBSCRIPTION NOW AND START ENJOYING THE ONLY ROMANCES THAT "BURN WITH THE FIRE OF HISTORY." YOUR GIFT OF A *FREE* BOOK IS WAITING FOR YOU.

Your FREE Book Offer Card

Zebra

HOME SUBSCRIPTION SERVICE, INC.

☐ YES! please rush me my Free *Zebra* Historical Romance novel along with my 4 new Zebra Historical Romances to preview. You will bill only $3.50 each; a total of $14.00 (a $15.80 value–I save $1.80) with *no* shipping or handling charge. I understand that I may look these over *Free* for 10 days and return them if I'm not satisfied and owe nothing. Otherwise send me 4 new novels to preview each month as soon as they are published at the same low price. I can always return a shipment and I can cancel this subscription at any time. There is no minimum number of books to purchase. In any event the Free book is mine to keep regardless.

Name _____
                        (Please Print)

Address _____ Apt. No _____

City _____ State _____ Zip _____

Signature _____
            (if under 18, parent or guardian must sign)

1112186

Terms, offer and price subject to change.   PRINTED IN U.S.A.

A FREE ZEBRA
HISTORICAL
ROMANCE
WORTH

$3.95

BUSINESS REPLY MAIL
FIRST CLASS   PERMIT NO. 276   CLIFTON, NJ

POSTAGE WILL BE PAID BY ADDRESSEE

ZEBRA HOME SUBSCRIPTION SERVICE
P.O. Box 5214
120 Brighton Road
Clifton, New Jersey 07015

table next to the bed.

Amanda couldn't take her eyes from the bed's occupant. He was without doubt the oldest-looking human being she had ever seen in her life. A living skeleton. A tangled mass of gray hair sat atop a skull-like visage of sunken eyes and spidery wrinkles. A white satin coverlet that seemed more a death shroud buried the creature up to its chin. The only other visible patches of flesh were the long claw fingers jutting from the sleeve of his nightshirt.

"Who is he?" Amanda gasped.

"Welford's grandfather, I suppose. I heard a lot of talk about how sick he was."

So this was J. T. Welford. Sick? She shuddered. The man had long ago surpassed sick.

The old man's eyes fluttered open slowly, as though it were a great effort even to lift the lids. "Philip, please, don't just stand there," he rasped. "Say something. You know how I hate it when . . ."

"I'm not Philip," Jace said.

The man gasped. "Who . . . who . . ." He twisted his thin neck, trying to focus toward the sound.

A horrid rattling sound rumbled low in his throat. "No, no . . . How . . . how did you? . . ."

"Where's your grandson?"

"Philip! Philip!"

Amanda doubted the pathetic call for help could be heard across the room, let alone elsewhere in the house. Nevertheless, she tugged on Jace's arm. "We have to get out of here. Someone probably checks on him all the time."

"No. He's going to tell me where Welford is."

"He's right behind you, Montana," came the velvet-smooth voice.

Amanda whirled, her eyes falling on the revolver Philip held in his right hand. "Philip! Oh, Philip!" she breathed. "I'm so happy to see you!" She bolted toward him, wrapping her arms around him, praying he wouldn't pull the trigger while she was in his embrace.

"So you were stupid enough to come here, Montana," Philip said, "and to bring Amanda with you. How very thoughtful."

"Send one of your men for the sheriff," Amanda offered quickly, terrified Philip was about to finish Jace's execution here and now.

"I'm so glad to see you're all right, my dear." He crossed the room, turning up the light. "Where's that drunken old mountain coot?"

"Isaiah is dead," Amanda said quietly.

Philip laughed. "One down. One to go." He cocked the gun.

"Philip, for heaven's sake. Not here. Your grandfather . . ."

Philip glanced at the bed, seeming to vacillate, then let down the hammer slowly. "Very well." To Jace he said, "You can give your gun to Amanda. Butt first."

Jace lifted the .45 from his holster and held it out to her. Her fingers trembled as she took it from him. His gray eyes were unreadable.

"Get away from him, Amanda," Philip said.

Quickly, she did as she was told, returning to Philip's side.

He stuck the gun in his pocket, giving Montana a triumphant sneer. "You can feel that rope tightening

242

around your neck already, can't you, boy?"

"Philip, please . . ." Amanda pleaded.

"Sorry, my dear, but after your days in his company, I would think you would be more than . . ." He paused, eyeing her critically for the first time. "My God, Amanda, what's happened to you? What has this beast done to you? And what on God's earth are you wearing?"

Her hand flew to her throat, her gaze darting frantically from the outlaw to Philip. "They're . . . they're just trousers, Philip," she managed. Odd, how she'd forgotten she even had them on, they had become so much a part of her. But she could tell by the look on Philip's face that his question went deeper than her attire. Surely he couldn't tell by looking at her that she had been more than a quiescent hostage.

She hurried over to the mirror above the dressing table, staring at the reflection that gazed back at her. How could it be? Jace kept calling her beautiful. The apparition in the mirror was anything but. Her exposed skin, especially her face, was like burnished oak, her hair paler than she had ever seen it. Her eyes looked almost bloodshot from her constant squinting in the harsh sunlight. And still he called her beautiful. She smiled.

"I guess I do look a little worse for wear," she said unsteadily.

"Keep those hands in the air, Montana," Philip warned. To Amanda he hissed, "What else did he do to you?"

There was no mistaking the meaning behind that question.

"Philip, please, I'm exhausted. I need to lie down."

He was immediately contrite. "I'm sorry. Of course, you must rest." He settled his left arm around her waist, gesturing with his gun hand for Montana to move toward the door. "Please forgive me, Amanda. I'll waken one of the servants. She'll prepare a room for you at once."

"Is Delia here?"

"She thought it best to stay in town. The poor woman is worried sick about you."

Jace stopped in the doorway. "Any particular direction?"

"There's only one direction I want to send you, Montana. But Amanda's presence demands I be discreet."

"Philip . . ." came the rasping voice. "Philip, what's happening? How did . . . how did he get here? Where? . . ."

"Don't talk," Philip cautioned, and Amanda had the strangest feeling the request was not out of concern for his grandfather's health, but a warning to be silent.

"Aren't you going to introduce me to your grandfather, Philip?"

"He needs to rest. He's quite ill." He prodded Jace in the back with the gun. "Down the stairs. Quickly."

Amanda didn't object to leaving the oppressive room. She had been about to become physically ill herself. In the breathable air of the living room she could concentrate on how best to get Jace out of danger.

"Sit down in the chair, Montana," Philip said. "And don't even so much as twitch, or I'll forget about

244

Amanda's delicate sensibilities and blow your brains all over that bearskin."

Jace sat down, but Amanda could feel the bowstring tenseness in him. As Philip headed toward the front door, Amanda turned toward Jace. She put every ounce of feeling behind her "I told you so" glare.

He only shrugged.

Pacing the lavishly furnished room, she took scant notice of the exquisite glassware lining the mantel, the oil paintings gracing the adobe walls. All she could think about was what Philip intended to do with Jace. She glanced toward the door to note Philip still standing in the doorway. He was holding a lantern, lifting it up and down as though signalling someone. His back was to her.

Amanda dared take the chance to walk over to the fireplace, barely two feet from the chair in which Jace sat.

"Don't do a damned thing, Andy," he said, running his hand over his chin as though scratching his day's growth of beard.

She jabbed at the logs with a poker, stirring the flames to life. "I'm not going to let him kill you."

"Neither am I."

"Amanda!" Philip snapped sharply, striding back into the room. "Keep away from him."

She jumped, backing toward the settee opposite the chair. "Philip, please, we have to talk. I know you're not going to believe this. But I . . . I really don't think this man committed any murder."

"Oh, my God!" Philip shouted, his handsome face purpling with rage. "What lies has he been telling you?"

He stormed toward Jace, backhanding him across the face.

"Philip, don't!" she cried. "Please."

"What did you say to her, Montana? What? To have my own fiancée doubt me?"

"Philip, I don't doubt you," she said quickly, wincing inwardly at the scathing look Jace gave her. "But there could have been a mistake."

"Mistake!" he cried. "Mistake? He raped that poor girl. Beat her. Stabbed her."

"He said someone stole his knife."

Philip swore.

Amanda instinctively cringed away from him. She had never seen him so enraged.

"What would you expect him to say? Did he also tell you that Gabe Langley, Jack Bates, and I found him in her room? That his clothes were torn and bloody? That Juanita whimpered his name right before she died!"

Amanda gasped, staggering to the settee. "No. No, he didn't say that." She looked at Jace, but his eyes were stony, unreadable.

"Oh, my dear," Philip said, coming over to her, drawing her hand into his. "Please, you must discount any lies this vermin told you. He and Benteen would have said anything to win you to their side, don't you see?"

"Oh, Philip, I'm so confused. It's been such an ordeal. Please understand." She shook herself, her spirits sinking even lower as she looked up to see Gabe Langley stomp into the house.

"Seen the lantern . . ." He stopped in mid-stride, an evil grin spreading across his ugly face. "Montana." He shot a glance at Philip. "This mean we're gonna have ourselves a hangin' after all, boss? Want me to get the rest of the boys?"

"No. No lynching, Gabe. We're going to see this all done legally and properly. Saddle my horse and yours. We're taking him to the sheriff."

"Whatever you say, boss." Langley stalked out of the house.

Amanda watched Jace's hands clench and unclench. He was furious, helpless. And she was agonizingly bewildered. If Jace was innocent, then it was no honest jury's mistake that condemned him to the gallows. It was Philip's perjury. But if Philip was telling the truth, then Jace was incontestably—she swallowed the bile that rose in her throat—a murderer.

"Amanda, darling," Philip said, diverting her from her tortured thoughts, "I've decided against waking any of the servants. I don't want them involved in this. The room at the end of the hallway upstairs is a guest bedroom. Why don't you go up and lie down?"

She bit her lip nervously. "What are you going to do, Philip?"

"I told you. Langley and I are taking this murderer to the sheriff."

"Is the sheriff in town? Had the posse given up looking for me?"

Philip stiffened. "After Stark's ludicrous attempt at tracking this animal, I'm afraid we had no choice but to call off the search, my dear."

"But you did find them."

"By accident," Philip grated. "Unfortunately, Benteen spotted us before we spotted him. I was terrified

247

you might be hurt." His brows furrowed. "Where were you that day anyway, Amanda? We never did figure out how Benteen smuggled you out of there."

"He was quite adept at living in the wilds," she said, praying it would be explanation enough.

"Well, thank God you don't have to suffer such torment any longer."

Langley stomped back into the room. "Got the horses saddled, boss. Three of 'em. Right out front."

"Thank you, Langley." He waved the gun at Montana. "On your feet. Now."

Jace stood up and moved toward the door. Amanda's eyes were on Philip. In that instant she knew Jace would not reach San Antonio alive. Knew that innocent or guilty, Philip would see him dead. Padre Manuel's words rose to haunt her. If she had to choose between Jace's freedom and her marriage to Philip, which would it be?

She twisted her hands together. Somehow she had to manage both. Right here. Right now. Innocent or—God help her—guilty, she was in love with Jason Montana. Innocent or guilty, she would marry Philip.

"Philip," she choked, "you're not going to leave me. Not after all I've been through with this . . . this beast." Her lips quivered as the tears spilled down her cheeks.

"Oh, my dear," Philip soothed, striding over to assist her to the settee. "I'll be back as soon as I can. But I can hardly allow Langley to take him in alone. Think of it, Amanda, the coup of my political career. Capturing a dangerous criminal like Montana. Rescuing my fiancée from his depraved hands."

She sobbed harder, clutching her stomach. "Oh,

Philip, I think I'm going to be sick."

"Not in here! I mean . . ." He whirled, shouting at Langley. "In the kitchen. Get a bucket. Anything."

The foreman rushed out of the room.

In the next instant Jace sprang at Philip. A chopping blow to the side of his head sent him sprawling to the floor. In one swift motion he grabbed Philip's gun, then yanked his own gun from Philip's pocket.

"Langley!" Philip screamed.

Jace hauled Amanda to her feet, wrapping his arm around her throat, levelling the pistol at her head. He didn't cock it.

"Oh, God, no," she cried, her resurrected doubts about Jace's innocence helping her play the scene for all she was worth.

"Son of a bitch, Amanda!" Philip exploded.

"Want me to shoot, boss?" Langley yelled, rushing back into the room.

"No!" Philip held up a restraining hand. "Let him go." He struggled to sit up. "Let him go."

It was at that moment that Amanda realized her engagement to Philip was secure, no matter what he suspected Montana had done to her. Her part of the bargain was as important to him as his was to her. If it hadn't been, she was certain he would have told Langley to call Jace's bluff. Instead he let them pass.

"You won't get far, Montana. There's not a rock big enough for you to crawl under."

"I'm not leaving without a little return for my efforts, Welford," Jace said.

Philip stiffened. "Money? Now you're going to out and out steal from me?"

Amanda's eyes watered as she stood on tiptoe trying not to choke. Was that why Jace had chanced coming into the house? To rob Philip?

"Get it," Jace said.

Philip reached into his pockets. "I don't keep much cash in the house."

"Why don't you open the safe I found in your study and tell me that again." Jace jerked the gun toward the study door, indicating both Philip and Langley were to lead the way. Inside, Philip worked the combination on the big floor safe, jerking open the door and extracting a black box. He emptied its contents, stuffing the cash in a small canvas sack.

"Just go ahead and throw everything in the safe into the sack, Welford," Jace said.

Amanda could feel the rage in Philip. But he did as he was told, shoving the remaining papers from the safe into the sack and thrusting it toward Jace.

"Don't try anything stupid," Jace warned, grabbing the sack and backing out the door with Amanda. "Or she's not going to make a very pretty bride."

"Don't hurt her."

"Another stalemate, eh, Welford? Don't open this door. Don't follow." He pulled the door shut and bolted toward the main entrance.

Amanda streaked after him.

"Stay here," he snapped, vaulting onto one of the horses, grabbing up the reins of the other two.

"No. They'll put more bullets in you than Santa Anna put in the Alamo." She mounted one of the horses, slamming her heels into its sides.

Swearing, Jace roared after her.

"I guess Welford really does love you," he shouted as

250

they pounded away from the ranch. "I would have sworn we were both dead."

"You underestimate my charms, Mr. Montana," she shouted back.

"Not on your life, woman. Not on your life."

But as they plunged on through the darkness, Amanda had to wonder if she had just chosen sides with a murderer.

Chapter Seventeen

Hard and fast Jace and Amanda whipped their horses away from the J-Bar-W. Only when they'd put ten miles between themselves and the main ranch house did Jace allow them to slacken the murderous pace. Still they continued to ride as long as it was dark. They rode over bedrock, up and down streams, hiding, disguising, confusing their tracks until even Amanda was certain they were heading two directions at once. Finally, near dawn, Jace pulled up near a small river. "We'll rest the horses for a while."

"Thank God for horses," Amanda groaned, practically falling from the saddle. Every bruise she had believed to be on the wane on the lower part of her anatomy was now reborn and fighting for its life.

She stretched out on her right side in the lush grasses, watching Jace duck his head into the swift current then yank it back, tossing off the cool water with a violent shake that sprinkled across her like a spring rain. She smiled. There were times he really did look like a stallion. But she couldn't think of things like that just now. There were too many new unanswered questions between them.

"Jace," she began, her voice tentative, "about what Philip said . . ."

He was on all fours beside the water, his hair still dripping wet. He twisted his head to give her a look she could only describe as wary. "He said quite a bit. You'll have to be more specific."

"He said Juanita named you her killer. How could . . ." The cold light that came into his eyes made her wish she had kept silent. And she knew it wasn't the question that affected him but the implied meaning behind the question. If she was asking for an explanation, in Jace's eyes she had again questioned his innocence.

Amanda tugged at a blade of grass. "I'm sorry." She let out a long sigh, then abruptly sat up. "No, I'm not sorry!" she snapped. "I'm not sorry at all."

His eyes narrowed, but he said nothing.

"Why do I always end up the one feeling guilty in this fiasco? You'd think *I* killed Juanita." She crawled over to Jace, poking a finger at his face. "I don't have to believe anything you say just because you say it. I didn't attend most of your trial. I didn't hear your testimony or Philip's or anyone's. I only heard part of the summation to the jury by the prosecutor. And maybe I would have voted guilty myself, based on what I heard."

His lips compressed into a grim line. But she did not halt her tirade. It had been too long in coming.

"And you know something else, Jason Montana. You're just as much an arrogant jackass as Philip. You dare tell me how innocent you are, then you prove yourself a thief! You steal me from my fiancé at gunpoint, you seduce me, you reach a part of me I thought I'd locked away forever when my brother died, you . . ." The anger drained out of her in a long, quivering shudder. "Damn you. I know you didn't kill that girl. But don't you see what my knowing that means?"

He reached out and pulled her across his chest. "Tell me." There was no anger in him now.

"It means Philip perjured himself. He told a jury you killed someone, knowing you didn't. Knowing the jury would believe a respectable citizen like himself. Knowing he was killing you, as surely as if he shot you. How can a man value a piece of land that much?"

He stroked her hair. "I've seen men kill over a piece of meat."

"Why did you rob him, Jason? Why?"

He pulled the reward dodger out of his pants pocket and showed it to her. "He claims I already have. It seemed like that made the money mine."

"Jason . . ."

"I wanted to hit him where it hurts. With Welford that could only mean his money."

"But now you *are* a thief."

"I consider it a loan. I'm going to need money to find out where all this leads."

She kissed his chin, though she knew he hadn't told her the whole of his reasons for robbing Philip. "I'm glad you got away."

His lips grazed her forehead. "And now that I have, I don't need a hostage any more. I want you to ride out of here, Andy."

"No."

He closed his eyes. "Damn, I told you you were a spoiled brat. Always wanting your own way."

"So you might as well give it up."

"Not when it could mean your life." He shifted, wincing slightly. "I could sleep for a week."

"Not here. It's not safe."

"I know. About an hour. Rest the horses."

She frowned, pressing her hand across his forehead. "You all right? You feel a little warm."

"Headache. It's nothing."

"Too much lovemaking?"

"Like hell." He kissed her soundly, feeling the tightening in his loins despite the continued pounding in his head. His hands glided down her arms, shifting to her middle, then up to snare the lush swell of her breasts. "Did I thank you for being foolish enough to be my hostage again?"

"No," she murmured as he tugged open her shirt buttons to take his mouth where his hands had been. "You didn't mention it."

He kissed a pink tip. "Thank you." He kissed her throat. "Thank you." He kissed her mouth. "Thank you."

His arms surrounded her, achingly glad to have her back. He hadn't really known until he was about to leave Amanda at Welford's just how much he wanted her with him.

"We'll go back to the hollow," she said.

"I will. Not you. It's too dangerous. If anything happened to you because of me . . ."

She skated her fingertips around his nipples, then down to his navel, and down again to rest against the taut bulge in his Levi's. His low, throaty moan thrilled her, challenged her, enticed her to be bolder still. She slid her hand beneath the waistband of his trousers, capturing the hard heat of his sex.

With a curse he yanked open the buttons, shifting instinctively to offer her easier access. His whole body shook. She stroked him, teased him, pleasured him, until he cried out, reaching over to free her of her own restraining clothing. Then he rose above her, bore her down into the grasses, thrusting inside her, making her need match his own.

"I didn't kill her, Andy," he rasped against her ear, his body at war with his heart over what he felt for this woman. He wanted her, needed her, yet the haunting spectre of Dawn Wind would not allow him the final step he ached to take. He could not love her. But he sought with everything in him to make her love him. "My hand to God, I've never killed anyone."

She kissed his cheeks, his nose, his chin, his mouth. "I know," she whispered, riding with him to the edge of forever. "I know."

In the quivering aftermath of his release he collapsed to one side of her, his body trembling long after he thought it should have ceased. He tried shaking his head but stopped, as shards of agony seemed to burn through all points of his skull. Sleep. He needed to sleep. He closed his eyes.

"Jason, what is it?" She stroked the side of his face. He was still too warm.

"Tired," he croaked. "Just tired. You do that to a man, woman." He tried to smile but didn't quite manage it.

"Are you sick?"

"Only about you marrying Welford." His eyes stayed

closed. "You're still going to do that, aren't you?"

"Yes," she said quietly.

"Damn. I don't understand you at all."

"It's not required that you do."

"Perfect. Smart mouth . . ." He winced as he jerked his head too quickly, exacerbating the pounding pain. "Why, Andy? Why?"

"I want to be the governor's wife." It was the only answer she dared give him, and she said it with every ounce of feigned pretense she could manage. And he believed her.

"What the hell are you going to do if the voters of Texas aren't stupid enough to elect him?"

"Oh, they'll elect him. I have no doubt of that. None. Philip can be so very charming."

He let it pass, lest his temper push him past enduring. Charming? Charming Welford in her bed?

"I can't ask you to understand."

"Good. Because I don't. I, ah, hell . . . it doesn't matter. I'm too tired for it to matter. I've got to sleep." He dragged in long, deep breaths, trying to ignore his slashing headache. But a half hour passed before he finally did sleep.

Amanda watched him for a long time, realizing how much they had been through together in only a few short days. How much she had had to learn about herself, what she was capable of, how much she had unwillingly come to learn about him. What she had learned, too, about her capacity for love. A capacity that was boundless were she to judge it by how much she now loved Jason Montana.

Until he physically chased her back to Philip, she would stay with him. She would savor every moment

258

they had together, before she condemned herself to a loveless marriage for the rest of her life. With a bittersweet smile she nuzzled against him, hugging him close until she, too, fell asleep.

She woke to the sound. She lay there, listening, hearing only the rushing water, the twittering of birds, the throaty song of a bullfrog. Then what had wakened her? Stiffly, she pushed herself to a sitting position, casting a glance at Jace. He was still asleep.

An hour, he'd said. Then why did it feel like she'd slept forever. She studied the sky, her brows furrowing. The sun was about to set! They had slept over twelve hours! Jace would never . . .

A sudden panic seized her. She touched the back of her hand to his cheek. It was like sticking her hand in an oven. "Jace! Jace!" She nudged his shoulder. He didn't respond. Scrambling to her knees, she shook him, called to him over and over.

He came awake then, dazed, groggy. He looked at the sky and swore, though even the curse seemed a great effort. He sagged back. "Why didn't you wake me?" Biting back a groan, he lurched unsteadily to his feet and aimed himself toward his horse. "Got to get going."

Amanda was at his side instantly. "Jace, you're sick."

"No, I'm all right."

"You are not all right."

"Whether I am or not, I'm leaving. And so are you. In the opposite direction." He lifted his foot as if to put it in the stirrup, but he lowered it again, leaning his head against the saddle. Gripping the pommel, he tried again to find the stirrup. "Help me . . . up, Andy."

"Jace, please, just lie down. We'll stay here tonight."

"Got to go. Got to. Help me. Little boost." He didn't get his boot even halfway to the stirrup this time. Sagging back, he collapsed against her. She caught him under his armpits and eased him the rest of the way to the ground.

"Dammit, Jace, what's wrong with you?"

"Don't know. It'll pass. Go. Go back to Welford. Don't want you"—her breath caught until he finished the sentence—"hurt."

"I'm not leaving you like this."

"Dammit, Andy." His eyes rolled back, his breathing raspy, his body quivering. "Son of a bitch. I'm cold." He levered himself to his hands and knees. Using the stirrup, he hauled himself to his feet. "Get me on my horse. Can't stay here. The cabin. Take me there."

Somehow she helped him mount, then climbed up behind him, tying the sorrel by a lead rope. "I'll try to keep my hands off of you," she murmured against his neck.

He chuckled, but his head listed to one side. She shook out the blanket and settled it around his shoulders, then kicked the horse into a trot. He was shivering violently by the time they finished the three-hour ride to the hollow.

Amanda slid over the horse's rump and was about to come around and help Jace dismount, when he sagged to one side and fell heavily to the ground.

"Jace!" She ran her hand over his face. How could he be so hot and cold at the same time?

Quickly she saw to the horses, then by tugs and pulls and barked commands she got Jace to his feet long enough for him to stumble into the shack and sag to the floor. It was fully dark now, the temperature in the shaded hollow dropping quickly. Near exhaustion, she stood not far from the sprawling willow under which Isaiah's grave seemed so peacefully to rest.

She stepped nearer the wooden cross. "Help me with him, Isaiah. Tell me what to do."

"Andy! Andy, where are you?" She whirled at the sound of Jace's voice coming from the cabin. Quickly, she grabbed up the canteen and ducked inside the small room. She struck a match and lit the kerosene lamp on the ledge in the corner.

"I thought you finally left," he said. He was propped up on his elbows on the lumpy pallet.

"Are you sorry I didn't?" She knelt beside him, handing him the canteen.

He took a long gulp, then lay back. His eyes burned into hers. "No, I'm not sorry."

A few sticks still lay beside the potbellied stove. In minutes she had a toasty fire going.

"Tell me how you feel," she said, coming back to sit beside him. "Exactly."

"Yes, Doctor Morgan."

She planted her hands on her hips. "Tell me."

"My head hurts."

"That's all?" She could tell he was trying to make light of it, but she didn't miss the concern in his gray eyes.

He shrugged. "I don't know. I just kind of ache. Hot. Cold. I'll be all right." He closed his eyes, his breathing seeming more ominously ragged.

With trembling fingers she loosened his belt, unbuttoned the top few buttons of his shirt. Her emotions were far different than they would normally have been were she disrobing him.

"Are you taking advantage of my condition, madam?"

She smiled. "I'll take advantage of your condition any time, sir." Gently, she caressed his forehead, her fear mounting to find it warmer than ever.

"I'll be all right, Andy. Honest."

"You'd better be." She snuggled next to him, holding him close when the chills came. "We're going to need more blankets. More supplies. I don't know how long you're going to be sick."

"I'll be fine by morning. Just need a little sleep, that's all." But his low groan put the lie to his words. Whatever was wrong with him seemed intent on staying with him. He hadn't been sick much in his life, and he didn't like his body's betrayal one bit. The only other time he remembered feeling this awful was the time he'd eaten some bad bear meat. He'd been ten, and Isaiah had liked to skin him.

"How could you eat meat smelled that bad, boy?"

"I was hungry."

"Hungry? A buzzard woulda thought twice about eatin' such as that."

"I'm sorry, Isaiah. I didn't . . ." Oh, his stomach hurt. Hurt bad for three days. But Isaiah had taken him to the Blackfoot, and he had been all right. That was the first time he'd ever seen Dawn Wind. She was eight and skinny and she gave him her special stone to help make him feel better.

"Shhh," Amanda soothed, spreading a cool, wet cloth across his forehead. Her heart caught as he called out Dawn Wind's name, but she never left him. His head lolled from side to side, and Amanda knew this was no ordinary sickness. She called his name, shouted it, and he looked right through her.

She lay down beside him, trying to get some sleep herself, jumping at each sound he made through the night, praying the morning would find him well. And when the dawn came, he did seem better. His head still ached, but he knew who he was, where he was.

"Told you I'd be all right."

But before the morning was over, the fever had returned. She stepped outside, needing the fresh air. Less than a day of having him sick, and she was already exhausted herself—from his constant haranguing that she leave him. If he said it one more time, she was going to gag him.

She walked wearily over to Isaiah's grave and sank beside it. "What am I going to do with him? How did you ever deal with such a bullheaded, stubborn, obnoxious, boorish . . ." She smiled, trailing a hand over the wooden cross. It was as if she could hear Isaiah chuckling.

She stood up, feeling oddly comforted. Too, thinking of Isaiah made her realize it was time she took a more pragmatic approach to her situation. She was no Dawn Wind. She knew precious little of how to survive in conditions other than tea parties and political dinners. But Jace's life might well come to depend on what he had taught her, often against her will, during her days as his hostage.

It took her over an hour, but she was justifiably proud of the snare she constructed in the brush. Now if it just yielded a rabbit for dinner . . .

Every few minutes she checked on Jace, but there seemed little she could do but change the cool cloth on his forehead. He was lucid for the most part, but weak.

He was also so hot that she stripped him down to all but his drawers. Cradling his head in her lap, she forced him to drink down plenty of water.

To pass the time and to take her mind off her mounting anxiety, she decided to wash out his clothes. Emptying the pockets of his trousers she found a hard, round piece of buckskin. Turning it over in her palm, she studied the exquisite detail of the snarling cougar and knew at once who had made it for Jace. With a wistful sigh she set it gently among his other things.

It was late afternoon, and she was running the cloth across his chest when he opened his eyes, suddenly alert. He ran a hand up his bare arm. "Damn."

"What is it?"

"The tick. The damned tick."

"What about it?"

He spoke more to himself than to her. "Tick fever."

"That ugly little beast made you sick?" She swallowed, ill at ease by the worried glimmer in Jace's gray eyes. "Is it, I mean . . . you'll be all right, won't you? It's not serious?"

"I'll be fine."

But she knew at once he was lying. "Jason, tell me the truth. I have to know how to take care of you."

He tried to smile. "Glad he bit me, not you."

"People die of this, don't they? Don't they?"

"People live too. No bug's going to kill me."

"Damned right," she said, but she had to fight off the tears that stung her eyes. "Stupid tick. One taste and he should've . . ."

"He paid the price." His chest heaved as he tried to laugh. "Damn . . . damn. The fever will get higher. I might be delirious. There'll be spots . . . a rash. I don't

264

know." He tried to think. "Maybe it isn't. Maybe . . ."

But he knew. Knew too that as quickly as the fever had come on after the bite, he was in for a long siege. The quicker the onset the worse . . . "Andy, this thing could last for weeks. Two, three, four. I don't know."

"Weeks?" She hardly recognized the sound of her own voice. Weeks of seeing him like this?

"I'm sorry." He reached for her hand, but his once strong grip was already tellingly debilitated. "This is going to be hell for you."

"I'll manage." She raised his hand to her lips. "I'll manage." She brightened, hoping to distract them both from what lay ahead. "I'll have you know I set out a snare for a rabbit."

He groaned. "I forgot all about food. I won't have to worry about the fever. We're going to starve to death."

She stuck out her lower lip in what she hoped was an attractive pout. "Beast. I'll have you know I have a stew cooking out on the campfire right now."

"Rabbit?"

"I'm not precisely sure what it was actually. But it wasn't a skunk." She described the sharp-snouted creature that had been her snare's first victim.

"Possum," he pronounced. "I've eaten worse." He caught her hand. "I know it's not easy for you to kill . . . anything. And I'm sorry you're being backed into that kind of corner."

Her eyes misted. She would never have thought he could understand that, a man raised to live off the land. And yet he did, and she loved him all the more.

"I'm glad you're here, Andy. For more reasons than you know."

His breathing grew ragged as his fever climbed

higher. By late afternoon of the second day he was so weak he could no longer do even the most simple tasks like shave or feed himself. She'd just finished helping him with supper, when she noticed he was looking decidedly uncomfortable, embarrassed.

"Damn." He tried to shift, to move.

"Don't try to get up, Jace. Just tell me what you want. I'll get it."

"This isn't something you can . . ." He didn't look at her.

Her face heated as she realized what he was talking about. But she buried her embarrassment lest she make it worse for him. "We'll . . . we'll figure something out."

The fever rose, and then it didn't matter because he didn't even know she was there. And to spare him his dignity, she was grateful he did not.

The days settled into an ongoing battle to bring down the fever. In the mornings he would often seem to be getting better, but by noon the fever would always be back, worse than ever. By the fifth day the rash had started, breaking out first on his wrists and ankles, but spreading rapidly to the rest of his body. She lay whiskey compresses on the sores to help dry them out, but many blistered painfully.

On the sixth morning, he couldn't move at all. He groaned and lay back, trying unsuccessfully to hang on to what was left of his pride.

"Andy, I want you to leave. For God's sake . . ." He blinked back tears of angry frustration.

She kissed a three-square-inch patch on his forehead unaffected by the rash. "No. Us spoiled bitches always get our way, you know."

"Some spoiled bitch," he rasped. "You look worse than I do."

"You do know how to turn a lady's head, Mr. Montana." But she knew she had to look like she'd been dragged through the brush on the wrong end of the rope. Surviving in the wilderness left her no time to nurture a perfect manicure or pamper delicate skin or even wash her hair as often as she would like. *Godey's Ladies' Book* would be appalled to find one of its favorite readers in such a state. It seemed she was forever setting snares, chopping wood, cooking meals, cleaning game, or simply tending to Jace.

On this particular evening she was helping him get down a little soup. He coughed, choking, calling out as he had so often lately to Dawn Wind, to Bright Path, to Isaiah.

What frightened her most was that all three of those people were dead. And it was as though he could see them, touch them.

"Isaiah, you said he was mine," she whimpered, exhaustion robbing her of her own senses as she lay her head on Jace's heaving chest. "Two rivers. Two halves of the same whole. He doesn't belong to Dawn Wind. Not any more. Don't let her take him. Please, don't let her take him."

She fed him, bathed him, kept him alive. She shook him, shouted at him, swore at him, terrified at the glazed look in those gray eyes.

"Dawn Wind can't have you. She can't!" She wiped at her sweat-covered, grime-covered face. "She's dead. And I'm alive. You hear me, Jason Montana. You're mine!"

Chapter Eighteen

Jace was more nervous than he had ever been. Today he rode alone to the Blackfoot encampment bearing gifts for Tame Bear, gifts to exchange for Tame Bear's daughter, Dawn Wind, so that she could be his wife. Behind him on a lead rope trailed six of the gifts, the finest pieces of horseflesh he had ever seen in his life. But he knew they would not be enough. Not that he had any doubts that Dawn Wind would marry him. It was just that he was certain Tame Bear wasn't going to make the experience of asking easy on him.

He lifted his beaverskin cap, running a hand nervously through dark hair that brushed his shoulders. It had been a long time since Isaiah had taken his knife to it. He studied the village he had visited scores of times in his twenty-eight years. About two hundred families lived in the camp, their tipis scattered across the high plain just east of the Rockies, just below the Canadian border. Tame Bear was their chief, father to one daughter and two sons, though the eldest of his sons, Dancing Eagle, had been killed three years ago in a battle with the Shoshoni to the south.

The Blackfoot were not the friendliest of tribes to whites, but as far back as Jace could remember neither he nor Isaiah had ever been considered white in Blackfoot eyes. Those few times he and Isaiah had come in contact with other human beings, it had mostly been the Blackfoot. Jace spoke their language as easily as his own.

He reined his horse toward the tipi near the center of the village. The conical deerhide structure was decorated with paintings of running horses, but the dominant picture was of a massive black grizzly bear slumbering peacefully in a grove of aspen.

Jace grinned as the flap of the tipi slapped open and a slender, bronze-skinned woman stepped out. Her coal-black hair hung in two braids that ended just above her high, firm breasts. Her doeskin dress hid the shapely curve of her hips.

Jace dismounted, clearing his throat. "Is Tame Bear here?"

"Shall I tell him you wish to speak with him?"

"No, I was just checking to see if he was here," he said. Then he grimaced. "I'm sorry. I think I'm a little nervous."

Dawn Wind giggled. "You are a strange brave to tell a woman you are sorry." She ducked back into the tipi, emerging a minute later behind a tall, gray-haired Indian in fringed buckskins and full headdress.

"My daughter tells me you wish to speak with me."

Jace straightened, wishing Isaiah hadn't backed out of coming along. Tame Bear would be less likely to practice any of his more notorious chicanery with Isaiah present. Jace loved Tame Bear like a favorite uncle, but the wily old Indian never missed any opportunity to use his position as Dawn Wind's father to his advantage. The look of deviltry in the chief's dark eyes left no doubt in Jace's mind that this day would surely test his patience.

He wiped the sweat off his upper lip. Nothing would be gained by stalling. "I'm here to bring you gifts, Tame Bear," he began. "I trade you horses and furs for your daughter, Dawn Wind, that she might be my wife."

"Have you spoken with her of this?"

"Yes."

"And her answer?"

"Was yes." He looked at her, his chest swelling to see the love in her brown eyes.

"Dawn Wind is a daughter to prize. She is not cheap. You have many horses?"

"Six."

The chief folded his arms across his broad chest. "Not enough."

"I also bring Tame Bear a half dozen buffalo hides and two dozen beaver pelts."

"Not enough."

Jace stiffened. It was twice more than enough, but he kept his tone reasonable. "What would be enough, Tame Bear?"

The Indian smiled, and Jace knew that he would not secure Dawn Wind's hand this day. "I wish hunting knife with bone handle and sharp blade. On bone handle is picture of bear."

Jace grimaced. Isaiah's knife. Tame Bear had had his eyes on that knife for years. But he could never talk Isaiah out of it. "It is not mine to give, Tame Bear. You know that."

"You will find a way, or you will spend long winter alone. No grandchildren for Tame Bear by spring."

Dawn Wind giggled again.

Jace handed Tame Bear the lead rope for the six horses, crediting Dawn Wind's presence with forcing him to keep his voice mild. "I'll see what I can do about the knife."

Tame Bear nodded, slapping Jace on the back. "You make good, strong grandchildren. You get knife. You have Dawn Wind. She want bear you children. She say you be good under her robes."

Jace's eyes widened. He stared at the ground, not believing that he could be blushing. But he felt the heat in his face. "I will be a good husband to Dawn Wind," he managed. Though how she could know that he would be good "under her robes" he would have to discuss with her later. He would have no chance to sleep with her until their wedding night. Tame Bear had made damn certain of that.

Jace rubbed a hand across the back of his neck. Isaiah had told him of chaperones who protected a maiden's virtue in the white man's world. Such chaperones could take a lesson from a Blackfoot chieftain named Tame Bear.

"Will you walk with me, Dawn Wind?" he asked, grateful to leave the gloating chief behind.

She nodded shyly.

He took her hand and together they strode toward the meadow of wildflowers that skirted the village on the west. Without preliminaries Jace pulled her down into the knee-high grasses, his mouth hot and wet against the sweetest lips he had ever known. "Would your father really keep us apart for that knife?"

"No, my love, he will not. But he is enjoying watching the mountain cat dance for his mate."

"Oh, he is, is he?" Jace sat up, one hand on an upraised knee, grinning ruefully at the four squaws who had followed them into the meadow. They kept a respectable distance, he had to grant them that. But their presence assured Tame Bear of his daughter's virginity until Jace could come up with Isaiah's knife.

"I love you, Dawn Wind," he said, tugging on the end of one of her braids.

"You are a good man, Jason. I will be honored to be your squaw."

Jace plucked a flowering stalk of bear grass, trailing the silky bloom down the side of her face. "You sure you won't mind living apart from your people?"

"Wherever you will be, my husband, is where Dawn Wind will be."

He kissed her, a hard, probing kiss that fired the heat in his loins. Damn, but he wanted to take her. His near hermit's life with Isaiah had left him precious little opportunities to explore the wants of his sex. But he would not have traded his life for a satyr's. He was at peace in this meadow with this woman, in spite of her scoundrel of a father.

Much later, he rode back to the cabin he and Isaiah shared near the Flatheads.

"Get your woman?" Isaiah asked.

"Nearly," Jace said, not certain how to bring up Tame Bear's additional piece of demanded booty. "We'll be married before winter."

Isaiah grinned. "Here. Have an early weddin' present." He shoved a piece of folded buckskin into Jace's hands.

273

Frowning curiously, Jace unwrapped the buckskin, the bone-handled knife sliding into his palm. He stared at it, knowing the store Isaiah had set by that knife all his life. "Isaiah, I can't let you do this. Tame Bear will come around. He's just being stubborn."

"And so am I. It's done. I want me some grandkids, too."

Jace smiled. "All right. Thank you. It looks like the old bastard finally got his way."

Two weeks later Dawn Wind was his wife. Isaiah and Tame Bear spent most of the time after the ceremony making wagers on how long it would be until Isaiah won back the knife.

But Jace's thoughts were filled with Dawn Wind. There were no squaws to chaperone this night, their wedding night. He pulled her down into the three-deep pile of buffalo robes that lay across the floor of the tipi. They would spend this first night here, then travel tomorrow to the new cabin he and Isaiah had built in the mountains. A cabin big enough to accommodate the houseful of children he hoped one day to have with this woman who was now his wife.

His loins tightened, white hot heat spreading like fire through his body as Dawn Wind stood beside him, raising her dress above her head and tossing it at her feet.

"I want to please you, my husband," she said, her supple bronze skin aglow with the light of the lantern that hung from the center pole of the tipi.

"You already please me, Dawn Wind," he whispered. He reached up a hand, grasping her wrist and pulling her down beside him. "You please me very much."

He explored every inch of her, as she denied him nothing. Never had he known the true power of the mating of a man with a woman. She was passionate, eager to please him.

And oh, how she pleased him that night. He drove himself inside her, feeling for the first time in his life that he had made love to a woman, not had sex with her.

"I love you, Dawn Wind," he murmured, kissing her hair as she nuzzled against him. "We'll have a good life together. I promise you that."

She fell asleep in his arms.

For a long time afterwards, Jace lay awake. He could only marvel, as he had countless times, that his life could be so full, so good. He knew the story of his beginnings, the tragic deaths of his parents, but he couldn't imagine any other life than the one he had led with Isaiah.

Isaiah. The old trapper had done his best to be mother and father to him, though there were times he might have gone a step too far. Jace grinned in the darkness, remembering his first woman, a young French widow to a trapper friend of Isaiah's. Isaiah had brought Mazie to him as a "present" for his fifteenth year. It was a night he would never forget. He laughed. It was a week he would never forget. The few women he had had since had been much like Mazie. But he had grown tired of lovers who did not love. He wanted a family. And he had known and loved Dawn Wind since they were children.

The next morning Dawn Wind kissed him awake. "I have a gift for you, my husband," she said. "For our new life as one." Almost shyly she handed him a small present wrapped in deerhide. He opened it to discover a round buckskin medallion with an exquisitely made beaded cougar's head in its center.

"It's beautiful," he said.

She took it from him, settling it around his neck. From beneath her dress she pulled a duplicate medallion. "I have made one for myself, Jason. The spirits will always know we are husband and wife."

That day he rode out of the Blackfoot camp with his new wife at his side, ready to begin their new life together. It was a three-week journey to the new cabin, a magic time filled with excitement and love. Jace made a point of watching Dawn Wind's face when they reached the cabin, set in a clearing surrounded and sheltered by an ancient stand of lodgepole pine. The awe and wonder in her soft brown eyes made him feel much like a king, pleasing his queen with a new castle.

"Best I go my separate way now, boy," Isaiah told him as the old trapper helped unload their cache of supplies from their three pack animals. "Don't need an old reprobate like me gettin' in the way now that you got yourself a good woman."

"Isaiah, we built the extra room onto the cabin for you. You're not going anywhere. I have no intention of setting that trap line alone."

"Mountain's gettin' trapped out."

"But you know how to trap beaver and still leave enough animals to trap next season."

Isaiah sat himself down on a tree stump thirty yards from the house, rubbing his bushy beard. "You're a married man with a wife to look out for now. You'll be startin' a family. . . ."

"You're my family, Isaiah." Jace gripped the old

man's shoulder. "And don't you ever forget it."

They settled into a routine of hard work, sometimes back-breaking work. But they were happy. Dawn Wind especially took to cabin living, preferring it at once to a tipi. And when they went out to set traps, often leaving the cabin for weeks on end, Dawn Wind proved an invaluable third pair of hands, as adept at trapping and tracking as either himself or Isaiah.

It seemed nothing and no one could intrude on their isolated paradise.

"It's a damn good life you've given me, Isaiah," Jace said, pausing in between swings of his double-headed axe as he worked to lay in enough firewood for the winter ahead.

Isaiah set down his own axe, stifling a nagging cough that had been with him for weeks now. "It's always a good life when you work hard for it, boy. But I think we've had it better 'n most."

Jace sliced through a short length of pine, tossing the cleaved logs onto the growing woodpile. "Sometimes I feel strange, though, wondering how different it all might have been if my parents had lived. I don't know why but I've been thinking more and more about that lately."

Isaiah swiped a sleeve over his sweat-drenched face, seeming to take an extra minute before answering. "A man can always wonder what his life would have been like if he took one path over another. What if I wouldn't have been trackin' that buck? You would've died with ma and pa."

"I guess you can 'what if' yourself to death, huh?"

Isaiah ran a hand over his beard. "What's really eatin' at ya, painter?"

Jace hesitated before bringing the axe down across another log. He straightened. "What do you mean?"

"This is Isaiah you're talkin' to, not Dawn Wind. You may be able to palaver your way out of a corner with her, but you ain't foolin' me none. Ya got the itch, don't ya? You want to leave the mountains."

"What the hell are you . . ." He stopped, propping the axe against the woodpile. "Damn, I don't know what it is. Sometimes I just think I'd like to know what the rest of the world looks like. Not that I'll want to stay. . . ." He raked his damp hair away from his face. "And I sure don't mean to hurt you or Dawn Wind."

"I know that, boy. And I don't ever want you to stay here because of me."

Jace blew out a long breath, hefting the axe once again. "Well, I don't have to worry about it today. What say we finish this?"

He had seen the hurt in Isaiah's eyes in spite of the old man's efforts to conceal it. Dawn Wind, too, had been reluctant to discuss any thoughts of leaving the mountains. He supposed he could understand her fear of white man's cities. Even in the wilderness he had had occasion to view too many whites' vicious bigotry toward the Indian. He couldn't justify satisfying his curiosity about what lay beyond the mountains at the cost of Dawn Wind's peace of mind or Isaiah's happiness. He loved her, and he owed the old trapper everything.

The first heavy snow had fallen when word reached them that Tame Bear had been hurt. Jace immediately started them on the arduous trek to the Blackfoot village. But they were too late.

Tame Bear was dead. It was the irony of his death

278

that struck Jace. That Tame Bear would be mauled by a grizzly. The Blackfoot chief had managed to kill the bear with Isaiah's knife, but the bear's death had been at a high cost. Tame Bear had lost an arm and a leg to the beast, and Dawn Wind accepted his death as a blessing.

"I'm sorry, Dawn Wind," Jace said, pulling her close as they waited out a storm in Tame Bear's tipi before beginning the long journey back to the cabin.

"His death was with honor," she whispered, though Jace heard the quiver in her voice. "I regret he did not know of his first grandchild before he died."

"I'm sure he . . ." His eyes widened. He pulled back to search her face. "Child?"

She smiled, nodding even while tears for her father slid down her cheeks.

He held her, kissed her, joyously happy. And, though he too felt the pain of Tame Bear's death, he knew the old chief would have been pleased. He pressed her down into the buffalo robes, making love to her gently, passionately.

"I have pleased you, my husband?"

"Don't ever doubt it, Dawn Wind."

What had promised to be a sorrowful ride back home was instead a thoughtful one. The coming reality of being a father resurrected the need to know more than the world of the Flathead Mountains. He wanted his child to have a choice. At the same time he would not press Dawn Wind during her time of grief.

"She doing all right?" Isaiah asked as he rode up behind Jace, while Dawn Wind rode alone to the rear.

"She will be." Jace gave Isaiah a lopsided grin. "We're going to have a baby."

Isaiah gave Jace a hearty slap on the back. "About time, painter." He sat back in the saddle. "I'm going to be a grandpa." He pulled his knife out of its sheath on his belt. "Tame Bear left word I was to have it back. I think I'll give it to the child, when he's old enough. Teach him how to clean a pelt, like I taught you."

"He?" Jace said, arching his eyebrows. "What if it's a she?"

Isaiah chuckled. "Then I'll teach *her.*"

Jace was as nervous as the cat Isaiah had always named him when the time came for Dawn Wind to give birth. He had gone to the Blackfoot village in late summer to bring back a squaw to act as midwife, but even so he couldn't stop pacing outside the cabin as he waited to hear the healthy wail of his child.

"Take it easy, boy," Isaiah cautioned. "You'll wear a trench in the ground."

"Take it easy?" Jace snorted. "I notice you haven't sat down in the last six hours either. It's a good thing . . ."

The cabin door opened, the stocky, square-shouldered White Crow hurrying over to Jace. "Dawn Wind asks for you."

"The baby?" He felt the blood drain from his face.

"She asks for you," she repeated.

Jace bolted into the cabin, crossing to the bed in the far corner of the room. He stared at her face. She seemed tranquil, serene, her full lips curving into a gentle smile when she saw him. "Dawn Wind," he blurted, "the baby?"

She lifted the edge of the bundled wool blanket that lay against her breast. "Our son."

He was on his knees beside her. "He's all right?"

"He is strong, like his father."

"Then why didn't he cry? Babies are supposed to cry, aren't they?" He couldn't take his eyes off of the scrunched-up little face. His son. His son, who seemed to be extremely content to lie atop Dawn Wind and chew on his own tiny fist.

"He is happy. Why should he cry?"

Jace grinned. "Yeah, you're right. Why should he? He's going to have the best life a boy ever had." He leaned over, giving Dawn Wind a swift kiss on the forehead. "I love you."

"I love you, my husband."

"Is it all right if I bring in Isaiah?"

"Of course. He must meet his grandson."

He rose and crossed to the door, but before he went outside he turned to look again at his wife and son.

Her smile seemed sad, but he didn't think of it again as he rushed out to tell Isaiah the news.

And for the next three years he tried with everything in him to give Bright Path the best he knew how. But as the signs of winter settled over the mountains and his son's third birthday passed, Jace came to realize that the mountains that had nurtured him all of his life weren't enough any more.

"I don't know how I'm going to do it, Isaiah," Jace said, hefting Bright Path onto his shoulders as they gathered berries. "But somehow I'm going to convince Dawn Wind that going to a city, any city, won't be the end of our family."

"I kept ya from a lot, boy."

"I don't mean it that way, you know that. I have no regrets about my own life. But I want more for Bright Path. I guess I want him to have a choice. To know both worlds and choose which one he wants. To go to school.

"We could head down to San Franciso. Or Santa Fe. Or east to places I've heard about . . . Chicago, Philadelphia."

Jace made little progress convincing Dawn Wind that everything would be all right in the white man's world.

"I have heard stories, my husband. I would not be welcome, nor would our son with his white and Indian blood."

"We won't know until we try it." He pulled her close, inhaling the healthy woman scent of her. "I'll never let anyone hurt you."

Strangely, it was Isaiah who suggested where they might go.

"Texas."

Jace frowned. "Why?"

"Just think maybe a cattle ranch would be to your likin'. Talked to a drifter who runs cattle up the Goodnight Trail; says Texas is wide open. Cattle roamin' for the takin'. We could gather up a few head. Start us a ranch."

"Well, it would sure as hell be different," Jace said. "I'm not saying I wouldn't come hightailin' it back to the mountains. I just want to see what else is out there."

"We can give Texas a look-see anyway."

Jace shrugged. "Why not?"

Later, when he told Dawn Wind, her reaction was much as he expected—a kind of sad resignation. Jace pulled her close, made love to her, but he sensed her fear, her withdrawal.

He decided finally that the longer he put it off the

worse it would be. It was late February when he approached Isaiah as the old trapper sat on a tree stump repairing in iron-jawed trap. "I want to leave soon."

"We've got the traps to clear."

"We'll bring 'em in, then go."

"If it's what you want." He let the jaws snap shut.

"Damn, I wish everybody would stop making me feel like I'm putting a gun to their heads."

"Sorry, painter."

"I know." He gave Isaiah a rueful smile. "If it doesn't work out, I'll be the first one to drag us back here, all right?"

"Uh huh." Head bowed, Isaiah resumed his task.

It was then Jace realized the burning fear that Isaiah must have carried with him for years—that if Jace ever left the mountains, he would never come back. Jace wanted to tell him such a notion was ridiculous, but for some reason he couldn't bring himself to say it.

Instead he wandered over to where his son was busily constructing a mound of mud and pine needles.

"I'm making a castle, Father," he beamed. "I'm going to be a knight like in King Arthur."

Jace hoisted the boy into his arms, giving him a swift hug. "Maybe someday you can see a castle just like King Arthur's."

"Oh, could I?" The boy kissed Jace on the cheek. "Can we go now?"

"Not just yet," Jace laughed.

"You're going away with Grandpa Isaiah?"

"For a little while."

"Can I go this time? You promised one time I could."

Jace tousled the dark hair so like his own. "Not this

time, Bright Path. Your mother's going to need your help getting ready for our trip to the castle."

Dawn Wind stepped out of the cabin, crossing over to them. She held out her arms, and Bright Path went eagerly into them.

"Father's going with Grandpa hunting," he announced proudly.

Dawn Wind gave him a wistful smile. "Yes. Our last season, my son."

Much, much later, Jace remembered her words and the odd melancholy that had been in her voice, as though she had had some kind of premonition that gave them a tragic double meaning.

But for now he couldn't suppress his excitement as he readied the horses for the three-week trek to collect the traps. "It'll be all right; you'll see."

It was a thoughtful ride. Isaiah kept his own counsel most of the journey, saying little on either the trip out or the trip back.

"You don't want to go either, do you?" Jace probed as they rode the last few miles toward the cabin. Three weeks away from his wife made him anxious to see her, see his son. But he wanted to settle things with this man he loved as a father.

"It had to be sometime, painter. Whether I want you to go ain't important. You want to go."

"You are coming along, aren't you?"

"Stay here and not see my grandson? Just try to keep me here."

Jace grinned, but the smile vanished as he looked ahead on the path that led home. Even before they crested the final hillock that wound down into the clearing, Jace saw the smoke, thick, black, clawing the air like the arms of a beast.

"My God! The cabin!" He savaged the sides of the horse to reach the clearing. But it was too late. Yesterday would have been too late. The cabin was a smoldering shell.

He leaped off the horse, seeing the body of the man first. Vaguely he heard Isaiah thunder into the yard behind him. Jace threw the man over onto his back. A stranger dressed in buckskins. Panic seized him. He screamed for Dawn Wind.

"Jace. Oh, God."

He turned to see Isaiah standing over a small body on the ground lying near the woodpile. His guts turned over. Like a walking dead man he crossed to Isaiah, not wanting to see, not wanting to know. A cry from hell was torn from his throat as he dropped to his knees beside his son. The side of the small, precious face was black with congealed blood. His small body was already stiffening in death. Very, very gently Jace lifted Bright Path into his arms, crossing the yard to lay him on a bed of pine needles next to the boy-sized castle.

Tears blinding him, he stumbled toward the burned-out remains of his home. "Dawn Wind!" He found her in the corner of the cabin, her breathing labored, her body beaten, naked. Scrambling like a wild man, he scrounged up a scrap of cloth and some clean water.

"Bright Path," she whispered. "My son. Where . . ."

"Who did this? Who?" He squeezed the water against her swollen lips.

"Not leave mountains. Not leave Bright Path."

"Dawn Wind, please. I have to know."

"White men. Three. Strangers."

He smoothed the water over her face, dabbing gently

at the cuts, the bruises. "The dead man. Was he one of them?"

She shook her head feebly. "Him here before other men. Just want food." She clutched her stomach, gasping. "I must be with my son."

"No!" He closed his eyes, forcing his voice to steady. "Did these three men know the other one?"

"They call him a name. Not his. He told me his name was Gage."

"Did any of them call each other by a name? Anything?"

"No." Each breath became a struggle. "They shot Gage. Then they grabbed me, dragged me toward cabin. I see Bright Path. Scream for him to run." Her eyes widened, and Jace read the terror, the agony in them as she relived the horror. "He see man hit me. Bright Path run over to hit him. Man kick him. Man kick Bright Path." She screamed, her face contorting with grief, anguish. "I must be with my son. I must."

Terrified, Jace clutched her hand. "Stay with me."

"No." She gave him a look filled with sadness, with tenderness. "I cannot." She closed her eyes, her chest heaving in a long, shuddering sigh. She was dead.

Jace had never known pain like this. Never. For the first time in his life he realized his parents had been lucky. If they loved each other, they had at least died together.

In the first days of his rage and grief he neither ate nor slept as he and Isaiah followed the trail the three men had left on their way down the mountains. But a spring blizzard ended his hopes of tracking them. Even then he wouldn't turn back. Isaiah had had to clip him on the side of the head with his rifle butt and tie him to his horse to force him to return to the cabin.

For the next seven months his life was a blur of whiskey and tortured nightmares.

"I'll find them, Isaiah. I'll find all three. And before they die, they'll be cursing God that He ever let them be born."

And always he thought of Dawn Wind. *I'll never let anyone hurt you.*

She was dead. His son was dead.

And, though Isaiah never left him, he was alone.

Chapter Nineteen

Amanda listened to Jace's grief over his wife until she thought she would go mad hearing it. She could feel his agony as she sat beside him in the small cabin, running a cool cloth over his sweating body. It had been ten days. Ten days of seeing him like this. Hearing his fevered nightmares. She wondered sometimes which of them would be broken first by his illness, Jace or herself. As he called out his wife's name yet again, she thought surely it would be herself.

"Let him go, Dawn Wind," she begged, lifting his hand to her lips. "Let him go. Please."

He twisted his head, his eyes opening. "Andy?"

"I'm right here."

"Did you say something?"

"No. No, nothing important." She wrung out the cloth and lay it across his forehead.

It had been the same every morning. For about two hours he would seem better. The fever would be down, and though extremely weak, he would be alert and lucid. And it drove them both mad because it was so.

That he could seem well and then have the fever return time and again was more to bear than if it just went on and on without relenting.

And yet she would not have given up the two hours. Because in that tiny space of time each day a bond had grown up between them that Amanda longed to believe even Dawn Wind could not have breached.

"I don't want another day of this," he rasped. "I can't take another day of this. I remember finding them . . . over and over again. Finding them. Savaged. Beaten. Bright Path, dead. Dawn Wind nearly dead. And then she dies in my arms. Every day. Every day."

That he remembered the nightmares seemed more cruel still. She stood abruptly and walked over to the small basin she had arranged in the corner of the shack. Dipping the cloth into the fresh water, she stepped back over to him. It was time for a change of subject.

"I was thinking," she said, forcing a false cheeriness into her voice, "that it's about time we got rid of that scraggly looking beard of yours. Abraham Lincoln you're not." Whether he saw through her diversion didn't matter. It only mattered that she distract him from thoughts of the fever's return, distract them both from thoughts of Dawn Wind.

"You're saying it doesn't give me that proper Baltimore image of gentility."

"It gives you the image of a gorilla."

"The one who taught Mozart to play the piano?"

She brought over the pan of water and sat down, regarding him thoughtfully. "We haven't always been polite to one another, have we?"

"I, uh, wasn't real comfortable with your calling me a savage." He fingered the edge of the blanket beneath him. "Maybe because I am one. At least to a proper lady like yourself."

She had collected his shaving supplies from his saddlebags and mixed the soap in a small tin cup. She couldn't meet his eyes as she scooped out the lather with his shaving brush and began working it into the eleven-day growth. The beard might have looked striking if he was healthy, but his sickly pallor and his loss of weight made him look all the more gaunt.

"The proper lady was scared to death of the savage," she said, her voice shaking so much she had to stop applying the soap to his face to take a steadying breath. "I meant to insult you to keep you away. I think I knew what would happen if you didn't."

He gripped her wrist, though his hold was no longer a strong one. "I wanted you to be afraid of me. And when you were, I hated it." He turned her hand over in his. "Are you still afraid of me, Andy?"

She shook her head, suddenly feeling very shy.

He smiled. "Good. Because I want you to believe this, if you never believe anything else I ever tell you: I'll never hurt you, Andy. Never." He closed his eyes as a sudden pain shot through him. "Son of a bitch. This can't last much longer. It can't."

She kept hold of his hand, glad suddenly for all those years of pretending after Matthew's death, as Jace would not have guessed how great the pain in her heart to see him so near despair.

The pain subsided, and he opened his eyes again. He tried to smile. "From a proper lady to a trapper and now a barber?"

"I'll take care not to slice you too much," she said, taking aim with the razor as though she meant to carve his face for a jack-o'-lantern.

"Watch yourself, woman. You leave me no lips and I'll not be able to kiss you."

"Then I'll take especial care," she promised huskily. The rash had ulcerated on some parts of his body, faded on others. The spots on his face were mostly gone, but she used the razor cautiously nonetheless. He never took his eyes off of her hands while she worked. She felt warm and found herself thinking of the price the fever had wrought beyond ebbing his strength. She pushed the thought away. He might not say it aloud, but·the way his thoughts were filled with Dawn Wind, Amanda had to wonder yet again if his need for her body was merely a way to find surcease of his need for the other.

"I think your mouth has survived intact, sir," she said softly. "Might you put it to good use for me?" She leaned forward, impulsively brushing her lips against his own.

"How can you stand the sight of me after what I've put you through?" He threaded his fingers in her pale hair. "You look like you've had the fever yourself."

"Thank you, sir. It's compliments like that that make me realize why I've never had any inclination to be a nurse."

She went outside to empty the wash basin, returning with a bowl of tepid soup. At least in the morning she could get him to eat. If not for these lucid times, he would surely have starved.

"You haven't seen any sign of Welford in all this time?" he asked.

"Do you think we'd both still be here if I had?"

"Don't make me think. Just answer yes or no."

She smiled. "Yes, there has been no sign of Philip."

He raised up a hand, as if to touch her face, but the effort proved too great and he dropped it back to the floor beside him. "Damn, I hope this ends soon."

"It will. You'll be fine. You said two weeks."

"Or three, or four."

"Well, why not settle for two? No sense bein' a hog about it."

"Yes, ma'am." He gripped his stomach and looked away. She knew the signals by now and saw to his needs with little discomfort to either of them. He was beyond being humiliated. He just wanted it over as quickly as possible.

Amanda made certain he finished eating well before noon, because it was then the fever would start to rise. She busied herself around the camp, checking the snares and cooking down meat into soups that were easier on his digestion. Even so, the pickings in the hollow were becoming thin. The animals seemed to have grown wary of her traps, and she didn't know enough about such things to do them any differently. Besides, she was getting almighty tired of rabbit.

It was late afternoon before she reentered the shack to check on Jace. She wasn't up to another siege of his wanting Dawn Wind, but she didn't like leaving him alone too long either. She noticed the difference in him at once. He was prisoner to a new dream. It took her a while to understand him, and when she did she wished to God she had not.

Jace was reliving the time they had first made love, if such it could be called considering its ending. And in his fever he called her every name he must have thought but not said that afternoon.

"Welford's whore. She's Welford's whore, Isaiah. Okay, she was virgin, so what? So she's keepin' him in knots until the wedding. He's still buyin'. And she's still sellin'. Whore. Such a pretty little whore."

She whirled, running, stumbling away from the cabin, not stopping until she reached the creek. Sobbing, screaming, she stripped off her clothes and plunged into the shallow water. She sank to her knees on the pebble-strewn bottom, scrubbing the gritty water across her naked flesh until she rubbed her skin raw.

"I hate you! I hate you, Jason Montana!" she shrieked. "I hate you!"

How could he still think such things? Say them after what they'd shared these past weeks? Try as she might to convince herself it was the fever talking and not Jace, the words clawed at the very core of her. To care about him, to love him, was to be so very vulnerable. And to be vulnerable was something she had only recently permitted back into her life. Now she had to wonder at the cost of those resurrected emotions.

Wonder because she knew what Jace did not. That his fevered ramblings weren't so very far from the truth. Not that she was a whore with Jace. Because she loved him. But Philip . . . oh, what would she be with Philip?

Feeling drained, bereft, she climbed out of the stream and not wanting to pull on the same grubby clothes as before, she hurried back to the camp naked. Quickly she pulled on a clean pair of trousers and a shirt, then crossed to the canvas sack Jace stole from Philip's ranch. If there was one way Jace's sickness could be counted as a blessing, it was because it had kept him from going through the sack's contents. She had seen the look on Philip's face when he had been forced to empty the safe of more than just money. A look she would have shared had she known what Jace had then had in his possession.

She unfolded the note she had signed promising to be Philip's wife. If only tearing it to bits would end that promise. But the knowledge Philip held about her, about her family, would not be destroyed by destroying the note. She folded it and stuffed it into her pants pocket. The other papers were merely legal forms and things that Amanda could see no use for. Though one of them was a copy of Philip's father's and grandfather's last will and testament. She imagined Philip's lawyer had the original documents. She gave them only a cursory glance. Philip the principal heir. With mentions of beloved servants and such.

Out of curiosity she counted the money, gasping to find twenty thousand dollars. If Philip didn't have enough of a motive for coming after Jace before, she was certain nothing would stop him now.

As darkness fell she resisted her usual habit of settling down for the night in the cabin with Jace. Even though the air was much stuffier in the cabin, especially with the excessive body heat of his fever, she had remained near should he need anything. But tonight Amanda spread her blankets outside the open doorway. She could still hear him if he called out, but she could not bring herself to be near him.

She had thought he would be too sick to notice her absence. In fact, she wasn't even certain he was aware she spent her nights in the cabin. But when she woke the next morning it was to find him lying beside her on the hard earth. She had been so exhausted she hadn't even heard him moving about. Reflexively, she felt his forehead.

Her eyes widened. Perhaps it was wishful thinking, or perhaps it was only because he had slept in the cooler outdoor air, but he didn't seem as warm this morning. "Please, God," she whispered. "Please."

Wanting nothing more than to snuggle close to him, she forced herself to get up to start breakfast. An hour later she brought a soupy portion of rabbit stew over to him. She reached to shake his shoulder, terrified she would find that the fever had returned. Instead, he came groggily awake.

"Good morning," he mumbled, painstakingly levering himself into a sitting position. He leaned against the side of the building. "I'll be damned. I feel almost human."

She said nothing, handing him his soup. But she grew cautiously optimistic as for the first time in well over a week he was able to feed himself. Perhaps the fever had run its course at last. She prayed it was so. Still, as she set about cleaning up the dishes, it wasn't the fever that occupied her thoughts but his fever-driven words of the day before.

"Something wrong, Andy?" he asked as he set his coffee cup down beside him.

"Nothing, why?"

"You seem different. Sad."

"Tired," she snapped, stiffening. "The word is *tired*. I have never been so stinking tired in my life!"

Color rose in his pale cheeks, and it wasn't from

anger. "I'm sorry," he said quietly. "I know I've been . . ."

"No," she sighed. "I'm the one who's sorry. That was awful of me. I am so very tired, Jason. Forgive me. I think I'll just lie down for a while."

She walked over to a cottonwood twenty feet from the cabin and lay down. But she didn't sleep. Everything had changed. No matter how she told herself he would never say those things to her face, she had heard them and they hurt. They hurt because she loved him. And there wasn't a chance in heaven that he would ever love her.

He loved a ghost. Loved Dawn Wind. And try as she might, Amanda was finding it more and more difficult not to hate the Blackfoot woman she had never known, would never know.

She was grateful Jace slept most of that day and the next, grateful especially that it was a natural sleep, not delirium. But when she woke him to eat, she could tell he was concerned about her new dispiritedness, so she made an extra effort to be cheerful around him. She didn't want to upset him, didn't want any chance of a relapse. Only when he was free of the fever for three days did she allow herself to truly believe he was going to be all right.

"You're getting to be a damned good cook," he said, finishing off his first solid meal in two weeks, a supper of fried rabbit and wild onions.

"I'm still not as good as the teacher, but I'm getting there." She sat down cross-legged beside him, wishing there were a way to ask him about the dream, ask him what he really thought of her. Instead she kept the conversation light. "Actually you were lucky you were delirious a few days back. I caught a raccoon in the new snare you told me how to make. I felt terrible, but it was dead, and I couldn't very well just let it have died for nothing."

"You cooked raccoon?"

She rolled her eyes, remembering. "Oh, Jason, the smell. The little beast got his revenge. I'm surprised the posse and half the state of Texas didn't come to investigate. It must have been sick."

He chuckled. "There are two glands in the rear of a raccoon you have to cut out before you can cook it. Otherwise it does have its vengeance. If you catch another, I'll show you what to cut before you cook it. Then it'll taste just fine."

"I did feel terrible about it though. I lost sleep over the bunnies. But the raccoon, oh, Jason, it was so cute."

"Damn, you are one strange woman."

"You're welcome."

"I suppose if you hadn't had my life to concern yourself with, you would have chosen to starve rather than sacrifice the . . . bunnies."

"Quite honestly, I don't know if I can answer that."

He pulled her onto his lap but just as quickly released her. For an instant she thought he was thinking of her betrothal to Philip. Instead, he only looked at her sheepishly and said, "Sorry. I must not smell too good."

"Better than most mountain goats, I imagine."

"That's mountain lion, woman."

"You haven't been downwind of yourself lately. I've done my best, but sponge baths can only go so far."

"Show me to the creek."

"With pleasure."

Amanda helped him to his feet, and in spite of her personal hurts she was achingly glad to see that he was getting well. She came under his arm, letting him use her for support as they made their way to the stream.

"I'll forgo my usual modesty," he said as she began out of sheer habit to undress him.

She backed away at once. "I'm sorry."

"I'm not." His gray eyes darkened, and he made no move to finish the task she had begun.

No, she thought despairingly. She couldn't renew that part of their relationship. It would make going back to Philip that much more painful. And after what Jace himself had called her in his dreams . . .

"Dammit, Andy, are you going to tell me what the hell is bothering you or not? You've been damned strange ever since the fever broke. Why?"

"I have not been strange. I don't know what you're talking about."

"Fine," he gritted, jerking at the buttons of his shirt. "Don't tell me." He shrugged out of the shirt, then slid his pants off, and she was amazed at how casual, how comfortable he had become in being naked around her. And before he trudged into the three-inch deep water he made certain he stood looking at her long enough, so that she became very pointedly aware of that part of his anatomy that seemed to have recovered most completely.

"Damn you," she whispered, tearing off her own clothes and splashing into the water to join him. "Damn you."

He sat very still while she turned the soap over and over in her wet hands. Then ever so slowly and lingeringly she caressed the slippery lather across his broad shoulders, down his back, and up the tight muscles of his arms. He closed his eyes, arching his head back, his breathing growing shallow. Gently, gently she eased him down into the shallow water. Her hands never stopped moving.

"Andy. Andy, please . . . I need . . ." He gasped, his fingers digging into the streambed as her slick fingers found that part of him so rigidly aroused with a fever of a different sort.

She watched his face, his eyes, all the while continuing to stroke his turgid flesh until she was certain he was more than ready for her. Seeing him like this, so passionate, so alive, let her forget for the moment at least that it wasn't she whom he craved, but another lost to him by fate.

"Jason, oh, Jason, hold me," she whimpered, pressing her breasts against his chest, kissing him, loving him, crying out when his arms surrounded her, crushing her to him. Sensing he was still too weak to take the lead, she straddled him, moving her hips against him.

Even in the whirling rapture of her need, she held back, making certain he reached the summit before she followed. For long minutes afterward neither moved, neither wanting to sever the link as the water rippled past them both.

She stroked the side of his face. "I'm sorry. Maybe I shouldn't have done that. You're not well enough."

"I'm a helluva lot more than well." He gripped her arms, his eyes locking on hers. "I love you, Andy."

She pushed herself away from him lest he see the quick tears that sprang to her eyes. He was throwing

300

her a bone, likely relieving his own conscience about Dawn Wind.

"Did you hear what I said?" he asked quietly.

"I heard."

He swallowed, feeling his face heat. "I see. The feeling is not mutual.

Oh, yes, it is, she longed to say but instead she shrugged. "I hadn't given it much thought."

"Then what the hell was all this about? What just happened between us?"

"The same thing that's happened on more than one previous occasion. You didn't say you loved me then."

"Andy . . ."

"Don't call me that!" *Oh, please, don't call me that.* She had grown to love the name, as she had grown to love the man. And now she couldn't bear either one. No matter if Jason loved her; it was obvious from his delirium he had no respect for her. And the cruel reality was it didn't matter anyway.

She laughed, a mirthless, sick laugh. She wasn't a whore with Jason, because she loved him. But what would she name herself after she married Philip and he beckoned her to their bed? What would she call herself then?

"I'm sorry, Jason. Truly."

"No harm done," he said.

She winced at the anger in his voice.

"I don't know what I was expecting. But it all comes back to the real world, doesn't it? Savage Jason. Civilized Amanda."

"Don't push it all back on me!" she cried. "You don't love me, Jason. You love a ghost!"

"That's not fair." He struggled to sit up, reaching for

his clothes but falling back. Amanda had to help him dress.

Maybe it wasn't fair, but the hurt she felt pressed her to be anything but. "You love Dawn Wind! You always will. And I leave you to her. I've had all I can take of trying to measure up to that sainted savage!"

He said nothing, his features tight with what it cost him to be silent. How dare Amanda attack Dawn Wind! How dare she! He jerked away from her when she reached out a hand to help him walk. Instead he picked up a fallen branch, twisting off the twigs along its five-foot length. Using it as a crutch, he hobbled back to the cabin.

"I'm so sorry, Jason," she murmured, knowing he was too far away to hear. She sank to her knees in damp earth, tears streaming unheeded down her cheeks. Why? Why had she said such a thing? But she knew. She'd said it partly out of her own impotent anger, anger at a woman brutally murdered, a woman who had had Jason's heart. A woman against whom Amanda constantly measured herself and came up wanting.

Dawn Wind would have been at home in the wilderness, at home in Jason's world. Amanda couldn't tell Jason, but she still got nauseous every time she cleaned one of those damned bunnies.

But she suspected there was more to her ill-considered remark about Dawn Wind. To attack someone so precious to Jason was to virtually assure his rage, assure his welcoming the end of whatever odd symbiosis had grown up between them since that fateful moment on the gallows in San Antonio.

I love you, Andy. The words echoed and reechoed in

her mind. But she could not, would not, believe they came from his heart.

She climbed to her feet, letting out a shuddering sigh. Jason was well enough to take care of himself now. It was time to go back to her world. Time to be what she was. What she had to be.

She would leave Jace to his vengeance. To his ghosts.

Back at the camp, they took great pains to avoid each other in the cramped closeness of the glen. When she readied her blankets to sleep near the house, she was grateful he reacted as she'd hoped, stomping into the cabin to sleep alone. Still she waited until it was well past midnight before she dared saddle the sorrel.

A thought struck her as she left. She pushed it away, but it stayed with her. He wouldn't know. How could he? She crossed to the canvas sack. What would it matter if he did?

Jace woke, instantly alert. Something was wrong. He bolted to his feet and clambered out of the cabin, glancing warily about the camp. It was well past dawn. He didn't have to check the horses to know. Amanda was gone.

He wouldn't find her at the creek, wouldn't find her scouting them up something to eat. She was gone. Still some part of him wouldn't believe it.

"Andy!" He stuffed his shirttail into his pants as he stalked barefooted toward where she'd tethered the horses. His jaw tightened. The sorrel was gone.

He stood there for a long minute. What the hell was he getting so angry for? He'd wanted her gone from the first minute he'd laid eyes on her, hadn't he?

Raking a hand through his sleep-tousled hair, he found himself heading toward Isaiah's grave. Fighting off a strange feeling of desolation he sank down beside it. "She's gone, Isaiah. Gone."

"You told her to go."

He almost jumped, as the voice his mind conjured sounded so much like Isaiah's own. But he could hardly fear that much-loved voice. "I'm on the run. What kind of life can I give her?"

"Do you love her?"

"She's from another world, Isaiah. She's going to marry Philip Welford. It's like I told you; she's nothing but a spoiled bitch. She called Dawn Wind a sainted savage, for God's sake."

"Haven't you made Dawn Wind a saint, painter? A saint no human woman could ever measure up to? Because you blame yerself for her dyin'?"

"I loved her."

"And now she's dead. But you didn't kill her. She held no blame for you on that. And she'd skin ya herself for makin' her into something she wasn't. You had your go-rounds."

"No. No, we didn't fight. We loved. I loved Dawn Wind. She loved me."

"She didn't want to leave the mountains. You did."

"NO!"

"Amanda Morgan ain't no spoiled bitch. Amanda Morgan's a she-cat who's as scared of lovin' you as you are of lovin' her."

"Shut up, old man."

But in his mind Jace could see Isaiah grinning.

"Son of a bitch," he snarled, levering himself to his feet. "I'm well rid of her!" Then why did he feel like a steer just gored him in the gut?

Swearing, he stomped over to his saddlebags. To hell with Amanda. It was time to pay a visit to her beloved fiancé. He reached for his gunbelt.

"I wouldn't," a familiar voice grated.

Sheriff Jon Stark strode toward him, his .45 Colt levelled at Jace's middle. "You look like pure hell, Montana." He kicked Jace's gun away. "But then she told me you would."

"She?" The steer twisted.

"Miss Amanda Morgan. She told me right where to find you."

Chapter Twenty

Jace stuck his hands out in front of him, every muscle in his body tightening with rage as Stark locked a pair of handcuffs around his wrists. His disposition didn't improve as Philip Welford and Gabe Langley stepped out from behind the trees.

"Let's string him up, Jon," said Langley. "Save the citizens of San Antone the expense of buildin' another scaffold."

"No lynching," Stark said. "I won't have no one going around the law." He looked at Welford. "Not even you."

"Take it easy, Jon," Welford said, "I'm not about to lynch a man. I have only the greatest respect for the law. You know that."

A muscle in Stark's jaw jumped. "What I know is that you've done some fancy dancin' *around* the law and made it so this man . . ."

"That's enough," Philip snapped, then instantly smiled. "I wouldn't want to spoil our surprise for Mr. Montana." He slipped a hand into the pocket of his brocade vest, extracting a gold watch. "Time's wasting, gentlemen. I want Mr. Montana disposed of by noon. I have to be ready for my speech in San Antonio tomorrow." To Langley he said, "Get his horse saddled."

Langley grumbled but trudged toward the gelding.

Welford crossed over to Jace. "I want what you stole from my ranch."

"Amanda?" Jace sneered.

Welford drove his fist into Jace's stomach, doubling him over. "The money. The papers. Now."

Jace straightened painfully. "I lost 'em."

Welford arced back his hand as if to hit him again, but Jace brought up his handcuffed wrists and slammed both fists into the side of the rancher's head. Welford stumbled back, reeling, cursing.

Stark cocked his pistol, shoving between the two men. "That's enough! Both of you." He poked his gun in Jace's belly. "Touch him again and you're dead, Montana!"

"I don't think that will be necessary," Jace said. "I think he got the message."

The sheriff shoved Jace toward the horse. "You all right, Mr. Welford?"

"You should have shot him!" Welford seethed.

"He's an unarmed prisoner."

Welford visibly controlled his anger. "Whatever you say, sheriff. Whatever you say."

Welford's capitulation surprised Jace. Something was not right here. Not right at all. "Should I ask where you're taking me, Stark?"

"You can ask."

Jace mounted the bay, keeping a wary eye on his

captors. He might be a fool, but Stark's presence gave him some hope that he would not be murdered. What he couldn't get out of his mind was the lawman's comment that Amanda had given him away. Why? It didn't make any sense. She wouldn't stay with him, keep him alive for two weeks, then hand him over to the law knowing he was sentenced to hang.

As much as they both might fight it, they had grown to care about each other. She'd even accused him of still being in love with Dawn Wind. He remembered the hurt in her blue eyes when she'd said it. That had to mean something, didn't it?

Before they rode out, Welford took the camp apart searching for his money sack. Jace watched with studied fascination as the man tossed the currency onto the ground, looking through the documents first. The rancher's face purpled.

"Where is it, Montana?" he raged, stalking over to the bay. "Where the hell is it?"

Jace kept his face carefully neutral. "Something missing?"

"You know damned well what's missing."

"I haven't had time to spend the money."

"It's not the money and you know it, though I notice half of that is missing, too."

"What?" This time Jace was certain he had not hidden his astonishment.

"You stole twenty thousand dollars, Montana. There's only ten here. Now why don't you just save me and my men all the hard work of digging up this hollow and tell me where you put it."

"Whiskey and women."

"You bastard! Sheriff, I demand you get this

murderer to talk. Now!"

"You're the one says you want him taken care of by noon, Mr. Welford," Stark reminded him.

"But he's still got ten thousand dollars of my money! Not to mention legal papers that are of the utmost importance to me . . ."

"What papers would those be, Mr. Welford?" Stark asked.

Welford took a step back, seeming to collect himself. "They would only be of interest to my attorney and myself. Legal details that need to be worked out for my candidacy, that sort of thing."

"Well, if you want to stay here . . ." Stark began.

"No, no, no," Welford snapped. "Never mind."

"All right then," Stark said. "Let's go."

As they rode, Jace soon became aware that they were not heading for San Antonio. He wasn't going to give the posse the satisfaction of betraying his edginess. The odds were not in his favor should Welford decide to circumvent the law. They weren't even in Stark's favor. Welford would have no qualms about adding Stark's murder to the list of crimes in Jason Montana's obituary.

Damn, had there really been twenty thousand dollars in that sack? Or was Welford just trying to convince the sheriff that half the money was missing? He grimaced. What would that gain him? He wished now he would've gotten around to counting it. As for the papers, he'd seen the copies of the wills, but nothing else.

The thought that popped into his head was so absurd that he didn't even want to credit it his full attention. But the notion wouldn't go away. He had been out of his head for nearly two weeks. During that time only one person had had access to everything in the camp. Everything.

But it was ludicrous! Why would Amanda? . . . No, no, he wasn't even going to think about it. Welford had to be lying.

The sun wasn't yet overhead when they reached a dilapidated line shack no doubt meant for use by Welford's hands during cattle roundups. At the moment it was deserted.

"You wait outside, Stark," Welford said.

Stark started to object but apparently thought better of it. "Just see to it he's still alive when we leave."

"By all means," Welford said.

Langley pulled his rope from his saddle horn, keeping his gun on Jace. The foreman followed Jace and Welford into the shack.

"Tie him up over there," the wealthy rancher ordered, waving the gun at a rickety slat-back chair with most of its slats missing. To Jace he said, "Sit."

Between the handcuffs and Welford's gun Jace had little choice in the matter. He sat down. Langley immediately wrapped the rope around his chest, then proceeded to secure him to the chair.

"Now that I have your attention," Welford said, a sly smirk playing on his handsome features, "I think it's about time you and I had a little talk."

"If you insist."

"Get out, Langley."

The foreman stiffened but said nothing, turning to stomp outside.

"There are certain things big ears shouldn't hear." Welford lit a cigar. "Smoke?"

"No. Thanks."

Welford shook his head. "It's too bad, really, that you and I must be adversaries. But I can't permit interlopers. The J-Bar-W is mine. Only mine."

"I checked the surveyor's office. You don't have a deed for half the acres you claim. They're still public range."

"I say they're not."

Jace saw no point to the discussion. "Is Amanda all right?"

"Miss Morgan, my fiancée, is just fine. After suffering through her terrifying ordeal of being your hostage this past month she is, of course, in seclusion on my ranch. But that will not be any more of your business."

"Why Welford? Why all of this just to see me dead?"

"You don't ask the questions, Montana. I tell you what you're going to do, and then you do it."

"And what exactly are you telling me to do?"

"You're going to Huntsville."

Jace frowned. "Is that supposed to mean something? I've never heard of . . ."

"It's a prison, Montana. A Texas prison about a hundred fifty miles or so from San Antone. I've gotten you a room there. A cell to be precise. Very cheap. Very solitary. Very easily misplaced in the guards' minds."

"Why not just hang me?"

For an instant Jace could have sworn he saw a flash of rage in Welford's normally cold features. But Welford's voice betrayed no such emotion. "I said you don't ask the questions. And you'd best learn to do as you're told. They're very strict about that at Huntsville. Now, I want you to tell me what you did with my money. And those papers. Those papers are meaningless to you."

"I lost 'em."

Welford stubbed out his cigar, extracting a foot-long leather strap from the inside pocket of his jacket. Holding it in his right hand, he slapped it again and again into the palm of his left in a slow, methodical rhythm that matched the cadence of his speech. "Don't make me angry, Montana. I may yet see you hanged." He stepped closer. "Now where are those papers?"

Jace said nothing.

Welford drew in a long breath. "You won't be able to use them, you know. They're useless without . . ." He stopped. "Damn. Maybe you don't know." A slow smile spread across his face. "Amanda."

Jace's eyes widened. Then there really was something missing from that sack. Damn, that meant Amanda had seen what was in it! But she hadn't mentioned anything about it. When he'd gone through the papers and found them worthless, he'd been disappointed, hoping to find something, anything that would point to Welford and why the rancher was trying so hard to frame him. He'd stolen the money only to make it seem his goal. Had Amanda stolen something back to . . . No. The bile rose in his throat, but his mind finished the thought anyway. To protect Welford?

"Now we really do have something to talk about, Montana." He continued to thump the leather strap against his palm. "And I want the truth. Did you sleep with Amanda?"

Jace made certain his expression was unreadable.

"Did you sleep with Amanda?" Welford repeated, the leather strap slapping harder as he circled the chair.

"Did you rut with my fiancée? Did you defile her with your . . ." He stopped behind Jace, rubbing the strap across the back of Montana's neck. "Please don't spare her virtue on my account, the poor dear sobbed hysterically about it for hours. I believe she mentioned the word 'rape.'"

Jace gave Welford no reaction.

The rancher stalked around to face Jace, a sly smile playing on his lips. "Of course I had to cuff her a little bit. She was terribly uncooperative—not at all the refined young lady I've come to love. But when you know how not to leave bruises . . ."

Jace tried to lift himself chair and all from the floor, every muscle in his body bulging to break the bonds that held him. "If you hurt her, I'll kill you."

Philip smiled. "I thought as much." He tipped Jace's chin up with the strap. "I didn't touch her. I wouldn't strike my own fiancée. Amanda is very precious to me. But I had my suspicions about your feelings for her and I just wanted them confirmed."

"If I ever find out you hit her . . ."

"You're in no position to make threats, Montana. None." He brought the strap down across the side of Jace's face.

For an instant Jace thought Welford might have broken his jaw. He felt his rage building as he tasted the salty sweetness of his own blood.

"You're not going to see her again. In fact, you're not going to see much of anything again. This is going to be better than hanging you. To know that you'll spend the rest of your life in prison. To have you thinking of Amanda in my bed, pleasuring me, giving me children. She is so very pretty, isn't she?" He licked his lips.

"How does she like it? Maybe a little pain. Maybe she likes to beg for it . . . maybe . . ."

"Prison won't hold me, Welford," Jace snarled. "I'll get out. I'll find you. Even if you're in your governor's mansion. And I'll kill you."

"It's that hopelessness that I want to instill in you, Montana. You won't escape. You'll never escape. And you'll never see Amanda again."

He walked to the door and called Langley back in. "When we get back to the ranch, remember to tell Bates I want that loose end taken care of in the near future. Oh, and give our friend here a little taste of what prison life is going to be like."

Jace fought the ropes but couldn't move, couldn't fight, couldn't do anything but sit there as Langley crossed over to him, backhanding him across the face. The pain was sharp and deep at first, then settled to a dull throb as Langley rained blow after blow across his head and his upper body. Then he felt nothing at all as the blackness claimed him.

His memories of the days that followed were vague, filled with the jarring motion of a prison wagon, darkness, and beatings. He felt hands lifting him, dragging him, but his eyes were swollen shut and he had no idea where they threw him when the motion of the wagon ceased.

"Welcome to Huntsville," came the cackling laugh. He heard the sound of a door grating shut. Wherever he was, he was alone. And it was hot. So stinking hot.

The darkness lifted, and through the slits of his battered eyes he could just make out the tiny window

315

on the door. Sunlight crept through that four-inch-square opening. Struggling to his knees, biting back a groan when the pain sliced through his ribs, he peered out the hole. His muddled senses gradually made sense of what he saw.

He was in some kind of box, hardly bigger than himself, in the middle of a huge, dirt-covered yard, a prison yard. And he was hot. Damned hot. Sweat dripped from every pore of his body. He tried to lick his lips, wincing to find them twice their normal size. He sagged back, curling against the rear of the box, the stifling heat making any movement at all not worth the effort.

Sometime during the day the door opened and a cupful of water was set beside him. "It's all you're getting, bucko. Better drink up."

He brought it to his parched lips, thinking of Amanda. Had she really given him up to this? Turned him in to Welford? He slumped against the wall again, remembering the last time they'd made love. The water had rippled all around them. Water. Oh, God, what he wouldn't give to be in that creek right now. . . .

But he wasn't. He was on a desert. There was rain up ahead, but he couldn't reach it. He walked, ran, staggered, fell. Always the rain splashed down just out of reach.

Then a beautiful woman appeared. Blond hair, mountain-lake eyes, beautiful, so beautiful. She was holding a glass of water, melted snow water. She was smiling. A beautiful smile.

"Thirsty, Jason?"

He nodded, his tongue too swollen for speech.

"I have water, Jason."

He crawled toward her. If he could just reach out a hand he could touch her. But his hand weighed a thousand pounds. She tipped the glass, pouring the water into the sand.

"Philip didn't want you to have any. And I have to do what Philip says. I love him so."

"No!"

"He's so good to me. He buys me pretty things. Like this dress." She skated her hands across her full bosom. "Do you like the dress, Jason?" She lowered the bodice, exposing her breasts, feathering her fingers around the nipples.

"Andy," he rasped, "Andy, don't go with him."

"I love Philip. He's rich, powerful. Why would I marry someone in buffalo robes who didn't even learn how to read until he was fifteen?"

"I was twelve!"

She laughed, soft, silky, lilting. "It doesn't matter, does it? I'm the governor's wife. Can you be the governor? Can you be president? I must have my silks. My satins. My servants."

She waved a sheaf of papers in his face. "I could have proved you innocent, you know. But that would have ruined Philip's career. I just couldn't take that chance. Poor Jason. Poor Jason."

Wrinkling her nose, she pulled on a pair of thick gloves, lifting a dead rabbit by its hind legs. "You're the savage. You eat it." She threw it at him, her face twisted, ugly. "You lived with savages. Loved a savage. You are a savage! A savage!"

"Andy . . . Andy . . ." His mouth was dry, his voice cracked, hoarse. He couldn't think. It was as though he had the fever again, except that this time Amanda wasn't there. Wasn't there.

Days later, he couldn't guess how many days, hands dragged him out of the box, out of the sun. They took him inside the cell blocks, down a long, dark corridor, then shoved him inside a walled cell. The thick iron door with its tiny barred window protested on rusty hinges as two burly guards forced it shut.

He was alone then, and he used the time to get to know the twelve by twelve room with its lumpy, straw-stuffed mattress and its two buckets, one to relieve himself, one with drinking water the guards might bother to refill every third day or so. He found two candles. But no matches. He had to ask for matches.

He picked up a piece of stone that had chipped off the rear wall and scratched a two-inch-high mark above his mattress. For the hell of it he scratched thirty more, making it a month's worth. He wondered bleakly how many years the wall would hold, then shoved away the thought. He would get out of here, some how, some way, he would get out.

A big, blank-faced guard brought him his supper.

"Step back," the man grunted.

Jace did so, listening as the man jammed the key into the lock and opened the door. The guard set the plate on the floor, then relocked the door.

"Room service for you, Montana," the guard said, his mouth splitting into a near toothless grin. "Warden wants to keep you private for a while."

"When can I talk to him?"

"The warden? Prisoners don't talk to the warden, Montana. 'Specially not a prisoner in solitaire."

"How long am I going to be . . . in solitaire?"

"Long as the warden says so."

There were ten more marks on the wall before the guard spoke to him again.

"Warden gave you permission to speak, huh, Dealey," Jace said, his eyes skirting past the guard to try and judge how far he could get if he attacked the man and headed down that corridor.

"Not just speak," Dealey said, stepping inside the cell, a strange look on his usually emotionless face. "Warden says it's time to remind you why you're here."

A second guard stepped into the cell. Jace's guts churned. Both men outweighed him by fifty or more pounds. Still he launched himself at Dealey, gaining some measure of satisfaction by feeling his fist smash into that smug face. But the second guard slammed an iron rod into the small of his back, sending him to his knees. He felt a boot in the side of his head, an explosion of white hot light, then nothing, nothing at all.

"How many days?" he demanded the next time he was aware of his food plate. "How many days?"

"Eight," came the guttural reply. "Nothing personal, bucko. You remember that now."

With trembling fingers he scratched eight more lines on his wall, then with a frustrated sob he hurled the stone chip across the room, listening to it shatter into a thousand bits of dust. "Andy! Oh, God, Andy, why? Why didn't you just let them hang me?"

No. No. This wasn't her doing. It wasn't. She could not have been a party to putting him here. But what had she taken back to Welford? The thought tormented him unmercifully.

But even more unmerciful were the times he imagined her naked in his arms, holding her, touching her, tasting her. He wondered if he would ever again know the pleasure of making love to her. Love. He had told her he loved her, the words torn from him in the thrall of wondrous rapture. Did he mean them still?

Amanda had accused him of loving Dawn Wind, and he knew there had been some truth in that. He supposed he'd felt guilty when he'd first been attracted to Amanda. Even Isaiah had seen it. But Amanda had drawn him out, proving his damning judgment of a spoiled white bitch wrong at every turn. Her grit and her courage amazed him still as he remembered how she had kept them both alive while he lay helpless with fever.

Dawn Wind would always have a special place in his heart. But she was dead. That part of his life was over.

Now he sometimes tried to deliberately conjure the image of Dawn Wind in his mind. But while she was there and she smiled, it was not a solid image any more. She was moving away, vanishing. She wished him well. She let him go.

And he let go of Dawn Wind.

In a stinking cell in a stinking prison in which he might spend the rest of his natural life, he acknowledged what his heart had known from the first. He was in love with Amanda Morgan.

Chapter Twenty-One

Amanda ran a hand over the smooth satin of her dress, caressing the fine material. It was so good to feel clean again, even to feel pretty again, her hair done up in a stunning French twist, her body scented with the finest perfume. In the two months since she'd left Jace, she had lost much of the unfashionably dark color the sun had wrought on her face. And now as she stood in front of the mirror above her maple vanity in Philip's guest bedroom, she was certain the transformation was complete. She was once again Jason Montana's version of a spoiled, pampered . . . lady.

Her throat constricted just thinking of him. Thinking of him? Her every waking moment was obsessed with him! Wearily, she sank onto the brocaded bench seat in front of the vanity.

"Dear God, Jason. Did I do the right thing?" She didn't even know where he was. All she knew, all Philip would tell her, was that he was alive. She was supposed to content herself with that, but she could not. She had to see him. Had to touch him. Had to know for herself that Philip had kept his word.

The door to the bedroom opened and Delia swept into the room. "You're looking mighty pretty today, Mandy."

Amanda smiled grimly. "I'm glad to hear that. It'll make things easier with Philip."

"What easier? Have you called off the wedding?"

"Of course not," Amanda gritted. "And I am getting very tired of your asking me that question every single morning of my life."

Delia plopped herself down on the chair beside Amanda's bed. "You don't love him. What do you expect me to ask?"

Amanda turned toward the mirror, feigning interest in her hair style. "Philip and I are going to be married in two weeks, and that's all there is to it."

"Even though you love that outlaw?"

"Delia, for God's sake," Amanda cried, "please, stop it. Just stop it."

She bolted out of the room and hurried down the hallway toward the stairs, wondering yet again why she'd been foolish enough to agree to stay here, even with Delia to safeguard her reputation. To reach the stairs she had to skirt past J.T. Welford's bedroom. Just thinking of the old man behind that closed door gave her the shivers. The doctor had been out to see him again yesterday. Amanda had to wonder if the medical man weren't some sort of sorcerer to keep J.T. alive in his emaciated condition. She had to admire Philip, though. He certainly took excellent care of his grandfather.

She felt a stab of guilt, remembering how she'd read through J.T.'s last will and testament, which had been among the papers Jace had accidentally stolen along with Philip's twenty thousand dollars. The will gave Philip complete control of the J-Bar-W fortune—not just the ranch, but shipyards, banks, railroads, and more. Given such temptation many a man might have been tempted to hurry nature along. But not Philip. He was constantly fretting over his grandfather's condition.

Amanda just hoped Philip would be as compassionate toward her this morning, especially since her request would involve Jace. Taking a deep breath, she hurried downstairs and crossed over to the study.

She was about to rap on the door, when the sound of raised voices from within stopped her. Leaning closer, she discerned Philip's voice and that of his ferret-eyed lawyer Elliott Wickersby. She tried to make out what they were saying, hoping finally to discover any tiny shred of evidence that would free Jace from wherever Philip had sent him, but the thickness of the door muffled the words. When the voices stilled, she knocked, fearing they might open the door and find her standing there.

"We'll speak of this again, Philip," Wickersby was saying as the door swung wide. He halted abruptly to see Amanda.

"Miss Morgan," he said, politely inclining his head. "I'm so glad to see you're looking well."

"Why thank you, Mr. Wickersby. I didn't know you cared."

Philip chuckled. "I do wish you two would stop sparring and be friends."

Amanda said nothing, only watching as the lawyer settled his top hat on his head and let himself out of the house.

"Come in, Amanda darling," Philip said, gesturing toward the interior of the study. He closed the door behind them. "And what can I do for such a vision of loveliness this fine morning?"

"My, aren't you feeling chipper!" Amanda said, her hopes soaring. Maybe he would be cooperative after all.

"I'm feeling more than chipper. I'm feeling on top of the world."

"And can I ask what brought on these good feelings?"

He chuckled, perching himself on the corner of his desk. "Money, my dear. What else?"

"A good investment?"

His gaze grew sly, though Amanda doubted anyone but she would have noticed it. "A very good investment indeed." His lips curved into a pleasant enough smile. "But you don't care about my monetary adventures, so why not tell me why you've sought me this morning? You've pretty much avoided me these past weeks."

Amanda stared at the floor, then straightened defiantly. "We have a bargain, Philip. You know it. I know it. We need no pretenses when we're alone. That is, of course, unless you would like our bargain called off. Perhaps you don't wish to marry me any more."

"Oh, we'll marry, darling. It's a marriage made in heaven. Both parties benefit."

"Exactly."

"Why else do you think I've forgiven you for falling in love with Montana?"

She blinked, incredulous. She wouldn't have given him credit for being so sensitive. But then, how much sensitivity did it take to read something that was all over her face? She no longer made it a practice to hide her feelings, because it was no longer second nature for her to do so.

"He is alive, isn't he, Philip?"

"I promised you that, didn't I?"

"You wanted him hanged. You won't tell me where you've sent him. And I won't believe you set him free." She stepped closer to the desk. "Just remember, I bargain from a position of strength, too, at least until we're actually married."

His green eyes glittered dangerously. "Don't threaten me, Amanda. Don't ever threaten me."

"It's not a threat, Philip. I just don't want Jace hurt." She sighed, her shoulders slumping. "Is that really so much to ask? Isaiah is dead. I'm sure Jace would be content to go back to his mountains and be left alone."

"You are so naive. The man is a thief and a murderer, whether you choose to believe or not."

"He robbed you, yes. And I don't pretend to know why. But he is no murderer. And you have your money and your papers back."

"Yes, I have it all back. But you'll recall it wasn't Montana who had all of it on him when Stark arrested him."

Amanda recalled only too well. Philip had come at her in a rage, and for an instant she had feared for her life that day he had returned from recapturing Jace. She had thought Philip would think Jace had hidden the papers and the money. But, though she was certain Jace had told him nothing, Philip had deduced who had J.T.'s will and his ten thousand dollars.

"I only wanted another bargaining chip or two,

should I ever have needed them," she said quietly. "I thought a will promising you a fortune would gain your attention."

"Those are only copies, my dear. As I told you. Besides, I do not like to think of my grandfather passing on. Please . . ."

"But Philip, he's so sick. Perhaps it would be a blessing. Can't you see . . ."

"Enough! Tell me what you want. As if I couldn't guess. My God, for you to love him that much, he must be very good between your legs."

She swallowed her revulsion. She could not afford the luxury of telling Philip what she thought of him. "I won't discuss my private life with you. It's none of your business."

"It will become my business when you become my wife. I'm not certain I want used goods."

"You won't mind, Philip. Not really. I thought you might. But I saw it in your eyes that night when Jace robbed you. You weren't going to let anything happen to me, even though you weren't at all certain that I hadn't walked into his gun deliberately."

"Bright," he mused. "So very bright you are, my dear. I should have looked for a more stupid woman. But, alas, one can't always be that selective."

"Let me see him, Philip."

"You push me too far."

"I want to see him. Only once. Alone. To make certain he's all right, then I'll never ask to see him again."

Philip stood up, reaching for her, trailing his fingertips down her arms.

She jerked back, the feel of his flesh revolting her,

reminding her absurdly of how she had once wished she could care about him, since they were going to be married anyway. But she felt nothing for him but hate. "I want to see him," she repeated evenly.

"Then of course you shall, my dear. Of course you shall. It's about time you see firsthand what happens to someone who challenges the J-Bar-W. And why by now Jason Montana wishes you hadn't been so successful in persuading me to spare his life. That you would have let me hang him."

Amanda paced the sparsely furnished warden's office in Huntsville prison, straightening the sash on her exquisite lime silk dress. It was past midnight, and she was alone. Philip had kept his word. Money had changed hands and in minutes the bribed guards would be arriving with Jace. She would have six hours. Six hours locked in this room alone with him. She glanced around, checking to see that everything was ready, hoping she'd forgotten nothing. Her heart beat faster. Dear God, what would his reaction be to seeing her again? What if he hated her?

She jumped as the door to the office creaked open. A dark, hooded figure in tattered clothing was shoved into the room. A burly guard yanked off the hood, and Amanda watched the figure's hand rise automatically in defense against the light. She turned toward the dim lantern. For such minimal light to hurt his eyes, this man must have been in total darkness.

"I told you to bring me Jason Montana," she snapped at the guard. "What do you mean by . . ." She stopped, feeling as though a hand were squeezing her heart, her chest, until she couldn't breathe. No.

"Jason?"

The guard laughed wickedly. "Enjoy yer pleasures, little miss! Personally, for what you're payin', I could give ye a lot more for your time."

"Get out!" she shouted. "Get out!"

Still cackling leeringly, the guard shuffled out of the room.

Jace's gray eyes still hadn't focused, and he seemed to be having a hard time staying on his feet. Her own eyes blurred with unshed tears as she stepped closer to him, gasping to see the marks of faded bruises on his face, bits of straw clinging unnoticed to his matted hair and dark, shaggy beard.

"Six hours," she murmured, crossing to bolt the door from the inside. "I have you for six hours, and by God, I mean to have you in better condition than this!"

Ripping her clothes off down to her chemise and pantalets, she came under his arm and steered him toward the tub of steaming water she'd arranged to have in the room. She had thought he would enjoy an extra bath. Tears streamed down her cheeks. Extra bath? Likely his only one since he'd been here.

She sat him on the small stool beside the tub, dipping a clean cloth in the water and dabbing it at his face.

"Don't touch me," he rasped, jerking away. "Don't touch me."

"Jason, please . . ."

"Please?" His eyes narrowed to slits, as though he were trying desperately to focus but could not. "Andy? My God, is it really you? Or am I dreaming? The same nightmare I have night after night. That you come to me, make love to me, and then jerk the lever on the trapdoor at my hanging."

"It's me, Jason." She cradled his head against her breasts, holding him, not caring how filthy he was. Only caring that he was here with her, and he was alive.

His eyes opened, wide. He tilted his head back, staring at her. "It is you. Oh, my God." He twisted his head, seeing the tub filled with water, seeing, too, that he was still somewhere inside Huntsville prison. He was not dreaming. "What is this? What the hell is this?"

"I just . . . wanted to make certain you were . . ." The word was a mockery, ". . . well."

His lips curved into a sneer. "Well? If I was *well?* Why, Amanda, darling, I've never been better." He lurched to his feet, glowering at her. "This is your doing, isn't it? Yours and Welford's. Why didn't you just let them kill me? Or do you derive more pleasure from seeing me like this?"

"I find no pleasure in your pain, Jason."

"Then unless you've come to aid in my escape from this hellhole, I'll just ask you to leave. Now."

She shook her head. "No."

"Damn. It was you. I didn't believe it. But it was. You turned me in." He sank back onto the stool, looking more defeated than Amanda had ever seen him. "Didn't you?"

"I didn't come here to talk about . . ."

"Why did you come here, Andy?" He dropped an arm into the tub, swirling his fingers through the clear water. "Why?"

"To see you."

"All right. You've seen me. Now go."

"Not yet."

"Dammit, what do you take me for? Only Welford's

money could have gotten you in here."

She pressed the damp cloth to his forehead, but he pulled away. "Don't."

"Let me. Please. Let me do this for you."

This time he didn't pull away as she started to unbutton what was left of his shirt. She tried not to touch him, because it hurt her to feel him flinch away each time her fingers brushed his flesh. Gently she peeled the shirt away, biting back a scream of outrage to see the massive purple, red, and yellow bruises that marred his back and his ribs.

She feathered a hand across the worst one, a long, wide streak that looked as though he'd been struck with some sort of club. "I'm going to get you out of here," she whispered. "Some how, some way I will. I promise."

He laughed without humor. "They'd shoot us both. You can be certain Welford knows exactly what's going on." He angled a glance at her, "Exactly. Which is why I have to wonder just what the hell you're doing here."

"If I promise you I'll explain at dawn, will you give me this night?"

He made a low, rumbling sound in his throat that Amanda took for an attempt at a chuckle. But there was no humor in his gray eyes.

"Take the night, Amanda," he said, waving his arm wide in a sweeping gesture of capitulation. "It's yours. I'm at your complete disposal."

She ignored the sarcasm. "Fine; I'll take you at your word then." She helped him to his feet. While he held himself rigidly still, she tugged off his filthy trousers.

"Does madame have anything particular in mind for her night's entertainment?"

"As a matter of fact, yes. Get in the bath."

Shrugging, he climbed into the tub, wondering to heaven why he didn't just strangle her and be done with it. For all he knew she was Welford's wife. But he couldn't yet bring himself to ask. And when she began to bathe him, running her velvet-soft hands across his aching shoulders, he didn't care. He closed his eyes.

It wasn't until she was almost finished that Amanda realized he had fallen asleep. She didn't stop the sobs then as she washed his hair and shaved him. No, Philip had not had him killed. But he'd sentenced him to a living death instead. She knew Philip had no intention at all of ever allowing Jace to leave this place.

He woke with a start when she accidentally nicked his cheek with the razor. He studied her warily, while she pressed a cloth to the cut, then wiped the remainder of the shaving soap from his face. "Why? Why did you tell him?"

"I thought we'd agreed on no more questions for a while."

"I have to know." He stood up, deliberately flaunting his nakedness as he accepted a towel from her and only settled it across the back of his neck.

Amanda smiled wanly. At least he was feeling a little better. But there was no way she could chance telling him the truth. To tell him would only make his being here all the more intolerable. Better he blame her, hate, her, than know what had ultimately brought him to Huntsville.

"And while I'm asking, why did you steal back his

money? And those documents. Dammit, Andy, I wanted to see what kind of papers Welford had in his safe."

"It was only his grandfather's will. I promise you."

He raked a hand through his damp hair. "Somewhere there has to be proof that he's framing me. Not that it matters. Just being here instead of hanging from a rope proves how much power Welford has." He walked over to her and gripped her arms. "Why?"

"Philip promised he wouldn't kill you."

"So you told him where to find me?" His grip tightened.

She looked away. "Of course not. I would never do that. Oh, please, Jace, at least believe that of me. But once he did know . . ."

His big hand captured her chin. "My God, what kind of deal did you make for my life, Andy?" His eyes tracked up and down her body. "No. Please, no."

"It's not what you're thinking. It's nothing of what you're thinking. And I can't explain. Please, don't ask me. I just can't."

She pressed a hand against his bare chest, teasing her fingers through the dark hair, skating over the numerous droplets of water still clinging there.

He sucked in his breath, and her eyes dared trail lower to see that at least he was giving in to the passion that had consumed her since the instant she'd seen him again.

"Are you his wife?" he rasped.

"No."

He buried his hands in her hair, pulling her to him. "Andy, please. Why are you here? Why am I still alive? No one tells me anything. Please . . ."

Her arms surrounded him, revelling in the feel of the rippling muscles of his back. And then his lips found hers, and answers didn't matter any more. Nothing mattered but the sweet, sweet surrender of one to the other.

"Damn you," he breathed as he gathered her to him. "Damn us both."

He ripped away her chemise and her pantalets, dragging her down to the blankets she'd arranged on the floor.

He had lost his mind. He was insane. The guards, the prison—he was mad. He was dreaming. But he didn't care. Didn't want to be sane. Didn't want anything but the wonder, the magic of her soft, supple, magnificent body in his arms.

Her pale hair draped like a shimmering curtain of silk across her arms and down to her hips. His eyes devoured her, like a starving man set before a feast. She was even more beautiful than he remembered. She had not been in the sun. But the creamy white of her skin looked healthy and glowing.

"Oh, Jason, Jason, I've dreamed of this, ached for it. I love you so."

"I love you, Andy. God help me, I do. I love you, love you, love you." His hands were everywhere, his mouth following, his tongue teasing, tasting.

She gasped, her eyes flying wide open when his lips trailed past her navel and down. "Jason, what? . . ."

"Shhh, let me. Let me, sweet angel. Let me. I need you. I need you so much."

And then she had no thought for caution, no thoughts at all, as his mouth drove her past this world and into another, where the only reality was this man who whispered over and over and over again that he loved her.

She hated to give up any of their time together to sleep, but the ecstasy-born lassitude in her limbs demanded at least that she snuggle into his arms for a languorous moment of blissful contentment.

He kissed the top of her hair. "How am I ever going to bear that cell after this?"

"I'll get you out of here. I promise." She trailed a hand around his nipples. "But not tonight."

"You can't get me out of here, Andy. No one can. Except Welford."

She closed her eyes. They still had two hours until dawn. She wasn't going to risk an argument. "Did I ever tell you about the time I thought of you as the big bad wolf?"

He sighed. "All right. No Welford. For now."

"Do you remember the time I was laughing and you thought I was laughing at you?"

"I thought you were laughing at me on more than one occasion."

She kissed his nipple, then tilted her head to kiss his jawline. "You were dressing out that steer carcass, and you had blood up to your elbows. You looked just like a wolf must on a kill."

He stiffened. "So I'm still an animal to you."

She kissed his cheek. "I don't mind your being an animal. A stallion. A cougar." She grinned. "A big bad wolf." Her finger feathered around his eyes, caressing his dark, silken eyebrows. "What big eyes you have."

His hand captured the side of her head. "The better

334

to see you with, my dear." He joined the game. "Your eyes, your lips"—his gaze seared her—"your breasts, your lovely, lovely breasts."

Her voice was low, throaty, as he propped himself up on one elbow beside her. "Such a big mouth you have. . . ."

"The better to taste you." His lips circled her nipples, suckling until she whimpered from the sheer intensity of the emotions he roused in her.

"What . . . what big hands you have. . . ."

He smiled, cocooning her breasts, then gathering her to him.

"What big . . ." Her hand closed shamelessly around him, savoring the hard meat, savoring too his gasp of pleasure.

"Love me, Andy. Love me." He rose above her, and suddenly he wasn't in prison at all. He was in a shady hollow and he was with this golden-haired angel who had woven a spell around his heart.

With a cry of savage joy he drove himself inside her, giving her his body, his heart, his soul. "Andy, Andy, I love you. I love you."

Tears streamed down her face and he kissed them away, driving, thrusting, moving inside her, never wanting to be apart from her. At the instant of their final, primal, explosive release he brought her with him to a realm of shattering pleasure, a place he'd never been, knowing that only with Amanda would he ever be there again.

Gasping, he rolled over, pulling her on top of him. "I don't know how or when, but I am getting out of here. And you and I are going far, far away from Welford, from Texas, from everything." He kissed her hard.

"Damn, I love you so much."

"What about Philip? What about finding your wife's killers?" Surely, it was just the rapture of the moment that made him willing to leave his past behind.

"I don't expect I'll ever find the beasts who killed my family. Once the snow wiped out their trail, they could have gone anywhere. I have no clues, no hope. I was only deluding myself, because I felt so guilty that I wasn't there when they needed me."

"And now?"

"Now I love you." He kissed her upper lip, then her lower lip, then captured her mouth to explore the warm, moist recesses with his tongue.

She moaned, though her heart was breaking. Was he really releasing the ghost of his wife? For her? How could life be so cruel that she could never have this man she loved, this man whom she at last believed loved her?

He lay back, studying her intently as he brushed away her tears with his thumbs. "It's almost dawn. It's time for the truth."

"I'm not an Indian."

"What the hell does that mean?"

She drew back, climbing to her feet and reaching for her dress. "You keep forgetting that I am at home in parlors and sitting rooms. That I favor tea and fancy cakes over hardtack and biscuits."

"So I'll build us a cabin with a parlor, and you can cook whatever you like."

"Jason . . ."

He levered himself to his feet, grabbing her arm. "What the hell is this, Andy? You come here, you make love to me. Dammit, I want the truth."

"I wanted to make sure you were all right," she said, pulling away, knowing the excuse was as lame as it sounded.

"What else?"

She couldn't meet his eyes. "If you ever escape from here, don't come for me."

His jaw tightened, his hands curling into fists at his sides. "Why did you come here? Why did Welford let you come here?"

"He . . . he said I should be the one to tell you the news."

He was trembling, aching. Why did he know this whole night was about to become the nightmare he had believed it to be from the first? "So tell me."

"In three days Philip and I are getting married."

It was as though she had shot him. She had no gun, but it was a bullet just the same.

"What was this?" he shouted. "What the hell was this? A wedding present!" He shoved her against the wall, more angry than he had ever been. More hurt than he ever knew he could be.

"I care about you, Jason. I . . . I wanted to make sure you were still alive. Philip promised . . ."

"God damn you! You did sleep with him, didn't you? Didn't you?"

She jerked away, rushing to the door, pounding for the guard. "I'm sorry, Jason. I'm sorry."

And then she was gone. Leaving him bleeding, agonized, lost.

Chapter Twenty-Two

Amanda did not marry Philip three days after leaving Jace in Huntsville, because three days later she was violently ill. For nearly two weeks the doctor confined her to her bed, and she would not have left it even if he had not. She didn't know what sickness had seized her body, but her heart was in danger of never recovering after what she had done to the man she loved more than her own life.

"Please, stop fussing, Delia," Amanda pleaded as the woman bustled about the guest bedroom in Philip's ranch house, adjusting the windows for fresh air, fluffing her pillows, and generally making Amanda exceedingly weary just watching her.

"I'll fuss if I like," Delia said, stepping up to the bed, her eyes reflecting both sympathy and a mild annoyance. "How long are you going to do this to yourself, lass?"

"What are you talking about? I'm sick."

"Heartsick." The woman sat down, giving Amanda's hand an affectionate squeeze. "Why did you go to see him, Mandy? Why?"

"See whom?"

"Amanda, stop it!" Delia snapped. "Who do you think you're talking to? I love ye. I feel responsible for ye what with your ma dead and your pa gettin' ready to head for Europe with Mrs. VandeKellen."

"Don't remind me," Amanda gritted. It wasn't that she was upset about her father's increasingly serious relationship with the wealthy widow. But she was upset by the fact that he had made no plans to attend her wedding. The fact that he didn't approve of her choice of husbands was singularly ironic, considering her reasons for marrying Philip. If her father only knew . . . No. That was one of the reasons she was marrying Philip. So that her father would never know.

"Please, Delia, I just want to be alone."

Delia stood up, though she was obviously reluctant to go. "If you ever do want to talk about it, Mandy . . ."

"I know," Amanda said, her voice shaking. "Oh, Delia, I know."

Amanda lay back, watching the door close as Delia left. Thank God for Delia! Philip had been positively livid when Amanda had taken ill. But Delia had kept him from following through with his elaborate plans to have the wedding anyway. "You can't have her gettin' sick on the walk down the aisle now, can ye, sir?"

Amanda was all too aware of what it cost Philip to postpone what he considered the social event of the decade in the state of Texas. A cost he measured not only in money, but in embarrassment.

Even so, he had not gone so far as to cancel the wedding altogether, just as Amanda had known he would not.

Against her will her thoughts floated back to that steamy summer night in Baltimore just a little over a year ago. Her father had invited all of the great and near-great to one of the truly exclusive social gatherings of the season. Gloria VandeKellen had assumed the task of being the perfect hostess, a chore Amanda had happily relinquished to the society-conscious matron.

Everything was in tight order that evening with extra servants brought in just for the banquet alone. Amanda would have preferred to spend the night in her room, but she didn't dare. This was going to be her father's most important soiree since her father had taken over the sprawling estates of an antebellum plantation four years ago, not long after her mother's death.

"Mrs. VandeKellen is beside herself," Amanda giggled, coming up to give her father a swift kiss on the cheek as she joined him inside the lavishly decorated main ballroom. Amanda had thought the red, white, and blue bunting a bit much, even considering it was the fourth of July, but she had managed to keep her mouth shut. "Cook just ran out of sweetmeats."

Zachary Morgan's handsome face distorted in a mask of mock horror. "Gloria will have my hide for that one."

"Well, she shouldn't. The party is a smashing success. Fourteen senators, seven governors, and heaven only knows how many representatives and judges and . . ."

"You're being sarcastic again, Amanda. And I do wish you would call Mrs. VandeKellen *Gloria*. You make it sound as if I'm courting a married woman. Mr.

VandeKellen has been under the sod for twelve years."

"And a greater blessing the man never received."

"Amanda!"

"Yes, Papa. I'll try. Honestly. But you know I hate these parties."

"Perhaps you could try being a little extra nice to some of the more eligible bachelors."

"Don't start, Papa. Please. I want no crushing bore of a husband."

"You want no husband at all, child. And that worries me more than a little. How am I have to to grandchildren? With Matthew gone . . ." He stopped, his face frozen. "I can't believe I said that. It's been so long."

"Twelve years," Amanda supplied quietly.

He put his arms around her shoulders. "Try to have a good time, Manda, please."

"Yes, Papa." Instead she had gone out on the veranda alone. She was alone a lot these days now that Delia had gone off to be with her ill sister. But it was just as well. She had her sewing, her books, her long walks.

"A lovely woman shouldn't look so sad."

She jumped, startled by the unfamiliar male voice somewhere behind her. "Who's there?" she snapped, whirling to see a tall figure coming out of the shadows.

"Oh, I doubt you remember me, my dear. We were introduced at a party your father gave last year. The name's Philip Welford."

She relaxed a little, placing the tall, sandy-haired giant. "Yes, I do remember, Mr. Welford. But if you don't mind, I'd like to be alone."

"I'd always admired your candidness."

Amanda felt an odd uneasiness begin to stir in her. "I

don't recall having spoken to you sufficiently for you to form any but the most superficial opinion of me one way or the other."

"I know you're extremely lovely."

"You're not the first man to tell me that."

He stepped closer, and she was struck by how truly handsome he was, though there was a strange, hovering coldness about him as well.

"What I find peculiar," he went on, as though they had been lifelong friends, "is that I don't think there's even a trace of conceit in what you just said. It's as if you don't appreciate how truly lovely you are, Amanda Morgan."

"Mr. Welford . . ."

"Philip, please."

"Mr. Welford, I am not at all interested in continuing either this conversation or our acquaintance. So if you don't mind . . ."

"Ah, I do like that tough streak. No one is going to hurt you. At least, you won't let them know it if they do."

She swallowed, struck by his intuitiveness. He was arousing her curiosity, too. There seemed to be more to him than the casual flirt. "You're a rancher, as I recall?"

"Among other things."

"Yes. Definite political aspirations, if I remember correctly."

"You see, you weren't so unimpressed by me after all."

"I'm getting more unimpressed by the second."

He laughed, a pleasant, polite laugh. Ah, yes, he would make a fine politician.

"Actually, I have a purpose for approaching you

here, alone, Miss Morgan."

"Which is?"

"Can we sit down?"

"I don't intend to give you that much time. . . ."

"Oh, I think you will."

She caught the warning note, and she felt a sudden chill. Wanting only to rush back into the ballroom full of revelers, instead she allowed him to lead her over to a stone bench canopied by a trellis loaded down with the cloying aroma of dozens of blooming roses.

"I'll get straight to the point," he said, sitting at the opposite end of the four-foot bench. "I want you to be my wife."

Amanda gasped. She would have laughed out loud if not for the strangest glint in Philip Welford's green eyes. "This conversation is over." She started to rise. His iron grip on her wrist forced her to sit back down.

"You'll hear me out. And then you'll give me an answer."

"I already know the answer."

"Then you have nothing to lose but a few moments of your time."

"This is absurd."

"No, it's business. Pure and simple. I want to be president of the United States. And you will be my First Lady."

Now she did laugh. "You've been at Mrs. Vade-Kellen's punch, haven't you, Mr. Welford? And this is all some sort of preposterous joke."

"I am not laughing, my dear. You will marry me."

"I most assuredly will not."

"I understand you loved your brother a great deal."

She stilled. "I'll have you removed from the grounds

at once."

"I think not. Matthew was a Union spy, correct?"

Amanda felt gooseflesh rise on her arms, followed instantly by a rippling heat. "You're not to speak of my brother, sir. Not to me. Not ever."

"Your father went to a great deal of trouble to have the proof of your brother's guilt, even mention of his trial, such as it was, removed from any historical records."

"Get out of here!"

"I can have it all over Washington in a week that Matthew Morgan was more than a traitor. He was a murderer. He killed three Confederate soldiers in cold blood to prevent them from sabotaging his mission."

"You're a liar! A scoundrel and a liar! If Matthew killed anyone, it could not have been murder." And at that moment she hated Philip Welford for forcing her into defending a brother that she had successfully excised from her memory for years. "Why are you saying these things?"

"Your father is a very wealthy man. You are his sole heir." He sidled closer to her on the bench seat. "It costs a great deal of money to become president. And a pretty bride doesn't hurt a man's chances at all. It keeps questions at a minimum, you might say. And if Matthew isn't reason enough, there's more."

She shot to her feet. "I'm not going to listen to any more of this."

"You will listen. Oh, yes, Miss Morgan, you will most certainly listen. And you will marry me, or I will destroy not only your brother's precious reputation, but your father's as well."

"My father is above reproach. He's one of the most

345

successful, respected . . ."

"Haven't you ever wondered how your father came to be so very, very rich after the war, when so many of his friends were bankrupted?"

"My father has all sorts of business interests. Shipyards, freighting, railroads."

"Exactly. And he used every one of them to run guns and supplies for *both* the Union and the Confederacy."

"Liar!' she shrieked.

Philip stood, towering above her. "It's true. And I have the proof, more proof than any court of law would ever require. Your father was worse than a spy; he was a mercenary, making money off of the living and the dead on both sides of the war."

"How do you know all this? How?" Her mind reeled. This couldn't be happening, couldn't be true.

"It's quite simple really. I know it because your father was in business with my father. Bartholomew Welford. Oh, you've never met him. In fact, your father would never have allowed my father into your home. When I was here last year, it was only because your father didn't realize who I was until it was too late to ask me to leave. And, no, he doesn't know I'm here tonight. Zachary Morgan and Bartholomew Welford were both thieves, Amanda. But I've made certain my father's culpability can't be proved. Ever."

"If any of this outrage is true, then you must have plenty of money of your own from your father's treachery."

"Oh, I have enough. Unfortunately, my father had a bit of a penchant for gambling, and your father ended up with much of the money that rightfully—or wrongfully, depending on your point of view—belonged to

346

my father. Now I want that money back. And I'll get it . . . through you."

"You're despicable!"

"And you're lovely. And very wealthy. And we'll make an enviable couple." He paused meaningfully. "Or I'll destroy Matthew's memory and destroy your father utterly."

Amanda tasted despair that night, total, irrevocable despair. She couldn't go to her father. She couldn't go to anyone. Who could she trust with Welford's information? If she went to the law, her father might even be arrested, or ruined legally.

Amanda twisted on the bed, turning away from the memory. She couldn't let Philip defame Matthew, couldn't let him bankrupt her father, no matter how despicable his wartime behavior had been. And so she had signed the legal document Elliott Wickersby had drawn up, agreeing to be Philip's wife, agreeing that every cent of her eventual inheritance from her father would belong to Philip.

She sat up, reaching for the glass of water Delia had left on her nightstand. Philip's victory had been postponed, but the inevitability of it bore down on her. He would never free her of her promise, because to do so was to cost him an uncounted fortune. Money gained by men dying. Nor could she free herself, because though her father's crime far exceeded any imagined wrong of Matthew's, she loved him.

Still in all, it had been a kindness for her body to stall for time, and she wondered if she hadn't somehow brought the illness on herself. If she had married Philip so soon after Huntsville, she had little doubt Philip would have had Jace killed. As long as she was not actually Philip's wife, he could not take the chance of murdering Jace. He knew she would go to almost any lengths to protect her father and brother, but he was not so much a fool that he didn't know that Montana's death would change everything, change her.

Just knowing Jace had changed her, reawakening her to a world of feeling—ecstasy and despair. But rather than run away from her feelings, she had learned to accept them and deal with them. And because she also accepted the heartache of loving Jace without ever being able to have him, she was determined to at least give him back his freedom, no matter what the cost to her or her family's reputation.

And on that determined note she climbed out of bed, feeling, if not precisely well, then much, much better. And the first thing she had to do was talk to her father before his trip to Europe.

"You're not going home alone," Delia protested when she told her of her plans.

"I am," Amanda said. "And I want you to stay here and keep Philip off his guard, so he barely has time to know I'm gone."

Still, she was surprised when Philip raised no more than a token argument against her leaving. At home Amanda tried to be comfortable around her father, but ever since Philip's devastating revelation a year ago, she had been unable to look at him without remembering his self-righteous condemnation of Matthew's behavior in the war without ever circumspecting his own.

"I'm sorry we won't be able to make the wedding, Manda," Zachary Morgan said. "But Gloria wants to be off to the continent before winter takes hold."

"The wedding would have been last week, Father. It's barely October."

"Yes," he cleared his throat of an imaginary frog. "Well, we have a lot of packing to do. It's likely we won't be coming back home for a long time."

"Home?" Amanda had never considered the elaborate estates home. "Father, I want to know the name of the man you hired to cover up everything about Matthew."

"You're not to bring up that time of shame, child."

"I'm not ashamed of Matthew. He did what he thought he had to do. I can't fault . . ."

"He was my son! He betrayed the South! Broke your mother's heart."

She wanted to scream, *And what did you do, hypocrite?* But if he knew she was aware of what he'd done, it would destroy him.

"The name of the man you hired. Please."

"He was a Pinkerton. Went into business for himself. A detective agency, he calls it. But why would you want? . . ."

"His name, papa."

He frowned. "Eric Tibbs. His name is Eric Tibbs."

"I also want the name of the very best lawyer in Washington, D.C. I have a friend, who will one day benefit from his services. And then there's only one other thing you will ever have to do for me, Father."

Three days later she started the journey back. She couldn't postpone the wedding any longer. She would have to become Philip's wife. But once she'd done so, she would use that very position to uncover evidence that could free Jace. She'd never found any proof around the ranch that indicated there had been manufactured evidence in the Juanita Melendez trial, but there wasn't a doubt in her mind that Philip had used the poor girl's death to rid his ranch of a man he considered a squatter. She would contact Eric Tibbs and her father's lawyer, and soon—very soon, she told herself—she would have Jason Montana walking out of Huntsville a free man. Even though he would be walking out of her life.

A month later she was Philip's wife. The San Antonio wedding was a blur of forced smiles, endless kisses on the cheek, and leering winks at her groom from supposed statesmen who attended the excruciatingly painful affair. It had been two and a half months since she'd seen Jace. Four months since he'd been sent to Huntsville.

As she stood next to Philip in the receiving line, all she could think about were the bruises on Jace's body. She had yet to hear from Eric Tibbs since she'd first posted him a letter four weeks ago, detailing everything she knew about Jason Montana, Isaiah Benteen, the trial, and Juanita Melendez. As for Philip, she could only permit herself to hint to the detective that he was capable of blackmail. She didn't want Tibbs going off on a tangent in his investigation and unearthing things about her father or Matthew. Once she and Tibbs had gathered enough evidence, she would contact the attorney.

That night in her hotel suite Amanda cringed to think of Philip coming to her rooms. If he tried to touch her, she would scream the hotel down. A man in as sensitive a public light as Philip would risk no lurid gossip. But to her surprise when he did stop by before retiring, he made no move to touch her.

350

"We have one side trip before we begin our honeymoon, dear."

"What are you talking about?"

"Why a visit to your beloved, of course. It's been over two months since you've seen him. I'm sure he's pining away."

"I don't want to see him."

"Of course you do, my dear."

"Philip, you and I have an agreement."

"Exactly. And now that you're my wife, there is nothing in heaven or earth that can stop me from reaping the benefits of your end of the bargain. You're my wife, my property as it were, finally and at last. All that you have is mine."

"And because that's true, you agreed to let Jason live."

"I may have changed my mind."

"Philip, please . . ."

"Please? Please? I have grown so weary of your sad face these past months. I suggest you cheer yourself up and very soon. I have all I need from you. And I still have yet to play my ace."

Don't be too sure I don't know how to stack the deck, Philip, she fumed inwardly. But she dared not say anything. Not yet.

It was all she could do not to be physically ill as she waited in the warden's office with Philip to see Jace. Blessedly the warden had excused himself. Even so, how was she ever going to survive this confrontation with Philip posturing as her blissfully contented husband?

"Remember," he warned, "convince him you're happy, or I swear to you Matthew Morgan will be

351

right next to Benedict Arnold in every schoolchild's history book."

"Matthew was a hero."

"This is no time to defend the traitor. Besides, there's always your father."

"I'm not going to hurt Jace. Not any more. It isn't necessary. And it's not part of the bargain. Besides, for you to bring down my father, you'd have to bring down your own delusions about being governor."

Philip paced back and forth in the Spartan room in which Jace and Amanda had last made love. "Maybe it's time you did know the whole truth. Then we'll just see how far you're willing to go to protect Montana's feelings."

"Shut up, Philip. I have an ace or two of my . . ."

"Who do you think your precious brother Matthew stumbled onto in his spying?" he snarled, gripping her arms, his green eyes fired with spite. "He came home wounded. Your father and my father were arranging one of their bigger arms shipments. Matthew begged your father to stop. He even threatened to expose him. So your father had him arrested. Your father, not mine."

"No! For the love of God, Philip, do you know what you're saying?"

"I know exactly what I'm saying. Maybe your father didn't know what the end result would be, but it happened. Your brother was arrested. And then he was hanged. Your father killed him as surely as if he put the noose around his neck himself."

She almost collapsed. Matthew. Oh, Matthew. How could her father have done such a thing? Worse, he never seemed to have displayed the slightest guilt over having been virtually his executioner? "Does . . . does my father know . . . what he did? Does he?"

"Actually, that's something I've never quite been able to figure out. From everything my father said afterwards, it was as though your father wiped the memory from his mind. He doesn't remember. He honestly doesn't remember. But I will be very, very happy to send him the documents that would, shall we say, remind him." Philip's smile at that moment must have been very much like the devil's own.

"You'd ruin your career," she managed weakly, still reeling from his devastating revelation.

"On the contrary, my dear. I would make certain the public felt sympathy for me, caught by a conniving, rich brat—daughter and sister to two of the most reprehensible creatures to claim allegiance to the Confederacy."

"Don't you say a word against Matthew! My father put his principles aside, not my brother."

"Just make certain you behave when Montana is brought in. Or your father will discover he murdered his own son."

Amanda wanted to run from the room, screaming. Instead, from somewhere deep inside her she called on the Amanda she had been before Jace. The Amanda she had never wanted to be again, but now must be for the very man who had been so much a part of her transformation.

She almost lost her carefully neutral facade when the door opened and Jace was shoved inside. In fact, the look he gave her all but sent her to her knees. Hate. Pure venomous hate sparked from those charcoal depths as he looked first at her, then at Philip.

353

At least he didn't appear as abused physically as he had the last time. His biceps rippled with suppressed strength, as though he had been hefting a great deal of weight for a prolonged period.

"Enjoying your stay?" Welford chuckled.

"Go to hell."

"I can still send you there." He kissed Amanda on the mouth, while she barely managed not to vomit. "I'll bet you miss that, don't you, boy?"

"Actually she was always a little too much of a lady for the likes of me. If you know what I mean."

Amanda saw the uncertainty in Philip. He wasn't sure whether Jace was baiting him or speaking the truth.

"I'll let Amanda tell you for herself how much she's enjoying being my wife." He gave her a painful nudge to the small of her back. "Tell him, dear."

"There's not much to say, really." At Philip's warning look, she added, "Except, of course, that I'm very much in love with a very special man." *Oh, damn you, Jace*, she thought miserably. *Why did you have to look away when I said that? I was talking about you.*

"I'm . . . pleased you're happy, ma'am," Jace said. "I never wanted anything else for you."

"Happy?" Philip mocked. "Did you ever expect a woman of Amanda's breeding could be happy with the likes of an animal like you?"

Jace stiffened perceptibly and Amanda hurt for him, knowing Philip had gouged a sore spot in that sometimes sensitive hide of his.

"Could you buy her clothes like this, Montana?" Philip leered. "Or jewelry, furs, trips to Paris? Could you really expect to make her happy in your bed? Tell

354

him, dear, tell him who pleases you more."

"He is very good, Jason," she said in the barest of whispers, because if she dared speak any louder she would have cried.

The contempt in his eyes broke her heart. But she knew the look in her own eyes was coolly detached, disdainful.

She stepped up to him, trailing her fingers down the side of his beard-stubbled cheek. "You know what I think of when I think of you?"

"Careful, dear," Philip chided. "Not so close."

She swallowed, fixing her gaze on Jace, his hate chilling her to her soul. Her tone was cruel, designed to wound, but she prayed to God he would hear the words and not the way she said them. "You were an animal. Frightening, terrifying, like poor Red Riding Hood and her big bad wolf."

Philip gripped her arm. "Come, dear, it's time we leave this vermin to his fate."

The expression in Jace's eyes hadn't changed. He hadn't understood. Or maybe it didn't matter. She was Philip's wife. Jace could hardly be blamed if he wasn't impressed by her alluding to a teasing game in their lovemaking past. With a shuddering sigh, she allowed Philip to guide her from the room. Jace must have been waiting for just that moment. To savor the parting shot. His words carried down the corridor after her. And she thought she would die from the pain of them. She was certain she only imagined the bitterness that laced that husky voice.

"You were right, Andy," he called. "I was thinking of Dawn Wind. Every time."

In town they spent the night in a hotel rather than

355

start the tedious journey home. She was still fearful Philip was going to make the wedding official, but he didn't come near her, even to ordering separate, though adjoining, rooms.

Philip must have been working late on some speech or other, because the desk clerk was forever traipsing back and forth to his room. At the same time, Amanda found sleep impossible, tossing and turning fitfully, remembering Jace's cruel words, remembering her own. Hoping, praying that somehow he would get past his anger to understand that she loved him.

Sometime in the night she fell asleep but woke to an odd sound coming from Philip's room. Creeping carefully she cracked open the door.

Revulsion ripped through her. Stifling the urge to gag, she made her way back to her bed. *Maybe I do have some leverage left after all, Philip. Maybe I just do.*

Chapter Twenty-Three

Amanda tugged at the frayed threads of the red silk covering on the settee in the sitting room of her Austin hotel suite. It was well past noon, and Philip had told her he would be by to take her to lunch. Last night had gone exceedingly well for him. At a gala ball he had at last announced officially his candidacy for the governorship. The elections were barely ten months away.

Soon, very soon now, she thought, she wouldn't have to involve herself actively in his campaigning any more. It was an announcement she was most thoroughly looking forward to, for more reasons than one.

Philip sauntered in an hour later. "Sorry, dear," he said reflexively.

"There aren't any witnesses, Philip. Elliott and your other constituents went ahead to the cafe. That means you can drop the pretenses."

He chuckled. "Always so pleasant, my dear. But I'll continue my pretenses, as you call them. If I don't practice being nice to you, I may forget one day at a most inconvenient moment"—his words now came through clenched teeth—"it wouldn't do at all for a governor to put his fist in his wife's face."

"I'll have to remember that, Philip," Amanda mused. "It would be worth a black eye to destroy your career." She smiled as his fist clenched. "But not here. I'll kill you, if you try to hit me here. No witnesses, remember?"

He stomped across to the wardrobe and extracted a clean shirt and tie, tossing them onto the bed. "Aren't you ever curious about why I haven't come to your bed in our two months of marriage, beloved? To exercise my husbandly rights."

"I'm too grateful to care."

"It's just that I know you were defiled by Montana. Who knows what sort of diseases a savage like that might carry?"

She felt a scalding rage course through her. "Be glad you don't want me, Philip. You would never be able to please me after I'd had Jason Montana."

"Temper, temper, dear. You've proved to be a lovely asset to my campaign strategy, but don't forget, I own everything now. With you or without you. Imagine the sympathy votes for a bereaved widower."

"You may not believe this," she said, stepping over to her travelling bag. "But I was waiting for you to make that little threat, Philip. It seems the perfect opportunity for me to tell you about a letter I received from my father three days ago."

She smiled to see that she now had his undivided attention.

"You recall that visit home I made a while ago? Well, I asked father for one tiny favor—a wedding present, you might call it. And considering who I was marrying, father has seen fit to indulge me. He doesn't exactly admit to having known your father, but I think you could call this the work of a troubled conscience."

She crossed the room to wave a folded piece of paper under Philip's nose. "Do you recognize the sort of document this is a copy of, Philip? Not unlike the one you hold so dear to your heart, signed by your sickly grandfather."

"You didn't . . ."

"Oh, but I did. This is a copy of my father's will. There are two conditions you'll find especially fascinating. First, if my father precedes me in death, everything he owns will go to me. That is, if I choose to accept it."

"Which you will."

"Well, that brings me to the second condition, Philip. You see if anything happens to me after I inherit this vast wealth, well, then every penny is to go to the Smithsonian Institution, which I'm certain will be exceedingly grateful for my generosity. Every penny, Philip. All businesses are to be sold at auction and the proceeds also given to the Institute. So, you see Philip, it behooves you to see to it that I'm kept in the best of health."

His face turned purple. "You bitch! You conniving little bitch!"

"I can't spend all this time around you and not learn something, now, can I? Oh, and if something should happen to my father *and* me, the same applies. The Smithsonian will be ever so pleased."

She didn't need her other announcement after all. Philip immediately made arrangements that she head back to the ranch. She had to admire his excuse. He told his political backers that he didn't want to exhaust his new bride so soon after her harrowing ordeal with that outlaw Montana. Even that lie brought no objection from her. Anything to get away from Philip.

Back at the ranch Amanda took comfort in having Delia with her. She began the difficult task of making good on her promise to do everything she could to free Jace.

Often she would prowl the house at night, opening drawers, peeking through cracks in the floorboards, seeking out any place that Philip might have hidden papers that could incriminate him in any way at all. Papers that, for whatever reason, he had to keep in his possession. She also used the time to secret away a derringer in her vanity—just in case.

She wrote several more times to Eric Tibbs, making sure on each occasion to remind him to address all replies to a fictitious person in care of general delivery in San Antonio. Amanda then arranged for Delia to pick up the fictional character's mail.

The detective had assured her he was working hard on the case, but he'd also been straightforward about the fact that it could take a long time to unearth evidence covered up by the likes of such a powerful attorney as Elliott Wickersby. Besides, there was only so much he could do from his home base in Washington. He suggested one lead she might check out for herself in the person of Father Manuel. Astonished, Amanda hitched up one of Philip's buggies and started toward the priest's San Antonio mission at once.

"Ah, Senora Welford," the rotund padre intoned,

"what brings you to my humble church?"

"Jason Montana."

He stared at her quizzically.

"You said once that you had something to give to Jace. You told him to come to the church. Well, he's . . . indisposed. And I would like to at least see whatever it is you have for him."

"I'm afraid I cannot show it to you, Senora Welford."

"Please, call me Amanda."

"I cannot help you."

"Father, I'll do anything for Jace. I love him. Please, believe that."

"Senora, I am a priest. You are married to one man, yet you tell me you love another. I do not know how to advise you on this, because truly you have not asked for guidance. But I must presume your first loyalties are to your husband. . . ."

"No!"

The padre took a step back, obviously surprised by the vehemence in her voice.

"Please. If you could just tell me what Isaiah told you. I remember he seemed very agitated about something right before he died. That he didn't think Jace could forgive him for whatever it was."

"I cannot talk of this to you. Please, understand."

"I understand that Jace's life may depend on something you know but aren't telling anyone."

"All I can tell you is that Isaiah gave me this." The priest held up a leather-bound Bible.

"But Isaiah couldn't read."

"Si. But it was he who gave me the Bible to keep for him. It seemed very precious to him. He was glad I had it, because when he was in town during the trial, his room at his hotel was ransacked."

"He thought someone might steal the Bible?"

"He did not know what to think at that point, senora. And believe me when I tell you, there is little else I am at liberty to speak of."

"Do you think I could have the Bible?"

"I would not feel right . . ."

"Please. You helped Jace once because you believed him innocent. I believe the same, padre. But I will need your help if I'm ever to prove it."

"I believe you. And may God forgive my earlier misjudgment of you."

"Don't be too hard on yourself, father. You may well have been right. At the time. But not any more."

He nodded his understanding.

Amanda turned to leave, but paused at the door. "How well did you know Juanita Melendez?"

"She was a member of my church."

"I understand her family was an important one in San Antonio."

"Her father was one of the great dons. But he died many years ago. Juanita's mother sold off the properties. I'm afraid she was taken advantage of. Juanita was a very angry young woman."

Amanda had the distinct impression that the priest wanted to say even more, but for whatever reason chose not to. "She had to become a seamstress just to put food on the table, is that right?"

"Si. After she lost her job with Mr. Wickersby."

"Philip's attorney?" Amanda gasped. Juanita once worked for Philip's attorney? Could this at last be the link she was looking for in Philip's attempt to frame Jace?

"Si. She worked for him for several years. He said he caught her stealing money, but I do not believe it."

"She didn't do anything else to make money, did she, padre?"

The priest looked away.

"I'm sorry. I'm afraid I'll say, think, anything that might help Jace. If Juanita sold her . . . herself . . . I mean, then someone else could have easily been there that night . . ."

"Juanita Melendez was not a prostitute. She was a fine young girl. A little mixed-up, perhaps . . ."

"About what? Father, please . . ."

"It was nothing. She was just alone. Her mother died in poverty, after having known such wealth, such status. Juanita would have been all right. She was strong. . . ."

Amanda sighed. "There's nothing she said, did, that you could tell me that would help Jace."

The padre again turned his back on her. "She was making curtains and serapes for them. That's what I can tell you. Nothing more."

"Thank you, padre." Outside in the small rear court of the mission Amanda opened the Bible.

On the flyleaf was a penned name. Grace O'Brien. Something else had been written after it, but the ink had blurred and the word or words were unreadable. Jace had mentioned missionaries among the Indians; perhaps one of them had brought Bibles. Amanda flipped through the pages, finding no other inscription, only a deerskin bookmark with Indian beadwork decorating its fringed ends.

Resigned, she climbed into her buggy and headed

back toward the ranch. Once there she put the book in her bureau drawer. Then, strangely, she thought better of it. Her nocturnal forays about the house had shown her more than one place to hide something if one didn't want it found. Lifting a loose board in the floor of her bedroom, she tucked the Bible away for safekeeping.

Just before she did, she looked more closely at the deerhide bookmark. The beadwork was similar to the cougar medallion she had found in Jace's pocket, and Amanda knew then that the bookmark was the work of Dawn Wind.

She caressed the soft, exquisitely worked hide, feeling no more of the anger and the hate she had once imagined she felt for Dawn Wind. The woman had loved Jace, even borne him a child. How could she hate her for that?

Amanda touched her distended abdomen, a wistful smile touching her lips. In five months she would do the same.

Chapter Twenty-Four

Jace stared at the scratchings on his cell wall. Six months. He'd been in Huntsville six months. That is, if he'd given a fair estimate to the days he'd been unconscious or locked in the sweatbox or buried in deep, solitary cells with no way to tell day from night. But if he'd added in an extra day or two, he really didn't mind, because for each one of those marks Philip Welford was going to pay hell.

The sounds of prisoners rising and moving about in their cells along the rest of the cellblock signalled the start of another mind-numbing day. It was dawn, and just as it had happened these past two months since Welford had stopped by with his lovely bride, the guards came by to let him out of his cell to head to the prison yard and another backbreaking day on the rock-pile. Not that he objected to the physical labor. It helped pass the time, and it gave him a much better idea of the layout of the prison. One day soon he would make his break, and Welford and Amanda would both pay hell for what they had cost him.

He hefted the sledgehammer, bringing it down with bone-jarring force on the slabs of rock. Though it was January and the air was crisp, in minutes he was sweating. He pulled off his shirt and continued slamming the hammer into the rock, the hammer his fist, the rock Philip Welford's face.

"Got a smoke?" a stringy-haired inmate asked nervously.

"Don't smoke," Jace said. "I've told you that often enough, Selby."

Luther Selby was a lifer, in jail, he'd said, for busting some guy's head in a saloon fight. Ever since Jace had been set into the general prison population, Selby had followed him around like an unwanted but persistent stray mutt.

"If anybody can get me some good cigars, it'd be you, Jace."

The man's obsequiousness was beginning to wear extremely thin. "I don't think I can get anything for you this time, Selby. The air's bad enough in those cells without adding to it."

Luther ran a hand over tobacco-stained lips. "I seen the way you don't take no crap from the guards. They respect that."

"Any more respect and they'd bury me." Jace swung the hammer back and brought it down hard, sending shards of rock chips in all directions.

"I been in prisons before," Selby said, obviously not leaving until he'd had his say. "It's like they break up into wolf packs with leaders and followers. And then every once in a while there's a lobo wolf who cuts out on his own and makes everybody sit up and take notice. That's you, Jace."

366

Jace eased the hammerhead to the ground and leaned on the handle. "What do you really want, Selby?"

Nervously, Luther hefted his own sledgehammer, though his scrawny build made the task difficult.

"Spencer's after me."

Jace recognized the name of one of the more brutish prisoners. "What did you do to him?"

"Nothin'! I swear, Jace. But I got the word he's out to get me."

"You're likely imagining things. Everybody's out to get you, Selby."

"No, no, please, Jace. Please." The man turned furtively, making certain the guards were paying only cursory attention to them. "You help me out of this and . . . and maybe I can do you a favor sometime."

"The only favor someone can do me is getting me out of this hellhole."

"Exactly."

Jace straightened. "What are you saying?"

"I got me a compadre on the outside. I wrote 'im. We got us a kind of code so when they read my mail they can't tell we're plannin' nothin'. Only trouble is he can't make a move for another five days at least. He wants to wait for the new moon, so's it'll be pitch-black that night. But Spencer's after me now. I don't want to be kilt when I got the chance to get out."

Five days, Jace thought. The chance to be out of here in five days, just for protecting Luther Selby. "All right, Selby. You see that I join you and your friend, and I'll see that Spencer doesn't come near you."

Muscles bulging, Jace drove the hammer against the stone. Five days. Five days to Welford. He looked at

Selby. "I never did like Spencer."

"Thanks, Jace. You won't be sorry."

Jace watched the little man move off to his own section of rock, though he made sure he wasn't out of Jace's line of sight. Likely Selby was imagining Spencer's vendetta. Selby was such an insignificant little weasel that Jace couldn't picture Spencer wasting his time.

Still, whenever they were in the prison yard over the next few days, Jace kept a watchful eye on Selby. He was beginning to think Selby had made up the whole story about the jailbreak just to get himself a personal bodyguard, when he saw the thickset Newt Spencer maneuver his way into the noon chow line so that he could be behind Selby.

Jace was several prisoners behind both men, but he immediately stepped out of line and walked toward Selby, his muscles tensing. He had to be damned careful about this. If he did have to take on Spencer, both he and Newt could be in the sweatbox for a week, leaving Selby to escape alone.

But he didn't have time to think about it. The prisoners parted as a wave, allowing Spencer access to Selby. The closest guard very deliberately turned his back. It was in that instant Jace knew Selby's fears had been justifed. Selby must have sensed something wrong. He turned, shrieking to see Spencer advancing on him, a prison-fashioned knife in his massive fist.

Jace launched himself at Spencer. He wrapped his arm around the big man's neck from behind, thrusting Spencer's chin upward, using his own free hand to grab Spencer's wrist. Again and again he slammed the man's knife-wielding fist into the rock wall, until finally

Spencer howled with pain and let the knife drop free, his hand broken.

"Damn you, Montana. You had no right to interfere. None."

Jace drifted back among the crowd of prisoners as several guards closed in.

"What the hell happened?" Dealey demanded.

No one said anything, including the guard who had turned his back.

"How'd you break that hand, Spencer?"

The tall giant said nothing, merely holding his broken, bleeding hand as he was led toward the prison infirmary. The prisoners' code. Jace was safe. For now. Until Spencer's hand healed. But by then Jace wasn't planning on being in Huntsville.

Selby sidled up to him. "I told ya."

"Yeah, and you made me a promise."

"Tomorrow night."

Jace felt his heart pump faster. He was going to have a chance to be free again. "How do you get me out of my cell?"

"I'll do it. Don't worry. You saved my bacon. I'll save yours."

Jace didn't know whether to believe the man or not. But he had a helluva time waiting for the following night.

Around midnight the key turned in the lock of his cell. Jace hugged the wall warily, approaching the door. He spied a dark figure in the corridor of the cellblock.

"Jace?" came the harsh whisper.

Selby. Jace edged toward him. "Right here."

"Come on."

Jace followed Selby, stepping over the dead or unconscious body of Dealey. Keeping to the shadows, they made it to the twenty-foot walls that surrounded the prison. Selby approached a water barrel abutting the wall in the main yard, and from behind it he produced a rope and a grappling hook. In minutes he and Jace were over the top of the wall, dropping to the ground on the opposite side.

As they ran, hunched down, away from the prison, Jace's whole body tensed waiting for the alarm to sound. But there was no sound save their boots on the hard-packed earth. Damn. This was almost too easy. The hair on the back of his neck prickled.

Selby led him to a stand of trees. "My compadre should be here."

"Who the hell is this?" a voice out of the darkness demanded.

"He's okay," Selby said quickly. "He's in for murder. He's a friend of mine."

"All right. All right. This isn't the time or the place to argue."

Jace mounted a big chestnut, Selby climbing on behind him. In seconds they were riding away from Huntsville at a hard gallop.

They rode for two hours, until Selby's friend called out that his horse was pulling up lame. Chafing at the delay, Jace dismounted, pacing.

"All right, Luther," the shadowy figure said, "you want to tell me why you brought company along?"

"He saved my life. I owe him."

"It was stupid. You could've messed up everything. The boss had it all planned to the last detail."

"Nothin' happened," Luther said hurriedly. "No

alarms. No nothin'. We're safe. You did good."

"Yeah, well, the boss ain't gonna like it."

"So don't tell him."

Jace's brows furrowed at the continued exchange between the two men. There was something about Selby's friend that wasn't right. Jace wished suddenly he had a gun.

"I guess it ain't gonna matter," the friend said. "Not really. You see the boss was gettin' worried about ya, Luther. You sent 'im that letter threatenin' to tell what you know about too many things. We tried to have Spencer do the job for him, but . . ."

"No!" Selby shouted, backing away in the darkness, reaching for the reins of the chestnut. "No, you can't mean that. I'd never tell! I just wanted out of jail. I'd never . . ." The sound of the shot echoed and reechoed in the still night air.

Jace had a chance for only one step toward the gunman before the man squeezed the trigger again. "Sorry, mister. No witnesses."

A blinding pain exploded inside his skull, and then he knew no more.

Jace was facedown in the dirt. Something heavy was lying on his back. He couldn't move. Neither could he seem to open his eyes. Again something thudded onto his back, not so heavy this time.

His head hurt, throbbed, white hot lightning shooting through it. He tried to think, to remember what happened, as something else sifted over him.

Shot. Yes, Selby's "friend" had shot him. Shot him and killed Selby.

Something grainy and crumbly spattered down over his head. Dirt. He was lying awkwardly on his stomach, his hand twisted up over part of his face. Though the dust made breathing difficult, he didn't cough, didn't move. He heard a strange scraping sound somewhere above and to the left of him. A shovel. And more dirt.

God. He was being buried.

"Don't much care if the coyotes get ya." It was the voice of Luther's friend. He was certain the man was just talking to keep himself company. There was something vaguely familiar about the voice, but Jace couldn't place it.

If he moved, the man would simply put another bullet in his head. The grave was shallow. Maybe . . . maybe . . . It was his only chance.

His head was on fire. He was finding it harder and harder to breathe with Selby's lifeless body halfway on top of his own. Several fist-sized stones were being tossed into the hole to fill in the gaps between the dirt and the bodies. Even then his grave digger stood around whistling, perhaps smoking a cheroot, for what seemed an eternity after he'd finished his ghoulish task. Finally Jace heard the man mount, leading away the other horse.

Still he waited.

He must have passed out. When he woke it was dark again. But the stones and the dirt had wedged in such a way to allow him a small tunnel to the surface to breathe. He listened. He could hear nothing. Gathering every ounce of his strength, ignoring the stabbing pain in his head, he pushed upward.

Nothing happened.

He tried again.

Still nothing. He fought down a mindless panic. Again he heaved himself upward.

The exertion caused his head wound to bleed freely, and he had to hold still to allow a wave of nausea to pass. Again he pushed up, this time feeling the barest movement. Or was it a trick of his rapidly deteriorating senses?

Selby's body wasn't so much directly on top of him now as it was wedged off to his left side. A heavy stone seemed to be pressing in at the small of his back.

Calling on every ounce of strength he had left, he pushed again, crying out against the pain and the terror of being buried alive. He thought of Amanda. Thought of her in Welford's bed. Rage, fury, agony ripped through him. He swore, cursed, screamed, and pushed.

Big bad wolf.

He'd show her a wolf. He'd show her an animal. All the better to see you with, caress your breasts . . . "Andy, why? Why?"

A hellish fury gripped him as he drove his body upward, feeling Selby sliding off, feeling the stone rise up and drop away. Crawling, fighting, clawing for every inch, he shook himself loose of the earth that had sought to bury him. He was free.

For the longest time he lay beside the grave not moving, unable to summon the strength to do anything but breathe. If Selby's friend had still been there, Jace would have been a dead man. But the man was gone. And Jace was alive.

Finally the sound reached him, the sound of water rushing somewhere nearby. He had to get to it. On his hands and knees he dragged himself toward the sound, the smell of water.

When he reached it, he shoved his head in the shallow creek, gliding a hand over the deep gouge in the side of his head. Then he passed out again. Jace lay there beside the water for a week, maybe two, not daring to leave. The water kept him alive. That and the insects he ate. Frogs, roots, anything. Anything at all to keep him alive.

And he dreamed of Amanda. Dreamed of her in his arms, laughing at him in her silks and finery as she went off always with Welford.

Finally he gained a measure of his strength back. Staggering to his feet, he started walking. He wasn't sure where he was. But it didn't matter. He was free.

He stopped at the grave. The coyotes had been at Selby's body. Jace scraped out the rock and was about to rebury what was left of the man, when he caught sight of something around Selby's withered neck. He'd never noticed it before because Selby must have worn it under his shirt. But the tattered cloth had been torn aside and now . . .

Jace lifted it, held it in his hand, his eyes glazing like some mad-crazed beast. Raw hate filled him, so foul he thought he would choke and die of it.

A medallion.

A beaded medallion on buckskin.

With the image of a cougar.

Chapter Twenty-Five

Amanda trailed a finger over the typeset name—Jason Montana—the name that figured so prominently in the newspaper article she had read and reread these past four months. The headline above the name smacked of sensationalism, but she imagined it had helped sell extra copies of the day's edition:

Convicted Murderers Flee Huntsville in the Dead of Night; Gubernatorial Candidate Pleads: Hide Your Women. Convicted murderers Jason Montana and Luther Selby stole out of Huntsville sometime about midnight on Tuesday last. Prominent statesman and rancher, Philip Welford, charged outside help was likely involved and will seek a full investigation of . . .

She lay the paper aside. Jason was free. Free of that monstrous place. When she'd first read the story, she'd prayed he'd gone back to Montana, back to his mountains. To find the peace he deserved. But she knew that had been too much to hope for. And though she feared for his safety, she could not bring herself to regret the increasingly obvious fact that he was still somewhere in Texas, obvious because of Philip's increasingly erratic behavior.

Her pregnancy, now in its eighth month, had been reason enough to keep her discreetly out of the public view, but since Jace's escape Philip had kept her a virtual prisoner on the ranch. Her comings and goings were closely monitored by Bates and Langley. No one was allowed to answer any but her most innocuous questions.

She winced as the baby kicked, crossing to the vanity in her bedroom. "You miss your papa, too, don't you?" she murmured, patting her swollen stomach. "I just hope he has sense enough not to get himself killed."

Picking up a hairbrush, she began to work it through her pale tresses, her thoughts still filled with Jace. No, he had not left Texas. He was too busy harassing the hell out of Philip. She'd heard the rumors about rustled cattle, stolen payrolls, even leaflets defaming Philip's parentage. She supposed Jace had gotten an especially perverse pleasure out of that one. On the few occasions she'd seen Philip of late, his closed-door meetings with Elliot Wickersby told her more than any ranting harangues might have. Jace's tactics were succeeding.

She remembered Wickersby's tight-lipped, "That outlaw could cost us everything," as he and Philip exited the study a couple of weeks ago.

"I have an ace or two left to play," Philip had grunted, before he'd seen her on the stairs and ushered Wickersby toward the door.

She had no idea what new lies Philip would have circulated about Jace, but she knew the reward for his capture had risen to thirty thousand dollars. If he stayed in Texas, he couldn't continue to openly challenge Philip and still remain free. Too many men with guns were looking for him.

With a shuddering sigh she set down the brush and walked over to the glass doors that led onto the small balcony outside her bedroom. She pushed the doors open, stepping out to inhale deeply the warm, fresh late spring air, trying not to think about the danger Jace could be in even now. Philip was in Dallas, playing another ace even as he sought additional backers for his political candidacy. His story now was that Jason Montana was not only an outlaw but a vicious gunman hired by Philip's opponents to harass the Welford campaign.

She worried that Philip's new tactics would make Jace reckless, make him close for the kill. What broke her heart was that he had made no attempt at all to contact her. She thought about his parting words at the prison—that he had thought of Dawn Wind when he made love to her. The words had stung for weeks afterwards. But the bitterness and pain in his voice when he said them had allowed her to consider them suspect. She had to or she ran the risk of believing the only alternative message in the words—that he hated her.

She gripped the filigreed wrought iron rail that skirted the balcony, studying the gray clouds moving in from the north. The air was changing, growing heavy with the scent of rain. Her gaze shifted absently to the barns and corrals beyond the courtyard. Nothing moved but the few horses penned in the far corral, now milling restlessly as they sensed the approaching storm.

She frowned as she watched the bunkhouse, expecting to see Bates emerge to stable the horses. But there was no sign of him. Probably curled up with a bottle of whiskey, as was his habit whenever Philip was away. Langley was gone, accompanying Delia on a trip to town.

"I don't see why I have to put up with that brute escortin' me," Delia had grumbled before she set out this morning.

"Because if you didn't, you couldn't go," Amanda soothed. "And your going is the only chance I possibly have of learning any more news about Jace."

"Aye," Delia said. "But I don't like leavin' you here alone with the likes of that Bates either."

"I'll be fine. I've lost my appeal to the man since the baby."

Still fussing, Delia had settled herself in the buckboard seat beside the equally chagrined Langley. He didn't much care for his chaperone duties either.

Amanda peered north but spied no dust plume to indicate the buckboard was returning. She hoped Delia made it back soon. Mostly, she was hoping for word on Jace. But neither did she relish staying in the house alone with J. T. Welford. Philip had dismissed the old man's nursemaid, forcing Bates and Langley to look in on him. Out of pity Amanda had sometimes answered his pathetic calls for water, when neither Bates nor Langley responded. But even looking at the wizened, deathlike visage gave her nightmares.

The wind caught Amanda's hair, tugging several wisps free of its tight chignon. Maybe she should have tried harder to convince Langley to allow her to accompany Delia to San Antonio.

"I just do what Mr. Welford says," the tobacco-chewing foreman had told her. "And so should you."

Doing Philip's bidding had gotten her into this whole complicated mess. Still in all, what choice had she had? Jason was a fugitive, yet his freedom surpassed her own.

"Oh, Jason, where are you?" she whispered into the wind.

Did he stay away because he feared she would turn him over to Philip? Just as he likely believed she had those ten long months ago after his fever had broken and she had left him. The memory of that day had never permitted her any peace.

She'd ridden up to the ranch, pleased she'd been able to find it in the dark. She had done her best to disguise her tracks, remembering what Jace had said about Stark not being much for reading signs.

Her hopes that Philip was not at home were dashed at once, as she'd entered the living room and found him standing in front of the fireplace alone, a glass of brandy in his hand. His handsome features mutated at once to a mask of hideous fury.

"Where is he?" he snarled. He had no use for any tender welcome-home scenes. There were no witnesses to impress.

"I'm very tired, Philip. I'd like to lie down."

He stomped over to her, gripping her upper arm. "An outlaw kidnapped you. Again. Held you hostage for over a month. Do you know what that's going to look like in the newspapers?"

"So call off the wedding. I wouldn't want to tarnish your image." He could hardly destroy her father if it were he that ended the bargain.

"Oh, no you don't. We've been all through that. And

you're going to be my wife." His hand moved to her hair as he tangled his fist in it, twisting viciously. "Where is he?"

Involuntary tears stung her eyes, but she stiffened defiantly. "You'll kill him."

"Exactly."

"I'd let you ruin my family before I'll let you hurt Jace."

"*Jace* is it?" He stared at her in utter disbelief for a long minute, then flung her away from him. "You'd really let me ruin your father over Montana, wouldn't you?"

"Try me."

He paced to the fireplace and back. "I think we can affect a compromise, my dear. You tell me where he is, and I promise you I won't kill him. I'll just have him put where he can't do any more damage."

"Jail?"

"Maybe. But he'll be alive."

"How could you manage such a thing? He's been convicted by the courts of killing someone."

"I can manage just about anything. It's about time you realized that."

"Including framing him in the first place?" She sank onto the settee. "Somehow I had hoped Juanita had been killed by some transient, and you had merely used it as a convenience to rid yourself of Jace. But you had her killed, didn't you?"

"You don't expect me to answer that, do you?"

She shook her head. "You don't have to."

"Where is he?"

"I can't betray him."

"You can and will. If destroying your family name

isn't enough, how about arranging for the death of your father or Delia or anyone else you hold dear?"

"You wouldn't!"

"Try me."

"Oh, God, Philip, what kind of a monster are you?"

"Tell me where to find Montana, or Delia is dead. Today. And I'll send word to Europe. Your father will be dead in a month."

She had sobbed for days after she'd told Philip where to find Jace. She had tried to get to him ahead of the posse to warn him of her betrayal, but Philip had anticipated her attempt and had Jack Bates stay behind to guard her.

"I can make threats, too, Philip," she screamed after him. "If Jace is killed, my hand to God, I'll never marry you. I don't care who you threaten to kill. Because I'll kill you first!"

Somehow she had made it through that awful time, realizing Jace had no chance at all if she fell apart.

Fell apart. There were days now when she felt dangerously close to doing just that. If only Delia were here to cheer her out of her mood. But there was still no sign of a returning buckboard.

Oh, thank God for Delia, Amanda thought for the thousandth time as she crossed to the horsehair rocking chair near the foot of the bed. She had finally broken down one night soon after reading of Jace's escape and told Delia everything, even about her father and Matthew.

"You can't stay married to such a beast," Delia had said, practically wearing a path in the Persian rug that lay next to Amanda's bed.

"He'll ruin Papa," Amanda cried, propping herself

up against her three feather-ticked pillows, her hand absently caressing her abdomen.

"Your father wouldn't want ye to do this, lass. Ye must know that."

"But Papa is happy now. He's married to Mrs. Van . . . Gloria. And they're in Paris and they're in love. He doesn't even remember what he did—in the war or to Matthew. It's like he erased the memories."

"Doesn't remember?" Delia gasped, flabbergasted. "That he had his own son arrested?"

"I wrote to him, told him most of what I knew. He was so upset that someone would tell such lies about him, I thought he was going to come straight home to confront Philip. But Gloria penned me a note herself, advising me Papa is much more ill than he lets on. She begged me not to trouble him further with any of this.

'He has something wrong with him. In his head, the doctors say. Nothing can be done. He even thinks Matthew is still alive, living in the states, happy." Her voice broke. "Papa's dying, Delia. Dying. And I can't allow Philip to destroy the time he has left by showing him proof of what he did to Matthew. I have to let him die in peace."

Delia planted her hands on her thin hips. "But there has to be something we can do to help you, lass. It isn't fair you should bear all the grief your father caused, no matter how much he's put out of his head."

"There's nothing. Philip took me to Wickersby's office and they showed me everything. Papers, documents, sworn affidavits. Papa betrayed the North and the South. Betrayed himself. Betrayed Matthew. But as long as he's alive, I have to protect him."

Delia sat on the bed, her brown eyes so very wise.

"And who's going to protect you? Or your outlaw. How is this fair to him?"

"I love him, Delia. More than life. But . . ."

"It's his babe, isn't it?"

She nodded, the tears streaming down her cheeks.

Delia hugged her, rocking her as she had done when she was a child. "We'll get through this. We will. And though it may sound cruel, if it's God's will to take your father, we'll confront Mr. Welford the very next day."

Confront Philip? Amanda had long since decided the only way to bring Philip down was to put him behind bars himself. She sank into the rocking chair, listening to the approaching storm. She had heard nothing from Eric Tibbs for weeks and was beginning to wonder if even the very thorough detective would be unable to unearth any substantive evidence against Philip. She had to ruin him legally, defusing his threats of blackmail. In jail Philip could no longer hurt Jace, hurt her, or hurt their baby.

The chair creaked against the wooden floorboards as she rocked. At least Philip's only comment about her pregnancy was that she had best never ever say the child was not his. At times he had actually used her condition to glean more sympathy and support from voters. Women would tell their husbands to vote for that wonderful family man, Philip Welford, who doted on his expectant wife.

Sighing, she brushed back a stray tear, berating herself for feeling so melancholy. She tried to chalk it up to being so heavy with the child, but she knew part of it was her desperate loneliness. "Jason, where are you?"

A long while later she stood up. The storm was

bringing with it a drop in temperature. Moving awkwardly because of her size, she changed into a billowy cotton nightdress and pulled her shawl tight around her shoulders. Delia must have decided to stay overnight in town. The scent of rain was heavier than ever. Late spring storms could be pretty nasty, so it was just as well Delia had not chanced coming home. Still Amanda would have liked the company.

She settled back into the rocking chair, liking the feeling of rocking herself and the babe as the storm picked up outside. The sound of the glass doors rattling caught her ear. She supposed she should get up and secure the latch, but she was so comfortable. It was pitch-black now, outside and in. She had lit no candles this night. The moisture-laden breeze sifted about the room, sending the curtains undulating inward. She sighed, shifting her woolen blanket to one side. She didn't need a wet floor.

Pushing herself up from the chair, she ambled over to the balcony doors. Lightning streaked across the sky, illuminating a ghostly apparition on the opposite side of the glass. She screamed, bolting back into the corner of the room, then stared as the shadowed figure stepped inside. She collapsed into the rocker, reflexively hugging her blanket in front of her.

Jason.

She was shaking so badly she couldn't have stood up even if she'd wanted to. "You scared me to death."

"Where's your husband?"

"He's not here."

"I know that," he gritted. "Where is he?"

"Houston. Dallas. Austin. I don't know. I don't care."

"Loving marriage."

"I never said I . . ." She stopped. Yes, she had told Jason she loved Philip. She'd said it when her feelings for Jason were new and frightening. But then she'd told him so many lies. Why should he believe anything she had to say now. "Why are you here?"

"Thought he might have some more money laying around the house. He did once, you'll recall."

"I'm sure he does."

"Get it."

"You're not going to break him, Jace. Not financially. He has more than you could ever steal."

"I'll find a way to bring him down."

I wish you well she thought, but said nothing.

"Did you miss me, An . . . Amanda?"

"Why would I miss you? My life is full, happy. What more can I ask?" All she could think of was Bates checking on her, finding him here, killing him. "Philip is all but assured the governorship. He sees to my wants even in this place. And I've been to Baltimore, Philadelphia, next year it'll be Paris. . . ."

"Sounds like just your kind of life."

"It is. And I don't intend to apologize for it. I don't ask you to apologize for yours." *Please, get out of here,* she wanted to scream. But if she warned him about Bates, she was certain Jace would be perverse enough to stay around for the fight.

"No, I guess you don't."

"Especially now that you're a thief, cattle rustler, and God knows what."

"Come with me, Andy."

She gasped. "What did you say?"

He crossed over to her, though not close enough to

touch her. "I didn't come here to rob Welford. I came here because I couldn't stay away from you."

"I'm his wife now, Jason."

"I don't care. It couldn't have been a lie. What we had. I won't believe that."

"Your male pride?"

"Damn you!"

"I'm sorry."

"Look at me and tell me you don't love me." He knelt beside the chair, reaching up to her face, turning it toward him. "Tell me you don't."

Lightning splashed across the room, allowing her to see for the first time in months the face of this man she loved so very much. Her lips trembled. "Get out. Oh, please, get out."

"I want to make love to you." His hand shifted to the nape of her neck. "Let me. Let me show you how much I . . ." He kissed her, and if she had thought in her condition such emotions would be dormant she found at once how mistaken she was. Her pulse leaped, her senses blazing to life with the devastating pleasure of his mouth on hers. She moaned, reaching for him, just as his hands slid to her abdomen.

"Oh, my God." He said it again, even more softly, strangled, and she didn't have to see his face to know the anguish she would find there.

She groped a hand toward her dressing table and lit the kerosene lantern. On legs threatening to buckle she stood to face him, smoothing her hand over her belly, trying to speak, to explain. But no words came against the agony in his eyes.

His breathing was shallow, rasping, as he stared at her middle. "God, how you must have enjoyed this.

Listening to me tell you how much I loved you. What a fool I am. What a fool you've made me."

He turned on his heel, closing the distance to the window in three long strides. "I won't be offending you with my presence again," he paused, "Mrs. Welford."

He slammed open the glass, shattering it, and was gone.

For a long time she stood there staring at the scattered shards, the wind snapping the curtains like whips. "Don't leave me, Jason. Don't leave me."

With a tormented scream she ripped out of her nightclothes, dragging on a dress and grabbing up her cape. Allowing no rational thoughts to intrude, she climbed over the balcony rail and down the trellis, the sodden leaves of the climbing vine almost making her lose her grip time and again. The feel of the solid earth beneath her feet bolstered her courage as she hurried toward the barn.

She spotted Jace riding up the ridge leading away from the house. She stumbled into the barn, gasping at the slumped figure in a corner of the first stall. Bates. With a nasty welt on the back of his head. Giving the unconscious ranch hand no further consideration, she saddled a horse and rode out as the rain began to fall harder.

In minutes water was coming down in sheets, the horse's hooves slogging through the wet grass. She rode slowly, fearing for the baby, for herself. She should have stayed at the ranch. What could she hope to accomplish?

No, she had to tell Jace the truth, tell him why they couldn't be together. Not until Philip was in jail. She had little illusion that Jace would ever want her now.

She had no proof he was father to her child. She had given him up to the law when the chance had existed, however remote, that Philip would kill him. She had put him in hell. How could she expect him to forgive that?

She couldn't see his tracks any more. She wondered if she dared chance the shack. He wouldn't be foolish enough to go there, would he? He knew Philip was out of town. Maybe . . . maybe to visit Isaiah's grave.

Isaiah. It was like she could feel him beside her. Yes, Jace would go to Isaiah.

She called out to Jace.

The wind answered. The howling, screaming wind.

Hours passed. She thought surely she must be lost, when a twisted, jagged bolt of lightning allowed her to see through the fearsome blackness long enough to spy the hollow just ahead. With a joyful cry she reined the gelding toward it, but the horse balked as she tried to force him down the steep incline.

The horse took a bad step. Amanda felt herself being catapulted into space, the ground coming up to meet her with a sickening thud. She lay there in the wet grass, watching the gray-black sky twist in circles above her head, feeling suddenly, strangely at peace. Was this what it was like to die?

She couldn't move. Couldn't.

Strong, gentle hands scooped under her, lifted her, straining against the added weight of her soaking wet clothes. She cried out as a sharp pain sliced through her, then she closed her eyes and felt nothing more.

She woke to the feel of the shack's wooden floor beneath her, the thin pallet doing little for her comfort. She was desperately cold. Shivering. Wet. She felt her clothes being peeled off one layer at a time, but she had neither the strength nor the inclination to protest.

She forced her eyes open only when she felt the heat of his gaze. He was staring at her distended abdomen. She winced to see so much pain in those gray eyes. Pain she had put there herself. She had to tell him, had to . . . She tried to speak, tried . . . But then everything was dark once again.

Jace couldn't take his eyes off her, a mix of emotions in him so raw he didn't know what he thought or felt anymore. Except that he loved her. Oh, God, he loved her. Was it possible to love someone and hate them at the same time? Welford's baby. She was going to have Welford's baby.

He remembered the time just after his escape from Huntsville, when he'd considered chucking it all, going back to Montana. Selby was dead. There'd be no talking to him about where he'd gotten Dawn Wind's medallion. Jace couldn't even be certain the man hadn't won it in a poker game, or taken it off the real killers. Anything.

Even his vengeance against Welford waned against the powerful pull of the mountains. After all, he was free. Wasn't he?

Free of everything but what he felt for this woman.

It wasn't Welford that had kept him in Texas. It was Andy. Even though he couldn't bring himself to go to her, neither could he bring himself to leave. And so he had stayed to play his cat-and-mouse games with the J-Bar-W.

Sporting a full beard and mustache he had ridden into more than one small town to observe Welford and Amanda on the bastard's political forays. She'd seemed so at ease in the company of wealthy and influential people, even though she'd soon stopped accompanying Welford. Jace hadn't questioned why, he was only glad it had happened.

His own legend was growing to rival that of Attila the Hun. As the crimes charged against him mounted, he stopped looking at the newspapers altogether. But he did start earning his reputation. First a few of Welford's cattle, then his money. There was something to be said for being an outlaw. He found it damned exhilarating to harass the man who had put him in Huntsville for six months.

But for the past three weeks he'd confined himself to watching the J-Bar-W ranch house itself. He had decided Amanda must be there, because she wasn't with Welford. And because he had seen Delia Duncan coming and going. But never had he seen Amanda. Still he hadn't been able to bring himself to break into the house. To go to her.

Finally, this morning he'd followed Langley and Delia to San Antonio. It was apparent the woman was being escorted as though she were under guard. Jace's concern about Amanda's whereabouts gave way to a nameless fear. He'd waited until Langley drew even with a copse of trees and then he'd ridden out, gun drawn.

Langley had no time to resist. In minutes Jace hog-tied him, then walked Delia out of the foreman's hearing range.

"What the hell's going on?" he demanded. "Where's Amanda? If Welford's hurt her . . ."

"So you're Amanda's outlaw," the woman said, giving Jace a thorough appraisal. "I can see why she frets so. I'd fret, too, if you were mine, Mr. Montana."

He grinned, impressed by the woman's brassiness. "Jace."

Delia darted a glance at Langley, then gripped Jace's wrist, speaking in quick, hushed tones. "She misses ye so. She's worried sick." There seemed something else the woman wanted to tell him but decided against it.

"Why did she marry him?"

"She's got a lot of pride." Delia twisted her hands together. "She'll have my skin for me tellin' ye. But I love her so. And I can see it in your eyes that you love her too." She took a deep breath. "Mr. Welford is blackmailing her."

Jace stiffened with rage. "About what?"

Briefly, Delia had told him about Amanda's father and brother.

"So she put me in jail to spare her family's reputation?" he gritted. "Damn, how could . . ."

"No, there's more to it," Delia interrupted swiftly. "I'm sure of it. Maybe a few months ago she would've done that. But not any more. She's changed. Come out of herself. I think there's a lot of you to do with that. She told me you had her cleanin' rabbits. My God, Jace, what I wouldn't have given to see that."

He chuckled. "It was a sight."

"Go to her."

"What?"

"Go to her. I'll make sure this one doesn't bother ye," she inclined her head toward Langley. "And I'll stay in town tonight. Maybe talk to the sheriff. I doubt he'll believe me, but it's about time he started thinking twice about Philip Welford." She took Jace's hand in hers. "She's alone. The third bedroom on the second floor, but there's a balcony in front of the window."

"I don't want to see her."

"Don't ye? Then what are you doing kidnapping me and tryin' to find out every scrap of information you can about her? She loves you."

It was those words that had driven him to her bedroom tonight. And then . . . then he had found her heavy with Welford's seed. He'd known the Duncan woman was keeping something from him, but this . . .

"Jason!"

He turned toward Amanda's agonized cry. "I'm here." No matter what, he hated to see her hurting.

"I'm sorry," she whimpered.

"Don't talk. Save your strength. When the storm breaks I'll take you to a doctor."

"No time."

"What?"

She cried out again. "The baby's coming."

His eyes widened. "What? It can't."

She gripped the blanket, twisting, writhing. "It hurts."

Jace scrambled out of the hut, getting water from the stream to boil. Then he gathered more blankets to keep her warm, but as she thrashed about she only kicked them off. He remembered how she'd cared for him during his fever.

Hunkering down he held her hand, talked to her, coaxed her. Hours passed and he thought he would go mad listening to her hurt. And still the baby did not come.

She screamed, a soul-chilling sound that scared him to death. She was getting weaker. Something was wrong. The baby should have been born by now.

Again he washed his hands and examined her. He had birthed a foal or two in his time. How much different could it be? Her struggles lessened, but there was no baby. She was stuporous, exhausted. He stared at her ash-gray face. She was dying.

"Andy! Andy!"

"I can't. I can't do it any more."

"You have to."

"No."

Praying to God, he worked his hand inside her, feeling for the babe. A back? The baby was sideways. Andy screamed in agony, the sound tearing him apart, but he didn't stop. Gently, gently he worked with the infant. "Don't hurt your mother, baby. Don't hurt her. Please."

Like a slippery foal, the baby seemed to turn all at once, and in seconds the tiny girl slid into his palms. Jace stared mesmerized at the awesome sight of the life he held. Then when he realized the baby was not moving, he rubbed her back, massaged her body. When she let out a piercing wail, he grinned like a fool.

"Andy? Andy, you've got a daughter." She made no response. "Andy?" He lay the baby carefully onto the blankets he'd arranged, then scrambled up beside Andy, staring at her waxen face.

"No!" He shouted at her, shook her, realizing he only started to breathe again when she did. He sank back, tears of relief stinging his eyes. He swiped at them with his shirtsleeve, then finished up the birthing, bundling the baby and laying her next to Andy on the pallet.

Welford's baby, came the unbidden thought. No. Andy's baby. Gently he stroked the tiny forehead. Beautiful. Like her mother.

When the baby started squalling several hours later he nestled her to Amanda's breast. Amanda was still exhausted. She didn't wake. With trembling hands he stroked her breast, drawing out the milk and helping the babe suckle, all the while cursing the throbbing ache in his loins. Finally, nature took over and he was able to slump away from her. The baby sucked greedily, while Amanda slept.

The next morning he helped Amanda drink down a little of the broth he'd made.

She was groggy, but she smiled. "Thank you. You saved my life."

He shrugged. "Seems fair."

She bit her lip. "You're certain the baby's all right?"

"You heard for yourself what a pair of lungs the little lady has. We'll have to get out of here and soon. Anybody passing within a hundred miles is going to hear her."

"I love her already." She watched his face. "Like I love her father."

His jaw clenched, an explosive epithet rising in his throat. But the words never came.

"No, Jason. Not Philip. Your wedding present at the prison, remember?" Her eyes were shimmering with unshed tears. "The babe is yours."

Chapter Twenty-Six

Jace paced the room like a caged lion. He didn't believe her. Not for one minute. The baby couldn't be his. And yet . . . And yet . . . He would give his life to make it true.

How well he recalled her nocturnal visit to Huntsville, one which had given him nightmares for weeks afterwards as he imagined her married to Welford, imagined her sharing his bed, crying out Welford's name instead of his own.

His voice dripped acid, in spite of his resolve to consider her condition. "Three days after your . . . wedding present . . . Welford was your husband. How can you know which of us is the lucky father? Or is it simply mother's intuition?"

"The wedding was postponed," she said quietly. "I was ill. Not that I had to be married to Philip to sleep with him."

He blanched, but did not interrupt.

"I married him six months ago. But, truthfully, it doesn't matter what you believe. The babe is neither yours nor Philip's. She's mine. And I'm very tired. I just want to sleep." She closed her eyes.

"No." He bent down beside her. "Don't sleep. We have to talk." But she had already drifted off. He stood, pacing again. When the baby started to cry, he picked her up, carrying her, talking to her, soothing her.

His child? His daughter? Sweet heaven, how he wanted it to be so. He held the baby and rocked her until she slept peacefully in his arms.

"I swear," he whispered, hunkering down beside Amanda, "I swear by everything holy, you and I are going to have this out when you wake." Then he snuggled the sleeping babe against her and went outside to chop wood for the evening's cookfire.

The physical exertion eased some of the tenseness in him. No matter what the truth of the babe's paternity, he could not deny his aching desire for Amanda. Yet it would be weeks before she could be with a man. Long before that he would take her back to her husband.

Cursing, he slammed the axe blade into the log he'd been splitting and stalked over to Isaiah's grave. If Amanda had not been pregnant, he would have stolen her out of Welford's home last night and taken her away with him. Instead he had ridden away alone, after she'd all but thrown him out. And then, heavy with child, she had braved the storm to follow him. He raked his sweat-dampened hair out of his eyes. As usual, his life since meeting that woman didn't make one damn bit of sense.

"What the hell am I going to do with her, Isaiah?"

This time there was no answer, as he sat beside the mound of earth now covered with new grass. The wooden cross had fallen away, and in time there would be no evidence at all that a grave had ever existed in this secluded spot.

"I guess this is something I've got to work out on my own, eh, old man?" He tugged at a tall blade of grass, pulling it free, and sticking it between his teeth. "Damn, I am not taking her back to that bastard."

He levered himself to his feet, traipsing deeper into the hollow, walking along the heavily shadowed creek. He stared at the rushing water, remembering the heated passion he and Andy had shared in its rippling coolness.

Dropping to his knees, he scooped a handful of the sweet wetness, bringing it to his lips. He drank deeply, then ran a dripping hand across the back of his neck. No, she was not going back to Welford.

Now all he had to do was convince her that she felt the same.

He shook his head ruefully. Not an easy task when dealing with a willful, temperamental, pampered, spoiled, and thoroughly wonderful woman. But then, *she* had followed *him,* hadn't she? Maybe she wouldn't want to go back.

Squaring his shoulders, as if he were about to enter a grizzly's lair, he turned and headed back to the cabin.

"Hungry?" he asked, seeing that she was awake, seeing also that her ice-blue eyes had narrowed ominously when he walked through the doorway.

"Not especially, no."

"Good. Because I haven't cooked our supper yet."

He crossed to the room and sat down on the floor beside her. The baby was nestled contentedly in the crook of her arm. "Thought of a name for her yet?"

"Grace," she mused, thinking of the name she'd

read in Isaiah's Bible.

"It's a nice name."

"You approve?"

"I don't think my opinion matters much. . . ."

So that was the way it was going to be. "Take me back to the ranch, Jason. Now."

"No. You're not well enough to sit a horse."

"So I'm just going to stay here and let you make my life miserable?"

He brushed back his breeze-tousled hair. How had this degenerated so quickly? But he knew. He could not accept her blunt assertion that he was the child's father, when it could as easily be Welford. And just the mere suggestion of her being in Welford's bed made him see red.

"I have no wish to make you miserable, Andy. I just don't understand why you came after me, when now you want me to take you back."

"No, that isn't what you don't understand. You just can't believe she's your daughter."

He picked at a long splinter of wood along a cracked floorboard. "I can believe there's a fifty-fifty chance. Obviously, she's almost a full-term baby. So just as obviously . . ."

"How decent of you!" she spat.

"Then you tell me how you can be so damned positive. . . ."

"Whatever you believe doesn't change what is," she said, pushing herself to a sitting position while keeping her hold on the baby. "She's yours, because I have never slept with Philip. And I don't give a damn if you ever believe that or not. If you can't accept her, you don't deserve her."

He snorted contemptuously, bolting to his feet. "My God, Andy, what kind of a fool do you take me for? Do I have *idiot* tattooed on my forehead?"

"I don't know," she said, "I'll have to take a look!"

He crossed to the door, but halted this side of it. He slanted an angry look back at her. "You're a beautiful woman. As much as I hate his guts, Welford is a man."

The baby squirmed restlessly. Amanda opened her chemise, letting the infant suckle, aware of Jace's heated gaze. "Philip has other lovers to please him."

"He has a mistress? The man must be out of his mind to choose another woman over . . ." He stopped, as he realized what he was saying.

"No, he didn't choose another woman," she said softly. "He chose another man."

"What?"

"His bed partners are male. And I thank God they are. If ever he would have touched me . . ."

Jace was still trying to assimilate what she just said. Welford took men . . . "You're never going back there. Do you hear me? Never."

"Actually, I've found some of Philip's lovers to be very kind human beings. It's Philip who's twisted."

He sagged against the door jamb. "Andy . . . Oh, God, I want so much to believe you."

"If it's such a terrible strain, Jason, please, don't bother yourself." She stroked the tiny fuzzy head, tracing the small, perfect features of her daughter.

"We're talking about my child."

"You can look at this tiny babe and love her *if* she is yours. And if I say she's Philip's, you look at her and feel what? Hate? Indifference? Yet the child has not changed. Only the eyes you see her with."

"You have a real way of making a man feel like a jackass."

"I'm sorry. That was unfair. It's just that I love her so. I've never felt this way before. So . . . I don't know, protective. Like I would attack the world to save her."

He pushed himself to his feet, striding over to her and settling himself beside her on the blanket. "I love you. I don't want to fight. I just want to love you."

Tears drifted down her cheeks as she nuzzled against him. "She's yours. My hand to God, she's yours."

He kissed the top of her hair, her forehead, her cheeks, salty with the taste of her tears. And because he could not make love to her, he contented himself with just having her in his arms, watching the baby nurse.

The next day he rode off to find a new, safer encampment. He worked like a dozen men, preparing a shelter for Amanda and the baby in a mile-long ravine a half day's ride from the hollow.

"It won't be safe," Amanda protested. "Having us to worry about makes it that much more likely you'll be discovered."

"I want you with me."

"I want you alive."

"I've stayed free this long. No one thinks I'm crazy enough to camp out on Welford's ranch."

She'd wanted to argue further, but being with him was too great a temptation. No matter what words she used, she wanted only that he convince her to stay.

Ever so gently, he helped Amanda mount the horse, then held the animal to a walk as he took her and the babe to the small lean-to that he hoped to convince her was home. For the time being at least.

"All the comforts of a bush," she pronounced

saucily. "But then I'm getting used to such amenities where a certain outlaw is concerned."

He gave her a swift kiss on the cheek. Just having her agree to stay was enough. He had ridden into San Antonio, to visit Father Manuel, and discovered that Philip had reported Amanda's disappearance to no one. He was living his life, continuing his campaign as though she were safe at home at his ranch.

"He's probably relieved," she sighed, staring up at the star-studded sky. Grace was asleep in her blankets under the lean-to, but Amanda had come over to spend a few precious minutes alone with Jace. "I doubt he wants a baby in his house."

"Especially mine," he said, spreading his long, lean length on the blankets beside her.

"What did Father Manuel have to say?"

"He told me he gave you Isaiah's Bible."

"I hope you don't mind."

He shrugged. "No. I didn't even know he still had one. I thought he'd traded it or lost it. It never made much sense, since he couldn't read it."

"But Father Manuel didn't tell you why Isaiah might have been . . . upset about something when he died?"

"That's what's peculiar. He said it was tied up with the privilege of the confessional. He couldn't tell me anything. But Isaiah wasn't a Catholic."

"Maybe I could talk to . . ."

"You're not going anywhere."

She circled her arms around his waist, pressing herself hard against him. "If you say so." It had only been a week since Grace's birth, but she sensed his passion, felt it fire her own. But for once common sense overrode desire. She giggled, trailing her hand over the taut evidence of his need beneath the well-worn denims.

"I never knew you to have such a cruel streak, woman," he rasped, though his eyes shared her humor. "Just for that, I'm going to save this just for you." He gripped her hand, curving his own scandalously over the back of it, forcing her to knead the aching flesh of his sex.

She knew he was teasing, but knew also that he was fearfully aroused. With a soft moan she continued her erotic massage, watching his neck arch back, his lips part.

"Damn, Andy. Have mercy!"

She unbuttoned his fly, tugging his pants down past his hips. "I will have mercy, Jason," she purred. "I will."

Her hands did for him what her healing body could not. And at the final, thrusting moment of his release, watching the almost excruciating pleasure reflected in his face, she gloried in a different kind of oneness with this mountain man she loved.

Long minutes later, he pulled her against him. "I may not have mentioned this lately," he whispered, nipping at her ear. "But I am very fond of the ground you walk on."

She kissed him, then rose to collect Grace. Snuggled in her blankets, their daughter slept on the grass between them.

As the days passed and Amanda gained her strength back, she noticed how Jace seemed to be making an almost superhuman effort to keep the subjects of their conversations neutral, often settling on the new pride of their lives—Grace Morgan Montana. But Amanda could feel the tension rising as the days slid into weeks, and she knew a decision had to be made. Philip might pretend to ignore the fact his wife was missing, lying to the newspapers and his supporters, but he couldn't keep up such a front indefinitely.

Grace was six weeks old when Amanda decided she had to return to Philip, if only to find out what he might be plotting against her family, against Jace. But she was most assuredly not looking forward to telling that much-adored outlaw of hers.

"The hell you say!" he roared, instantly regretting his volume when Grace's little arms flailed in startled alarm, and then she let loose with a piercing screech of her own.

"Very good, Papa," Amanda mocked, rocking the frightened child in her arms, cooing and soothing her. "There, there, Grace. Papa snarls, but he seldom bites."

He glowered furiously but resisted the urge to smash his fist into the wall of the cabin. "You are not going back to Welford. End of discussion."

"I'm going today."

"Andy . . ."

"Jason, look at us. We've only been fooling ourselves that everything is all right, because we've been so isolated here. Like a little piece of paradise all our own. But how long can it last? I know Philip. There's a trait he has that's remarkably similar to one of your own. You are both ungodly pigheaded. When you want something, you don't stop until you get it."

"I trust you'll at least credit our methods with being vaguely different. Delia told me how the bastard blackmailed you into the damned marriage in the first place. If you had just told me . . ." He stopped, noticing

403

how deathly pale she had become.

"When did you talk to Delia?"

Briefly, he told her about the day he had intercepted the woman on her way to San Antonio.

"Delia had no right to tell you such things! None! Is that why you came to the ranch that night? Because she told you I was pining away for you?"

She stalked through the grassed-in front of the small shelter, holding the squalling infant, refusing to shed the tears that trickled forlornly down her cheeks anyway. She had thought he came to her because he wanted to. She could well imagine the tale of woe Delia had woven for him.

"Don't you dare get angry over why I came to the ranch that night. I should think these past six weeks have settled . . ."

"They've settled nothing! Don't you see that. We've been like a couple of damned ostriches, sticking our heads in the sand. . . ." She bit her lip. "The point is I am married to Philip Welford. I have to go back, if only for that reason. And thanks to Delia, you know I have other reasons as well."

"According to her you married Welford to spare your father's bank account."

"I doubt she put it quite so coldly."

"And you also turned me in to the law for the same reason."

"I can see the truce has ended. How long have you been carrying that little question around in that self-righteous gut of yours?"

"*I'm* self-righteous!" he bellowed.

"Stop shouting!" she screamed. "You're frightening your daughter."

"And you're scaring me to death. How can I let you go back to him, knowing what he's capable of?"

"Jason, neither of us can ever be free, as long as Philip is free. You'll be running from the law the rest of your life if we can't find some proof that he arranged your arrest. Please understand why I can't leave him yet."

"Oh, yes, your father's precious reputation."

"My father is dying. I owe him . . ."

"You owe him nothing. He made his own choices. You have to make yours."

"Please, I can't bear this. Take me to the ranch, or I'll take myself. It doesn't matter any more."

"It matters to hell and back, woman. I love you! God spare me from my own idiocy, but I love you!"

"I have to go. I expect you to respect that."

"You'd let Welford be father to my daughter?"

"Philip pays little attention to me. You said yourself no one's even noticed my being missing. I'm sure he's sworn people like Bates and Langley to secrecy. As well as threatened poor Delia."

"This is insane. Look at me, Andy. Do you love me?"

"Of course, I love you."

"But not enough. Not enough to turn your back on that bastard and stay with me. Your father's reputation means more to you than I do."

"Please, try to understand."

"No. I lost one family. I won't lose another. You'll do as I say."

Even though she felt the pain that fired his words, she could not back down. For both their sakes. "I'm leaving, Jason. That's all there is to it."

"No."

She thought of Philip, how terrified she was that he was plotting some terrible vengeance against Jace and that she had to find out what it was. But with Jace hovering over her, protecting her, she could do nothing when all she wanted to do was protect him. But she said none of that, looking him straight in the eye, knowing exactly where to wound him to make him let her go.

"If nothing else, Jason, think of Grace. Think of the life Philip can give her. Money, a home, travel, education. Compare that to life as a hunted animal."

He didn't talk to her, didn't touch her, didn't come near her, as she saddled the horse, bundled up Grace, and left him standing beside their cabin, alone.

Chapter Twenty-Seven

The J-Bar-W looked deserted. Amanda breathed a
sigh of relief, even as she fought back her rising fear of
how Philip would react to her return. Nestling the
sleeping Grace against her chest, she gigged the horse
the last several hundred yards toward the barn. It
seemed more a lifetime ago than six weeks that she had
ridden away from the main house in that dark, driving
rainstorm. Her heart still ached to think of how she had
hurt Jace. But she would do it again if it helped keep
him alive.

Tying off the horse inside the barn, she hurried past
the corrals, praying Grace continued to sleep, praying
too that Delia was in the house. Delia would know if
any messages had come from Eric Tibbs. Amanda's
hopes waned as the eerie silence of the ranch yard
carried over into the house. Still she held her breath as
she crossed the living room and headed up the stairs.

Her heart almost stopped as a loud moan echoed
through the deserted corridor ahead of her. She backed
against a wall, hugging Grace tight, listening. The

moan sounded again. She expelled a long, shuddering breath. J.T.

Glancing toward his room, she noted the slightly ajar door. She was afraid to move, afraid not to, as she waited for Langley or Bates to appear. But no one came. Her alarm mounted. It wasn't like Philip to leave J.T. alone.

Nudging the door open further, she peered cautiously inside, nauseated by the cloying smell of sickness that hovered everywhere. J.T. held up a skeletal hand, his rasping voice sending a chill through her. "Help me."

She longed to turn and run, but she couldn't just leave an invalid to fend for himself. Listening for any sound at all from the corridor, she hurried over to the bed, helping its emaciated occupant drink down a small glassful of water.

"Where are Bates and Langley?" she asked, as loudly as she dared, soothing Grace when the infant stretched restlessly against Amanda's too-tight grip.

Watery smoke-black eyes more alert than she had ever seen them glowered back at her. "They didn't get a chance to drug me today."

"Drug you?"

"Philip has 'em give me sleeping potions."

Amanda gasped. "Why?"

He made a pathetic attempt at a chuckle. "You should know why by now, little lady. Because he doesn't want me to talk to anyone."

Amanda leaned closer. "About what?" My God, had she had the proof she needed to bring down Philip under the same roof with her all those months?

"Philip killed Bart, you know."

"Bart? Bartholomew!" Amanda straightened. Bartholomew Welford, the man who ran arms shipments with her father during the war! "Philip killed his own father?"

"It was an accident," the man wheezed. "They were fighting. They were always fighting. But Bart was weak. I wasn't surprised. He never was like Jonathon."

"Jonathon?" She watched the odd glassiness in his eyes grow more pronounced. What she had perceived as alertness was J.T.'s withdrawal into his own world of memories. He wasn't so much talking to her as talking to himself, talking to his two dead sons.

"Jonathon . . ." The man coughed violently. "Philip is killing me. Only it won't be any accident. Wouldn't have given him credit for that much backbone. Or maybe he's just doing what his father always did. Panic."

"Please, what do you know of all this? His framing Jason Montana . . ."

The man coughed again, and Amanda quickly gave him another drink of water. She wanted desperately to get Grace out of this horrid room, but if J.T. could tell her anything at all that might help clear Jace . . . "Please, Mr. Welford . . ."

His eyes moved along the shadowed corners of the heavily shuttered room. "You know, I haven't been out of here for"—his bushy brows furrowed on his leathery face—"for maybe six years now."

His words staggered her. Had Philip locked away a healthy man, turning him into this creature, drugging him, starving him?

"Doesn't matter. I would've done the same. I got a lot of money. A lot of money. Philip wanted it. Bart didn't stop him. But I wouldn't change my will. . . ." His eyes closed as a hacking seizure gripped him. "Time to get rid of old J.T. Poor Philip. Just like Bart. Neither of 'em worth a hair on Jonathon's head."

Amanda listened to the rambling story of the favored son, who had died long ago. Would it have hurt this old man to give a little of his praise, his attention, to his living son? His grandson? Maybe Philip wouldn't have become so twisted. . . . How pathetic people were to worship the dead in favor of the living. She brought herself up short. Hadn't she done much the same with Matthew?

She spoke more urgently, hoping to break through J.T.'s haze of remembrances. "Why does Philip hate Jason Montana? You saw him, the man who was in your room last year with me."

"Here? He was . . . real? My God . . ." J.T. made a feeble attempt at saying something else, but then he coughed once more and lay still. Her hand flew to her mouth. He was dead.

For a long minute she just stood there, relieved the man no longer suffered, furious he had taken so many unanswered questions with him. Then fearing that someone still could come by at any moment, she fled the room. Her every instinct cried out that she leave the house, leave the ranch at once. J.T. had accused Philip of panic. Philip in cold, calculated control of himself was a dangerous enough enemy. Philip on the defensive, striking out blindly, was an enemy whose ruthlessness she hardly dared contemplate. And now she had a daughter to protect.

She started down the stairs, pausing when she remembered the derringer she had once hidden in her vanity, insurance against Philip's ever deciding to exercise his husbandly prerogatives. She might need a gun. She raced into the room, almost dropping over in a faint to find Delia bound and gagged in the rocking chair.

Swiftly she removed the gag. "How long have you been like this?"

"Too long," the older woman grumbled, slapping the ropes to the floor as Amanda finished untying her. "That blasted Langley trusses me up every morning, lets me loose twice a day for half an hour, then trusses me up again." She grimaced painfully as she rubbed the circulation back into her wrists.

"Why would he do such a thing?"

"Philip Welford's orders. Why else? He was pretendin' like you weren't even gone." Delia stood, wincing at the cost to her ankles. "What are you doing back here? Are ye daft? I thought you'd be long gone with . . ."

A squalling protest from the wrapped bundle in Amanda's arms stopped the words in Delia's throat. "What?"

Amanda smiled at the dawning realization in Delia's eyes. "A girl," Amanda said quietly. "Grace."

Instantly Delia gathered the babe to her, peeking under the blanket at the tiny pink face. "Ah, she's a beauty, like her mother." Her voice grew stern. "I just hope she's got more brains than her mother. What are you doing here, lass? I wouldn't put it past Philip Welford to lock you in one of these rooms just like that

411

poor man down the hall."

"J.T.'s dead," Amanda said, quickly explaining what had happened in the old man's room. "He said something about not changing his will, and yet the copy Jace stole had been dated only months before. I might be able to use it to prove Philip is a thief. If I can confront him with that . . ."

"You don't dare face Welford," Delia said, her eyes widening with terror. "He's plumb out of his mind, he is. He was here two days ago. Ranting and raving like a madman about your outlaw. I couldn't make sense o' none of it. Said nobody takes his land. Nobody. He'll kill you, Jace, the babe, one and all. He's not right in the head, I tell ye."

"No. He won't kill anybody." Amanda looked at Grace, looked at Delia. "I think it's time I went to the sheriff."

"And what about your father?" Delia probed softly.

"Whatever happens happens. Philip has to be stopped."

Delia gave her a swift hug. "It'll work out, you'll see. You're doin' the right thing."

Amanda could only pray Delia was right. "Do you know where Langley and Bates are?"

"I heard 'em ride out this morning. Langley wasn't due back to let me loose 'til around dusk. I just had to sit here listening to that awful moaning from Mr. Welford's grandfather. When I tried to go to him yesterday, Langley wouldn't let me."

"They would have been kinder just to shoot him. But none of that matters now. I have to make sure Grace is out of Philip's reach, then I'll see the sheriff. I just hope he'll listen."

"I've already had a start at him myself. I think maybe he will."

Amanda chafed on the journey to San Antonio that she had to hold the buckboard to such a slow pace, lest she endanger Grace and Delia. It was nearly noon the next day before they arrived at Stark's office. From the first, she had sensed Jon Stark's respect for the law, even if it meant standing up to Philip and the J-Bar-W empire.

"I'll hide 'em away, Mrs. Welford," Stark promised. "But I'm still going to have to bring Montana in. And I'm going to have to know more about this whole plot you say your husband has put together. Forgery? Blackmail? Extortion? Maybe murder? Them's mighty serious charges. I can't believe it of Mr. Welford."

"Believe me, I wish it weren't true. Very few people know the real Philip." She gripped the sheriff's hand, smiling to herself to see the red stain creep up his craggy cheeks. "Just take care of Delia and Grace. Please."

"And what are you going to be doing?" Delia demanded.

"Philip doesn't dare hurt me. Not yet." Swallowing her anxiety, Amanda took Grace from Delia's arms and gave the baby a gentle kiss on the top of her head. "You mind your Aunt Delia now," she whispered. To Delia she said, "She's all fed. I'll be back as soon as I can."

"Be careful."

She gave Delia a hug. "I will." She turned to Stark. "If you see Jason, promise me you won't just shoot him."

"I'll do my best. I swear."

Holding onto that promise, Amanda made her way

413

to Father Manuel's mission church. Taking a deep breath, she pounded on the mission's rear door. In seconds it creaked open.

"Senora Welford?" the burly priest gasped, his eyes wide. "You should not be here. There is talk that you are in grave danger."

"Not me, father. Jason. And somehow I think you know why." She stepped inside the church, pushing the heavy door shut behind her, her lips twisting in a curious frown to find a plump Mexican woman pacing nervously on the opposite side of the room.

"This is Teresa Perez," Father Manuel offered, "housekeeper to Doctor Adams."

"You know who I am, senora?" Amanda asked.

"Si." The woman did not meet Amanda's eyes.

"Were you ever aware of the reasons for the doctor's frequent visits to the J-Bar-W ranch?"

"There was sickness." The woman wrung her hands together, her agitation increasing.

"Please, Senora Welford," Father Manuel interrupted, "I don't think there is anything to be gained . . ."

"We're talking about Jason Montana's life. And I think both of you know that." She turned again to Teresa Perez. "I understand your son was the one who brought Isaiah the horses the day he and Jason kidnapped me."

The woman stiffened with the first measure of defiance Amanda had seen in her. "I assure you, senora, Estaban meant no harm to you."

"I'm sure he didn't," Amanda allowed. "I doubt Estaban even knew what would happen. But I'm wondering if you did. . . ."

"What are you saying?"

"I'm saying I am a very desperate woman, Senora Perez. And I am seeking any tiny shred of evidence that might help clear Jason Montana. As a mother, I can only believe you let your son take Isaiah those horses, because you believed Jace was innocent." She turned toward the priest. "Just as Father Manuel does."

The priest looked away, crossing to a small altar and genuflecting in front of an exquisitely made porcelain statue of the Virgin Mary. Amanda was now certain she had interrupted a very telling conversation between these two people. Now if only she could convince one of them to talk.

She gripped Teresa's hands in her own. "Did you know Juanita Melendez? Do you know anything at all about her death?"

"I am very frightened."

"So am I. Believe me."

"Juanita was very unhappy," Teresa said, turning her eyes imploringly toward Father Manuel. Amanda thought she saw a barely perceptible nod. Teresa sighed. "Just before she died, she told me she was going to be rich, just like her madre and padre had been."

"Do you know how she was going to accomplish this?"

She nodded slowly, seeming to be grateful at last to unburden herself of the guilt of silence. "She had stolen some papers from Senor Welford's attorney. Juanita was once housekeeper to Senor Wickersby. I do not know what the papers said. But I know Juanita expected Senor Welford and Senor Wickersby to pay her a great deal of money to have those papers back."

"Blackmail?" Amanda gasped, adding almost to

herself, "How perfectly poetic."

"Senora?"

"Nothing. Really. Please, is there anything else?"

"No. Except that I am certain they did not pay her in the way she thought they would."

"And you never said anything?"

"They had Juanita killed, senora. What would they have done to me? Or my son?"

Amanda nodded her understanding, turning to face the padre.

"You've known more about this whole sordid story from the first, haven't you? Otherwise, you never would have agreed to help Isaiah Benteen free a condemned murderer from the gallows."

"I must prepare for mass later this morning. Please . . ."

"No, father, it's you I ask 'please'. I beg you. If you know anything that can end this nightmare for Jace, for us all, please tell me." She touched the wooden crucifix on the altar. "Jace said you mentioned something about confessional privilege. I'm not sure I understand. . . ."

He looked away, and she was certain he knew where this was all leading. Still, he surprised her by answering. "When a priest hears a sinner's confession, it is as though the sinner speaks to God. I cannot betray anything I have heard in confession. Ever."

She paced to the end of the room and back, then stopped, grimacing, realizing she had taken on one of Jace's most nerve-wracking yet endearing characteristics. "Can I pose a question to you, padre?"

"I am very sorry, senora, but if it is something from the confessional . . ."

Amanda plunged ahead. "Suppose someone committed a murder. If that person told you about it, you could do nothing?"

"If a sinner confessed a murder under the sanctity of the sacrament of penance, I could say nothing to no one. Not ever."

"But if the person just told you. As one person to another . . ."

"That would be different. Then I must do as my conscience directs me."

"Father, how well did you know Juanita Melendez?"

"Please, no more questions."

"She was a Catholic, wasn't she?"

"Si. She went to church here, but I'm afraid I can discuss it no further."

"Not even if innocent people are going to die?"

"Please leave, Senora Welford."

"I beg you. If there is anything at all you can tell me without betraying your faith, please . . ."

"Ask God, senora. Ask God to help you."

Unable to hide her frustration, she turned to leave. "Maybe I will." She opened the door but paused one last time. "Padre, Jace said Isaiah was not a Catholic. Did he say anything? . . ."

The priest shook his head sadly. "He gave me his Bible. That is all I can tell you."

Amanda nodded. "Thank you." She turned back to Teresa Perez. "Senora?"

"I know nothing more. I swear."

Amanda walked back toward the sheriff's office, feeling more confused now than ever. Father Manuel knew something, but he wasn't free to tell her. *Ask God. Ask God.* The padre's words came back to her again and again. As though he were trying to tell her in the only way he could.

Like a thunderbolt it struck her. Isaiah's Bible!

She didn't stop for the sheriff, didn't stop for anything. She hired a horse and rode hard and fast to the ranch, secreting herself in the rocks above it, waiting to see if anyone was about. Langley and Bates no doubt would have been on the prowl once they found Delia was missing.

When everything seemed quiet, she decided she had to take the chance. Her heart thudding against her ribs, she crept up the stairs to her room, barely noticing that J.T.'s body had been removed from his bed.

Moving the vanity and lifting the loose boards underneath it, she picked up the leatherbound book in her hands. Could it possibly tell her anything it hadn't already?

She opened it, poring over it, flipping pages from front to back. Nothing. Then what? What? She lay it open on the bed, staring at it. *Ask God.* Ask God what?

"What?" The pages fluttered in the breeze of the open window. Amanda frowned, as one particular page was not lifted by the wind. It seemed thicker, heavier than the others. Gently, she poked at its edges with a fingernail. It wasn't one page. It was two. Two pages sealed together to look like one, effectively concealing the two facing pages between.

Working with extreme care she eased them apart. For a long time she studied what was written on the pages that had been hidden, their awesome power not registering at first.

And then she knew.

My God, my God . . . Jason!

He was in mortal danger.

She twisted, starting violently, hearing the hammer of a gun drawn back.

"I've been waiting so very long for someone to find that for me. So very long."

She glared at Philip, a cocked pistol in his right hand.

"I'll take the book now, Amanda dear. And then, of course, since you know the truth, I'm afraid I'll have to kill you."

Chapter Twenty-Eight

Jace's rage at Amanda had settled to a simmering fury by the time he was within sight of San Antone. Damn her conceited bitch hide! How dare she find favor with Welford's blood money for raising their daughter! He was sick to death of her condescending attitude toward the way he lived his life.

His life? He'd thought she'd gone beyond tolerating sleeping under the stars to actually enjoying it. As he urged the gelding to a faster gait, he was careful to avoid taking his ill temper out on the horse. Maybe Amanda was right. Maybe their physical attraction for one another had only served to mask deep-seated differences that could never be resolved. But there was one thing he swore. Though she might never be his, neither would she ever be Welford's.

Using back streets and alleys that had become annoyingly familiar, he rode to the rear door of Father Manuel's mission church. Amanda had said something about talking to the priest. He didn't especially want to confront her right now, but he hoped the priest would tell him anything he had told her.

He was about to knock on the door when he heard the voice. The hauntingly familiar voice. Jace stiffened, lifting his revolver from the holster on his hip. The man who killed Luther Selby. The man who buried Jace alive.

Levering back the hammer, he gently eased open the door to the priest's quarters.

"You're going to tell me what Juanita told you in that confession of hers, padre," Selby's killer was saying. "Or you're gonna meet God face to face sooner than you planned."

The man had his back to Jace, as he stood in the center of the small room, his gun aimed at the padre.

Cougar-soft Jace padded into the room. "Don't move, mister. Don't turn around. Just drop the gun."

The man did not drop the gun, but neither did he turn around. "I got no quarrel with whoever you are. Just go on back out the door and forget you ever came in here."

"I don't think so."

"You're asking for more trouble than you know, mister."

"Did you know a man named Luther Selby?"

"If I did?"

"If you did, you're a dead man."

"Listen mister, I don't know what's stuck in your craw, but I just do what the boss tells me."

"Selby wore a medallion. A cougar medallion. Where'd he get it?"

The man seemed to relax. "Don't fret yerself. He got it off'n some squaw."

It took everything in him not to pull the trigger on

the .45. "You killed a woman and her son in Montana last year. You and Selby and who else?"

"I don't know nothin' about killin's, mister," the man said, his voice betraying a mounting nervousness. "Like I said, I just do what the boss tells me."

"Who else was with you?"

"Listen, mister, I don't know . . ."

"That woman was my wife. That boy was my son."

"You! Oh, my God!" The man whirled, his gun firing wildly.

Jace returned the fire, watching the man slump to the floor, blood spreading in a wide pool beneath his body.

Swearing, Jace flipped him onto his back with his boot. For a long minute he just stood there, staring at the face of the dead man.

Jack Bates.

"You must hurry, senor," the padre said. "Senora Welford will be going to the ranch. This man told me Senor Welford has returned. The senora is in great danger."

Jace shoved his gun back into his holster. "Why should Welford hurt Amanda? He hasn't in the past."

"She didn't know the truth before."

Jace's insides tightened. "What truth?"

"I cannot say."

"Padre, you're telling me Amanda could be hurt, and then you won't tell me why. . . ."

"I am sorry, senor. Truly."

Jace looked at the burly priest's face, feeling the anguish in the man. "She'll be all right, padre. I'll take care of her."

"I pray you're not too late already."

Jace stalked back out the door. Bates. *I just do what*

the boss tells me. The boss. Philip Welford.

Welford ordered Dawn Wind's death? Bright Path? What sense did that make?

I just do what the boss tells me.

Lunacy.

Amanda was with Welford.

Jace mounted his horse, a deadly calm settling over him. The cougar on a death stalk.

Chapter Twenty-Nine

Amanda turned a wary eye on the gun Philip had levelled at her back as he marched her across the ranch yard toward the barn. She thought about making a try for the derringer in her pocket but decided to wait. She wanted to find out as much as she could about Philip's expanding plot against Jace.

"Where are we going?" she demanded, as he led two saddled horses out of the barn.

"You don't ask the questions here. I do." He stalked over to her, gripping her arm. "So why don't you be a good girl and tell me where Montana is?"

"I wouldn't tell you even if I knew," she snapped, jerking away.

He slapped her. "Shall I repeat the question?"

With one hand Amanda reflexively rubbed her cheek; with the other she took a swing at Philip, narrowly missing as he leaped aside. "Repeat what you like; I'll tell you nothing."

His eyes narrowed. He looked feral, evil. "I think you'll change your mind, my dear. That is, if you ever want to see that daughter of yours alive again."

"Grace?" Amanda recoiled in horror. "No, you're lying! She's with Delia and Sheriff Stark." Her heart lurched as she watched him reach into his pocket, extracting a swatch of the blanket she had wrapped Grace in this morning.

"You bastard!" she shrieked. "What have you done with my baby?" She flew at him, fists flailing, more terrified than she had ever been.

He backhanded her across the face, sending her sprawling in the dirt. "You'll see soon enough."

Amanda tasted the salty sweetness of her own blood, but more than that she tasted the acid bitterness of despair. Philip had her child. He had Grace. Trembling, she pushed herself to her feet, no longer resisting as he shoved her toward the chestnut.

"This promises to be quite a memorable day for you, Amanda. You're going to watch Jason Montana die. Your daughter die."

"If you've hurt my baby, I'll kill you."

He chuckled, an evil sound that prickled the hair on the back of her neck, even as he offered her a hand up into the saddle.

"Go to hell," she spat.

"I must say, that man has certainly been an appalling influence on you," he said, mounting the bay. "But then, I should never have let him go to Huntsville. I thought I could arrange for an accident. One you couldn't trace to me. He would be dead, and I would still have all of your money. Who would have thought he'd escape? A most disagreeable man."

"Just take me to my baby, Philip. Please."

He holstered his gun, kneeing the bay forward at a

smooth trot.

"I'll take you there, don't worry," he called. "After all, I don't want your baby found at the ranch. That would never do."

They rode for hours, Amanda more than once finding herself scanning the passing rocks and trees for any sign at all of Jace. But there was no reason to believe he would have followed her from the camp, no reason to believe that if he saw her with Philip, he would even give a damn.

When they at last arrived at a dilapidated line shack, Amanda leaped off the horse and raced inside, gasping her relief to find Grace and Delia safe, the older woman sitting on the floor, holding the baby and rocking her.

"Are you all right, Delia?" she asked, rushing over to her.

"Aye, lass, don't you worry now. And Gracie's been busy sleepin' the past hour."

Any thoughts Amanda had of going for her gun ended when she spied Gabe Langley standing off in one corner, a malignant grin on his beard-stubbled face. He patted the gun in the tied-down holster on his thigh.

"Mighty nice of you to drop in, Mrs. Welford," the foreman sneered. "Just the little lady we needed to get this party started."

"Shut up, Gabe," Philip said, striding inside. "She's still my wife until I kill her. You'll show her some respect."

Langley's jaw tightened, but he said no more.

Amanda's gaze fell on Sheriff Jon Stark, bound and gagged against the wall opposite her, his eyes reflecting his profound regret. *Dear God,* she thought, *how were any of them going to survive this day?*

She gathered her sleeping daughter into her arms, finding comfort holding the small body, child of her love for Jason Montana.

"It's all so perfect," Philip said, parading back and forth in front of her, his face burning with an insane light. "So very perfect. I've worked it out to the last detail. Bates is in town killing that nosy padre. When he finishes with the priest, he'll kill the Perez woman. And the best part is that both murders will be pinned on Montana."

Using Delia's shawl, Amanda managed to discreetly bare her breast to her awakening child, all the while staring mesmerized at this preening wild man as he continued to unfold his tale of horror.

"The sheriff and I will have been out searching for you," he said, his arms moving in an exaggerated theatrical motion. "We stumble across this place by accident and shoot it out with Montana. But sadly, he gets in a lucky shot, killing our beloved lawman. Then like the coward he is, Montana bolts, making a run for his horse. I hesitate for just an instant, fearful of what I'm going to find, and then I enter the shack. My worst nightmare is realized. Montana has already raped and murdered my wife and slit my baby's throat."

Amanda felt the blood drain from her face.

"I, of course, am beside myself with grief. I climb on my horse and ride after the murdering coward, leaping from my horse to drag him from his. I grapple his gun away, and in a frenzy of righteous vengeance I put a bullet in his head."

"You're insane, Philip," Amanda murmured, scarcely believing the awesome scope of his depraved fantasy. "Insane. You'll never get away with any of this.

I have a detective investigating your past even now. He'll know what you've done. He's probably already found out what J.T. told me. That you killed your own father."

"Yes, dear J.T. He's dead."

She was surprised by the sadness in his voice. She continued to listen as she adjusted her dress, cuddling the dozing Grace to her shoulder.

"I always did my best, but it was never enough. Never. My father could never please him either. Always Jonathon. Always Jonathon."

"The favored son. I can see now why he was, considering what poor J.T. was stuck with in you and your thieving father."

Philip stiffened. "My father was no more a thief than your own! Though perhaps he was more of a fool."

"I admit my father was a thief. A mercenary. And I feel sorry for him. But I no longer feel any need to protect him from his own past."

"How sad that it's too late for you to come to such a grand revelation." He waved the pistol, indicating Amanda should sit down in a rickety-looking chair near Delia. "Bates should be here soon. And then you know what to do, right, Langley?"

"Yes, sir. But I still don't see how the hell you're going to get Montana here."

"Why that's the easiest part of all. Amanda's going to bring him here. She knows his habits, most especially his sleeping habits. She'll find him for us."

Amanda slumped in the chair. To buy Grace and Delia time she would be forced to bring Jace to his death. "You killed Juanita, didn't you, Philip?"

"That silly little bitch didn't know who she was

dealing with. A serious mistake not to know your enemy. You knew me, didn't you, Amanda?"

She said nothing. But the look in his eyes frightened her enough so that she handed her sleeping child back to Delia.

In the next instant Philip dragged her to her feet, propelling her toward the door. "I see anyone else coming back with you, and your Miss Duncan dies first. If you're not back in twenty-four hours, I'll kill Montana's brat."

"I'll be back," she whispered.

Philip opened the door, leaping back when a bullet splintered a fist-sized hole six inches from his head.

Jace stood in the rocks above Philip's ranch, his blood running hot with rage as he watched the bastard drag Amanda from the house. When he had dared strike her, Jace yanked his rifle from its scabbard and drew a bead on Welford's head. But Amanda was too close to take the chance. Thank God the priest had known she was coming out here.

When Welford and Amanda rode out together, he forced himself to hold back, to find out what the man was up to. Keeping his horse at a safe distance, he followed.

He crept to within fifty feet of the shack but ran out of ground cover and could go not farther without exposing himself to a bullet. He would have to wait for nightfall, still three hours away. Chafing at the thought of what Welford could be doing to Amanda, he hunkered down beside a cottonwood to wait.

Less than a minute later he was on his feet, assessing

which direction would be best to approach the shack. He could not let Amanda stay another instant with a crazy man.

He counted five horses hitched near the wooden building, knowing two belonged to Welford and Amanda, wondering who had ridden the others. It was possible the rancher had as many as three hirelings in there with him. Five men against Amanda.

He stepped away from the tree but instantly dove behind it as the door to the shack creaked open. Welford. Jace levered a cartridge into the rifle's chamber, deciding to take the chance. Without Welford his hired hands would likely give up or run.

Jace cursed feelingly when the shot missed, seething with an impotent fury as the door slammed shut. A minute later he heard Amanda's terror-filled voice, her words sending him back to that hell-born day when he'd found Bright Path dead.

"Jace! Jace, he has the baby! Please, he says to throw down your gun, or he'll kill her."

Damn Welford to hell! Jace stepped out from behind the trees.

Welford whipped the door open, shoving Amanda out of the shack ahead of him, holding a gun to her head.

"Forgive me, forgive me," she sobbed.

"It's all right, Amanda." He raised his arms high, hands empty as he approached Welford.

She winced at the coolness of his voice, winced that he had called her Amanda. She knew he cared, knew he didn't want her hurt, but ached to think that here now when they were in danger of dying, how cruel fate was that she had lost his love.

"Who else is in the shack?" Jace asked.

"Delia, Stark, the baby, and Langley," Amanda said quickly, crying out when Philip gave her arm a vicious twist.

"Search him, Gabe," Philip said.

Langley approached Jace, checking him for weapons. "Nothin' boss."

"Excellent. Now we'll just wait for Bates, and then the show can begin."

"Bates won't be coming," Jace said.

Welford pushed Amanda away from him, strutting toward Jace, stopping with less than five feet of ground between them. "What did you say?"

"Bates won't be coming. I killed him."

Welford's features contorted. "You shouldn't have done that. It wasn't in my plans."

"Just what the hell is your plan, Welford?" Jace snarled, still not ready to accept the inconceivable twisting of his life with this monster's. Surely not even Welford would order the slaughter of a stranger's family a thousand miles away. "Tell me you didn't know what Bates and Selby and Langley were doing in Montana two years ago. Tell me you didn't know they were there to kill my wife. My son."

Amanda gasped, holding a hand to her mouth to keep from being sick. "My God." She stared at Philip. "You did it. You did." She sank to the dirt. "Of course you did."

Jace glared at her. "What do you know about this? What the hell do you know about him killing my family?"

She didn't look at him. She just sat there, her eyes wide, disbelieving, staggered by such diabolical evil.

"Isaiah's Bible."

"Would somebody tell me what the hell is going on?" Jace shouted. "Why, Welford? In the name of God, why would you murder my family?"

"You still don't know, do you, Montana?" Philip's insane laughter filled the air. "It was because of your father. Because of your father! The long lost favorite son and heir to J.T. Welford. Your father was Jonathon Welford."

Chapter Thirty

Jace felt as if he'd turned to stone, his mind refusing to accept Welford's stunning revelation. "No one knows who my father was," he ground out, "least of all a son of a bitch like you."

"Isaiah Benteen knew," Philip cackled.

Jace took a step toward Amanda, halting when Welford's gun shifted toward her. Jace glared at her. "Do you understand any of this?"

"Isaiah's Bible," she repeated softly, looking up at him, her heart breaking to know what the truth would do to him. "It was there all along. Grace O'Brien . . ." She stopped, needing to take a long, shuddering breath before she could continue. "Grace O'Brien . . . your mother . . . wrote out her family tree and your father's in that Bible. Isaiah must have kept it all those years after he found you in the mountains."

"Isaiah couldn't read. He couldn't know . . ."

She shook her head. "Maybe someone read it to him. Maybe . . ."

"Maybe the two of you had best shut up!" Philip

raged. "The old coot had someone write a letter. Two years ago. Elliott Wickersby got hold of it. And he showed it to me. Imagine my . . . chagrin . . . to discover an interloper, a usurper to my throne, to grandfather's holdings. Someone who deserved none of it. Did nothing to earn it but be born of Jonathon's loins."

"You're mad," Jace said. "I would never have wanted . . ."

"J.T. kept the will the same, don't you see! Thirty-three years. The money, the property, everything to Jonathon and Jonathon's heirs. You had to die. You . . . and your heir."

Jace's voice was barely audible. "My God. Bright Path."

"The woman was just a bonus," Philip said, waggling the gun like some kind of demented preacher excoriating his congregation. "Langley and the others came back. Told me the job was done. No heirs. No heirs."

"I thought it was done, boss," Langley put in defensively. "We killed a man, a woman, and a kid."

Jace thought of the stranger, a man fated to be in the wrong place at the wrong time. A man who had died instead of him. He felt a soul-chilling sickness come over him. Philip Welford was his cousin. His blood cousin. And the man had spent two years taking his life apart piece by piece.

"I'm going to kill you, Welford."

"Not likely," Philip said, drawing back the hammer on the .45.

"No!" Amanda screamed, launching herself at Jace, wrapping her arms around him and at the same time twisting to face Welford. "Don't kill him, Philip. I beg you."

"Beg me?" Philip laughed. "I'm afraid that's not nearly good enough, my dear." He raised the gun.

Jace shoved her out of the way, but she rushed right back. He swore.

"You can't, Philip," she said, grasping, desperate, reaching for anything that would buy her and Jace more time. "If you kill him, I'll make certain you don't get my father's money. Remember, he changed his will."

"I'll just have a forgery drawn up. As I did with J.T.'s. I was very worried when you stole that particular item from my safe, Montana. I thought you might piece it together."

"It wouldn't have meant anything to me."

"Such a fool . . ."

While Philip continued to harangue Jace, Amanda slipped her hand very cautiously into the pocket of her trousers.

"Get away from him," Philip said. "Or I'll shoot you both."

Amanda started to back away, sliding the derringer into the palm of Jace's hand as she did so. Thank God for those big hands.

With a sudden, violent motion he crashed his shoulder into her, then dove sideways, hitting the ground rolling. He fired the small gun. Philip yelped with pain as the bullet caught his right arm, his fingers going slack, his gun thudding to the ground.

Langley's gun hadn't quite cleared its holster, when the foreman hesitated. Jace had the derringer pointed straight at him.

"There's one bullet left," Jace said. "You want it?"

Langley dropped the gun.

With long, dangerous strides, Jace crossed over to him. "This is for my wife." He drove his fist into Langley's face. The man started to crumple. "This is for my son." A second savage blow sent Langley to the ground. He lay still.

From the corner of one eye Amanda watched Jace, grateful his rage at Langley went no further. Quickly, she retrieved both Philip's and Langley's weapons, carrying them inside the shack, where she stooped to untie Stark. "I hope you heard most of that, sheriff."

"All of it," the lawman gritted. "The only hanging Philip Welford will be goin' to is his own."

"Is the baby all right, Delia?" Amanda asked anxiously.

The woman held a finger to her lips. "Just fine. Sleeping like an angel. It's you I've been worried about. What happened out there?"

Amanda was about to answer, when a strange shriek from Philip sent her bolting out of the shack, Stark following close on her heels. She stopped dead, Stark barreling into her from behind. She couldn't believe the macabre scene that greeted her.

Jace and Welford stood beneath the cottonwood some fifty feet from the shack. Jace had a gun levelled at Philip and was looping a rope around his neck. As Amanda raced toward them she heard Jace growl, "Get mounted. Now."

Awkwardly, his hands tied behind his back, Philip mounted the chestnut Amanda had ridden that morning.

"Jace, what are you doing?" she cried. "Let him go.

Let the law take care of him."

"I promised Dawn Wind. Promised Bright Path." He tossed the long end of the rope up and over a sturdy branch some eighteen feet off the ground. He tied it off around the trunk of the tree, then strode back over to Welford.

"Jason, don't." She reached him, grabbing his arm as he lifted his hat, as if to bring it down hard and send the horse bolting.

"Yeah, Montana, don't," Stark said, bringing his revolver to bear on Jace. "I don't want to kill you for the likes of scum like Welford. But you hit that horse, and I'll have to shoot you."

"No." Amanda stepped between the two men. "Let me talk to him. Please."

Stark waited.

Amanda turned back to Jace. "You can't murder him."

"He had my family butchered."

The raw agony in his voice tore at her. She didn't know if she could stop him, she only knew for his sake she had to try. "Let the law deal with him."

"The law twists and turns to Welford's bidding."

"Not any more, Jason. It's all fallen apart for him. Can't you see that?" Her heart pounded, even as she tried to keep her voice calm, reasonable. If Jace killed Philip, he would be killing any chance they had of ever having a life together. He would be killing himself. "Please, think of Grace. She needs a father."

Jace raised his hat again, poising it over the horse's flank.

Amanda's gaze shot to Philip, wincing to see the tears streaming down his face, to hear the pitiful whimpering he was making no effort to suppress. She looked again at Jace, at Stark. Jace's upraised arm, Stark's cocked gun. She had no words left. Jace had to decide his own fate.

She watched his jaw tighten, the fury dance in his gray eyes. And she knew even if he killed Philip, she would still love him. And Stark would kill him.

The longest minute of her life crawled by, the war Jace waged in his heart evident in the cold, hard look he drilled at her. He would hate her if she thwarted his revenge. Yet slowly, ever so slowly, he lowered his arm, releasing the gun. It landed with a soft thud in the grasses at his feet. He didn't look at her again as he stalked into the trees.

Amanda sank to her knees, weak with relief, not caring what his feelings were toward her right now, only caring that he was alive.

From somewhere behind her came the ominous click of a gun hammer being drawn back. She turned, terror searing through her. Langley. No one had been watching him. The man was staggering, half-dazed, but that didn't lessen the heart-stopping impact of the gun in his right hand—the gun he held to Delia's head as the woman gripped Grace protectively against her.

Amanda lurched to her feet, screaming. Stark whipped around, but he was too late. Langley fired, Stark slumping soundlessly to the ground.

"Don't move, Mrs. Welford," Langley grated, recocking the gun, Delia's eyes squinting shut against the sound. "One bullet should be plenty to kill 'em both."

"Don't shoot. Please, don't shoot," Amanda whispered. She longed to go to Grace. The baby was beginning to cry fitfully, in spite of Delia's best efforts to soothe her. Delia. She was shaking so badly, Amanda was surprised she could even stay on her feet.

"Great work, Gabe," Welford said, twisting in the saddle as he tugged at the ropes that bound his wrists. "Now come over here and get me out of this."

"Where's the outlaw?"

"In the woods," Welford said, jerking his head toward the trees. Amanda watched him wince nervously, as the motion tightened the noose still looped around his neck. "Get me out of this, Langley. Now."

"Montana!" Langley yelled. "You've got three seconds to come out with your hands grabbin' sky, or you're going to have three dead ladies on your hands."

Tears slid from Amanda's eyes as Jace stepped clear of the trees, tossing aside the rifle he had left near the cottonwood. "Your fight's with me, Langley. Leave the women and the baby out of it."

"Wouldn't you just love that." He jerked the gun toward Amanda. "Get over there, where I can watch all of ya at once." To Delia he snarled, "You get over there with 'em. And shut that brat up!"

"Let me take her," Amanda pleaded.

"You don't touch the baby," Langley said. "Don't even think about it."

Jace stepped close to Amanda, but he didn't look at her.

"What are we going to do?" she whispered.

"You're going to shut up!" Langley hissed. "Or I'm going to kill you right now. If you're all real quiet, maybe you can live another ten minutes whilst I have a little talk with the boss."

"All right, Gabe," Welford said. "You've got them.

Now cut me loose."

"I don't know about that, Mr. Welford," the foreman said, moving closer to the fidgeting gelding.

"What the hell are you . . ." Philip stopped, as the horse took a step forward. His eyes wide with terror, Philip hugged his knees tight around the horse's barrel, allowing himself to breathe again only when the animal halted. "Gabe, for God's sake . . ."

"It's like this, boss—" Langley said, close enough now to steady the chestnut but making no move to do so, "killin' witnesses like you been lately makes me wonder how long I'd last if'n I cut you loose. I never knowed what you was up to with Montana, but I still done like you told me. I killed his people, killed Juanita.

"Then when Luther got uppity, you sent Bates to kill him. And today you told me I was supposed to kill Bates when he got here. You even took away J.T.'s medicine. . . ." Langley scratched his beard-stubbled chin with the barrel of his Colt. "People dropping around you like steers in a slaughterhouse."

"I'd never hurt you, Gabe. We've been together too long. You know that."

"I'm afraid we're going to have to palaver a little longer. About money. And then I don't rightly think I'll be workin' at the J-Bar-W any more."

"I'll pay you whatever you want. Just get me down from here. I'll throw in plenty more for killing those two." He dared twist his head to glare at Jace and Amanda.

A slow smile spread across Langley's ugly features. He shifted the gun toward Jace. "You know, Montana,

442

Mr. Welford didn't tell me to kill your woman. Just you and your kid. But I couldn't leave no witnesses. Got a good piece of her first, though."

Jace's hands balled into fists at his sides.

"Mr. Welford wants his pretty little wife to get the same. You can be sure I'm plannin' to oblige." He swung the gun toward Amanda. "You always thought you was too high 'n mighty for my kind. But if you can take on a buck like Montana . . ."

"You hurt her," Jace said, "and I'll kill you."

"You're forgettin'—I got the gun."

"No. I didn't forget." Jace's voice was as cold as death.

Langley flinched noticeably. "I ought to gut shoot you right now."

"Langley!" Philip's voice was taking on a hysterical note. "Quit wasting time."

"Now, boss, that ain't no way to . . ." He turned suddenly, glowering at the squalling infant. "You shut her up"—he held the gun up meaningfully—"or I'll do it for you."

"She's hungry," Amanda said quickly. "If you'd just let me take her . . ."

A leering glint came into Langley's eyes. "Yeah, I'd like that. I want to watch you feed her this time, not hide them goodies from me like you did in the shack."

With shaking fingers Amanda unbuttoned the first three buttons of her shirt, then took the baby from Delia.

"Andy, don't . . ."

She looked at Jace. "It's all right."

Langley moved closer.

443

Amanda bared her breast, Langley's eyes locking for just an instant on the swollen mound. Just as she had known they would.

Jace dove at the man's legs, knocking him sideways, the gun firing wildly. Then both men were rolling along the ground, grappling for control of the weapon.

Amanda shoved Grace at Delia. "Run! Get her as far away from here as you can."

Their eyes locked for the space of a heartbeat, each knowing what had to be done, then Delia whirled and ran.

Amanda raced over to Jace's rifle, hefting the weapon and aiming it at the two men on the ground. "Give it up, Langley," she shouted, making certain a cartridge had been levered into the chamber.

"Amanda," Philip pleaded, "untie me."

She paid him no heed, skirting past the horse. Fighting down the fear that threatened to send her to her knees, she circled the two men and prayed for a clear shot. She watched in horror as Langley curled his fist around a small rock and slammed it against Jace's jaw. For the barest instant Jace fell back. Langley gained control of the gun.

"Drop it!" Amanda screamed, even as her eyes registered Langley's thumb drawing back the hammer.

"Jason!" She cried his name as he squeezed the trigger. The foreman's upper body jolted forward. As if it suddenly scorched her flesh, she let go of the rifle.

Jace shook off the haze of unconsciousness that had threatened to claim him, grabbing for Langley's Colt and deflecting the barrel. Even as he collapsed, the foreman squeezed the trigger one last time.

The chestnut screamed, rearing, his front hooves

pawing the air as the bullet grazed its flank. Instinctively, Amanda lunged toward it, but she was too far away. The pain-crazed animal bolted. Philip shrieked with terror, the sound abruptly cut short, his body arcing through the air at the end of the rope.

She collapsed to the ground, burying her face in her hands, unable to shield herself from the sickening snap that followed.

Jace heaved himself out from under Langley's body, leaping to his feet and grabbing at Welford's legs. Using Langley's Colt, he fired at the drawn-taut rope where it curved over the tree branch. The rope split. Jace went to his knees, Welford's limp body sagging beside him. With an anguished oath Jace twisted Welford's shirtfront, cursing the lifeless green eyes that stared skyward.

"You cheated me, bastard," he hissed. "You shouldn't have died that easy."

Battling waves of nausea, Amanda staggered over to him. "It's over," she said, sliding her hand over his shoulder.

"Over." He shook his head, as if to clear it, then climbed slowly to his feet.

Something about the finality in his voice sent an odd chill through her that had nothing to do with Philip's dying. "Jace . . ."

"Everything's over, Andy." He stalked toward the shack, and she knew he was heading for the nearest available horse.

She raced after him. "Jace, we have to talk. You can't just . . ."

"I've got nothing to offer you, offer Grace. . . ."

"That's not true." She touched his arm, but he jerked

away. "I said those awful things to make you angry. So you'd let me leave. I didn't mean any of it."

He stopped long enough to cast a sidelong glance back at her. "I think you did. Maybe you just don't know it. I can't . . . won't give up the life I live. And I can't ask you to give up yours. Grace deserves the best. It just wouldn't work between us, Andy. I think I finally understand that."

"What you have to understand is that right now you're angry and hurt, maybe even feeling betrayed . . . by Isaiah. Just give it some time. . . ." She stopped, staring at his broad back as he continued to walk away from her. Did he expect her to beg? Simultaneously furious and miserable, she crossed her arms in front of her. Let him make a fool of himself. Let him throw his life away. Let him . . . She tasted the salty tears that stained her cheeks.

She watched him stop beside a roan gelding, watched him check the cinch and inspect the animal's hooves, as though he intended to ride for a very long time. She hardly noticed Delia's return, except to gather her still unhappy daughter into her arms. The baby quieted almost at once as Amanda allowed her to nurse. But Amanda could do nothing for the aching emptiness in her own body. Jace was leaving her.

Some detached part of her noted Delia helping a woozy Sheriff Stark to his feet. But Amanda paid no heed to the words of comfort Delia seemed to be murmuring to the lawman.

With Delia's help Stark advanced toward Jace, Amanda finally gaining a measure of awareness as she eyed the gun the sheriff now held. No. Please, no. She had no strength left.

446

She whispered a heartfelt prayer of thanks when Jace, too, could summon no will to continue the fight. He spread his hands wide, stepping away from the roan. "Something I can do for you, sheriff?"

"You're not going anywhere, Montana," Stark said. "You got too many charges out on you. You're under arrest."

Chapter Thirty-One

For three weeks Jace sat in the San Antonio jail. The first few days Amanda went to visit him often. She hurt to see how much he was hurting, but he was moody and withdrawn, saying little, seeming to listen to nothing of what she said. She knew much of his pain stemmed from a feeling of betrayal by the man who had been his world when he was a boy, Isaiah Benteen. But he refused to speak of it, refused to speak of anything where Amanda was concerned.

When her pride couldn't bear his ignoring her any longer, she had taken up residence in the hotel across the street, sending Delia daily to check with Stark on whether any word had come from Eric Tibbs or the lawyers Amanda had hired to clear Jace. This morning's mail had yielded victory at last. The governor had granted Jace a full pardon, Jon Stark's testimony having helped considerably. Now Amanda paced the confines of the lavishly appointed room, waiting for Delia to return with word of Jace's reaction to the news.

She paused to peer down at her daughter, slumbering peacefully in the mahogany cradle beside the large bed. "Your papa's free, Gracie. Free." Amanda's voice quivered, as she blinked back tears. Free to leave her?

She whirled at the sound of the door opening, biting her lip, not daring to speak as Delia hurried into the room.

"He's out, lass. Free and clear."

Amanda only nodded.

Delia crossed over to her, taking Amanda's hand in hers. "You can't do this. You should've been the one to tell him."

"He's not coming, is he?"

Delia looked away.

Amanda expelled a long breath. "I guess that's the end of it."

"Just like that? You're going to let him ride out of town? Leave you and the babe? Just like that!" Delia crossed to the bed and sat down, gently rocking the small cradle. "You're daft, Mandy. You know that, don't ye?"

"He doesn't want me."

"You believe that?"

"Do you see him anywhere in this room?"

"You know what he's been through."

"What about what *I've* been through? What about that?"

Delia frowned. "He's the one put you through it, lass. That's just more of what's hurtin' him."

"Well, I hurt too!" Amanda raged, storming over to the window. Her heart lurched. Jace stood in front of the sheriff's office, talking to Stark. As she watched, the two men shook hands, then Jace stepped over to a

450

sorrel tied at the hitchrail and mounted, turning the horse to leave.

All she wanted to do was scream at him to stop, but she just stood there, her heart threatening to shatter into a thousand unmendable pieces. She gasped when he turned his head, for a long moment staring up at the room, then with a sudden movement he turned away, jerking his hat down over his eyes. She knew it was in that instant that he had seen her. He slammed his heels into the sorrel's sides and was gone.

"Well, that's the end of that," she said shakily, returning her attention to Delia.

Delia shrugged. "Just as well. He didn't even come up to say good-bye to Gracie. Man like that's not worth the time or trouble."

"He's worth the world. How can you say . . ." Amanda stopped, her lips twisting ruefully at the twinkle in Delia's brown eyes. "You said that on purpose, didn't you?"

"And who leaped right to his defense?"

"I know he wanted to see Grace. It's just that he didn't want to see me."

"And you're going to let him get away with that?" Delia shook her head. "The Amanda I saw battlin' life n' death at that shack wouldn't have let him. The Amanda who stayed with him and saw him through the fever wouldn't have let him. The Amanda who told me he had her guttin' rabbits wouldn't have let him."

"I can't make him love me."

Delia chuckled. "No, you can't. 'Cause he already does."

"Then why did he just ride out of here?"

"Why don't you go ask him?"

Go chasing after him? Amanda fumed. Why did she have to be the one? If he loved her, he wouldn't have gone. She sank onto the bench seat in front of the vanity. Yes, he would. She'd convinced him only too well that she wanted no part of his world, and that he could never fit into hers.

In the end it's gonna be you that's gotta go to him. Isaiah's words. She heard them now as clearly as the day he had spoken them to her. The day he died. *Go to him.*

Maybe she and Jace didn't have a chance together. But she couldn't let him make that decision out of pain and guilt. They had to talk it out. She stood abruptly.

"What time are you leaving?" Delia murmured.

Amanda gave her a sheepish grin. "Five minutes?" Quickly, she crossed over to the wardrobe, throwing open the doors. She selected a drab pair of Levi's and blue cotton shirt. With a smirk she pirouetted in front of Delia. "What do you think?"

"Just the thing for a lady to go outlaw hunting."

"Will you and Grace be all right?"

"I managed to take care of you, didn't I?"

"That you did." Amanda changed her clothes, grabbing up the letter from Eric Tibbs.

"Why didn't you give that to Jace?"

"Because, to be honest, it answers too many questions. I was hoping Jace wouldn't leave until he knew more about his past." She stuffed a change of clothes into a small valise. "Unfortunately, he's even more stubborn than I thought."

"How will you find him?"

Amanda stared out the window at the spot where the

452

gallows had once stood. "I know where he is, where he'll stay. At least for a while." She bent down to give her sleeping daughter a kiss. "I'll be back in a week—with or without a certain outlaw."

"Good luck to ye, lass. You deserve each other."

Amanda laughed. "I think I could take a statement like that two ways, Delia. And either way—you'd still be right." She hurried out the door.

She rode long and hard, surprised at how at ease she felt in the wild Texas countryside, especially now that Jace owned this particular part of it, whether he liked the idea or not. She found him where she had known he would be—sitting next to Isaiah's grave. He didn't look up.

Dismounting stiffly, she crunched through the weeds and grasses, brushing aside the trailing branches of the huge willow to reach him. The weeds around the grave had been cleared away. "Why wouldn't you talk to me in the jail?" she asked softly.

"I had a lot of things to sort out."

She sat beside him under the tree, not touching him. "And have you? Sorted things out?"

He turned red-rimmed eyes toward her.

She winced.

"Why didn't he tell me? Why? My God, his contacting Welford's people killed Dawn Wind and Bright Path."

"He loved you."

"He lied to me."

She extracted Eric Tibbs's letter from her shirt-pocket. "Isaiah didn't always know who you were." She unfolded the stationery, smoothing it across her knee. "This detective pieced things together pretty well, I think, considering how long ago a lot of this happened."

"Nothing can make it right."

"You're not being fair."

"Fair?" he exploded. "Fair?" He drew visible rein on his temper, leaned back against the tree, and sighed heavily. "Just leave me alone, Andy. It doesn't matter."

"*I* don't matter? *Grace* doesn't matter?"

"Don't twist my words. You don't understand . . ."

"No, you're the one who doesn't understand. Isaiah loved you. Think. Think! He found you, an eight-month-old infant in the middle of nowhere with two dead parents. He told you how he went through their gear before finding you. Well, one of the things he found was their Bible."

"He never told me that. Besides, he couldn't read."

She shrugged. "Neither could you. Neither could the only people he had contact with. The Blackfoot. So what was he supposed to do? He did what he thought was right. He kept it, planning one day to give it to you."

"It must have slipped his mind."

She ground her teeth together. He was determined to hang on to his anger. "You told me you learned to read when you were twelve."

He pulled another weed from the earth, twisting it in his big hands. "So?"

How could one little word sound so defensive? Steadying herself, Amanda plunged ahead. "That was the year the missionaries were with the Blackfoot. . . ."

"Are you going to tell me what I had for breakfast every morning?"

"I'm going to slug you if you don't stop being so sarcastic."

He turned a baleful eye toward her. "Now that you've thoroughly terrified me, I guess I'll have to listen. I wouldn't want to be beaten to a pulp by a . . . lady."

Amanda counted to ten before she continued. "Isaiah very likely showed the Bible to one of the missionaries. He or she read him the family tree so lovingly penned by a young bride named Grace O'Brien Welford. About her mariage, and later the birth of her son—Jonathon Thurlow Welford III."

"So he knew. Isaiah knew when I was twelve."

"And now he had to face giving you up to real people, real relatives. This man who'd raised you from infancy, loved you like a father would love a blood son."

Jace stared at his hands.

"He couldn't do it. Couldn't. And so when you learned to read that summer, Isaiah had those two pages of the Bible sealed together and the book itself hidden away."

"Why didn't he just destroy it?"

"I think you know the answer to that. He intended to tell you. One day, when he was ready."

"What was Jonathon Thurlow Welford II doing in Montana?"

"He'd had a falling out with J.T. Over his marriage to your mother. Grace O'Brien was an Irish immigrant, a peasant girl to J.T.'s way of thinking, unworthy of his favorite son. But your father loved her. So he left behind his wealth, his family, everything, to have her, to have you."

Jace's arm went around her, pulling her against him, and she had to wonder if he were even aware of the comforting gesture. "God, what a mess," he murmured.

Amanda lay a hand against the hard muscles of his chest, savoring the strong, steady beat of the heart beneath her palm. "Isaiah felt finally that you were getting restless in the mountains. So he had someone write a letter. He had no idea what a nest of snakes that letter would set free. He just didn't want to tell you about any kind of possibility of a family without checking into it first. He didn't want to get your hopes up unnecessarily. I mean, they could have all been dead for all he knew."

Jace said nothing, but she sensed a heightened tenseness in him as the chronology led inevitably to Philip.

"The letter wound up in the hands of Elliot Wickersby. Wickersby didn't go to J.T., who was already being kept a virtual prisoner on his own ranch by Bartholomew and Philip. He went to Philip.

"Philip went crazy. All of his life, he'd heard about the favored son, Jonathon. Lived in the shadow of a ghost. And that Jonathon had a living son, who would be sole heir to everything Philip had helped build all of his life, was just too much for him. He went to Bartholomew for support in his plan to send Bates, Langley, and Selby to kill you and your family."

Jace flinched, but did not interrupt.

"But Philip's father surprised him. Bart didn't want you killed. He wanted to welcome you back, to share everything. Bart believed you wouldn't just usurp control. Philip couldn't accept that. He killed his

456

father, then told J.T. it was an accident. And that's when Langley and the others rode out for Montana."

"My God," Jace said. "My God."

"You know most of the rest of it. When you and Isaiah showed up to start a ranch, it was the very thing Philip feared most coming true. Isaiah hadn't been able to bring himself to tell you the truth, partly because Wickersby told him it was all a mistake. Isaiah didn't know what to believe. He should've talked to you, but the real and awful possibility that he had brought about Dawn Wind and Bright Path's deaths however accidentally had already occurred to him. He had to be certain before he chanced your hatred."

"Hate? Isaiah? I could never . . ." His heart ached to think of the tortured hell Isaiah must have put himself through. He shook his head wearily. "What part did poor Juanita play in all of this?"

"She worked for Wickersby. She went through his files, found out bits of the truth. She was trying to blackmail Philip. He went along for a while, then used her death to frame you, get rid of you legally. As strange as it sounds, Philip really did love J.T. He longed for his approval."

"It's all so incredible."

"You remember J.T.'s reaction to seeing you that night in his room? I thought it was fear of seeing Jason Montana, outlaw. But he'd never seen you, in fact, hadn't been out of the house in six years. He was seeing Jonathon, looking at you. He thought his long lost son was back from the grave."

Jace kissed the top of her hair. "Thank you for coming here."

She tilted her head back, her lips brushing his

457

jawline. "You're welcome." Oh, how she loved this man. But how was she ever going to convince him? "Got any bunnies you want me to clean?"

He gave her a slight smile. "At the moment all of the bunnies are safe. I'm not hungry. For food." His gray eyes darkened, his lips skating across her forehead, his hand coming up to twine in her hair.

Taking a deep breath, she pulled back. "What are we going to do?"

He let his hand drop away. "I don't know. Isaiah . . ."

"Isaiah loved you," she gritted.

"I know," he said softly. "What I was going to say was that Isaiah told me I was in love with you that day I first looked at you in the courtroom."

"Oh." She swallowed nervously. "And were you?"

"In love with a spoiled, conceited white woman who didn't even know how to cook a rabbit?"

"Uh huh."

"Yeah," he murmured, "I was in love with her. It took me a while to get over my guilt about Dawn Wind, but, oh God, I was in love with her."

Amanda closed her eyes against the tears that had welled inside them. "Then why did you leave her? Leave the child you had with her?"

"Because I can't give her tea parties and fancy dances."

"Can you love her?"

"Forever."

"Can you put a sitting room in the cabin you build in the mountains?"

His voice grew hoarse. "I, uh, think that could be

458

arranged. But . . ."

She put her fingers to his lips. "Love me. Now."

With a groan he pressed her back, his body driven by weeks of self-denial after the baby, driven by desperately erotic dreams in jail, when he would not allow her to pierce the barrier of his hurt and confusion.

"Grace deserves the best," he groaned, hating himself but needing to push her past her passion, to know if she truly meant she would give up her world for his.

"Grace deserves her father. And so do I."

"I'm not staying at the J-Bar-W. I haven't decided what I'm doing with the money, but I'm not made for that kind of . . ."

"I didn't fall in love with a wealthy rancher." Her hand caressed the side of his face as he staked himself above her. "I fell in love with a mountain lion. . . ."

His body was on fire, but he would not take her, would not make her his, until he truly believed it was what she wanted. But he was hers. Sweet heaven, he was hers. If she asked him to live in the city, he would. If she asked him to give up the mountains, he would.

"I love you, Jason Montana."

"I was thinking. We would live in California. It has mountains and cities."

She drew him down, taking her mouth to his, knowing exactly the torment he was putting himself through. "All you have to do is promise me I never have to clean another bunny."

"You'll make a vegetarian out of us both."

She giggled. "What big eyes you have, my outlaw."

His eyes seared her as he undressed her.

459

"What big hands . . ."

His hands were everywhere, caressing her, loving her.

"What big . . ."

He silenced her with his mouth as he drove himself inside her. Two rivers. Roiling, boiling, coming together as one.

Afterward, she lay in his arms, sighing contentedly. "You are a wonderful lover, Jonathon Thurlow Welford the Third."

He grimaced. "I think I'll stick with Jason Montana."

"I appreciate that."

"Andy . . ."

"Have I ever told you I love it when you call me that?"

"I want to go get our daughter. We've got a home to find. One to please us both."

"Just be in it. That'll please me just fine." Her hand trailed down the side of his face. "My outlaw. My beloved outlaw."

Much later they rose to leave the hollow behind forever, Jace pausing long enough to collect two sturdy branches to form another cross. He bound them together with something he pulled from his pocket, then staked the marker at the head of the grave.

Amanda studied the cross, then looked long and lovingly at Jace.

"Quite an old man," Jace said. "He sure knew how to pick his hostages."

"That he did," she whispered. "That he did."

Jace mounted the sorrel, Amanda clambering on behind him. "You have your own horse, remember?"

"Uh huh. I kind of got used to riding this way, though." She hugged her arms tight around his middle. "I love you."

"I love you, Andy. I wonder if you'll ever know how much."

"Feel free to convince me all you like."

He gigged the horse forward. Together they rode toward San Antonio. Toward a new life.

Behind them on the small wooden cross two beaded cougar medallions shifted gently in the breeze.

MORE HISTORICAL ROMANCES
from Zebra Books

PASSION'S FLAME (1716, $3.95)
by Casey Stuart

Kathleen was playing with fire when she infiltrated Union circles to spy for the Confederacy. Then she met handsome Captain Matthew Donovan and had to choose between succumbing to his sensuous magic or using him to avenge the South!

MOONLIGHT ANGEL (1599, $3.75)
by Casey Stuart

When voluptuous Angelique answered the door, Captain Damian Legare was surprised at how the skinny girl he remembered had grown into a passionate woman—one who had worshipped him as a child and would surrender to him as a woman.

WAVES OF PASSION (1322, $3.50)
by Casey Stuart

Falling in love with a pirate was Alaina's last thought after being accused of killing her father. But once Justin caressed her luscious curves, there was no turning back from desire. They were swept into the endless WAVES OF PASSION.

SURRENDER TO ECSTASY (1307, $3.95)
by Rochelle Wayne

A tall, handsome Confederate came into Amelia's unhappy life, stole her heart and would find a way to make her his own. She had no idea that he was her enemy. James Henry longed to reveal his identity. Would the truth destroy their love?

RECKLESS PASSION (1601, $3.75)
by Rochelle Wayne

No one hated Yankees as much as Leanna Weston. But as she met the Major kiss for kiss and touch for touch, Leanna forgot the war that made them enemies and surrendered to breathless RECKLESS PASSION

Available wherever paperbacks are sold, or order direct from the Publisher. Send cover price plus 50¢ per copy for mailing and handling to Zebra Books, Dept. 1944, 475 Park Avenue South, New York, N.Y. 10016. Residents of New York, New Jersey and Pennsylvania must include sales tax. DO NOT SEND CASH.